TINY GODS

NATE TEMPLE SERIES BOOK 6

SHAYNE SILVERS

This is a work of fiction. Names, characters, businesses, places, events, and incidents are either the products of the author's imagination or used in a fictitious manner. Any resemblance to actual persons, living or dead, or actual events is purely coincidental.

Shayne Silvers

Tiny Gods

Nate Temple Series Book 6

Formerly published as The Temple Chronicles Series

ISBN: **978-0-9980854-8-7**

© 2017, Shayne Silvers / Argento Publishing, LLC

info@shaynesilvers.com

ALL RIGHTS RESERVED. This book contains material protected under International and Federal Copyright Laws and Treaties. Any unauthorized reprint or use of this material is prohibited. No part of this book may be reproduced or transmitted in any form or by any means, electronic or mechanical, including photocopying, recording, or by any information storage and retrieval system without express written permission from the author / publisher.

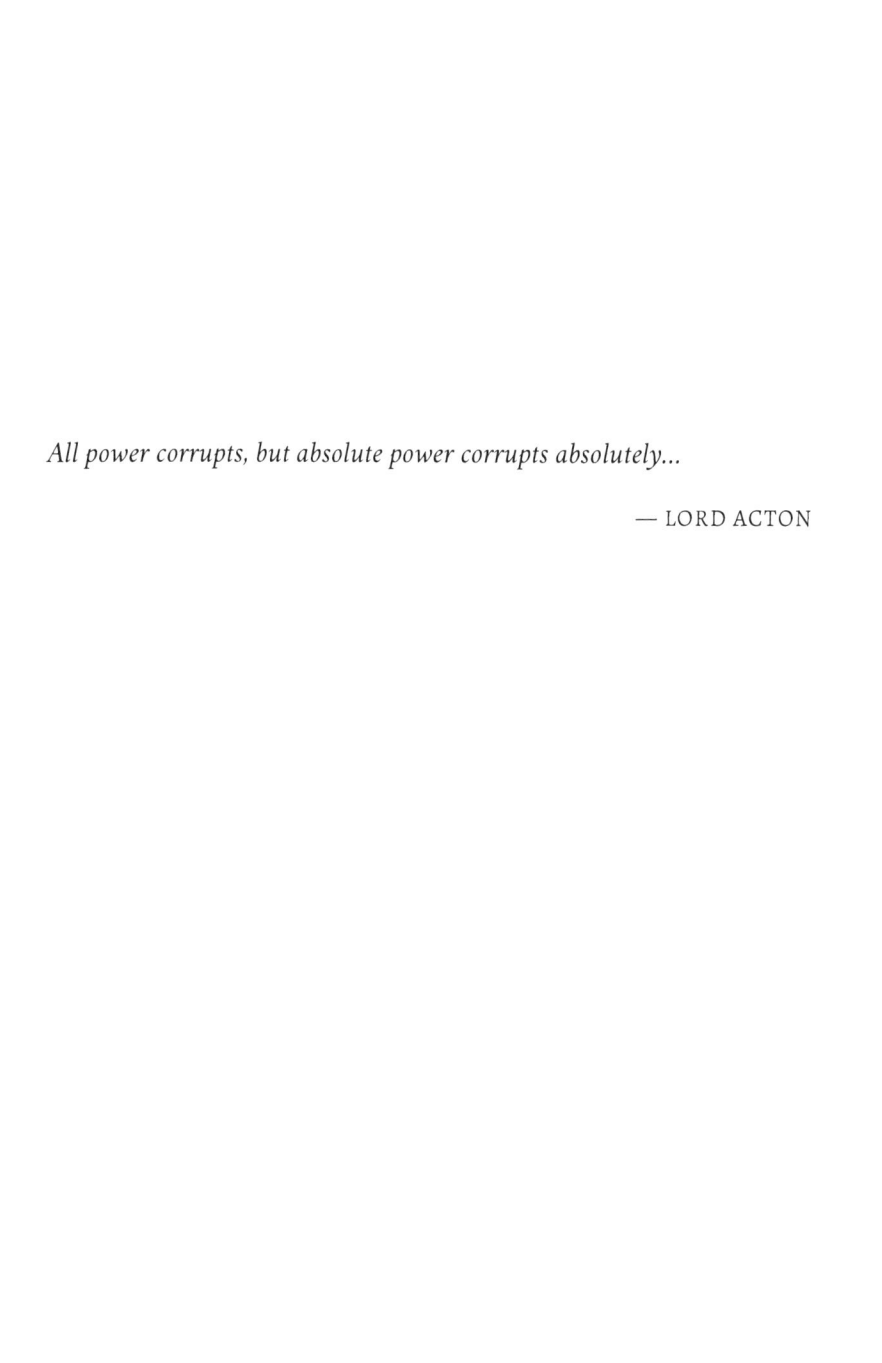

All power corrupts, but absolute power corrupts absolutely...

— LORD ACTON

THE NATE TEMPLE SERIES—A WARNING

Nate Temple starts out with everything most people could ever wish for—money, magic, and notoriety. He's a local celebrity in St. Louis, Missouri—even if the fact that he's a wizard is still a secret to the world at large.

Nate is also a bit of a…well, let's call a spade a spade. He can be a mouthy, smart-assed jerk. Like the infamous Sherlock Holmes, I specifically chose to give Nate glaring character flaws to overcome rather than making him a chivalrous Good Samaritan. He's a black hat wizard, an antihero—and you are now his partner in crime. He is going to make a *ton* of mistakes. And like a buddy cop movie, you are more than welcome to yell, laugh and curse at your new partner as you ride along together through the deadly streets of St. Louis.

Despite Nate's flaws, there's also something *endearing* about him… You soon catch whispers of a firm moral code buried deep under all his snark and arrogance. A diamond waiting to be polished. And you, the esteemed reader, will soon find yourself laughing at things you really shouldn't be laughing at. It's part of Nate's charm. Call it his magic…

So don't take yourself, or any of the characters in my world, too seriously. Life is too short for that nonsense.

Get ready to cringe, cackle, cry, curse, and—ultimately—*cheer* on this snarky wizard as he battles or befriends angels, demons, myths, gods, shifters, vampires and many other flavors of dangerous supernatural beings.

DON'T FORGET! VIP's get early access to all sorts of Temple-Verse goodies, including signed copies, private giveaways, and advance notice of future projects. AND A FREE NOVELLA! Click the image or join here: www.shaynesilvers.com/l/219800

FOLLOW AND LIKE:
Shayne's FACEBOOK PAGE:
www.shaynesilvers.com/l/38602

I try to respond to all messages, so don't hesitate to drop me a line. Not interacting with readers is the biggest travesty that most authors can make. Let me fix that.

CHAPTER 1

*B*ullets shattered the back windshield of the Tahoe, but I had already been ducking down in the front passenger seat.

"What part of *lose them* was unclear to you? And you're *still* going the wrong way," I shouted, peeking over the back of my headrest. "You girls okay?" I asked, loud enough for the Reds to hear me over the sudden street noise and roar of our engine, let alone the van chasing us. They nodded, slowly climbing back into their seats from the floor.

"I *know* I'm going the wrong way, but I had to go the wrong way to lose the first two vans!" Alucard snapped, tires squealing as he jerked the wheel to avoid another barrage of pistol fire. "You didn't have to break his damned arm! We could have just agreed to disagree."

"They surrounded me! All while you stood there doing a whole lot of *nothing*!" I argued.

"It's what weregorillas do when threatened! And you told me you needed a *driver*, not a *thug*!" he shouted right back, turning down a side street to get us going in the right direction.

Bullets sprayed the buildings beside us, their shots going wide as we changed course. "In my world, they're the same thing!" I snapped. "Just drive. Lose them. We'll sort this out after we escape the angry monkeys," I growled.

He just shook his head angrily, glancing in the rearview constantly, trying to predict their shots and keep us bullet-free. I turned around, watching the van chasing us. It seemed to be getting closer, and I could see a man leaning out the car window. "Tory is going to be so pissed. We're going to be late," Alucard whined.

"No, we're— Ah!" the man had pulled out a shotgun, aiming it our way. "Get down!" I shouted at the teenaged weredragons in the backseat, and let off a few shots from the pistol in my fist, trying to deter the van. The man ducked back inside instantly. One of my shots went wild, but one struck the front wheel, blowing their tire – just like in the movies.

The chasing van lost control and swerved right into the only parked car on the deserted street. I grunted satisfactorily, trying to both hide my astonishment, and maintain my devil-may-care reputation in front of the Reds. "Okay, you can get up now, but be ready to duck again." I changed my voice to the Count from *Sesame Street*. "Because like Sparkula said, there are *one, two, three vans of gorillas chasing us!* Muah, ha, ha, ha." They just stared at me, probably not getting the reference.

Kids.

"I do *not* sound like that," Alucard snarled. "And don't call me Sparkula!"

I chuckled, searching the floorboards now that we had a moment of respite. "We're not going to be late to the Gala. I have a—" I cut off, staring at the floor in disbelief. "Shit," I whispered, quickly leaning over the center console to check the floorboard in the back. The Reds moved their feet, confused looks on their faces. *Nothing*.

"What are we going to do when the other two vans find us? *Hmm?*" Alucard persisted. "You know they're circling the block. This is their neighborhood. And what the hell are you looking for?" he hissed, annoyed that I seemed to be ignoring him.

"I must have left it at the office," I said, feeling like an idiot.

"What are you *talking* about?" he yelled, eyes scanning the streets as we zipped by.

"My satchel. Our way out of here."

"Your man purse?" Sonya asked. "I saw it on the table. You left it there when Greta began showing you those pamphlets."

"Religious tracts," Alucard shuddered, saying it in the same tone someone else would use to describe a platter of steaming dog feces. Because he was a vampire. Although the whole religious thing didn't seem to bother him as much anymore, he'd still been zapped one too many times by them. Because vampires and religion got along like a dog peeing on an electric fence.

"It's not a man purse," I argued, pulling out my phone to call the office. "It's a *satchel*."

A harried voice answered the call, sounding annoyed. "Grimm Tech."

"Greta! This is Nate. Did I leave my satchel there?" I asked desperately, fear clawing at my insides. The contents of the satchel were unstable. Lethally unstable.

"Your man purse? Let me check," she responded. Alucard burst out laughing.

"You are literally the only one who calls it that. Just admit it," he said. Then he jerked the wheel hard to the right – almost making me drop the phone – and ducked into an alley. He had flipped off the lights before we even stopped. A van flew by on the street where we had just been, racing towards their stranded pals, most likely. I flashed him a smile as Greta came back on the phone.

"You left it here on the table. Yahn said he would take it to you at the Gala after his dance class in the old warehouse district. The Gala I'm trying to get ready for. The one *you* are supposed to be hosting..." her annoyance was blindingly obvious, because Greta didn't waste time on *feelings*. At least not when it came to me. "He said he called you."

"Dance class," I repeated dumbly, but my fear was slightly diminished by relief, because at least we were *in* the old warehouse district. "Okay. Thanks, Greta. See you there," I blurted, hanging up as she began reprimanding me about something else.

Because fear still gripped me. Yahn was just *walking around* with my satchel? Did he have any idea what was inside? One wrong move and he could blow up a building! I quickly scrolled through my phone, Alucard tapping the steering wheel anxiously.

5

"We can't just sit here, Nate. They're bound to find us. We need a way out. Now. Or we're going to be late to the Gala," he warned. "Or dead. I would rather get dead than be late," he added. The Reds chimed in their agreement from the backseat.

I saw the missed call, and realized my phone had been on silent. I immediately dialed it back, ignoring Alucard. "Fucking wizards," he muttered as I waited for Yahn to pick up.

"He's carrying around a freaking *bomb*, man!" I snapped. Alucard's anger evaporated.

Yahn answered. "Ya, this is Yahn," he said in a thick, cheerful Swedish accent.

"It's me, Nate. Hey, did you pick up—"

"Master Temple! *Alriiight!*" he shouted happily, voice laced with enthusiasm, happiness, and unicorn farts. His accent was so strong, so flamboyant, and so overly enunciated, that it was sometimes painful to talk to him for very long. He was Greta's grandson – a foreign exchange student – and she had convinced me to hire him as an intern for my new company. "I *toe-tah-lee* have yer man purse—"

Even the Reds burst out laughing at that.

"Satchel, Yahn. *Satch*—" I cut off my argument abruptly. "Never mind. Where are you?"

"Just leaving dancing class, we are putting on this show, and like, it's going to be toe-tah-lee awesome and stuff!" he answered, excitedly.

"Address. What *address*?" I pressed.

He told me. Alucard pulled it up on the screen, face going pale. It was back the way we had come, right through gorilla territory.

Yahn began speaking into the phone again, but I interrupted him. "Yahn, listen. I need you to get my… purse, and wait outside by the curb. Be very, very careful with the bag. Don't jostle it. We will be there in," I glanced at the GPS unit, "two minutes. Be ready to jump in. Fast."

He was quiet on the other end of the line as Alucard put the car in gear, backing up quickly and turning around. "Yoo want to, like, give me a *ride* and stuff?" he repeated, almost whispering, but sounding as if he had won the lottery. "That would be *toe-tah-lee cool!*" he squealed, piercing my ear canal with Swedish cheer. "See you soon!" and he hung up.

Alucard shifted back into drive, shaking his head the entire time, but he took the first left, running parallel to the street we had originally been on, sending us straight back to monkey-town. "This better not blow up in our faces, Nate." He realized his words after the fact, and shot me a sickening look. "Figuratively or literally, I guess."

"Just drive, Glampire. And avoid the weregorillas, or I'm blaming it all on you."

The Reds clapped in the backseat, as Alucard pressed the gas pedal harder.

"Call me Glampire all you want, but just remember which one of us has a pet unicorn…" he offered casually. The Reds sniggered in the back seat as I bit back a growl.

CHAPTER 2

*Y*ahn stood on the sidewalk, unconcernedly jamming out to music with his overly large headphones. He was wearing sparkly charcoal-colored tights, ballet flats, and a flaming pink spandex unitard over his pudgy frame. My satchel and a backpack sat on the ground beside him. His white-blonde hair was perfectly styled under his huge headphones, and his light eyebrows made him look perpetually surprised and enthusiastic, dramatically lighting up his face. We skidded to a halt beside him, and with his eyes closed, he didn't even notice us. I found myself stunned to silence, staring as he thrashed and raged, kicking his feet while he made odd flailing motions with his hands.

Dancing like no one was watching, and the world was his stage.

Alucard made up for my surprise. He jumped out of the car, jostling Yahn by the shoulders, which surprised the ever-living hell out of him, because he shrieked as if being murdered. Alucard quickly and carefully picked up the bags, and handed them to me through the window. I let out a sigh of relief, clutching my satchel tightly to my chest.

Yahn was now staring at us, silent for once. Alucard jerked his head to look behind us, a panicked look flashing across his face. He instantly turned to Yahn, and said, "Sorry."

Then he grabbed him by the unitard straps as Sonya opened her door, and flung him inside with more force than was necessary. Because, despite how big Yahn was, Alucard was a vampire.

"Yah!" Yahn shrieked in surprise, before landing face-first into Aria's love-pillows, his headphones clattering to the curb.

Alucard had already jumped back into the car, slamming on the gas before he had closed his door. And not a moment too soon, as another set of tires skidded around the corner behind us, engine groaning as the van of weregorillas stomped on the pedal in pursuit. Alucard gave it everything he had, mashing the pedal to the floorboard.

Sonya slammed her door while the car was in motion, and then slapped Yahn hard on the ass. He shrieked again, this time into Aria's boobs, but quickly repositioned himself so that he was sitting between them, eyes as wide as saucers. "What ees—"

Bullets peppered the car again, and Yahn let out a scream of terror as Aria shoved his face into her crotch, hunkering her upper body low over his head to avoid any potential bullets. This effectively made a Yahn sandwich that any hormonal adolescent would remember to the end of his days.

But not Yahn. He just let out muffled, panicked screams.

I slunk lower into my seat, searching through the satchel carefully, but urgently. I let out a breath as my hand closed over the two small glass spheres. I slowly pulled them out, thinking furiously.

"We're never going to make it. One of the other vans is right behind him. You better have one hell of a plan in that purse of yours," Alucard said, swerving back and forth to avoid the gunfire.

I did have a plan, but it wouldn't work with us moving this fast. I needed to break the spheres open at a safe distance. Because they were still prototypes, and liable to blow up three out of ten times.

Rather than open a Gateway like they had been designed to do.

I had put them in my satchel, wanting to take them home to tinker with later tonight. Alucard pumped the brakes, swerved to dodge a random shopping cart rolling across the middle of the road, and then punched the gas again. The motion sent the balls flying right into the backseat, and I gasped in horror, expecting a ball of flame to incinerate us in an instant. But my balls bounced off Yahn's pudgy chest, and dropped straight into his cleavage, burrowing under his unitard. I let out an anxious breath. We had been saved by Yahn's man-boobs.

"Be careful with my balls!" I screamed. "They're fragile!" The three in the back froze, each staring down at Yahn's sweaty chest, and the two perfect spheres that could be seen pushing out under the fabric.

Alucard began laughing so hard that he couldn't speak for a moment. "Nate's balls are fragile!" he finally hooted, pounding the steering wheel. "If I wasn't driving right now, I would *toe-tah-lee* Facetime Gunnar!" he roared, mimicking Yahn's voice.

Yahn managed to frown at the vampire, sensing the mockery, but I placed my palm on the vampire's face, slowly pushing him away to focus on the road as I climbed onto the console.

"Ack! I'm trying to drive!" he slurred, words impeded by my fingers up his nose and in his mouth. I ignored him, focusing on the Swede as I pulled my hand away. *Gross, vampire slobber.*

"Yahn, stay still. Sonya, Aria, I need you to grab my balls."

"*Jesus!*" Alucard shouted, roaring with laughter again. "I can't even—" he gasped.

"Yah, toe-tah-lee okay. I won't make a peep," Yahn insisted, jutting his chest out.

The Reds turned horrified faces in my direction. "He's so *sweaty,*" Sonya whispered.

"Great dancing class today, yah! Toe-tah-lee rad and stuff!" Yahn grinned happily, not understanding that it hadn't been a compliment.

Aria tightened her lips, face a mask of disgust as she slowly inched her hand into his cleavage and carefully retrieved the ball. She hesitated, and then her fingers began to slide across his sweaty chest towards the other sphere, trying to grab both balls. "*No!* Just one ball at a time. They're fragile, and sweaty. Sonya, grab the other one. Just hold it. Carefully. Like a baby bird."

Alucard was hyperventilating now, jerking the steering wheel. "Hold Nate's sweaty balls! Like a baby bir—"

A sudden burst of gunfire cut him off. He swerved forcefully, causing my gut to tighten. But Aria clutched her... *magical sphere* protectively in one hand. Sonya didn't need any more encouragement, the gunfire reminding her that time was of the essence. She closed her eyes as she slid her hand over the sweaty flesh, and carefully grasped my ball— *magical sphere*.

I let out a sigh of relief, motioning for them to hand them to me. Carefully. They did, and then leaned back with a shiver, each wiping their hand on the seat as they gagged. Yahn wore a weak grin, the gunfire slightly diminishing his cheerful mood. But like a puppy, that didn't last long, his enthusiasm shining through the storm of gunfire and high-speed car-chases. He peppered the girls with questions in his high-pitched voice. I began climbing back into the front seat, but my pistol was in the way. I wasn't keen on experiencing genital relocation surgery in a moving car.

"Help?" I asked Alucard.

He growled, retrieving the gun quickly, not even turning his head from the road. I needed to focus on my balls—

Magical spheres.

More bullets actually pelted the back of the Tahoe this time, and Yahn let out a very feminine shriek. Alucard shook his head, angrily reaching back to shove the pistol into the sparkly Swede's hands. "Bad guys are trying to kill us. Point this at them and shoot. It's okay if you miss. Just *distract* them," Alucard shouted, not looking back. Yahn's hands began to shake, but I tuned him out, turning to the vampire.

"Okay, I need to throw my balls on the ground, but we need to be far away. As long as they don't blow up, they will open a Gateway back to Chateau Falco where—"

"Nate, we're going ninety miles an hour, dodging bullets. I can't just *stop*. Can't you, I don't know, *magically* swing your sweaty balls or something?"

I shivered at the thought. "Not a good idea. They're unstable. And slippery."

A flash of fear shot across his face, his eyes flicking to the rearview mirror. He suddenly swerved again, avoiding another barrage. He hit a pothole, and the pistol in Yahn's hand went off with a thunderous *boom*, blowing a fist-sized hole directly through the ceiling of our car, causing all of us to shout out in terror, especially Yahn. But his was more of an feral shriek.

"*Christ*! Give it to me, dancer boy!" Aria hissed, snatching the gun away from him.

Alucard took a deep breath, and spoke without looking. "There's a slingshot in the glovebox. Will that work?"

"Why the hell do you have—" I let out a breath, shaking my head. "Never mind." I thought about it, opening the glovebox to take a look. Dangerous, but I didn't have any other options. I just had to be very, very careful.

I settled them into the leather strap, careful to hold it so that I didn't put any pressure on my balls—

Magical spheres.

"Alright. You're going to need to slow down for a second in case these blow up. *Then* you're going to need to floor it. The Gateway only stays up for a few seconds. Just aim for my balls— magical spheres," I corrected, with a weak grin.

Alucard shook his head in disbelief, but gripped the steering wheel tightly. "Do it."

I readied the slingshot for a quick release, and darted up to poke my torso out the sunroof. Alucard let off the gas, and I released the band the moment I was steady, aiming straight ahead of us, hoping I had given us enough distance.

But Alucard floored it while I was ducking back inside to avoid any bullets, which sent me flying into the backseat, landing face-first in Yahn's sweaty chest, taking his breath away.

"I hate sweaty balls!" Alucard shouted at the top of his lungs. Then, "Duck!"

We dove for the floor boards, trying to get as low as possible, as the sound of screaming metal and shattered glass exploded all around us.

CHAPTER 3

The car jerked, skidded, spun, and Alucard shouted, pumping the brakes as we all played human Twister in the backseat. I heard the crunching of gravel before the car finally struck something solid, coming to a complete and sudden stop. The vehicle wheezed and hissed, and I heard birds chirping in a cheery song. I found myself staring up at a clear blue sky.

Because the top of the car was *gone*. It must have been too tall for the Gateway. The back of the car, about a foot away from the backseat, was also missing. Probably a result of the Gateway snapping shut behind us, slicing through our car like a hot knife through butter.

If we had been a second slower…

Alucard let out a shout, pounding the steering wheel. "Nate's sweaty balls save the day!"

I heard someone clear their throat outside the car beside the backseat passenger door. I looked up to see Dean frowning at me, my home looming over his shoulder.

I smiled weakly. "Dean… Is my suit ready?"

"You hit the fountain," he replied, turning his back on us. "Your suit is hanging in the foyer. The Gala starts in twenty minutes," he said, shaking his head as he walked back to the house.

We piled out of the car, brushing ourselves off and checking for wounds. Everyone seemed to be fine. Until I got to Yahn, who was scratching at his chest with a thoughtful frown.

"You okay?" I asked nervously.

"Yah," his smile morphed back to his usual ray of sunshine look. "I think one of them, like, scratched me with their *fan-see* nails or something," he said, shrugging dismissively. "Didn't hurt my dancing suit, so I'm toe-tah-lee great and stuff," he added with one last rub at his chest.

I nodded with a faint, haunted smile, slowly turning my back on him as I shot Sonya and Aria a meaningful look. Their faces were ashen.

One of them had possibly scratched Mr. Ya-ya Sunshine.

And they were shifters.

Weredragons.

Sometimes their scratches and bites could transform a human into whatever flavor of shifter they were. It wasn't as common as with werewolves, but still.

They may have possibly just created a monster.

I could only imagine what color he would be if he became infected by the dragon gene.

Pink, silver, and purple. With glittering scales. Like a disco ball.

Then there would be nothing to save us from him. Because the Reds would become responsible for him. And Raego, the king of the dragon nation, would not be pleased with me. And Greta would finally have to kill me for harming her grandson.

I shook my head, shooting them a calming look. We had a Gala to go to.

"Can I, like, change and stuff?" Yahn asked, grinning widely.

"Yes. Powder room is down the first hallway on the right. Third door," I said. "Just hurry."

"*Alriiight!* Party time! This ees going to be toe-tah-lee awesome and stuff!"

Alucard was brushing off his clothes, already dressed for the Gala, and surprisingly, no rips, scrapes, or stains marred his suit. Although it was slightly wrinkled.

He met my eyes. "How are we going to get there in time?" he asked.

I smiled. "Shadow Walk."

Alucard's gaze latched onto Yahn jogging up the steps with his backpack, which was unpleasant to witness with his sparkly tights. "You're going to scare the living hell out of him."

I shrugged. "Worth it. Do *you* want to tell Tory we can't make it?"

Alucard just sighed. "Think she'll know what we were up to?"

"No way, man. We're sneaky. She won't suspect a thing."

"Famous last words…" he said absently. Then he flashed me an overly-animated smile. "This ees going to be toe-tah-lee awesome and stuff! I'm a sparkly dragon, ya?"

I smiled lightly, shaking my head with concern, hoping that wasn't the case.

CHAPTER 4

If I hear it one more time, I'm going to blow this whole Gala to ashes, Carrie-style, I thought to myself, meandering through the crowd and away from the guest that had forced me into conversation a few minutes ago. To wish me a happy upcoming birthday. Like every other guest here. Thankfully, the announcement of the keynote speaker had given me an excuse to exit. Because I was excited to hear Tory speak. And I wanted away from these bootlickers.

I was also very aware of the Reds, Alucard, and Yahn, studiously keeping as much distance as possible from them, so as not to raise suspicion of our earlier adventures. Especially Yahn, because Shadow Walking had both terrified him into silence, and then oddly *compounded* his excitement and cheer. He was unflappable. He had peppered me with questions until I had yelled at him to keep his voice down. But I did keep an eye on him now out of the corner of my eye. He was hard to miss with his red and yellow plaid suit, complete with bright red loafers. He waved happily at me, noticing my look. I smiled, nodded, and turned into the crowd, hoping no one else had noticed.

I still needed to share the update about our weregorilla adventures to someone here in the crowd. He wouldn't be having any more stalker problems. I hoped…

"Happy upcoming Birthday, Master Temple!" the Mayor bellowed in my ear as I stalked by.

Damnit all.

I plastered on a smile for him, and then pressed on. He nodded knowingly, understanding that I had duties as one of the hosts for this soiree. Despite us being inside Tory's newly constructed school – that still smelled of sawdust and paint – the heavy scent of barnyard animals permeated the air like a faint body odor. Tory had decided to hire a small petting zoo, making the event kid-friendly. All the miniature animals were outside, freshly-bathed, their hair styled, and with flashy ribbons covering every square inch of their tiny bodies. Still, not many kids had shown up to the event, but the animals had been a big hit to the adults.

Which was kind of cool. It was entertaining to see respectable, serious-faced business men and women from St. Louis letting down their guard to pet a pony, even take selfies with the mangy beasts.

I moved closer to the podium, wanting to be visible as a show of support for Tory. Because this crowd was intimidating. Quite a few donors had turned out, all dressed to the nines, representing the majority of the money in St. Louis. They were all very, very liquid.

By *liquid*, I meant *cash*. These people had dough. Scrooge McDuck money.

And we had set up this event in hopes to swindle some of that money for Tory's new school for Freaks. Well, we had obviously used our marketing hats to change the title to something less terrifying and monstrous. So, it was instead called *Shift*.

Transform your mind, was our marketing slogan, which was kind of clever, appealing to both the Freaks and the Regulars. An expensive graphic design company had come up with the logo, and it was pretty snazzy.

But let's be honest. It was a school for hyper-violent shifters with almost zero control. Good thing their Principal, Tory Marlin, was a Beast Master – able to control their powers until she could teach them to control themselves.

If she *could* teach them to control themselves.

And their part-time Vice-Principal was a werewolf with one eye, who always appeared to be scowling. Gunnar, the Alpha werewolf of St. Louis, and my long-time childhood friend. I had strongly voiced that he should also teach the cheerleading team, but I had been voted down.

Maybe Yahn would be up for the job, I thought with a faint grin, but it quickly shifted to anxiety. I really hoped he wasn't infected… I shook my head clear of the thought, focusing on the matter at hand. Only time would tell with Yahn. Nothing I could do about it now.

Gunnar was also their landlord, because he had bought the land where the school was located – the old Temple Industries property. I had given him a deal on it after my company had been shut down. He had also moved the kids into his apartment complex, where he and his pack of werewolves lived. We had hoped that the kids living surrounded by other shifters would make for an easier transition, and that any accidents would go unnoticed. Or at least unremarked upon.

Which brought us to the party. Gala. Charity dinner. Whatever. I was trying to raise money for them.

Because it would attract all sorts of the wrong attention if I simply wrote Tory a check. Which was also why I had sold Gunnar the land. His doggie supply business had taken off, and he was doing well financially. *Werewolf-owned pet supply business*, I rolled my eyes.

To be honest, I couldn't really write her a check right now, anyway. Because I was busy getting my new company, Grimm Tech, off the ground, and I sorely needed investors as well.

Which, surprisingly, was not all that easy. Especially after I had effectively destroyed a multi-billion-dollar company here in St. Louis not too long ago. One that had been in my family for generations.

Now, *I* hadn't really destroyed it. The Brothers Grimm had.

But like the true purpose of Tory's school, that didn't necessarily fit on the newspaper headlines, either.

Because… well, the Grimms weren't *real*. At least not to the general, *Regular*, population.

Must be nice to go to bed with thoughts like that. *Monsters don't exist.*

Rather than thoughts like, *the mysterious super-secret club of wizards known as the Syndicate wants to murder you, the pompous professional club of wizards known as the Academy wants to murder you, your great-great-great ancestor wants to murder you, your fiancée wants to murder you, and really, any Freak who has ever met you wants you six feet under...*

Tory cleared her throat from the podium, accepting a flute of champagne from a dark-haired, young female server holding an empty tray. I frowned, not recognizing the girl. After all, each of the servers was actually one of her students, one of the group of shifters we had saved from the Circus almost a year ago. I knew them all pretty well, because I had spent many months trying to help them. Maybe she had just changed her hair color or something. Or Tory had hired additional, more experienced help without telling me. That made sense.

The server departed, walking behind an older couple watching the podium. My frown grew when I didn't see her appear on the other side of the couple. I should have seen her as she made her way back towards the kitchen with her empty tray. But a *tinkling* sound blasted from the speakers, and I spun around to see Tory holding her champagne flute much too close to the microphone, tapping it with a small spoon. She blushed a little bit, but lifted up her champagne in a toast, and then took a big sip to cover her blunder.

More of a long *gulp*, actually.

She frowned down at the glass for a second, blinking slowly, and then lifted her gaze to the guests. Hushing sounds spread through the room. Her dark hair seemed to shine in the light, emphasized by the contrasting large diamond earrings she wore. She smiled a little too broadly, flashing her white teeth at the crowd a little too openly. She was all of five-foot-five and, even in heels, was noticeably short and thin. No muscle or bone bulk to add to her weight. But she was chiseled, in great shape, and this was elegantly displayed by the perfectly-tailored cocktail dress she wore, with just enough cleavage to catch a wandering eye. She wore a diamond pendant necklace to cover it up, but this only served to emphasize it in a classy manner, which had the added benefit of helping her appeal to both the money-hungry women and the questionably-moral men.

Which had been *my* idea.

Despite appearances, little ol' Tory was anything but fragile. She was a Beast Master – or some flavor of maybe-Fae that could control shifters and other monsters. And she was incredibly *strong*. As in, pick up a car with one hand, hammer you into paste, and not break a nail, strong.

The Principal of Shift.

Gunnar, scowling per usual, stood beside her. He wore a fancy, silk eye patch over one eye (which he hated), and generally looked like any Vice-Principal everywhere. Brooding. His eye locked onto me, and I could tell he knew something had happened. I don't know how, but I kept my face blank, casually tapping my eye and nodding in approval. He turned away, jaw clenching in frustration.

You couldn't tell by looking at him now, but he was excited, thankful, and terrified of his position. Even though he had argued that he didn't have time for such things, he had displayed a surprising amount of support in helping set everything up. Because he was a big softie. Or maybe he just didn't want his new residents destroying the city in a murder spree that led back to his land holdings.

It was probably a combination of a lot of things. Point was, he was taking his job seriously, even though he complained to me about it at every opportunity. Alucard stood on Tory's other side, looking guilty as hell. *Keep it together, Glampire*, I thought to myself. Gunnar seemed to be sniffing him curiously, too subtle for anyone in the crowd to notice, but I saw his nostrils flaring, and werewolves had darn good sniffers. He finally relented, eye darting back to me, but I pretended not to notice.

Alucard was a secretary of some kind to Tory and Gunnar. He had asked for all sorts of cool titles, all of which had been rejected in a vote. But he was basically there to help Gunnar keep the kids in line. With force, if necessary.

Because vampires were strong. And *Master* vampires were even stronger. But *Daywalker* Master vampires were a complete rarity, as in, I had never heard of another one. Having that kind of muscle around was a good precaution. It was why I had taken him with me today to meet with the weregorillas, too. Even though he had failed miserably. But between Gunnar and Alucard, Tory had plenty of additional muscle to keep the kids in line, and the kids were doing much better than anyone had expected after a life of fighting in the circus.

"I want to thank everyone for coming this evening," Tory began, interrupting my thoughts. I frowned, because it looked like she was swaying a little. She was either extremely nervous, or she had already sampled too many flutes of champagne. But I was pretty sure I had only seen her with the one glass. Well, before that server had given her another one. The paranoid part of me began to grow antsy, but I shook it off. Even though there were enough untrained shifters present to start an unparalleled murder spree, we also had enough Freaks here to keep everything civil.

Gunnar had hired on a dozen of his werewolves to help as security. And the Huntress – a possibly immortal assassin – was also lurking in the wings, ready for anything.

No one was going to be able to just waltz in here and fuck it all up. Because, there wasn't any reason to. This school would help everyone. Hell, we might even get requests for new students after word spread about what was really going on. What kind of students we were really teaching. It was probably just Tory's nerves, giving a speech in front of so many wealthy people.

Perhaps she hadn't run into that very often as a beat cop on the streets of St. Louis.

Everything is fine, I thought to myself as Tory continued to speak.

But my eyes tracked the room, watching the two dozen servers gliding through the crowd with trays of drinks and hors d'oeuvres. The two-dozen servers who might – at any moment – decide that the guests all around them were the real hors d'oeuvres…

CHAPTER 5

I realized I was subconsciously fidgeting with my lapel pin as I assessed the room for dangers, warning signs, idly listening to Tory speak about her school. The pin was a *GT* symbol my design crew had come up with for my new company, Grimm Tech. Sharp, sleek, and to the point. Not many knew exactly what the company would be doing, but all assumed it was basically a rebrand of Temple Industries.

Which was true. But it also wasn't *entirely* true.

The Research and Development group of Grimm Tech would maintain a lot of projects off the books, so to speak. Because I was building a magical arsenal of my own devising. Something to help keep everyone safe. Cutting edge stuff. A combination of science, technology, and magic. Over the past few months, I had swiped quite a few things from Pandora's Armory to study, returning them promptly only to borrow yet another set of doodads. Pandora had been pleased to see me finally playing with my toys, but I was still very careful. The things in Pandora's Armory were dangerous, deadly, and had been locked away for a reason.

Grimm Tech was just in the startup phase. I hadn't even looked at properties yet, let alone construction companies and architects.

I had hired Greta, her grandson, Yahn, and two other previous employees of Temple Industries so far. Othello – a hacker friend I had met in college – had performed due diligence on each of them, making sure they weren't corporate spies, they were good at their job, and that they were aware of magic. Yahn, being an intern, hadn't had the magical awareness, but he had received one hell of a crash course an hour ago.

The crew was already hard at work on some fun projects I had come up with. Like the magic balls I had tested today, in fact. We had an old warehouse – revamped and retrofitted – in Soulard, not too far from my bookstore, Plato's Cave.

Greta had been the only one I personally knew beforehand. One of the *Old Guard* from Temple Industries, she was a cantankerous, but lovable employee; one I could trust implicitly. She was only recently coming to grips with the magical side of the world – since no one believed in that kind of thing – but was well-versed in the traditional side of a technology company, so that we could eventually pursue projects for the Regular world, like many that Temple Industries had pursued. So that investors might see profit potential without me having to explain the crazily high R&D expenses on the books.

As if I had whispered her name, a voice suddenly spoke beside me. "Mr. Murdock," a crotchety voice murmured from my left. I turned to see Greta discreetly pointing her chin at a man standing a dozen feet away. He wore a sharp suit, and had beautiful young escorts on either arm, guiding him to the stage. I pretended not to notice them – the Reds – as he gave me a polite nod. I smiled, nodding back, wondering why the hell the Reds were hanging on his arm. He had been very adamant about wanting to invest into Grimm Tech, but I had yet to speak with him.

I nodded to Greta, putting Mr. Murdock on my list for later. Greta wore a matronly suit, bangles covered her arms, and hairspray had transformed her head into a helmet. Greta had been the Executive Secretary at Temple Industries, and had beaten me upside the head – literally and metaphorically – with her Bible for the brief time I had run the company. She had made sure I didn't screw up anything too badly. Like I potentially had with Yahn, her grandson.

Of course, after the Grimms had sabotaged my company, she had taken a hefty settlement, and retired to focus on spreading God's word. She had later adopted a stray pigeon outside my bookstore one day while hosting a bake sale with her Bible students.

I nodded at the man standing over her shoulder, thick, dark hair brushing the tips of his shoulders. His name was Eae, an Angel – or *pigeon*, as I called him – and his face looked cut from marble. To me, his eyes seemed to pick up the light like a mirror, creating a golden halo around his irises, and his black suit bunched up around his shoulders like he was wearing old-fashioned shoulder pads. "Sup, Pigeon. Shoulder pads went out of style a long time ago." He muttered something under his breath that I didn't catch. "Got your smiting paddle ready? Just in case any of these kids need an Old Testament lesson in manners?"

The Angel bit his tongue, flashing me a deep scowl. "One day, Temple…" he finally warned.

I batted my eyelashes at him. "And you'll be there, waiting for me, Feathers. It's why you took the job. You know, after you Fell—"

He stammered angrily, "I didn't *Fall*, I am being taught patience and humility."

"Right—"

Greta gripped my arm with an iron, old-woman claw, an inherited skill granted to all women once they became grandmothers. "Watch your tone when speaking with an Agent of Heaven. Have some *decency*," she hissed.

I smiled playfully. "He knows I'm just ribbing him. Sometimes my mouth just moves on its own."

"We've all sinned and fallen short—"

"Who's that?" I interrupted. Greta and Eae turned to look, and I slipped away. I heard a muffled curse, but kept walking as Tory continued speaking about the primary mission of the school. I found myself scanning the crowd, marking potential investors. Many had reached out to me expressing interest, but I had yet to accept anyone. Grimm Tech was a long way from that.

I had shaken many hands this evening, entertaining many offers, and none of them had set off magical alarm bells. Next step was Othello digging into every inch of their lives – without them knowing – to make sure they weren't a plant.

Paranoid?

Yup. And proud of it.

Because there was a lot of shit going on in the world right now, and—

"Watch it, you vile street urchin!" a thick, baritone voice shouted. I flinched, instinctively ready to fight my way out of a warzone, because the last few years, that's all my life had been.

But all I found was a portly white-haired man, sporting a red sleeve on his otherwise immaculate white dress shirt from where one of the servers had spilled a glass of wine on his way by. The server – one of Tory's more advanced students (read *less bestial*), was fumbling with the spilled glass, and in his effort, ended up dropping the rest of the carefully balanced tray of drinks all over the man, the remaining glasses falling to shatter on the ground. The beefy server was the weregorilla student I had been hoping to talk to about his stalker problem.

Everyone nearby turned, and Tory suddenly giggled into the microphone, noticing the action, her noise amplified by the dozens of speakers surrounding us. Tory regained her composure after a moment, picking back up where she left off after apologizing to the crowd.

"Now look what you've done! Do you have any idea how much this suit cost?" The portly man was seething, shaking a fist, his red cheeks puffing at the beefy server, who looked utterly embarrassed.

But even worse... He looked on the verge of shouting right back.

Or... something a lot more *primitive*.

I intervened before the situation escalated to the server slicing the man into banana bites. "Easy, Sir. Let's get you cleaned up. I'm sure he didn't mean—"

The man rounded on me, and his features immediately changed from anger to greedy anticipation. "Ah, Master Temple. I hear a Happy Birthday is in order." He waved a hand dismissively while he spoke, signifying that he was merely following etiquette to the letter, if not the intent. "Just the man I wanted to see. Bad enough to waste my precious time attending this sorry excuse for a charity, for a sorry excuse for a school." He reached out to attempt to place his clean arm on my shoulder, trying to deliver camaraderie by osmosis or something. I politely stepped just out of reach, masking my motion as trying to step out of the mess on the floor as I faced him.

I didn't smile. He rolled his eyes, grinning as if trying to console me. "Honestly, charities don't *have* to be hopeless. There are many groups that *our* type of crowd wouldn't mind throwing money at. You didn't have to concoct one of your own. We do have our dignity, you know." He winked at me, chuckling. "Now, about Grimm—"

"What. Did. You. Say?" the server whispered, interrupting him. I glanced over to see his arms quivering as he stared at the broken glass on the ground. Then his arms began to actually ripple beneath his tuxedo, and his hair began to grow longer, thicker, wilder. It was barely noticeable, but I knew what to look for.

The Freak was about to Freak out.

Shift.

But at least Tory's presence would prevent him from mauling everyone in sight.

Still, I didn't want to take any chances. I reached out to grab the portly man by the shoulder, "Right. Let's go find somewhere quiet to discuss Grimm—" but my fingers suddenly tingled where they had touched him.

I reeled back in surprise, staring first at my hand, and then at the portly man.

He smirked, and then winked with eyes that were much too deep and aware. Like an entirely different persona than the greedy businessman I had seen so far. Before I could speak, he rounded on the server. "What I meant to say was that I would rather toss quarters at the homeless than drop a penny to help the likes of *you people*," he sneered, leaning forward.

My shock and alarm was yanked away as Tory suddenly shouted at the crowd. "You people might want to get the… frick out of here!" Then she began cackling uproariously into the microphone. The crowd simply stared at her, frowning in confusion.

Gunnar and Alucard flinched, bewildered as they turned to stare at Tory. Then the fire alarms went off, and their postures shifted from confused to predatory in a heartbeat, gazes roving the room for threats. They simultaneously slipped from the stage in different directions like shepherd dogs, urgently ushering people outside as if they had planned it all along.

I risked a glance back at Tory to see she was clutching the podium as if it were the only thing holding her up. She frowned down at her champagne glass, wobbled a bit, and then righted herself, taking a deep breath.

Screams, arguments, and angry shouts rose like a tidal surge, because rich people didn't like being told what to do. This was punctuated by the bleating of the fire alarm, which seemed to send tiny spurts of adrenaline straight into my brain via my ear canal. Tory stared at the crowd, most of whom were being frantically forced out the room, and mouthed a single word.

No…

Then she collapsed like a sack of bricks, her eyes rolling back into her head.

I turned in horror to the server. Shit. No more Beast Master to keep the shifters at bay.

The kid was staring down at his wrists, which were suddenly sprouting long, wiry fur.

"The Academy says, *Hello*," the portly man murmured behind me. I had completely forgotten about him in the chaos. "Toodles, Temple," he said, and suddenly disappeared.

I heard Alucard and Gunnar, as well as a handful of his werewolves, shouting over the crowd, trying to calmly force everyone out of the building. The last of the guests were finally shoved out the door, and the doors closed loudly, blocking any guests from sneaking back in unannounced. Leaving me in a room full of panicked shifter servers, who looked just as terrified as I felt.

But for different reasons. They were scared of the alarms, the panic, Tory passing out.

I was scared of *them*.

I let out a sigh of relief to see Eae standing where I had abandoned him, in front of Greta, arms outstretched as his heavenly gaze flicked from one server to the next, the shoulders of his suit perched up higher than usual, like he had inflated his shoulder pads. He had chosen to stay behind, lend me a Heavenly hand.

Sweet. It was about time the Angel carried his weight.

The server in front of me cried out as his shirt ripped open, revealing a heavily furred chest. Then his shoulder seams burst open and he hunched over, hammering his fists into the ground, right into the broken glass, because his arms were suddenly as thick as my thighs, and twice their normal length. He completed his shift, clothes shredding and popping as they tore free from his now, much larger, body.

Weregorilla.

Why did it have to be the weregorilla? The one I had been planning on talking to anyway, about my earlier meeting in the warehouse district. And now I was going to have to *subdue* him?

He lifted one calloused fist, glanced down at the blood, and then gave it a long, wet lick between his ape-like canines. He lifted his head, his eyes rolling back into his skull for a moment as he let out a deep chuffing sound.

I spotted the Huntress carrying Tory off the podium, and I noticed Alucard and Gunnar had returned, and were now herding a large swarm of servers into one of the back rooms, trying to get them as far away as possible from the gorilla before he gave them any ideas. Gunnar shot me a panicked look as if to say, *it's the best I can do. I'll be right back.* Then he was gone.

Which left me and Eae with three servers. Two struggling against their shift, and my gorilla. But they all suddenly turned, as if sharing one hive mind, to stare at the doors where the guests had disappeared.

Because predators loved it when prey fled.

I was the only one who noticed the older gentleman standing in the corner. He winked at me, turned to face the wall, and extended his palm towards the surface.

But his palm was suddenly an extension of live, smoldering coals. And the wall instantly roared with flame, crumbling and cracking as it was engulfed. Then he turned his head to look back at me, and this time, all I saw was a face from hell, made entirely of red, white, and orange burning coals. His eyes and mouth were black pits, but I could still tell that he was smiling.

Then he also disappeared as the wall began to splinter and crumble, spreading the fire higher.

Shifters didn't like fire. It did something to their animalistic brains.

The other two completed their shift in an explosion of fabric that I didn't have time to study, because the gorilla suddenly rounded on me, roaring like this was all my fault. Shit.

CHAPTER 6

*I*gnoring the fire, I double-checked that no Regulars were present, and called Stone Skin around my fist. A handy – no pun intended – spell I had used to take on a group of gargoyles once. Basically, changing my skin from soft mortal squishy stuff to that of a statue. It wasn't permanent, more like body armor. But I pretended I was the Iron Fist. Because, why *not*?

I gave him a right cross straight to the nose while he was still roaring, feeling cartilage crunch underneath as his war cry abruptly became a squeal.

Before he could Donkey Kong me, I dropped to a crouch, and shouted, *"Hadouken!"* as I cast a blast of ice at his chest. It shattered on impact, knocking him back a dozen feet as the explosion of ice cubes ricocheted off him. His eyes were murderous, and he roared at me again, this time much more… invested.

Now, roaring might sound cliché. It's not. Ever heard a gorilla roar?

Those that have, understand me. For the rest, the sound was primal, ferocious, and struck a space deep inside my chest, trying to convince me on a biological level that I needed to flee while I still could. As if the gorilla had told each of my individual cells that he was going to tear them to shreds, slowly.

I pointed at his torn suit on the ground. "That was a rental. You're going to pay me back for that, kid. Or else I'm changing my mind, and giving you to the gorillas downtown like they so politely asked me to do earlier today."

Some part of him heard me, but he was too hyped-up to listen. Still, it bought me a few precious moments as he shook his head, silently fighting himself. Enough time to notice that the one corner of the room was burning hotter, and smoke was slowly filling the space. I took stock of the dozens of buckets and tubs near the tables, each full of champagne and other assorted beverages. And they were all brimming with *ice*.

I pulled heavily on my magic and connected the heat from the flames with the ice. The heat melted the ice in an instant, it was that hot. I cut the connection before the heat could set the water to boiling, possibly melting through the tubs. Then I took a deep breath for round two, groaning as I collected the moisture in the tubs into one large, quivering orb of water before me.

Through the floating water, I saw that the gorilla had regained his special purpose: to eat my face. But he was still a safe distance away, so I let out a shout, and cast the water like a tidal wave at the wall of flames.

Which, in hindsight, was pretty stupid.

The wall of water blew out the fire in an explosion of steam. But it *also* tore through the weakened wall, revealing a lawn of fresh green grass lit by the fading sun, and the sound of sirens in the distance.

Which was when the weregorilla tried to bushwhack me, having closed the distance quicker than I had anticipated. He swung his fists down at my outstretched hands, luckily striking the one with the Stone Skin. I heard his forearms snap, but I was still knocked on my ass from the force of the blow as he yowled in agony, beefy arms now useless tentacles of flesh. Chips of stone broke away from my armor, weakened by the blow. I couldn't take another hit like that.

"Stop taunting him, and shut him down!" Eae yelled in a tight voice. I turned to see him struggling against a weregoat of some kind, gripping it by the horns to keep it away from Greta – who was swinging her purse over his shoulder, hitting the goat upside the head with the metal buttons and zippers. The goat bleated in pain as one of the zippers caught his eye.

Eae used the distraction to twist his forearms and fling the shifter across the room into the podium, destroying it in a cloud of splinters. He flexed, and his wings burst out of his suit, shredding the fabric as they arced out above his back, trebling his size. His wings were a mottled grey, still impressive, but looked more weathered, beaten, and downright sickly than when I had first met him. Because when I had first met him, his wings had been made of elements: stone, ice, fire, and ether. But that was before.

He hadn't made Daddy happy when he blundered the demon situation that had plagued my city in the past. His Nephilim children had wrongly hunted me down to give me a whooping. Since then, he had been serving time on earth as penance. So, he didn't have his full mojo back yet. Still, half an Angel was a whole… *hell* of a lot, so to speak.

I ignored the whimpers of the gorilla behind me, walking towards the goat, eager to see an Angel kick ass. Like a Vision of Righteousness, his wings flexed out, and he soared straight at the weregoat, who was now scrambling to his hooves on the stage. The Angel clutched something to his chest, and I felt anticipation building in my soul. He was going to go all out. Smite the shit out of this kid.

Heh. Goats. Kid.

"Angel stuff!" I cheered, voice brimming with excitement. "He's going to do Angel stuff!"

Eae wouldn't kill – that wasn't his way – but I'd be lying if I said I wasn't anxious to see what the Angel could do when he put his Sunday School pants on.

And you would be right if you said it caught the goat and I entirely by surprise when he sailed just above the shifter's head and out the giant window, shattering the brand-new glass as he bravely fled the carnage.

Because he hadn't been holding some Heavenly power to his chest, ready to lay the smack down on the weregoat. He had been holding Greta, helping her escape the chaos.

I realized this, because on their way by, Greta got one last good swing in, decking the goat in the jaw with her million-pound purse, knocking the goat out cold. She must have had a Gutenberg Bible in there because the kid went down.

I felt the ground shaking, and turned to see the gorilla pounding my way, having overcome his injuries, or at least ignoring them long enough to attempt at least one successful strike while I was distracted by the fleeing Angel. I flung up a flicker of power, unleashing an elemental whip of ice at an exposed beam in the ceiling. I didn't want to play with any more fire, not in Tory's brand new building. I jumped, and yanked my hand on the whip, hurling myself over the gorilla as he raced to where I had just been standing. I dropped to the ground behind him, releasing my whip from the beam, and flung it at his legs.

Then I fucking *jerked* the whip like I was trying to start a stubborn lawnmower for the first time in six months. His forward momentum slammed his face into the ground, knocking him instantly unconscious.

I knew this because his body immediately shifted back to his now-naked human form. I looked over to the stage and saw that the goat was also just a skinny kid again, sans tuxedo.

"Who wants some?" I shouted to the empty room, holding up my arms, even though no one had been present to see my impressive display of magic. I heard bleating and shouts from outside, and cursed, hoping that none of the shifters had broken out of the room and gone about murdering the petting zoo…

Or the fleeing guests.

My suit was torn, and I was pretty sure I had split the seam of my pants, because I felt a cool draft in my danger-zone region. I craned my neck to try and get a look at my rear before I dared run outside.

That's when I saw the charging chimera racing my way in utter silence on her padded leonine feet, head down on all fours so that her horned ram's head was aimed directly at my back. Shit. Distracted by Eae's Divine battle tactics, I had forgotten there were *three* shifters in the room.

She hit me.

It hurt.

I flew.

I landed on my ass, bounced, flipped and hit my head before skidding across the floor on my back. I heard a leonine roar, and blinked stars from my vision. My kidneys ached, likely ruptured or something, but I couldn't do anything about it. The blow to my head had really rattled me.

I stared through the haze of stars and saw the chimera stalking closer – on two legs this time – her lion-headed chest snarling at me, drooling droplets of flame, and her cobra tail swaying back and forth over her back, dripping venom from its fangs. The hypnotic motion lulled me into a daze, and I just stared at it, wondering why I had been scared.

Because chimeras were both terrifying and beautiful. A merging of three beasts. Its tail was a serpent, the tip a hooded, venomous cobra. With the body of a lion, it could either crouch down on all fours and spit fire at you from its maned lion head, or it could tuck that head down and nail you with its third form, a horned ram head, which sat just above the lion's head. Or it could stand on two legs and make you pee your pants as you stared at three monster heads ready to roast you, poison you, then head butt you before eating you alive.

A red blur of shiny scales hammered into the chimera from stage left, interrupting my thoughts. I groaned, the sudden movement snapping me out of it, but I was still sluggish in the muscle department. I lifted my head to see how close I was to death, expecting to see a few ribs poking out from my side or a hole in my gut from the chimera's head-butt.

But all I saw was that I wasn't wearing any shoes. I blinked several times, head throbbing, as I frowned at my black dress socks in confusion. My big toe poked out from a hole that hadn't been there when I put them on earlier. Unable to comprehend, I instead looked up as the sounds of continued battle raged nearby. Two red dragons now darted back and forth, shooting brief, precise gouts of flame at the chimera, taunting it, keeping it distracted. As soon as the chimera lashed out at one, the other would hit it from the opposite side – by flame, claw, or even a sudden swipe of dragon wing.

The chimera roared, hissed, and bleated in frustration.

Then a single arrow hammered into its leg. But it was small. Not an arrow. A dart.

The dragons stilled, watching the chimera as it struggled for a few seconds, and then finally crashed to its knees with an exhausted purring noise. The dragons paced back and forth for a few more moments around the fallen monster, sniffing, grunting, and watching. Then the deadly beast shimmered, and suddenly a small, naked teenaged girl lay on the floor.

I heard racing footsteps, so I struggled to sit up. "You're awesome. Unstoppable. Your socks aren't ripped, and your pants don't have a hole in the ass," I slurred, trying to motivate myself for round two. "Now, where are your shoes?" I said, finally managing to prop myself up.

But it wasn't an enemy this time. I saw the Huntress sliding on her knees in her fancy dress, tearing her stockings on the way, and finally bumping into the naked chimera girl. She yanked out the dart, and slapped her ass hard enough to make her scream from a dead sleep.

"Heh. That was funny," I mumbled, glancing back at the massive hole in the wall. A gentle breeze carried in the sound of sirens, louder than earlier. I shook my head, trying to clear away the last of my dizziness. "Probably not smart," I grunted, loud enough for the Huntress to hear me. "Seeing as how shock and surprise often turns on beast mode…"

"Shut up, Nate. I've been doing this for a while." She turned back to Camilla, the young chimera shifter, who was panting, eyes darting about wildly. She saw the destruction, especially the missing wall, and began to sob.

"I was doing so well!" she moaned, dropping her face to her palms in frustration.

"There, there, child. It's okay. It wasn't your fault." The Huntress followed her gaze to the wall. "That wasn't you. The event was… tampered with."

With that, the two dragons abruptly flickered, and were suddenly healthy, nubile, naked young girls. The Reds. Tory's adopted daughters. They were at the age when I knew it was wrong to look – almost seventeen – so I quickly averted my eyes.

That being said, anyone who simply saw them naked wouldn't have had any thoughts about age. Because their, *erm*, developments kind of murdered that thought.

As if on cue, the weregorilla groaned, shaking his head slowly. I hadn't realized he had woken. He tried to prop himself up on his broken forearms, gasped in pain, and collapsed back to the ground. Instead, he turned his head from side to side, trying to see what had happened and who was talking. He immediately noticed the three naked girls, then turned to me. "Boobs," he whispered, entirely serious. Then he passed out.

I chuckled.

"Nate! Stop laughing at the boy and help him! And where are your damn shoes?" the Huntress snapped.

I growled, finally climbing to my feet. "I don't need no stinking shoes," I muttered, stepping over the naked boy. I'd have to wait until he woke up to tell him I had hopefully put a stop to any more talk of the weregorillas wanting to adopt him into their gang.

I approached the podium. I needed to get a sample of Tory's drink. Maybe even a fingerprint from the person who had given it to her. Amazingly, the glass lay on the ground, broken, but the stem was still intact. I found a napkin, and reached to pick it up so that I wouldn't contaminate the evidence.

Then I saw that the napkin had writing on it. Which was weird, because all the napkins at the event had been plain white.

I carefully flipped it over, since it had a damp wine stain on it, and I didn't want to rip it. Someone had scribbled on it with a ballpoint pen. And rage instantly consumed me as I read it.

@StLouis'FavoriteSon – How you like them apples? #SyndicateParty-Crashers

"Motherfu—" I began, but suddenly froze as a literal icy chill swept over the back of my neck. A minor ward I had set up had just been triggered.

But the ward wasn't protecting anything *here*. It was at Chateau Falco. My home.

Someone was trying to steal my book, *Through the Looking-Glass*. My direct journal to the Mad Hatter. A truly dangerous SOB. But to get to the room with the book, they must have already broken into my house and taken out my safeguards. Both human and magical safeguards. Which shouldn't have been possible.

Regardless, someone had just done it.

I ripped open a hole in reality, a Gateway, back to my house. A vertical ring of fire erupted before me, sparks spitting out from the edges, before being immediately sucked into the opening, indicating the intended direction of travel. I glanced over my shoulder to let the Huntress know what was going on. "I'll be back. I have to—"

"No!" the Huntress shouted, eyes wide as she stared past me. I was suddenly yanked sideways by an unseen force gripping my sleeve, ripping the fabric, but still maintaining their hold on me. I felt a sharp stab in my neck, and then the world faded to black.

But I was pretty sure I also heard my pants-seam tear further before everything disappeared.

CHAPTER 7

The blinding sun struck me like a ray gun, seeming to parboil my flesh. It felt like a hot summer day, but the sudden change made it feel like a thousand degrees. The remains of my tattered suit whipped in the hot wind, and the ground felt fiery to my feet. I looked down, squinting in the reflective glare to see my toe still peeking out from my sock as I lifted my feet off the ground. My other sock was simply gone now.

What the hell?

The ground was white, and I was sitting chained to a metal folding chair. And the hot metal chair did not feel good on my ass, seeing as how only a thin layer of underwear prevented it from immediately sizzling. Because now I was sure that my pants had been ripped down the rear. And that the chair must have sat out in the sun for a while before they plopped me onto it. Whoever *they* were. I squirmed a bit, trying to hide my discomfort. I squinted less now, eyes slowly adjusting to the extreme brightness all around me.

It was kind of similar to when it snowed outside on a sunny day, and staring out at the snow physically hurt your eyes at first, because it was almost like one giant mirror for the sun. This wasn't exactly the same, but it was close. The air was dry, torrid, and heat waves shimmered in the distance as I got my bearings, able to do a little more than squint after a few moments of struggling against the chains, which were also hot to the touch from the sun.

I noticed three robed figures suddenly before me.

"I feel underdressed," I muttered, ratting the chains loudly.

They didn't respond. Merely stared at me from behind their very familiar silver masks. Rings of color flickered here and there in my peripheral vision, and I wasn't quite sure if it was from my over-use of magic, or an after-effect of whatever they had pricked me with. Because I had a sharp headache, like a hangover. The colors weren't there if I looked directly at where they had been in my peripheral vision.

Almost like I had been pharmaceuticalized.

Yeah, I know that's not a word. But I stand by it.

I scowled at the nearest figure. He or she wore a silver mask that looked to be laughing. The other had a frowny face, and the last was a mask of surprise or horror. I knew them. These ass-clowns wore masks that signified human emotions. They were Academy Justices. The police of wizards everywhere. And I had pissed them off a time or two. Granted, most recently I had done it when I carried the title of *Maker*, and had been out of their... jurisdiction.

But now? Yeah, this wasn't good. Because I was once again a wizard.

I measured up the first one from head to toe with a genuine scowl. "I don't know if anyone has ever told you the truth, but you should know that your tiny prick was not impressive."

He took a step closer, but one of the others – frowny face – held up a hand, barring his advance. None of them spoke, but the wizard did take a step back, rolling his shoulders as if ready to fight the moment he got the go ahead.

"Seriously. Hats off. You *Templed* me. Sucker punch and all." I pointedly glanced down at my chains. "Just imagine I'm doing the world's longest slow clap." They continued staring back at me from beneath their masks. For a long time. "Right. Is this a staring contest? Because I can't tell if I'm winning." I managed to wedge my naked toe into a loose chunk of white salt rock, and flung it at the laughing-faced Justice. The chunk of stone struck his forehead with a *pinging* noise, but he didn't flinch. As I did this, I very discreetly slipped a hand into my pocket, since the chains were holding my hands at my sides, looped underneath the seat rather than behind the chair. I slipped on the piece of jewelry in my pocket and waited. For a whole minute.

Then I decided to run my mouth. "Where *is* the old bag? I presume that's why I'm here. To speak with the old crone." I glanced around us, taking in the white earth for miles in every direction, rock walls showing that we were in a canyon of sorts. "The Salt Flats? Utah?" I asked curiously. "Appropriate for murder, or *being* murdered," I added, suggestively. I hoped they took it as a threat, rather than an admittance of my position.

Because I wasn't dying today.

I began to whistle the Rolling Stones song, *Time is on my side, yes, it is!* I even crossed my ankles, leaning back in my seat, and allowing my eyes to drift closed.

"Cute. I can put that on your tombstone if you like. Ironic to the last," a new voice whispered directly into my ear. I flinched instinctively, my tune falling to pieces. I heard one of the Justices snicker. Probably the laughing, tiny-pricked wizard.

"It's the dame, head-bitch, Grandma herself—"

I felt magic surge beside me before her blow lashed out at my face. I smiled.

Because her blast of power struck an unseen force field around me, and she recoiled in pain. She stepped into view, cursing as she held her fist, which must have taken the brunt of the blow. Her Justices fidgeted as she shot scowls at them.

"Not their fault, lady. As much as I'd love to see you spank them. Because Smiley over there getting spanked in the salt flats would just plain do it for me," I chuckled, winking at him. I moved my fist as much as the chains would allow, showing off my bracelet. "I brought my fisticuffs, wench."

She glared down at it, then pointed at one of the Justices. "Remove it. Honestly, do I have to hold your hands?" she snarled.

The Fae cuff prevented magic from touching me. But I had made a few upgrades to it. Frowny stepped up and reached out to remove the bracelet. "I wouldn't do that," I began.

Like a curious moth to a bug zapper, Frowny went flying a dozen feet amidst an azure explosion of sparks. I wriggled a bit in my chair to avoid getting my ass scorched further by the sparks. They instead struck the salt earth and flared red for a second. I frowned at that, then looked up, shrugging at the Grand Master of the Academy.

"Science," I grinned, "is fascinating." If a look could ignite someone into a pile of ash, hers would have. Luckily, either she couldn't, or my fisticuffs were keeping me safe. "Well, as much as I'd love to stay and chat with magic's rejects, I really do have other things to do. And it seems we're at an impasse. You tried – like the brave cowards you are – to crash my party and kidnap me." I shook my head. "Honestly, it was for the kids. Have you no *shame?*"

The Grand Master watched me. "You are right. We cannot make you do what we want. We underestimated you." She shot a glare at her three Justices, who seemed to cringe. "But we could just leave you here." Frowny was stumbling back up to the group. His mask was askew.

I frowned. "That wouldn't be very nice…" I said, trying to show a little humility for the first time. Because she had a point. I was still chained up. And they were blocking my power. If they really felt like it, they could just wait me out. Let me die of heat stroke or dehydration.

"Then, let's get straight to the point," the Grand Master began.

"Look, do you have a name? I feel sexist calling you Grand Master."

"My friends call me Grand Mistress," she offered, deadpan.

I sighed. "Right. Okay. *G Ma* it is. So, why don't you tell me what we're doing here, and why you went terrorist on the Gala."

She scowled at me. "Insolent little shit."

"Thank you," I said, my tone and face as sincere as I could manage.

She inclined her face skyward, closing her eyes, and taking a deep breath. "I really wish I could just kill you—"

"There's actually a Facebook Group for that," I interjected. "Not the *Nate Temple Fans* one. Those guys like me. Make sure you join the right one, or you'll look like a crazy old—"

She stared daggers at me, cutting me short. "Luckily for you, it is not your time. Yet." She said this last part under her breath, but loud enough for me to hear. Intentionally.

"Okay. You're fishing for attention. Obviously, you said that because you wanted me to ask what you meant. Because you made it sound like you knew *when* my time was."

She lowered her eyes with a smile, nodding. I waited, but she gave me nothing. Just then, a thought hit me out of the blue, likely delayed as a result of my injuries, the tiny prick, and this surprise kidnapping. The ward had gone off at my house.

I hid my reaction well, suddenly very interested in concluding this little chat. I waited patiently, rather than snarking off back and forth.

She tapped her lips thoughtfully, noticing my change in demeanor, if not my anxiety. "So, you do have common sense. A bit," she teased. I nodded, grinding my teeth. "I'm here to deliver an ultimatum. Imagine my surprise to find out that you are once again a wizard, and thus under my jurisdiction. Especially after that chat we had outside your home when you helped me with Jafar."

I ground my teeth harder. I hadn't *helped* anyone. I had gone against her wishes and murdered him for his crimes. For the crime of working with the Brothers Grimm to take me out in a revenge scheme. Because I had hurt his pride in the past. The Grand Master had inadvertently been kidnapped by my well-meaning friend, and upon her release, had demanded that she handle the justice of Jafar's failure. Since I had been juiced up on a new power, and no longer a wizard, I had challenged her, and come out on top. I had taken matters into my own hands and murdered the psychopath. *Against* her wishes.

But I had also shown her that it was the *smartest* option, rather than her taking Jafar back and having to answer to her other wizards, who would be very interested to know why and how her most trusted Lieutenant had double-crossed her. It also prevented her from having to kill one of her own, which would have hurt her power base with the other wizards. It had been pure politics, but I had won, and she – although knowing I had been right – hadn't liked it. Not one bit.

Because G Ma liked to get her way.

But I bit my tongue, letting her have her day in court. Well, at least in part. "You sure about the whole jurisdiction thing?" I replied softly, casually, careful not to appear threatening.

She frowned at me, and then shot a look at her Justices, who merely shook their heads in response to her unasked question. They had no idea what I was talking about. She took a few steps closer, studying me. I nodded in invitation. She slowly held out her hand, and closed her eyes. I felt her power touch me. Since I had invited her to look, and it wasn't an attack, my fisticuffs didn't block her. A few moments later, she stepped back with a gasp, as I'd known she would.

Because I had a little bit of Horseman in me. "A is for Apocalyptic. B is for Biblical," I began, but she cut me off harshly, leaning forward so that she was only inches away from my face, staring deeply into my eyes.

"Stop babbling. Explain," she commanded.

But I really couldn't. I wasn't quite sure why the power tainted me, because I hadn't accepted the job. Nevertheless, something about merely being *offered* the job had marked me with potential, and in the magical spectrum, potential for power... *stained* things. So, I had a certain stink about me.

Horseman of the Apocalypse stink.

"I'm just lucky, I guess," I finally said.

"But you are no longer a Maker. Even now I can sense the break. Cleanly severed. But the trace remains. What in blazes *are* you?"

I blinked. "What?" I still had Maker taint on me? I had only meant for her to see the Horseman thing. "But... that's impossible."

I was getting really sick and tired of this shit...

CHAPTER 8

She sounded amused. "Don't get excited. The power is truly dead and gone inside you. Merely a decayed tree stump. But it..." I could see her searching for words. "Left behind some furniture before it moved out."

"Oh," I breathed in relief. "Okay. That's better, I guess."

She was nodding, pacing around me. "Just stained from your brief contact with it, most likely. I'll admit, I hadn't anticipated sensing any of it on you. But it will all be gone soon." She completed her circle, eyes seeming to see my soul. "You thought I was referring to the other thing."

I nodded, glad she had picked up on it. I thought my alphabet recital had made it pretty obvious. "Exactly. Which is why we should just wrap this up really quick—"

"The world does not need another Horseman. We already have Four," she murmured to herself, thinking, taking on a scholarly tone. "Why would we need a Fifth? The texts do not speak of such a thing."

I shrugged, mildly curious why she had been so nervous about the Maker thing if she had known about my possible Horseman power. "No idea. I guess they saw talent. Point being—"

"Point being, I should just leave you here to die. The world will have enough chaos and carnage without a fledgling Horseman mucking things up. I don't think anyone would object to my decision." She wasn't smiling.

"I would raise my hand to object, but…" I shook the chains, arching a brow at her. She sighed, and nodded at the chains. They instantly released my wrists and zipped into the air, hanging suspended between us, like a coiled snake ready to strike. I stared at her, ignoring the snake chain as I stood. She smiled.

"Precautions…" she said softly.

"Okay." I shrugged, the heat from the sun beginning to burn my bare shoulder where the Justice had ripped off my sleeve. "I get that. Now, you mentioned something about an ultimatum. Seeing as how I'm not a wizard. Well, not *just* a wizard, I think you see how that won't really work out between—"

"We are going to kill all of the students in the school."

I blinked. "You might be new to this, but negotiations usually start out differently. Because that's a horrible idea." She didn't react at all. "They're innocent," I began, knowing that she had the strength, backing, and ability to do exactly what she said.

"It is *necessary*. We can't have a colony of shifters loose in your city. Too much chance for error. If they overwhelmed your Beast Master, your city would suffer consequences the likes of which haven't been seen for centuries. I will not allow that. Because that would indirectly lead the world to learn that magic is very, very real."

"Right. Well, we have a Daywalker, a Beast Master, an Alpha werewolf, an Angel…" I trailed off. "Look, it's easier to list who we *don't* have helping keep this thing from going belly up. Your goons tried to prove a point today. But they failed. Suffice it to say, I won't allow anything like that to happen again." I paused. "To my city." I took a step closer to the coil of chain, not even sparing it a glance as I met her eyes. "Or to the children. They are victims. They didn't ask to be kidnapped, tortured, brain-washed, and *then* killed."

"I sympathize with that. But the fact remains." Her face hardened, considering consequences, blocking out any sympathy. "They are unbelievably dangerous." Then I caught a flash of anger erupt in those eyes as she continued. "And you should know that bringing up your list of acquaintances does not help your cause. It's akin to one nation showing another nation their vast array of nuclear weapons while explaining how peaceful they are…" I swallowed. I hadn't thought about it like that. "One such group was founded in a very similar way," she added in a low tone, too quiet for her Justices to hear.

I leaned forward, suddenly interested. This was new. She could see the question on my face, but she didn't speak, only let out a final grimace of disgust.

"Fine. Don't share. Let's skip the games. First comes the part where I stupidly ask you to help. You know, the whole point of the Academy in the first place. To *help* magical creatures. Then you say you *can't*, or *won't* because *blah, blah, blah, aren't we great?*" I leveled her with a judgmental glare. "But I'm still going to pretend you have a heart in that old, desiccated, flesh-suit you call a body, G Ma."

The Justices went rigid, prepared to do whatever they could against me. I flung up a hand at them, and nothing happened. Right, they were blocking my magic. One of them snickered. I scowled at him. "Why don't you try throwing magic at me so I can snicker back, douchebag?" I folded my arms and began tapping my foot. "I'll wait."

He folded his arms, but I could imagine him grinding his teeth behind his mask.

"See how unproductive that is?" I rounded on the Grand Master. "Well?"

She looked furious, but let out a frustrated breath. "We don't have the resources to aid you." If she had said it in any other tone, I would have mocked her up, down, left, right, and center. But she looked as if she was swallowing a live eel.

"Explain."

She began to pace, that coil of chain slithering through the air between us, keeping me in line. "When you unveiled Jafar's betrayal, we did some digging. We found… veracity to your claims about the demon incursion as well as the Grimm ordeal. And we found… many others complicit in aiding him. In fact, we found more than we had feared. In our worst nightmares." She flicked her gaze briefly at the Justices.

I slowly turned to look at them with a frown. Then I remembered that the last few times I had run into them… there had been a lot more than three. "You're not saying that this is all you have left of the Justices, are you?"

She scoffed. "Of course not." But it sounded a little too immediate and rehearsed. She let out a sigh as I stared at her, waiting. "But it is accurate to say that where before you saw *seven*, now there are *three*. Statistically speaking."

I gasped in disbelief. "You're saying that more than half of the Justices were in on it?"

She nodded in resignation. "Maybe not fully aware of the big picture, what they were truly doing, but, yes. They were all helping the other team. And not just the Justices. Many other… departments were infested."

"Holy crap…" I murmured.

"Which brings me back to my earlier statement. There is another party at play, and we don't have the numbers left to spread ourselves so thin."

My mind raced. They were speaking of… "The Syndicate…" I whispered.

She flinched, pinning me with her gaze. "What?" Her body was entirely too still, and I suddenly felt waves of power gathering around her. A *lot* of power. "Where did you hear that name?"

"That's what you're talking about, right? The Syndicate. It's what they go by."

She stared at me incredulously, and then let out a very amused laugh, releasing her power. "The Syndicate was destroyed decades ago. Their name struck from the books. Before you were born. Hell, before *I* was born. Did your *reputable* father steal a book with mention of them or something?" she asked, sarcastically. "And like the *wise* wizard you are, you have attributed this to these Boogeymen?" she chuckled, shaking her head. "Whatever you think you know is false."

You may think I lashed out at her mockery of my father. Or at her mockery of me. But I didn't. Because underneath her harsh words, I sensed a very deep well of concern. She was using words as a coping mechanism. That word had bothered her on a level that things typically never reached.

I grew very, very uneasy. But I needed to tell her the truth. "I... have reason to believe that they are alive and well," I said softly, pulling the napkin from my pocket. "Not as *reputable* as a stolen book, but much more *recent*..." The end of the message had been destroyed, leaving only the *#Syndicate* part.

I showed it to her. She shook her head, looking amused as she entertained my delusion and accepted the napkin. She began to read it with a dismissive scan, but froze, rereading it much more intently a second time. Her hands began to shake, and all traces of humor were suddenly gone as if they had never existed, her coping mechanisms firmly obliterated. "None should even *know* of this name. It's an extremely well-kept secret. Which means..." her hands began to shake slightly. "They never really left..." she sounded stunned, terrified, and very, very angry. "And they left you, specifically, a message..." her eyes were pits of merciless hatred as she inclined her head. "Where did you get this?" she whispered.

"At the Gala. Someone—"

"You invited them to your Gala?" she roared, eyes flickering with fire.

"No! They dru—"

"You're *working* with them!" she continued, not listening to me. "We will *destroy* you and *everything* you hold dear! The school will be ashes. I will *not* let the Syndicate get their hands on them *or* your other allies!"

And the world abruptly erupted in fire, the sky blackening as fiery red bolts of tree-trunk-thick lightning began hammering into the salt flats, racing towards us. The Justices and G Ma disappeared rather than risking their lives in the oncoming inferno.

Now, my fisticuffs are good, but I wasn't about to test them against the full outrage of the Academy's Grand Master.

And since they had fled in such a rush, one of them forgot to maintain my ward.

And I suddenly had access to my magic again.

As the lightning from hell raced my way, I ripped a hole open in the air with a hasty Gateway, and threw myself through without looking, gasping as the air of the salt flats filled with fire and ashes. I landed on thick carpet, instantly releasing the Gateway behind me, panting as I sucked in cool, clean air. A furry face head-butted me from inches away, purring like a locomotive, and I cried out in surprise.

But it was just Sir Muffle Paws. My cat. I was back in Chateau Falco. The carpet near my feet smoldered where some of the lightning must have snuck through. I blindly reached up to dump a glass of whatever was handy onto the embers.

It was alcohol, of course, causing the entire rug to burst into flame.

Sir Muffle Paws hissed and bolted as I yelped, scooting my bare ass away quickly.

I jumped to my feet, fumbled with a vase of roses, and dumped them on the flames, stamping out everything that steamed or smoked.

Dean burst into the room, a feather duster in one hand and a pistol in the other, ready to domesticate or decimate, I wasn't sure.

"Master Temple, is anything amiss?" he asked, pointing both weapons at the steaming rug.

"Alcohol is flammable," I mumbled, trying to gather my thoughts.

He inclined his head to look at me for a moment, frowning. "Science is fascinating, is it not?" and then he turned away, calling over his shoulder. "Your fiancée came by earlier to pick up some things. Some things that weren't hers to pick up. You should have been here to stop her."

My heart stopped.

Indie? *She* had been the one trying to break my ward? I opened my mouth to press Dean for an explanation. But he was gone.

Fucking butlers.

I raced after him.

I was terrified at how badly my meeting with the Academy had gone. Now they thought I was part of the Syndicate, and would do anything to stop me. Including killing all my friends.

And judging by the napkin, the Syndicate wanted a little vengeance for my past attacks, even though it had been a long time since id heard from them.

Both parties had shown up at the Gala to fuck everything up. But who had fire-face worked for? The portly dude was obviously Academy, and the young, dark-haired server had been Syndicate, leaving me the note. I had once heard that embers and sparks revealed evidence of the Syndicate, but I hadn't seen any today. I let out an angry breath, promising myself I would find out. After this home-invasion issue.

Because love conquers all.

My ex-fiancée was back in town, trying to break into my house and steal my stuff.

CHAPTER 9

Dean sighed, apparently more interested in dusting than explaining what had happened when the wards had alerted me. He began ticking off points as if reading a to-do list. "No serious injuries at the Gala, just some very angry attendees. Tory woke up, was told some news about Yahn that she wasn't happy about." *Fucking loose-lipped vampires*, I silently seethed. "She would like to speak with you tomorrow," Dean continued. "Miss Rippley came, she saw, she was vanquished."

"Yeah, about that last part. Let's get more detail."

Mallory spoke up. "Indie tried to take your damn book, had her fingers almost blown off, and then she left. After the Guardians gave her a polite message. They almost tore her to shreds. Of course, she took many down with her." He leveled accusatory eyes on me. "And the mansion did nothing. At all. Not even a purr."

For reasons I was entirely unaware of, my house was alive. Or it harbored a Beast of its own. Possessed. But it was friendly to me. In fact, it *obeyed* me. Not because it had to, but because it had deemed me worthy. Which was kind of cool. And very terrifying.

I dropped my eyes. "Yeah. I…" I let out a guilty breath. It was my fault. I hadn't informed my house to mark her as an intruder. Because I harbored the hope that every crime she had committed with Ichabod had been under duress. But deep down I knew better. I should have told the House to keep her out. With extreme prejudice. But it had been almost a year since I'd heard from her, and our last meeting hadn't been too great. Meaning, she had tried to kill my friend.

I had no excuse. Only… misguided hope.

As if on cue, Death came striding inside. "What the devil happened here?"

"That's saying a lot coming from you, Horseman," Mallory grouched.

Death sneered at him. "Want to share fireside stories, Old One? I think I have a really good one for Nate. He probably hasn't heard it yet…"

Mallory muttered something unpleasant under his breath, but he did back down.

Death grunted in satisfaction before turning back to me. "I love the project car in your driveway. Billionaire meets white trash lawn ornaments." He smiled, and I noticed Dean dusting more forcefully, also angry about the totaled car in the drive.

"Afternoon appointment went FUBAR," I replied distractedly.

He chuckled, waving a hand. "So, Hope led you astray… Ah, Irony…"

I threw my cup at him. He dodged it effortlessly. "Be useful, or get out. So, I have a blind spot. Sue me." He had once referred to me as the Horseman of Hope. A Fifth Rider.

He nodded. "As long as you know it, it can no longer control you."

I nodded, turning to Dean and Mallory. "I'll change the guest list so that the mansion knows she is no longer welcome. Under any circumstances. The Chateau will tear her to shreds unless she has my permission to be here." Dean silently poured another glass, approached me with soft steps, and handed over the drink, frowning compassionately. His fingers briefly rested on the back of my wrist, and then he departed to dust the other bookshelf, no longer angry about the car.

Which meant a lot. He knew how dangerous Indie could be. But he also knew how much it hurt me to admit this to myself. So, he understood how much it took from me to officially declare her an enemy. It was the right call.

But it still sucked.

Mallory piped up. "One other thing, Laddie. She kept muttering about her Brothers. She stopped by the tree on her way out. Spent a few minutes lurking 'round, and then left."

Concern instantly hit me like a fist in the gut. The tree was where we had buried the Grimms that had attacked my home. "Why would she care about visiting their graves? We searched all the bodies. None of them had anything special on them," I lied, hoping I sounded convincing.

But in fact, I had taken several items from their corpses, not knowing what they were, but not wanting anyone else to ever find them. In case they were dangerous. Then another thought hit me. "Where was Carl during her visit to the tree, or at *any* point during her invasion?"

Mallory shrugged. "I saw him after, but not during. He wasna' present. Probably sharpening his blades somewhere."

I called out in my mind, summoning the bastard. He appeared in the doorway almost instantaneously. "Yes, Master Temple?" Death shot him a wary look out of the corner of his eye.

I studied the Elder. I hardly knew him or his... friends.

He resembled a tall, bipedal, albino lizard-man. He wore clothes made of crisscrossing strips of thick leather, and twin ivory blades hung at either hip, along with several more pale-bladed daggers tucked into the various folds of his clothing. His milky-white scales reflected the light so that he looked perpetually wet, and his beady glacier-like blue eyes tracked any and all movement in the room, even though he appeared to be giving me his full attention. The tips of his inky black fangs protruded from the thin lips of his elongated jaws, like he had bitten into a printing press on his way over, but that was just their normal color. The absolute opposite of his scaled body.

"Where were you?"

"Guarding the grounds, checking the perimeter. I never sensed danger from Chateau Falco."

"Maybe you shouldna' rely on the house to point out the obvious," Mallory spat acidly.

Carl leered at him, as if welcoming a physical solution.

"Enough. Play nice. I need a minute," I said, standing with a groan of pain. I wandered over to my desk, staring out the floor-to-ceiling window at the gargantuan tree dominating my property. Indie's temporary tombstone. A silver and gold-leaved white tree, that sometimes seemed to have a bioluminescent glow to it. I took a drink, thinking furiously.

Ichabod Temple – a long lost relative of mine – had banished the Brothers Grimm hundreds of years ago. But a handful of them had found their way back – with Ichabod as their prisoner – hungry to kill the last surviving Temple. Indie had been murdered in the battle, the *War*, and some Fae had planted the pale tree on her grave. But Death had brought her back to life...

As a Grimm. The last surviving Grimm in our world.

She had left with Ichabod to master her new abilities after a run-in with Rumpelstiltskin, who wanted to use her powers to bring back the rest of the Grimms. Under the control of the Syndicate. Rumpelstiltskin was now serving a life sentence with the Mad Hatter, courtesy of me.

I had later been cursed by a wizard, and in an effort to save myself, had given up the fledgling power of a Maker – a practically extinct brand of magic that involved sharing headspace with an immortal, all-powerful Beast. This constant, internal struggle with our Beasts made Makers prime candidates for gods to use as tools to enforce their will on the world. It was why Makers had been hunted to extinction. Too dangerous. Rather than become anyone's sock-puppet, I had locked my Beast into a cane, promising to free him once the dust settled, because he was as much of a victim as I was in the Maker partnership.

But before I had been able to free him, Indie had stolen the cane from me, willing to do whatever it took to annihilate the Syndicate. Just like Ichabod.

I hadn't heard from her since. Until now.

I glanced at the book on the table, *Through the Looking-Glass*. The book that would lead her directly to the Mad Hatter and Rumps, the only one who could...

"They want to bring back the Grimms... They think they can control them. Gain an army… to take out the Syndicate," I whispered in disbelief. Death grunted in reply.

I realized I was grinding my teeth, because a bit of dust fell from the ceiling, letting me see that my mansion was duplicating my mood, grumbling ominously.

I ignored it, staring out at the white tree. The Fae hadn't told me it was also a Gateway. To the Elders. Carl and friends. Who had been booted off earth long ago for eating too many people or something. Since the tree was on my property, they obeyed me. But they had *come* searching for Indie's corpse, thinking she was the key to bringing the rest of their people back home. Here.

I looked at Carl now, remembering the numerous warnings I had received about his people, the Elders. *Don't feed them…* Death was studying the rafters, and finally let out a satisfied nod, deciphering that I had firmly committed to standing against Indie.

I scowled back. "You know this is indirectly your fault, right? You brought her back."

Death rolled his eyes. "Right. I should have just let her die. Because you are so rational about things like that. You do remember that you were only heartbeats away from trying to kill me. Because you thought I *had* killed her." He shrugged. "Damned if I do, damned if I don't…"

I let out a frustrated sigh, brushing my fingers through my hair, which was growing much longer. "I know. Just… sucks." I stared at Carl and Death. "Let's go for a walk." Mallory began to pipe up, but I held out a hand, remembering Death's comment. Mallory was hiding something. About his past. "Just us, Mallory. You and I should probably have a long-overdue talk soon…"

He dropped his head, but didn't agree about us having a talk. I strode out of the room, listening as my house began whispering to me. "Where are we going?" Death asked.

I grinned. "Down the rabbit hole, apparently."

He frowned, but Carl merely grinned, revealing his inky black fangs as his hand caressed the blade at his hip. The milky white blade that may or may not have been pure bone.

"Hey, Carl. What are those made of? I've been meaning to ask you," I said.

The holes where his ears should have been constricted as he listened. He shrugged as if it were the most obvious answer in the world. "The bones of my enemies. What was left of them."

I shivered in disgust, but Death nodded to himself, completely at peace with Carl's answer.

"Carl, have I ever told you how creepy you are?"

"Often," he responded with a frown, head cocked slightly in confusion.

I sighed, continuing on. "Okay. Just checking," I said, shaking my head.

Fucking Carl…

CHAPTER 10

I urged Carl and Death back a few steps as I plucked out my phone. I needed to call Raego about Yahn.

"Hey, you filthy reptile!" I said the moment he answered.

"Temple," he said flatly. "I hear the most unpleasant things about you from your friends."

"Yeah, about that—"

"That you let a Regular get scratched by one of my dragons. Or Tory's dragons, if she's there beside you," he added quickly, changing his tone.

"She's not here," I chuckled.

He let out a breath, and then asked me what happened. I told him my version, not trusting Tory's reiteration of Alucard's opinion. He was quiet on the other end. "Well? Do you think—"

"It's too soon to tell. I'll have a few of my men follow him around. You owe me."

"He might not even turn!" I argued.

"Oh, no. I meant for wasting my time to *watch* him. If he *does* become a dragon, we will have a balancing of accounts. Your favors will *rain* down on me," he sounded pleased.

"The Reds did it!"

"While working for you," he replied lazily. "Now, if you'll excuse me, I need to go babysit."

And he hung up. "Bastard," I muttered, pocketing my phone.

I focused back on the house, sensing her annoyance at me ignoring her for the duration of my phone call. *Jealous, jealous...* I smiled to myself.

Thinking on Yahn brought me back to the Gala, where both the Academy and Syndicate had unknowingly teamed up to ruin my day. That mysterious dark-haired girl had drugged Tory. The Academy had antagonized a shifter. Then that weird flame guy had tried to burn us alive.

I shook my head, letting those thoughts stew as I let the house guide me, listening intently as it whispered into my ears. No one else heard anything, but they probably noticed the faint rumbling in the walls. Nothing alarming. Just a soothing purr. The house did that when content. Like a giant feline.

Speaking of cats, Sir Muffle Paws trailed behind us, tail arched up in the air, flickering back and forth of its own volition. I had thought he was a Maine Coon when I first found him. But he was turning out to be much bigger. Like a mutant cousin of theirs. Or the Sabretooth version of his bloodline. I had heard that Maine Coons typically weighed in at twenty pounds.

Sir Muffle Paws was at least double that, and still had big paws, which typically meant he had a lot of stretching to do. Freaking cats. Why couldn't I have gotten a docile little tiny kitten?

But I hadn't really had a say in the matter. Because... well, Indie had fallen for the kitty, convincing me to keep him. Before she went rogue. Because a brief vacation with Ichabod had apparently been enough time to brain-wash her with his all-consuming hatred for the Syndicate.

And I had become the owner of a big ass kitty. A constant reminder of what I had lost.

"Maybe he'll come in handy someday," Death offered, studying the paintings on the walls as we walked, reading my thoughts.

"Maybe you'd like to watch him for a few years. You know, just to make sure you're a good fit. We don't want to make any hasty decisions.

I hear that's a bad idea when you're emotional," I trailed off, listening as the house spoke to me.

Through the doorway just ahead.

Except, there was no doorway. Just a textile forest scene the size of a rug covering the wall. A wall leading to the exterior of the house. So, there obviously couldn't be a door there, unless it led outside. Hallways continued off to either side.

"You sure?" I asked out loud.

I saw Carl cock his head, eyeing first me and then Death, who shrugged in response.

Yes.

"Okay, Narnia. Whatever you say." She purred in delight at being given a name.

I pulled back the tapestry, wondering what this was all about.

We were instantly pelted with screams and wails, as if we had opened the pits of hell. The stone blocks of the wall suddenly began sliding out towards us in random patterns, then several rotated in place, slammed back into the wall, rearranged themselves, and switched places with other stones. Some massive mechanism. The screams and cries grew louder until Death waved a hand, and they stopped. He looked very, very concerned.

He's no fun. Totally harmless, really, since you're here, Narnia whispered to me.

I frowned, watching the stones as they continued to spin, roll, rearrange, and slam back into new positions, like a 1980's pixelated videogame of a pond rippling after a rock was thrown into it. Except with each sudden movement of rock, different colors and shapes began to appear, revealing some purpose to the mechanism.

"And what would have happened if I wasn't present?"

Empty meat sacks would be all that remained, and their souls would have joined the orchestra.

Death jumped back a step, staring hard at the door that was beginning to materialize. "I thought I heard a voice..." Death murmured.

You needed to hear my warning, Rider. Only the Master can keep you safe here, Horseman.

I grinned at that. "What she said. *Master*," I enunciated. Death shivered, staring at me in disbelief. Carl merely squinted warily at the wall, which buckled one last time before all the cracks dissolved, forming one large, heavy-as-hell stone door. And a handle slowly slid outwards. A bone carving of the Temple Crest, and it was caked with what looked like dried blood in places.

The crest, very familiar to me, featured a large shield with a lightning bolt down the center, splitting it in two. One side of the shield displayed a mountain, the other a feather. Because death was as light as a feather, while life could be heavier than a mountain. A scythe and a spear crossed the back of the shield, banners flying from the tip of each. One read *Memento Mori*, and the other read *Arete*.

Memento Mori meant *remember you are mortal*, and had been included to encourage the Temple clan to live life to the fullest, never wasting a moment, because tomorrow we could die.

Arete was a lesson taught by Aristotle, defined as the *most excellent form of a thing*. As in, one should always strive for excellence, the best possible form of yourself.

The butts of the weapons protruded out from opposite ends of the bottom of the shield, where two ravens were perched, and their names were listed below each. *Hugin* and *Munin*. Odin's ravens. *Memory* and *Thought*.

I shivered at that, remembering Ganesh's warning of ravens hanging around my tree.

I hoped to all hell that the ravens in my tree weren't the real Hugin and Munin. And that they had nothing to do with my family crest. Just birds.

The lower tip of the shield bore a single, large star, but the top of the shield was banded with seven stars that I hadn't ever received much explanation on. My father had once told me that it related to some old prophecy that had long ago been disproven, but that we couldn't just remove it from our crest. So, it had stayed.

A giant closed fist rose up above the shield, symbolizing one holding the power of creation in the palm of a hand, or fist. Wizards. And my favorite part, the words *Non Serviam* rested on top of the shield. It meant *I will never serve*, signifying the refusal to submit or bow to anyone. Explaining that phrase often turned people off. Because in Milton's book, *Paradise Lost*, Lucifer had carried banners with those words as he marched against his Brothers. Angels. But our usage wasn't a religious slam. In fact, our crest was likely older than Milton's book. Just a coincidence that *Paradise Lost* used the same phrase.

I think...

Staring at the crest carved in bone and splashed with dried blood was unsettling.

I frowned. "A little macabre, don't you think, Narnia?" I said aloud, reaching for the handle.

All will be understood shortly, she answered.

My palm touched the crest, and I hissed in pain.

But I couldn't let go, as what felt like red-hot thorns pierced my palms, branding me until the stink of roasted flesh filled the hall. I could only gasp in pain, unable to detach my palm.

Which pissed Carl right the hell off. He swung his precious ivory blade at the door handle, no doubt intending to chop it off. Or my hand. Hopefully not the latter.

The moment his sword touched the door, there was an explosion of blue sparks, and he went flying, ricocheting off a wall, knocking over a table, and skidding on his ass a good thirty feet. In his hand was only the hilt of his bone sword. I hadn't even had time to cry out. Then the door handle released my palm, and I yanked it back with a relieved groan, staring down to find the crest neatly burned into my palm.

Yesss... Narnia purred as if having taken a sip of an exquisite wine. *Your blood is pure, Master Temple. You may proceed with your batman and the Rider... I have waited years for this...*

Death had torn off part of his sleeve, and abruptly took my palm in his hand, staring down at the wound with muttered curses before he began wrapping it. But all I had attention for was the liquid blood flowing through the crest on the door handle, and the sound of dozens of heavy locks and bolts disengaging, clicking, unclicking, and hammering into unseen new positions with resounding *thuds* and *clangs*.

Then the door opened, dust gasping from the frame, and a violet glow illuminated a sandstone hallway as torches flared to life with purple fire, burning away the darkness.

Carl had rejoined us and was staring down at the hilt of his weapon in disbelief. But I knew he had others to replace it. Death gave a sharp tug on the makeshift bandage on my palm, but other than recognizing the pain, I was transfixed by the hallway ahead.

"What are we doing, Nate?" Death whispered.

Carl grunted, tossing down his destroyed hilt, and idly checking himself for other weapons.

"I have no idea. I'm just playing follow the leader, here. The house wants to show us something."

"Some doors are better left unopened…" he whispered, eyes troubled.

"Memento Mori," I whispered back, finding myself surprisingly anxious to see what exactly was going on. *Tomorrow you may die…*

They joined me as I followed the violet-flamed torches.

I glanced back to see Sir Muffle Paws watching us from the hallway, his tail flicking back and forth in agitation. He didn't follow.

CHAPTER 11

Death followed directly behind me. "Have you been here before, Nate?" he asked softly. Carl brought up the rear, keeping an eye on everything. I trusted the Elder, despite not fully understanding what he was. But I did know that he served me. Because I had dominated him, and the gateway to his home was on my property. Hell, I had killed dozens of his friends to prove it to him.

I just wasn't supposed to *feed* him.

Whatever the hell *that* meant. But I did know that the last time I had taken him to a fight, he and his brothers had seemed to feast on the soul of their victim. But we were in my house now, which was also bound to serve me, and there was no one here to kill. Or eat.

I hoped.

I shook my head in answer to Death's question. "To be honest, I've had my hands full for a while now. Searching for Indie, practicing with Ganesh, getting used to my powers again, and starting Grimm Tech. I didn't even intend to explore right now. But it seemed like Narnia had other plans."

"Narnia..." Death murmured thoughtfully.

I shrugged. "Just came to me. Like the wardrobe C.S. Lewis wrote about."

I could feel him staring at me, but he didn't speak as we continued on.

"You heard her, right? The house?" He grunted in affirmation. "You hear her too, Carl?"

He hissed back, which I took for a *yes*.

I glanced over my shoulder at Death. "She knew what you were…" he nodded, and I turned back to watch where I was going. I had seen enough Indiana Jones movies. One wrong step was all it took before a bulldozer-sized boulder was chasing you down. "But you've never been here before," I continued, speaking to Death over a shoulder. "Maybe she can smell you?"

There was a long silence. "Perhaps. I'm sure my rarity gives off a particular… scent."

The house – Narnia – rumbled in what I took for an agreement. I shivered, imagining the stone hallway crumbling to dust, burying us underneath tons of rubble. By all laws of physics, we should be standing outside the walls of my house right now, not in a hallway that couldn't exist. Because I knew for a fact that we were above ground, and that the door had been on an exterior wall of the mansion.

Yet here we were. As we walked, new torches ignited ahead of us with faint *pops* and *crackles*, and those behind us were extinguished, keeping our section – and only our section – illuminated. Which didn't make Carl too happy, judging by the frequent hissing as he struggled to stay close to us, because looking back, I could not see the doorway in which we had entered.

Which was impossible, because we hadn't walked very far. Maybe a couple dozen feet.

"What does it take to smell like a Horseman? In fact, what exactly does it take to *be* a Horseman? You guys keep saying I'm one of you, but not one of you. That I carry the mantle, but I'm obviously not a Horseman. And I haven't accepted, by the way. I'm just curious."

Death chuckled, reaching out to wave a hand through the purple flame on one of the torches. His hand passed through without fanfare, other than for him to grunt. "Cold," he said thoughtfully. He cleared his throat after a moment, addressing me. "You have to accept the gift, or curse, whatever you want to call it." He was silent for a few more steps. "And you need a Mask. And a Horse, of course. A few other things…" he waved a hand dismissively.

I frowned, ignoring the last comment. "Because Grimm, the unicorn, bonded with me, I'm now a contender for the Apocalypse?"

Death nodded. "In a way. It was no small thing for the unicorn to… adopt you. Don't take it lightly," he warned. Then he let out a breath. "Well, don't disrespect it, at least."

I let out a breath of relief. "Good thing there aren't any more Masks, right?" I pressed.

But he didn't reply.

"Because there is no way in hell I'm becoming a Horseman. I'd be terrible at it. I can't even handle being a wizard. Or, whatever I am now." Again, he remained silent. "It's not happening, Pastey. Okay? I won't—"

And in the blink of an eye, my words left me.

Because we were suddenly in a massive cavern that stretched for hundreds of feet ahead of us, and fifty feet or more above our heads, making me feel suddenly very, very small. Tiny.

And it was a fucking *library*. The library of all libraries. The ceiling was curved at the top like we were in a giant tunnel, with gems embedded into the stone to represent constellations. The stones even glowed faintly, providing a dim, blue light. As I followed the ceiling further with my eyes, I realized that each section glowed with differently colored stones. A cataloging system of some kind?

Four levels of walkways clung to the walls of the cavern, leading up to the ceiling. Each walkway was almost entirely lined with shelves containing books and knickknacks. One shelf even contained dozens of musical instruments – I spotted a violin, flute, trumpet, and guitar, and a giant white piano sat beside it. Ornate, oxblood banisters and guardrails lined each level – complete with chairs, divans, tables with lanterns, and lounging areas. Hell, I almost thought I could see a bathroom on two of the four floors. Regardless, the shelves were broken up by doorways here and there, so there were at least reading rooms, or living quarters on each floor.

Marble statues were spaced every couple dozen feet, larger than life, and all representing different eras of human history. Different monsters, gods, heroes, even an Elder, and… beings I didn't quite recognize. On every level. Again, arranged almost like a cataloging system.

The base of the banisters protecting one from falling off the next tiers were carved with runes and ancient words in every language imaginable, with a star emblem between each.

It kind of reminded me of a Barnes and Noble I had gone to once. Near the café, a band of names had been painted on the wall. Last names of well-known authors in a giant banner that bisected the landscape mural.

Except the words on the banisters here were almost unrecognizable.

But I did see one that I knew. *Merlin*. As my eyes tracked the banisters, squinting, I spotted a few more that might be recognizable. *Odin. Thor. Zeus. Anubis.* But they were in different languages, so I couldn't be sure. Maybe I was imagining it. I even saw sections of Enochian script – the so-called language of Heaven – according to Dr. John Dee who had written about it in the late sixteenth century.

I shivered, glancing sheepishly at Death, who stared open-mouthed at the names. He probably recognized a lot more of them than me. And it wasn't comforting him.

"What *is* this place…" he whispered softly, flicking his eyes my way for a brief second.

I shrugged. The cavern stretched on in a massively-wide hallway, longer than a football field, but we currently stood in a secluded, circular area, apart from the rest of the library. No tiers lined the wall here.

One section of the wall was lined with more shelves, but the other half was bare rock, and a steady, crisp waterfall fell from high above, casting a fine mist to the air, opposite from where we had entered.

And I immediately feared for the hundreds of thousands of books lining the shelves. Because water was not the friend of the printed word. It was the nemesis.

Death held up a hand, taking a few steps closer to the waterfall as he tested the air. "Hmm…" he murmured, twisting it back and forth. "Dry. Completely dry." He shot me a look. "Where have you taken us, Master

Temple? An underground library – when we are not truly underground – complete with a waterfall that does not damage the books that have no doubt been here for hundreds of years…"

Carl was sniffing the air, and studying the main room itself. The circular area was cozier, like a study area in a traditional library. Still huge, but not as stuffy as the rest of the library looked.

A large fireplace sat in the center of the circle, before a giant star carved into the stone floor, and all around it were cushioned concave bowls set below ground level, where one could lounge in warmth while reading. Or take a nap.

One massive, ornate wooden desk dominated the study area. The back of the desk had been carved in such a way that it more resembled a separate cloth sheet draped over the desk – even bunching up where it touched the floor – than part of the desk itself. I bent down to lightly knock on it to be sure it wasn't actually cloth. That's how realistic the sheet looked.

Now closer, I noticed the carvings in the wood itself – faint, worn with age, but still clear enough to make it look even more like a decorative cover had been thrown over the desk. The carvings looked to have been done in the Middle Ages, by the Fae, tripping on acid, while watching Pink Floyd's *The Wall*.

Because it was complete with reliefs of dryads consorting with nymphs, centaurs, sprites, ogres, wolves, hawks, and the Fae themselves. Fornicating, bathing, resting, battling, or hunting. It was glorious. And chilling. I stood with a grunt, peeling my eyes away to study the rest of the room.

A massive, wide stone ring was carved into the floor near the waterfall, a different type of rock than the rest of the room. It sat alone, with no tables and chairs around it. Just a big empty space. And for some reason, despite the beauty all around me, this vacuum pulled at me, as if it's lack of furniture gave it dignity. But it wasn't just visual. Some deep, wild power tugged at me.

Runes were carved into the ring, pagan symbols, Druidic carvings, many unrecognizable, worn with age and the passing of boots. I walked closer to it, wondering why such a massive ring was carved into the floor, and curious why it looked to be separate from the floor itself rather than part of the floor. Like a thick wheel without spokes... As I neared, the ring slowly began to rotate clockwise, and then it began to rise up from the floor without a sound.

Just rising up like I had pushed a button on an elevator.

I stepped back and it slowly began to descend again. I halted, glancing over at Carl and Death. They stared, stunned. Death slowly motioned for me to step forward again.

I did, and it resumed rising up out of the floor, this time complete with massive stone chairs sliding out of the floor to surround the table. A few moments later, everything stilled. It was a massive round table, a wide ring of stone with no legs holding it up. Just. Fucking. Hovering.

The empty space in the center of the ring – which was at least twenty feet across – contained only a plain podium. The chairs around the ring each had different unknown symbols carved into the tall stone backs. And the chairs looked surprisingly comfortable, despite being made from rough-cut stone. I slowly approached the table, studying the odd carvings, and I noticed a band of metal now splitting the circle into two rings, one large, one small, like a ring within a ring. Except the metal ring was liquid.

Just a three-inch-wide river of golds and silvers flowing infinitely around and around.

And I could see shapes, movement, forms, figures, symbols, briefly rising up to the surface before sinking back into the metal for another obscure shape to replace it. Like magical alphabet soup. The inner ring flowed like a lazy river, endlessly circling the table.

Death was frowning down at it. Carl shook his head, and then continued scanning the room, searching for dangers. I shared a look with Death. "You think..." I trailed off.

"No. That isn't possible," he said, eyeing the table doubtfully.

"It *is* round..." I argued softly. He ran a hand through his hair, muttering under his breath.

CHAPTER 12

I sighed, and backed away to the carved desk, watching as the round table silently sank back into the floor. I finally turned away, shaking my head. There were a few small piles of leather-bound books, dried ink wells, and a decanter with an amber stain on the bottom, also dried out. Two feather quills lay on the surface, and a stack of ivory paper sat before the ancient leather chair. As if the owner had been writing something before he left for the last time.

I frowned, studying the drawers.

Because I saw a faint carving on one of the legs. I leaned closer, my eyes widening.

Ichabod, was written in a childish, juvenile scrawl, etched into the expensive ornate wood.

"Fuck me…" I whispered. "Ichabod's been here."

"Makes sense," Death replied coolly. "He was raised here in this house, like you."

I nodded, still amazed to see proof that he had been here as a child, getting into trouble while his dad worked away. "Well, our upbringing must have been completely different. Because I sure as hell never came here, and I'm pretty sure my father hasn't either."

He rubbed his chin thoughtfully. "Could it be because you are the true Master Temple of the house? You did say there hasn't been one in quite some time..."

I shrugged. "I have no idea. Narnia did say it had been a while..."

He grunted, slowly studying the room on his own.

I stood, flipping back some of the covers of the books. Two were written in Latin, and although I didn't recognize the title, I knew they were related to magic. One was in German, but the last was plain, without title. A journal of some sort.

A slip of paper fell out of the cover, and I snatched it up on instinct, fearing I had ripped it out of the old book. After all, this room likely hadn't been touched since Ichabod's childhood, hundreds of years ago. But the paper was different. For one thing, it was black paper, but veins of silver were embedded into the pulp, and the message was written in silver ink.

My dearest Matthias,

I've taken the liberty of penning this message in silver, on silver-laced paper. None too cheap, I assure you! Only the most pretentious materials could be used to address my most esteemed colleague, Master Temple!

As you warned us months ago, the situation has evolved into something that can no longer be ignored, and actions must be undertaken, posthaste.

We, the Men of the Mind, anxiously await your reply to discuss our Grimm futures. However dire our decisions may be, anything is better than our enemy gaining more power in these brave and wild new lands. We must acquire these Hands of God prior to the upcoming war.

I hope that your beloved boy – that rapscallion if there ever was one – Ichabod is well, and that he hasn't taken after the weres as he seemed intent to do. We must keep our bloodlines pure, after all... You of all people know the importance of this.

Ever your friend,

Castor Queen.

I flinched to discover that Death was reading over my shoulder. He was completely motionless for a few beats. "Let me see that a moment..." he whispered. I nodded absently, handing it over as I began to pull open the top drawer, rummaging inside to find frayed and worn artifacts, all magical focus items, but nothing particularly special. A scratched coin, probably worth a lot of money now, but still, just a coin. Not even wizardly currency. A feather. A sextant, a thread and needle, a small dagger – likely a letter opener – and a wad of wiry hair with bits of flesh still attached. I also found a small bone, but from what creature, I couldn't quite discern.

I pulled open the next drawer, and the next, but found nothing useful. Just more junk.

Carl pulled a book from the shelf and grunted as a torch sprang to life directly above his head. He dropped the book and had his dagger aimed at the torch, hissing in warning, but the torch merely flickered as it burned away the dust coating it.

Nothing strange.

Except it was also the purple flame.

And it had ignited when he withdrew the book.

I began to laugh after a few moments of silence. "A freaking reading lamp attuned to the books?" I walked over to a different shelf and reached out for a book at random. But I felt a physical prickle on my fingers as I did so. I hesitated. Nothing happened. I moved my hand closer to the book and the sensation increased until I pulled my hand back. I frowned. Carl hadn't seemed to have any issue picking a random book. I slowly extended my hand until I could just feel the tingling sensation, and took a few steps lateral, my fingertips hovering a few inches away from the dozens of book spines on the shelf.

Then the tingling sensation suddenly evaporated, and in its place, I felt warmth, like a hot bath on a cold day. I stopped, and reached out to grab the book. The sensation increased until my fingertips touched the book, and then it suddenly faded to nothing, and I felt the house purr, the waterfall splashing a little louder for a moment, as if affected by Narnia's vibrations.

I withdrew the book, and the nearest torch flickered to life beside me, bathing me in the soothing purple glow, illuminating the cover of the book in my hands. The book that the house had seemed to guide me towards.

"Nate, don't!" Death shouted. I released the cover and the book fell open as I turned to look at him in alarm. He was pointing a hand at me.

Well, the book.

I looked down to see that it was glowing slightly.

But nothing had happened.

I read the cover page of the book, written on ancient, leathery papyrus.

Deus Ex Machina, Fable or Fact?

I stared down at the page, frowning. Something about it tickled my memory, but I knew I had never seen the book before. Before I could think about it further, Death swooped in, slammed the book closed, and shoved it back into the shelf in one lithe motion.

Carl watched him, looked at me thoughtfully, and then slowly replaced his own book very carefully.

I scowled at Death. "It's just a book. What's wrong with you?"

He arched a brow. "Is the owner of an arcane bookstore truly telling me that some books are *just books*? I seem to recall you going after quite a few books that you deemed too dangerous for mortals to have access to. Let alone, supernaturals to have access to."

I shrugged. "Yeah, sure, but these things have been locked away—"

"Probably for a reason," Death interrupted, folding his arms.

"Look, Ichabod hung out here as a little boy, and from the looks of it, getting into all sorts of trouble while his dad worked. This place can't be that dangerous. At least not on this level. Perhaps up higher, or in one of those rooms, but not out in the open like this where a kid could wake up a demon or something."

I leaned closer to the shelf, scanning the titles, but none looked familiar.

"Pick one up."

I did, feeling no tingling sensation this time. I grinned, flipping through the pages quickly as I met his gaze. He began to smirk.

"And did fire spring up around the edges?"

I frowned. "Well, no."

"So maybe we should leave the fiery ones alone. Get a better feel for the place first. Test the magic in the room. I mean, none of these books have been affected by the moisture, or fire. There's an idea…" He pointed at the shelf. "Cast a small bit of fire at it."

I blinked. "Yeah, that's like asking a pediatrician to kick a kid in the face."

He rolled his eyes. "Just do it. Trust me."

I sighed, but complied, casting a very weak bit of fire at an unimpressive book. The fire splashed onto the spine, and instantly splashed onto the entire shelf, causing me to panic. I was about to rip the air away, dousing the flames, when Death yanked my sleeve, pulling me back as he pointed at the shelf with his other hand.

The flames quickly died out. On their own.

And not a single mark marred the surface of the books or the shelves.

"That's… not possible."

"It doesn't care that it's not possible, apparently. How about something a little more… *wild*."

And he flipped his keychain out of his pocket, the little scythe keychain dangling freely. A wall of green mist flew through the air between us and the shelves, hammering into it like a wave of water on the shore of the beach. Wails of agony, screams of despair, and maniacal laughter drifted out from the mist, but just as soon as the sounds were heard, the green mist evaporated, and the shelves were once again left unharmed.

"Who the hell laughs in hell?" I shivered, staring at the bookshelves, heart racing.

"Fucking Jared. I'll have another talk with him," Death responded coolly. I frowned at him, but realized he was being completely serious.

"Right. Talk to Jared. Again."

"And perhaps warn us *before* you open a portal to the damned, if you please," Carl grumbled.

I stared at the bookshelf, taking a few steps closer. No damage could be found. The shelves were truly protected. And I realized Death was right. We needed to test this out, because from the looks of it, this wasn't just a library.

It was a magical bomb shelter.

But I suddenly had something else on my mind entirely. The letter on the desk from Castor Queen had mentioned both the word *Grimm* with a capital *G*, and the *Hands of God*. And the strange book Narnia had encouraged me to open suddenly became very clear. *Deus Ex Machina*. Roughly translated to mean *Hand of God*. Coincidence?

Not likely.

"I think we need to go have a chat with a girl about her box."

Death groaned. "For once in your life, have some respect."

I blinked, and then burst out laughing as I realized how I had phrased my statement. "It's a gift. I don't even try. I promise. I need to see if she knows anything about these Hands of God."

Death sighed. "Just promise me you won't do anything drastic."

I winked at him, and slowly strode out of the cavern, the purple torches igniting ahead of me with faint pops and crackles. I might have glanced at the round table before I entered the hallway. *Surely not...*

Death and Carl followed me rather than risk being left behind in the dark. Or perhaps left behind entirely, judging by the odd disregard of spatial awareness and known physics. The cavern – by all practical purposes – had been on the outside of Chateau Falco, but also underground. Very far underground. But we hadn't walked *down*. Or *out*.

I stopped, and rounded on the two. "I need you both to swear to never mention a thing you saw here today. Now." I was deadly serious. Due to recent events, I was severely lacking in the trust department. Especially after realizing that everyone seemed to know something about Mallory that I only suspected.

They dipped their heads after a moment, and both swore. I wove them with magic, binding them to their oath. Then I nodded, gave them a weak smile, and resumed my exit.

I wondered how many other secrets the house had to share with me...

But this was an idle thought, trying to ignore my true fears.

The Syndicate drugging Tory. The Academy threatening war. But mostly, Indie and Ichabod.

And as I thought about it, I realized that I had more pressing matters to attend to before I met up with Pandora. The person I really needed to talk to was… different. One needed to tread carefully around him. For multiple reasons. I could see Pandora anytime, but this guy? You never knew what kind of mood he would be in. Not wanting to bother him late at night, I decided to handle him first thing in the morning, optimizing my chances of catching him in a good mood.

The Mad Hatter and his prisoner, Rumpelstiltskin.

CHAPTER 13

*A*fter our adventures in the cavern, I had decided to get some sleep. Death had left to get a drink with Achilles, promising to bring the Myrmidon over the next day so we could go talk to Pandora. He'd said he needed the drink after our walk.

Before I had gone to sleep, I had properly reprimanded Carl for his failure during Indie's break-in. After our talk, he had seemed motivated to make up for his failure, telling me he would spend the night checking every nook and cranny of the property to make sure we were secure. From his tone, I imagined he had been at it all night.

I had woken up to sunlight streaming through my window, feeling much better. Less stressed. I had eaten a quick snack before checking my phone, only to find that Raego and Tory had called multiple times throughout the night. I had called Raego back, only to be told that my presence was requested at his home. So, on my drive over, I had decided to call Tory back later.

Raego's mansion – inherited from his father, Alaric Slate – loomed in the windshield before me. I climbed out of the car, staring at the oddest assortment of lawn ornaments I had ever seen.

Life-sized obsidian statues. I shivered, readjusting my sunglasses as I continued on to the door, which was held open by a hard-looking man with green eyes that I had never seen before. One of Raego's dragons. Shifter. He smiled as I avoided looking at the decorations.

Because they weren't just statues. They were people who had displeased Raego, the Obsidian Son, the King of the Dragons. He was one of those unbelievably rare black dragons, able to breathe a dark mist that turned things into shining black stone. I ignored the dragon holding the door as I stepped inside. The punk thought I was scared. I was really just disgusted at such a tasteless display of power, fear tactics, and theatrics.

Raego exited a hall, noticed me, and grunted, motioning me to a side room.

I heard Pop music blaring from one of the distant rooms, and smiled. The Reds, most likely.

Raego motioned me to a couch, as another dragon delivered me a glass of water. I frowned, but then remembered it was morning. Still, a Bloody Mary would have been nice.

I took a polite sip, arching my brow at Raego. "Well? What did you find out?"

"Just a moment," he said, scrolling through his phone.

I waited, and then heard shouting in the main entryway by the door. I frowned, shooting a glance at Raego, but he simply watched me, tapping his lips with his phone.

"When the *hell* were you going to tell me about the high-speed-car-chase, Nate?" a voice shouted, stomping into the room with her ass-kicking boots ready to go. She wore jeans and a tee that bore the *Shift* logo on it. I shot a glare at Raego, who seemed quite amused. "Don't you *dare* look at him. Look at *me!*" Tory continued, stomping closer. "You took my girls with you to pick a fight with weregorillas! After you *told* me that you were picking them up early for the *Gala!*" she shouted, eyes flickering with green light.

I winced. "Tory, let me explain. I'm sure—"

"Don't bother lying. Alucard already told me the truth," she warned as she sat opposite me, propping her forearms on her knees. I saw Alucard's head duck out of the doorway where he had been listening to Tory's tirade. He was going to pay for this. As was

Raego. Setting me up for this without warning, first thing in the morning.

Raego mimed pointing a gun at me, and then pulled the trigger with a hidden grin.

"Fine! I lied," I admitted. "Last time I was teaching your kids, the weregorilla mentioned he was being watched, stalked. I did a little sleuthing and realized it was a local group of shifters, and they wanted him in their gang." I frowned. "Or whatever you call a group of gorillas."

"Troop," Alucard called out from the other room. Raego chuckled.

I scowled at the doorway. "Come on in, Glampire. I've got—"

"He can't," Tory smiled dangerously.

I frowned at her, but she didn't explain. "Okay, why *can't* he?" I asked, rolling my eyes. "He's just as guilty as I am."

"Guilty… such an interesting word," Tory smiled. Then she snapped her fingers.

Seeing motion by the doors, I looked up, and my sphincter tightened.

Three weregorillas strutted into the room, led by Alucard. Two males and a female, dressed in work clothes like they had just left their auto body shop. All dark-haired with tan skin. They were each thick with muscle, and looked rough, hardened by a life of work. Just like they had yesterday. I met Tory's eyes, and she nodded slowly. "You're going to help me make this right," she murmured in a low, threatening tone.

I sighed, but got to my feet, warily approaching the sour-puss gorillas. They looked uncomfortable at their surroundings, used to less decadence and more grime. After my meeting yesterday, I didn't trust them, but I extended my hand anyway, which they ignored. But they did take Tory's hand with polite, reserved greetings, and brief, but well-concealed looks of caution at the tiny woman.

Because she was a Beast Master, and could make each of them her bitch, if she so chose.

Raego cleared his throat. "Please, take a seat. Welcome to my home. I thought this place would be more conducive to a peaceful discussion."

The gorillas didn't look pleased about it, but they did nod their agreement.

A male and female dragon entered, nude, asking if anyone desired refreshments. Worded just like that, drawing out *desire* as they smiled at the guests. This changed the mood quickly, the gorillas each grinning unashamedly.

I rolled my eyes. Stupid dragons and their ability to mess with minds. I wondered if the apes even knew they were being toyed with. Raego shot me a very discreet shake of his head, warning me silently, reading my thoughts easily. I sneered back as Tory spoke conversationally to the gorillas, all smiles. After the drinks came, and a few minutes of idle talk, Tory cleared her throat.

"I think we may have had a big misunderstanding yesterday…"

"I call pursuit with machine guns more than a misunderstanding," I muttered.

"You broke my arm!" the bigger of the three gorillas, their leader, growled, idly rubbing his now healed arm. Shifters were like that.

I nodded. "*After* you threatened to teach me a lesson," I reminded him. Tory shot me a look.

"Like I said, I think Master Temple handled this poorly. He had the best of intentions," she shook her head slowly at the gorillas. "Our students have survived… a very trying ordeal."

"He's one of *us*. We can help him better than you, Beast Master," the leader growled.

She slowly lifted her eyes to look at him, and I caught a faint flicker of green light. "Is that so…" she asked softly, still smiling. He grumbled under his breath, but did apologize. Which she accepted without an ounce of judgment. *Booooooring*, I thought to myself.

"Now, Master Temple was looking after my student's best interests, against my knowledge, but still. He *meant* well. He heard…" she turned to me. "What, precisely, did you hear again?"

"That he was being watched. Followed. Stalked." I folded my arms.

"Right." She turned to the gorillas. "Is this true?" she asked sweetly.

After a long pause, they finally mumbled confirmation. "We just wanted to *see* him. Make sure he was okay. We had heard… about the circus," the woman shivered.

Tory nodded sadly. "That's the whole point of the school. To help with the trauma. While in captivity, they grew only to know – and fear – each other. I'm trying to keep their environment the same, let them discover – at their own pace – that none of their fellow captives are cruel, but that they were *all* victims. Forced to do unspeakable things. To kill each other."

"By another *Beast Master*," the leader argued.

Tory's eyes were fire now. "Yes. By a Beast Master…" she let the silence grow. "That I helped *kill*."

They hesitated. I smiled. "She is truly terrifying," I offered helpfully.

Tory shot me a look. I ignored it to scowl at the traitorous vampire standing near the door.

"After our rehabilitation," Tory continued, "if he decides to join you, I will not stop him." They smiled eagerly. "*After* rehabilitation, and with no further contact from you until I say otherwise. Do I have your agreement?"

They looked at each other a few times, and then the leader leaned forward. "Master Temple attacked us. For that, we want him to pay."

"I'm right here, Donkey Kong. Come collect," I said in a low voice.

His shoulders bunched up, and I heard his knuckles popping, but the other male – who had been silent up until now – placed a hand on his forearm. "Dad, it's okay. Let me talk."

The father finally let out an angry nod, leaning back to fix me with a threatening glare.

The kid looked at me, much more collected than his father. "We have heard of a… Fight Club in the city, but we can't find anything concrete about it. We heard you formed it."

"I don't know what you're talking about," I said, face blank.

"We heard about that, too. That no one is allowed to talk about it."

I grunted, neither confirming nor denying, but if they had heard that much, they knew it was real, so there was no point in me continuing to lie. "And?"

"We want to join."

Tory was studying me, waiting. "I'll have to check." Their faces began to grow angry. I held up my hands, frustrated. "It's not just up to me. I *started* it, but I don't *run* it."

The room was silent for a while. "Do this, and we agree to your terms," the leader said.

I nodded slowly. "I'll try."

The gorilla shrugged, turning to Tory. "Maybe we will *try* to leave the kid alone."

Tory nodded, tight-lipped. Then she rounded on me. "I'm sure Master Temple will *try* very hard to get you access," she warned, voice laced with venom. She politely escorted them from the room, leaving me with Raego and Alucard. They were both going to pay for this.

CHAPTER 14

*B*ut before I could yell at the two of them for collaborating with Tory and selling me out, Yahn entered the room, dressed in skinny red pants and a too-tight graphic tee of some band I didn't recognize. There was a lot of glitter on it. I stared, completely caught off-guard.

"Master Temple!" he squealed in delight, hurrying my way with a relieved look on his face.

"Hey, Yahn. What are *you* doing here?"

"Thees one told me he needed to, like, check my scratches and stuff," Yahn complained, shooting a very comedic-looking angry glare at Raego. I could tell that his heart was in the look. He just wasn't any good at it.

Tory entered the room, and seeing Yahn, she paused for a moment. Then she flashed me a very satisfied smile as she folded her arms, turning to look at Raego.

I found the dragon king glaring at me. "He's here for protection. Kept running off."

"Hees goons kept following me!" his thick Swedish accent was jarring to hear, drawing out every soft vowel sound as if purposely trying to make you gouge out your ears.

Raego nodded. "For your own good, boy."

"Master Temple, please tell him I'm fine and stuff. Geez, it was just a scratch!"

As if on cue, two red dragons silently prowled into the room.

"Are you trying to give him a panic attack?" I hissed at Raego. He shrugged, waiting for Yahn to notice.

Yahn followed Raego's look to see the dragons standing in the corner.

And he squealed like a stuck pig, darting behind me. "Grab yer magic balls and stuff!" he shouted in my ear, clutching the back of my shirt like I was his savior.

Raego let out a stunned laugh at the sunny Swede's words.

"Yahn. *Yahn*!" I shouted as he began frantically checking my back pocket. "Stop! *Look*!"

He did, peering over my shoulder. With a purr, the red dragons shifted into their human forms, revealing Sonya and Aria, utterly nude.

"*Ah*! Boobies!" he ducked back behind me in an instant. Then he stilled, as if just having registered that maybe their boobies hadn't been the point of the display.

"No way," Alucard stammered, shaking his head in disbelief. "Where did you *find* this guy?" Tory shot him a look, reprimanding him as she quickly handed the girls blankets to cover up.

"No more boobies, Yahn, but I think you missed the point," I spoke softly, trying to pry his fingers off my shirt and step to the side.

He stood there, shaking, as he stared at the Reds. They smiled, waving back innocently.

He turned to look at me, and then Raego. "Are you, like, saying I can do that, *too*?" he asked.

I shrugged. "It's possible. They're weredragons. They accidentally scratched you." I held up a finger to Raego and Tory. "While trying to save his life, I might add," I said, defending them.

The Reds shot me relieved looks.

"Because you put them all in danger," Tory growled.

"I had his sack of magic balls and stuff! He needed them bac—"

"*Satchel*!" I hissed quickly. "I got this, Yahn." I quickly interrupted, scowling as Tory fought a huge grin, trying to keep her face serious. Alucard actually left the room, coughing with laughter. I ignored them, turning to Yahn. "You might be infected."

"Ah! I don't feel sick! Are you *toe-tah-lee* sure?" he shrieked, pawing at his chest.

I grabbed his hands, and he looked up at me, wild-eyed. "We don't know. That's why you need to stay here and stuff."

Alucard burst out laughing from the other room. I sighed.

"What about my dancing class? My Grammy?" Yahn complained, referring to Greta.

I shook my head. "We'll tell her later. Once we're sure. Dance class might have to wait."

To be honest, I was stunned he was taking it so well. Hell, he had just seen dragons, and all he cared about was his Grammy and dance classes. The Reds sauntered up, and each took Yahn by a shoulder, speaking soothing words to him as they escorted him from the room. He shot quick, nervous glances over his shoulder at me, but I shot him a *thumbs up*, mouthing *boobies*. His face paled, but he was soon out the door.

Raego was scowling at me. "Thanks. A lot. Do you have any idea what kind of music he listens to? And how loud he must listen to it? Trying to turn it down results in him screaming like a banshee," Raego muttered. "Easier to keep it on."

I sighed, nodding. "Sorry, man. Let's just hope nothing happens, and he'll be out of your hair soon." Tory let out a dismissive huff and left, calling out Alucard's name.

Music suddenly erupted from one of the distant rooms, some kind of techno jazz remix. On full volume. I smiled weakly at Raego.

"You owe me. Big," he warned.

I left. I had things to do. And I wasn't very excited about them.

CHAPTER 15

*E*ven though it was late morning, I wasn't ecstatic about my to-do list, so I poured myself a stiff one. I took a deep drink of the absinthe, caressing the book in my lap. The ruined rug had been taken out this morning while I had been on trial at Raego's house, leaving my office more spartan than I was accustomed to. It wasn't a big deal, but when you've spent so much time in a room that was always decorated exactly the same way, and suddenly one item was removed, it was very noticeable.

I set the glass down and took a deep breath, attempting to calm myself as I closed my eyes, idly thumbing the cover of the book. The one Indie had tried to steal.

Through the Looking-Glass.

Even though I had failed to ward the house against Indie, I hadn't failed to ward this book. The ward had been made strong enough to prevent even the slightest of magic from touching it. With painful consequences for any would-be thieves. The ward also protected against Regulars and non-magical creatures, with less fatal consequences, because that wouldn't be very nice of me to incinerate a defenseless human. Or if Sir Muffle Paws decided to use it as a resting pad. If he did, he would get a nice, pleasant good morning electrical zap to the belly and groin, but would generally be unharmed.

Enough stalling, I chided myself. I focused my mind, and imagined a White World.

I felt a tug on my soul, and the familiar resting sounds of my house instantly ceased, to be replaced by the sound of soft wind chimes and a violin.

I opened my eyes. Slowly.

The Mad Hatter sat before me in an ornate white armchair, playing a violin. I had last seen him as a nine-foot-tall giant ginger, but now… he was only a larger than average man with reddish hair and a gnarly chest-length beard. Apparently, he could change his size. Then again, I knew almost nothing about him. So, he could probably do a lot of impossible things.

He wore no shirt, and was surprisingly heavily muscled. Where did he work out? Considering that thought, I realized that he had little else to do, being possibly the only person in this world. He watched me with intelligent, raptor-like eyes as he continued fiddling. I watched him, smiling lightly. I checked my outfit, not surprised to find I was no longer wearing my tee and jeans, but a crisp, silver leisure suit, complete with grey loafers. This was typically the case whenever I visited. I found myself in crisp, fresh, clean, grey or silver clothes. Didn't know why, didn't ask. Instead, I crossed my ankles, careful not to touch anything.

Because the room was entirely white, and in the past, I had stained anything I touched.

Despite magically wearing new clothes of his devising. Like hospital scrubs to protect him from my human plagues, and his house from my dirty touch.

My very *existence* had stained things. I touched a book – stained. Touched a windowsill to stare outside at the white trees, lawn, and milky ocean – stained. Literally, anything I came in contact with left a sooty stain.

Which did all sorts of things to my self-image.

Like when someone idly mentions you smell like body odor, even if you know you don't.

Because I can promise you one thing…

After someone says that, for the next few days, you will constantly be taking a quick, discreet sniff of your pits just to make sure. Because emotion rules reason. The fear of the *chance* that it was true almost always overpowered your knowledge of the fact that it *wasn't* true.

Preach.

I spent a few moments scanning the room absently, enjoying his tune as I studied the white environment before me: paintings, rug, wooden floors, bookshelves, fireplace, and potted plants. The shock of everything being white had worn on me by now, and I no longer found it eerie.

Well, *as* eerie.

I slowly swiveled my head back to the Hatter – my mysterious pen pal from my copy of *Through the Looking-Glass*, and found him staring at me intently, still playing for me, but not needing to apply any attention to the complicated task.

His eyes were cunning, intelligent, wise, and… *wild*.

Because he was – self-admittedly – *Mad*, with a capital *M*.

He finally drew out a long, lamenting note, and then lifted the bow away. I dipped my head in appreciation, but dared not clap. Some things startled the Hatter, and one didn't want to startle the Hatter.

I wasn't entirely sure how it was possible. I mean, the Mad Hatter was a character in a book, not real. But… here we were. He had identified himself as the Hatter, and in my world, sometimes you just had to go with it.

Was it any more ridiculous to believe in bloodthirsty unicorns than it was to believe in the Mad Hatter?

"Exquisite," I murmured appreciatively after a polite pause.

He bowed slightly, resting the violin on the table beside him as he took a drink from a glass. The drink, of course, was white.

"Would you like some…" he studied me pensively for a second, and then smiled. "Absinthe?"

I grinned back, nodding. "If it's not any trouble."

He briefly flicked his head to the table beside me, and I managed not to gasp to – without any magical warning – find a bottle of milk sitting beside an empty glass. Because he was a Maker. And could do things like that. I didn't correct him, or show any surprise at finding a bottle of milk instead of absinthe beside me. I just freaking poured some into the glass. It was chilled.

I set the bottle down and took a nice big sip of the milk.

And almost spluttered in shock as it burned my mouth. I instinctively swallowed, and the fennel and licorice-like flavor made my eyes water. Because I had taken a huge sip. I coughed, gasped, and swallowed several times, trying to nullify the unexpected flavor.

The Hatter was suddenly behind me, pounding me on the back as if trying to bring me back to life. "Easy, Lad. Easy," he grumbled in a very deep voice.

I finally caught my breath, slowly raising my hand to let him know I was fine. "I wasn't expecting…" I coughed again, clearing my throat. "It looked like milk."

He chuckled. "*Everything* looks like that, here," he rolled his eyes, unfolding back to his full height to walk back to his chair on large, heavy feet.

"I guess I should have seen that coming."

He nodded, leaning back into his chair. "You get used to it."

"You… look different," I said casually, just an observation.

"My world, my rules. I can look how I want." I shivered at the intensity of his look. "To what do I owe this pleasure? Have you come to play?" He winked.

I hid my shiver, forcing my mind not to run wild with thoughts on what he might mean by *play*. I had to be careful, here. "No, I'm actually here – for one – to check on… your *guest*."

He frowned. "Why? He is mine."

I opened my mouth, closed it, and then gathered my thoughts. *Doucement*, I encouraged myself silently. *Easy*.

The Hatter began to laugh, shaking his head. "You don't need to treat me like a startled deer, Nate…" he smiled, reading my face.

I bowed my head. "Right. I didn't mean to imply otherwise. I just had a few—"

"Peddler! Dealer! Devil! Come forth!" the Hatter suddenly roared, causing a few of the paintings to rattle against the walls.

And Rumpelstiltskin was suddenly there, standing before us. His eyes were glassy, terrified, and he twitched with each inhalation of the Hatter's chest. As if awaiting a beating.

"Will this suffice?"

I shivered as Rumpelstiltskin looked up at me. His eyes were wild, broken, terrified, and momentarily hateful. Because I had brought him here. His face was a mask of scars. *Traitor. Vile. Foul. Thief. Fraud. Cheat. Liar.* These words were all carved into his face, among many, many others. He instantly lowered his eyes back to the floor.

What the hell had the Hatter done to him?

CHAPTER 16

On Rumpelstiltskin's list of most hated people in existence, I had to rank in the number one spot. I had earned it. Banishing him to this world. With this monster, the Hatter, for his crimes against me and my friends.

But this... I hadn't meant for anything like *this* to happen.

The Hatter snapped his fingers, and Rumpelstiltskin was suddenly gone again. The Hatter wiped his hands as if they were soiled from Rumpelstiltskin's momentary presence. "Now that business is concluded, perhaps we can chat."

I nodded eagerly, wondering what to do next. I had intended to question Rumpelstiltskin, but judging by the look on the Hatter's face, that wasn't going to be in the cards. I had received numerous warnings not to even associate myself with the Hatter. Death had repeatedly warned me to avoid him. Which was why I hadn't told Death of my errand before he left last night.

Not counting that, I had also discovered that the Hatter had been a Maker. A Maker that had succumbed to his Beast. Not fully in control of himself. And, well, he was *Mad*. Whether as a result of his Beast taking control or something else, it didn't really matter. He was entirely dangerous. Dangerous enough to be sent to this world. Or to *Make* this world.

As if reading my thoughts, the Hatter began to frown at me. I hastily threw up a shield, barring my thoughts from intrusion. "I'm not hiding anything," I said respectfully.

"Typically, when people start off with a statement like that, they are very literally hiding something," the Hatter replied testily.

I held out a hand. "No. I have some things to ask you, and I don't want you jaded by my thoughts. I want to hear your opinions. Not your opinion of my opinions."

He frowned for a moment, and then nodded appreciatively. "That might be the wisest thing you've ever said to me."

I let out a relieved sigh, dipping my head in appreciation of his response. I didn't want to ask him about his position on being mad, because making a psychopath emotional was always a bad plan. Rationality was not a strong suit. Just emotional drive. Fight or Flight.

"You mentioned your day of birth was coming up," he smiled. "I have a gift for you."

I blinked, surprised at his interruption. Had I told him that? I met his smiling, violent eyes, and nodded, forcing a grin on my face. "You didn't have to—"

But I was suddenly holding something foreign in my palms, the glass of milky absinthe now resting on the table again. My fingertips thrummed as if I was holding a live but well-insulated wire. I stared down to find a stone bowl in my lap, my fingers clutching either side, shaking.

Shaking from the energy oozing out of the bowl. But as I stared inside, at a concave of crystals, I recognized the interior formed a familiar shape. Not a bowl at all.

Then they began to twitch and spasm in *fear*. I was holding a mask.

A goddamned *Mask*.

"Holy hell!" I blurted, managing to flip the Mask onto the couch beside me, urgently scooting away. I suddenly froze, turning my head to see if I had offended the Hatter.

He was grinning. "You just shat on my divan."

I stared at him, wondering if I could escape before he decided to imprison or kill me for my disrespect. "No, I didn't shit on your divan," I said, voice hollow, ready for anything.

"Could have fooled me, my boy!" And he burst out in laughter. I relaxed my shoulders, beginning to smile myself.

"It… caught me off guard," I admitted, glancing down at the crystal mask beside me. Its weight pushed it down into the cushion, but it hadn't felt heavy in my hands. It was face down, so I was staring at the inside. It reminded me of one of those rocks you buy from souvenir shops that are a hunk of normal-looking stone on the outside but are all purple and white crystals on the inside. Like it would grind my face raw if I ever wore it. And despite it not feeling heavy in my hands a moment ago, it sunk deeply into the cushion. You know, because it was freaking crystal.

"It is just a Mask. You haven't accepted the thankless job, right?" he chuckled.

"No, definitely not," I stammered, turning to look at him.

"Your face!" he bellowed all over again. "Perhaps you *need* to go take a shat!"

I frowned, embarrassed. "It's kind of a big fucking surprise, you know," I defended myself.

He wiped his eyes, chest heaving as he chuckled. "That's the best kind of gift, is it not?"

"Gee, let me think about that. Offering me a gift that would doom me to murder a fraction of humanity during Armageddon. I'm not sure I call that a *gift*."

He frowned at me. "That's the *job*. I didn't give you the *job*. I gave you the *Mask*." I frowned, finally holding up my hands to show him I didn't catch the significance. "The Mask is powerful, my boy. Without the job, it's still fucking powerful. I made one long ago. Before…" his gaze trailed off, and I swear I saw storm clouds flickering in his eyes. "Well, before a lot of things." His attention riveted back to me as he idly stroked his beard. "I have no use for it any longer. It will make things more… convenient for you. For example, visiting me. Here."

"But I can do that already," I replied, not understanding.

He smiled as a teacher would at a particularly daft student. "You project yourself here. Once, you managed to come here in the flesh with a guest. Bravo on that, by the way," he clapped his hands lightly. "The other times, you have either had a mask or the book. No doubt one of the damn Hindus taught you that Projection nonsense," he grumbled.

I just stared at him. "So, you gave me a key to your place… Do I get a drawer?"

He shrugged. "If you want one." He didn't get my joke. "It's not *just* a key." He sounded grouchy.

"Listen, it's a great gift. I just wasn't aware of those other things. I saw the Mask and instantly thought of the Horseman thing. Which I don't want a part of. At all."

He judged me skeptically for a few moments, before finally nodding, waving a hand. "Anyway, Happy Birthday, my boy." He stared intently at me as he said it, and I wondered what mad thoughts were running through his head.

But I didn't dare ask. And I was glad he couldn't read my thoughts right now.

"It's not my birthday yet, but thanks for such a thoughtful gift." I glanced over at it for a few moments. "I presume it's very dangerous…"

"Oh, yes," he grinned, leaning forward. "What kind of gift would it be if not *very* dangerous? Covet it. Like a dragon with his gold."

"Of course," I said softly, wondering where the hell I should hide it. But my face was smiling, a carefully controlled mask for the Hatter.

No pun intended.

CHAPTER 17

I snapped out of it, promising myself that I would immediately lock it away. Maybe get Mallory to hide it wherever he hid the Macallan stash. Because he had even managed to prevent the mansion from knowing where it was. Which was baffling.

Because the mansion was sentient.

"You're not wearing a hat," I commented.

He shrugged. "My hair looks nice today. No need."

I nodded slowly. "Sure does…" I paused, debating. Then thought, *hell, he got me a gift, surely, he wouldn't mind…*

"You seem… different today," I held my breath, ready to flee at the drop of… a hat.

He leaned forward with an amused grin. "Less *mad*, you mean…" He leaned back with an easy shrug. "It comes and goes. You help."

I discreetly let out my breath. "Oh. I'm glad to hear that… Look, I wanted to ask you a few questions. If you're willing." I had meant to ask Rumpelstiltskin, but it had been pretty obvious that conversing with his prisoner was off the table. The Hatter nodded absently, picking up his violin again.

"Do you know if the Grimms are secure?"

"You killed them," he answered distractedly, strumming the violin with his beefy thumbs.

"Well, sure. I killed some of them. Even their leaders. But... your guest led *all* the Grimms, or they reported to him, or something like that. I need to know the rest are truly locked away."

The Hatter looked up at me frowning. "Why?"

I forced myself not to wilt under his scrutiny. "I once saw Rumpelstiltskin open a gateway to their world, after I had killed all those in... my world." I managed to correct myself at the last moment, having intended to say *our world*, which would have been pouring salt on a wound, because the Hatter wasn't part of *my* world.

He frowned for a moment, strummed the violin once, and then stared down at it. "Shh... it's okay, my dear."

And I was ready to leave. Right then. I sat very still, waiting for a polite opportunity to leave. It was good to know that I wasn't physically here, though. That he couldn't actually hurt me. Supposedly. Unless this was a time I had come here in the flesh...

I wondered if I would even be able to leave if he didn't want me to. He *had* mentioned that the Mask would let me in and out at my leisure, but I didn't know – and didn't *want* to know – how to use it. He flicked his head up, hair flinging back. "Apologies. She gets persnickety when they are brought up." I nodded slowly, barely breathing. "The betrayer told me about that. He tricked you. An illusion," he said offhandedly. I blinked, remembering my first encounter with Rumps, when he had forced me to give him a Seeder Grimm amulet – one that could make other amulets – in exchange for saving Indie's life. By suddenly opening a portal to the Grimms.

I had heard the army of Grimms shouting at me, and had instantly complied. The Hatter continued now, snapping me from my thoughts, but I silently imagined doing worse to Rumps than the Hatter had done to him so far. "Only Jacob Grimm's amulet is strong enough to bring them all back." I nodded slowly, leaning forward to rest my elbows on my knees. "To create the link the fiend needs to find them." He strummed his violin again, and the sound was sad. "But you bested him and took him here to my world. Where he cannot call out to them. That's what the fiend told me, anyway." He frowned to himself. "Unless, of course, you were stupid enough to bring Jacob's amulet here, and the fiend escapes."

"No, of course not."

"Good. He and the amulet must be in the same world for him to call out to them. Which would call the Grimms to the world he is *in*." He grinned, looking feral. "And that would lead them *here*." He flashed teeth at me, looking anticipatory. "And I have *many* guest rooms…"

I leaned back with a shiver. He wasn't even remotely alarmed at the possibility of hundreds of Grimms showing up in his home. In fact, he seemed to *want* that. But the added benefit was that Rumps would have to be free from his imprisonment, and have Jacob's amulet. Which was never going to happen. Because even if he *did* break out, *and* somehow managed to best the Hatter – which was impossible – he needed Jacob's amulet, which was embedded in Indie's arm, and I was never going to bring her here. Since I had the keys to the place, I could guarantee it.

I felt much better now. Even not knowing Indie's intentions, the possibility of her bringing them over had been terrifying.

But there was always the chance that she had merely wanted to obtain some artifact from one of the fallen Grimms. Maybe something Ichabod knew of since he had spent so much time around them. But I had checked all their bodies, removing anything that may have had some power tied to it. And I had moved those items to a safe that Ichabod couldn't know of. That no one knew of. Not even Indie. Literally, no one knew of it, or would suspect it.

And now she couldn't even set foot on my property without all hell breaking loose.

So, with a billion safe-guards in place, I felt a very heavy weight lifting from my shoulders.

Now, I just had to figure out how to fend off the Academy and the Syndicate. And fire-face, whichever side *he* had been on. And I had to keep the shifters safe from the Academy. I sighed. It was like the universe was trying to guarantee that my birthday sucked donkey wang.

"We could always… kill him," I offered gently.

The Hatter snorted. "He's my roommate. I'm not killing my roommate." I opened my mouth to press the issue, because surely, he hadn't meant it like it sounded. He was torturing him, after all. The Hatter held up a fist. "No. He keeps me company in this…" his eyes grew stormy. "This *hell*. And with the Pale One no longer visiting, I prefer the company."

"Death doesn't visit?" I asked, surprised.

He shook his head, lips thinning in both sadness and anger. "No."

Death had warned me about visiting the Hatter, but I was surprised to hear of him practicing what he preached. After all, what did he have to be scared of? He was a freaking *Horseman*.

"Has your… roommate told you much about the Syndicate?"

He jumped to his feet, panting with sudden fury. "Those slimy, good for nothing bastards," he snarled, spittle flying in an arc. Then he began to pace, stomping loudly. I sat very still.

"Has he told you something that upset you?" I asked softly. Politely. Casually.

He rounded on me, pointing a beefy finger. "There is nothing I do not know about the Syndicate. I—" then he clammed up, deciding not to say whatever had been on the tip of his tongue. He closed his eyes, and let out a deep breath. "They are a failure. A broken dream."

I frowned. That was a very specific way to describe them. I tried a different route. "I'm trying to stop a man. A man who is willing to go to very dangerous lengths to destroy them—"

"Then maybe you should be *helping* him," the Hatter snarled, more spittle flying.

I nodded slowly. "I'll… take that into consideration. But the things he's done – and is willing to do – might be worse than anything the Syndicate has done."

He took a menacing step forward as if willing to rip me in half with his bare hands. "*Nothing* is worse than what the Syndicate has done. Nothing! You should be willing to break the *world* to stop them." His eyes literally danced with white fire now, and drool coated his beard.

What the *hell* had the Syndicate done in the past to ignite such ire from both the Hatter and the Academy? I mean, I wasn't on Team Syndicate or anything, but I also wasn't willing to destroy the world to expunge them. What didn't I know?

I gave him a few moments to compose himself. "What I meant was that I at least need to *speak* with this man, but I'm having trouble locating him. Maybe I can feel him out, and find another solution to help him destroy them," I lied, very glad he couldn't read my thoughts right now. "But I can't *find* him." I paused, letting my words sink in past the Hatter's emotions. I had no intention of talking to Ichabod. I was going to *end* him. "If I can track the Syndicate, maybe I can find this man."

The Hatter grunted, muttering to himself, but not answering me.

"He… has hurt someone close to me. Taken her, in fact. And in a very short time span, has completely changed her as a person. I'm not sure how or why, but I don't know how it's possible to make my… friend so completely different in such a short period. Like night and day."

The Hatter snatched up the violin, but then he froze, looking horrified at his action. He held it close to his lips and whispered an apology. Then he held it up to his ears. A moment later, a wide smile split his face, and he nodded gratefully. I stared in disbelief, not moving a muscle. Then he sat down and began plucking it like a mandolin. "Perhaps he told her the truth," he said to me.

I waited for more, but when I sensed no more was coming, I pressed. "The truth?"

He nodded, seeming to grind his teeth as he plucked away an angry, violent tune. "The truth about what the Syndicate does. Has done. And will do. That would make anyone change their stripes." He met my eyes, plucking a low-tuned string dramatically. "Anyone."

I shivered. The look in his eye made me almost believe him. Could it be true? That the Syndicate was so evil that Indie had chosen to compartmentalize our love in order to carry such a deep hatred? I didn't like the outcome, but it was a hell of a lot better than thinking she had just turned evil.

Problem was, that even if this were true, Ichabod was willing to go to terrible lengths to accomplish his goal, and that didn't sit right with me.

Actions speak louder than words. It didn't matter if you were taking out a bad guy by becoming an even worse guy. Thrasymachus was wrong. Might was *not* right.

But I wasn't going to tell the Hatter that.

"Well, if Rumps says anything that might help me find either party, could you let me know?"

The Hatter grunted affirmatively. I think.

I took a risk. "And whatever you do, *please* don't let him out of your sight. If he's the only key to finding the Syndicate, this man may find a way to break him free."

"I would like to see him try," the Hatter growled. I frowned in thought, because technically, if Ichabod and the Hatter hated the Syndicate so much, why *wouldn't* they work together? I grew very uneasy, replaying past conversations with Ichabod in my mind. Did he know about the Hatter? How to get here?

"Listen, Hatter. Could you do me a favor?" he nodded absently. "Don't let anyone visit you here. Lock the doors, or whatever."

He slowly turned to face me, frowning. "You want me to lock my prison… even *tighter*?"

"No. It's just… this man may reach out to you, and that could go very badly for me… and my friend."

"I already told you, my boy. I *hate* the Syndicate…" he trailed off, studying his violin with adoration, "but I hate poachers even more." He leaned forward suddenly. "And no one takes my toys. I'm not going to make an already near-impossible prison even more impossible to get into."

I opened my mouth, but he interrupted me, growling murderously as he met my eyes.

"Tell you what. I'll make it so that the only way here is through your Mask." I let out a soft breath, trying not to sound too relieved. But since I was going to lock up the mask, that would be perfect. Ichabod could never come here. "But if you die, I remove those walls," he added.

I sighed, finally nodding. It would have to do. "Thank you. Once this is all over, we can open the doors back up."

"If you promise me one thing," he said, studying me. I nodded, waiting. "*Listen* to him. *Objectively*. He may have a good point. Perhaps you can guide him on a different path to achieve his goals, but know that his goal *is* worthy of listening to." He cocked his head, turning to the door expectantly. "It's time for you to leave. I have a guest."

Now, I had no idea if he really had a guest or was just nuts, but I stood, and turned to leave. Then I remembered I didn't need to physically leave. Just send myself back. I closed my eyes.

But he suddenly latched onto me, his grasp circling my entire forearm, which wasn't large, but it wasn't that small, either.

And power like I had only barely tasted from my Maker Beast coursed through me in a rush like a waterfall. The true power of a Maker. *A Tiny God*, a small voice whispered in my ears, and I momentarily lost track of everything.

Tiny God.

That was what Shiva had called Makers. When he had told me that the Hatter had once *been* a Maker. Feeling his power now, I had a whole new respect for the title. And a whole new fear for Ichabod's abilities and intentions. Was he willing to wake a god? Or was he just intending to use the Grimms to take out the Syndicate? To be honest, the Grimms sounded a whole lot better.

I brought myself back to the present, the Hatter still squeezing my arm. Not a threat, just a ridiculously large amount of magic emanating from his touch. I opened my eyes and looked at him. "Don't forget your Mask," he grinned. "You can make it smaller, like this." He touched it, and it became a small coin. And somehow, I knew I could duplicate it. Change it, even.

I nodded slowly, then plucked up the coin, refusing to look at it while somehow keeping a gracious smile on my face. As a coin, there was no vibrating tingle to it. Just a coin. But I felt it calling out to me. I blocked out the feeling. "Thanks. I'll… see you soon, Hatter."

"Please, call me—" his head whipped to the door again. "God's hairy balls! Fine! I'm coming!" And he disappeared as if he had never been there in the first place.

But I saw his precious violin resting on the couch, proving that I hadn't imagined it all.

I just shook my head, not wanting to even consider what he had been about to say.

I had enough crazy in my life already.

CHAPTER 18

My phone rattled on the desk, snapping me out of my daze. I had sat in silence upon returning from the Mad Hatter, considering dark thoughts, toying with my new coin.

I slowly climbed to my feet and picked up the phone, pocketing my coin. Raego.

"Hey," I answered.

"He fucking turned," Raego growled angrily.

My shoulders sagged. I had just left his house! "Damn it all," I muttered. "What color is he?"

"We… don't know."

I blinked, waited for elaboration, but got nothing. "What do you mean?"

"Just… get your ass over here. You started this, you can finish this," he growled. I heard voices shouting in the background before he hung up. I pulled the phone away, staring down at it, confused. How did he not know what color Yahn was? And what did he need me to finish?

Rather than wasting time driving, because Achilles was going to be at my house soon, I Shadow Walked to Raego's house, appearing in his lawn directly in front of an obsidian statue of a man. I jumped back a step, in surprise.

Peter.

My childhood friend. He had betrayed me for power, trying to kill me and my friends.

Which just set my mood perfectly.

I saw something move out of the corner of my eye, but when I turned to look, I saw nothing. I waited a few seconds, scanning the area, but nothing moved. I took one last look back at Peter, the jagged wound across his throat, and then stormed away.

It wasn't a *statue* of Peter. It *was* Peter, forever frozen in stone, thanks to Raego breathing his smoke fire on him, in essence, saving all of our lives. Even if Raego was able to release Peter from the stone, he would bleed out within moments. So, he was both dead and not dead. I didn't feel sorry for Peter, but I did feel… something. Regret. Pain. Loss.

Come to think of it, very similar to how I felt about Indie.

I shook it off, looking up at the house for the first time. And let out a surprised gasp.

A large hole marred the exterior wall of the second floor, like something had jumped out.

I ran up the steps, entering the house to find naked men and women running around, searching everywhere. I simply stood there, staring. No one paid me any mind, they were so obsessed with their search. Raego stormed onto the upper landing that overlooked the foyer, glaring down at me.

"I heard you needed some help with a reptile dysfunction," I smiled.

One of the dragons snickered as he searched. Quietly. Raego just stared at me for a few seconds. Then he pointed at me, and then at the landing beside him. I jogged up the stairs, and stood exactly where he had pointed, waiting. He let out a frustrated breath and then began walking away. "Follow me."

I did, and we soon reached the open door to a guest room. He motioned me inside.

I frowned, peering inside. And saw the gaping hole in the wall that led outside.

"Yahn's room," Raego growled.

I continued to stare. Then I frowned at him. "I don't see Yahn. Is he hiding?"

Raego met my eyes, not amused at all. "As a matter of fact, he is. We need you to find him."

I blinked. "You guys can't find a big fucking dragon on your own? You're the Obsidian Son. The Dragon King. Just command him to appear," I said, entirely confused.

Raego folded his arms, and finally shook his head. "I can't. I never saw him as a dragon. He never saw me as a dragon. We are strangers. Fledglings must be dominated before they can obey. The parents typically take care of this, and since the parents are bound to me by my magic, their offspring *becomes* bound to me." I frowned, not having known that. Then I got it.

"The Reds are too young to dominate him," I said flatly. "That's why you wanted him close."

Raego grunted a confirmation. Then he leaned low, eye to eye. "He is a fledgling carnivore, likely hungry, confused, and terrified." He pointed out the hole in the house. I could see the St. Louis skyline in the distance. "And we *can't find him.*"

Shit. We were both silent for a minute, staring out at the city. Where would he have gone?

"He is something... new," Raego said softly.

"What does that mean?"

"It means that he shifted, tore through my house, injured my dragons," he paused dramatically, "and no one *saw* him."

I digested that very slowly. What had I done?

"You sure no one saw sparkles or anything?" Raego just stared at me. "Okay. What typically happens when they shift for the first time? Do they simply hunt?"

Raego frowned, thinking. "If there is food nearby, they typically go for that." He clenched his fists. "But we had plenty of food laid out downstairs, just in case he turned, knowing it would draw him like a fly to shit."

"Except it didn't," I said, thinking. He grunted. "You said *if*. What do they do when there *isn't* food nearby? Or aren't hungry?" I added, remembering his comment about food downstairs.

Raego met my eyes. "They go to a safe place. Something they remember as a human. Home. Did he have family nearby?"

I shook my head since he was a foreign exchange student, but then I remembered Greta, his *Grammy*. I instantly dialed her.

"Master Temple… did you crash any birthday parties today? Make any children cry?"

I rolled my eyes. "Greta, this is important. Have you seen Yahn? Or a dragon?"

The line went silent for a few seconds. "What in the devil are you talking about?"

Which was good. It meant she hadn't. "Okay, good. I need you and Eae to get somewhere safe. Somewhere you don't normally go. Just stay away from home," I urged.

"I am *not* leaving my home, thank you very much!" she snapped. "Where is my Yahn? What did you *do*?" she hissed into the phone. I heard a male voice speaking in the background.

"Do I sound like I'm playing around here?" I shouted in disbelief. "You are in *danger*!"

"The Lord is my shepherd," she said with sheer arrogance.

And that set me off my rocker. "You *will* get your happy ass out of the house, or I will come over there and, so help me *god*, I will *drag* your happy ass out of the house, wrap you up in a damned doily, and drop you off at a strip club!" I roared, seeing red.

I heard her squawking in the background as someone took the phone away.

"This is Eae," he shouted. "Can you hear me?" Louder this time. I had to yank the phone from my ear before he shattered my eardrums.

"Stop shouting, Pigeon! I'm right here!"

He lowered his voice, sounding angry. "Then why are you two yelling into the phone?"

I took a deep breath, and let it out. Raego was smiling for the first time today. "Eae, you two are in danger. Yahn was infected by a dragon, and he might be coming to visit his dear old Grammy. He's not himself, and we're trying to help him." I said, forcing out a calm tone.

I heard him speaking to Greta in the background. He came back a moment later.

"Greta doesn't want to leave. And what do you mean, *Yahn is infected?*"

I almost slammed my phone down on the ground. "Eae! *Listen to me—*"

"If she doesn't want to leave, I'm not making her leave. Nor is anyone else."

And he hung up. I stared incredulously at my phone. Then I met Raego's amused gaze.

"Do you think I would go to hell for killing him?" But he just chuckled. My mind raced. I needed to get to Greta's house. I began planning, wondering how many dragons I could take with me, how many I would need, how I might be able to see him, since he was apparently a ninja dragon.

A car horn honked outside, and I stared through the opening to see Tory pulling up.

I clapped my hands together excitedly, rounding on Raego.

"I think this might be a job for our resident Beast Master."

Raego nodded and began walking away. "Take care of it," he growled before disappearing down the hall. "You two take the House of God. We'll keep looking here."

CHAPTER 19

The Reds had called Tory to tell her about Yahn, crying and sobbing, blaming themselves for his turn and then his escape. Tory, being an awesome mom, had come to console the Reds. But also, she was the self-appointed shifter-whisperer of St. Louis, and wanted to help.

For which I was eternally grateful, having no idea how to find a dragon I couldn't *see*.

After she checked on the Reds, Tory and I Shadow Walked to Greta's house, landing in her backyard to avoid anyone seeing us suddenly appear out of thin air. I looked up to see the lacy pink curtains slam shut. I muttered something evil under my breath, but Tory just smiled.

"She's an old woman. Just let her be."

I let out an angry breath. "Fine, let the pigeon take the house. We should be able to find a huge freaking dragon out here without divine intervention."

She nodded with a faint smile, and we began playing hide and seek with Yahn. But there really wasn't anywhere to hide. "Yahn!" Tory whispered loudly. "It's me, Tory. And Nate! We want to help you!"

No response.

I looked at her. "Can you sense a shifter nearby?"

She focused, eyes faintly pulsing with green light. After a minute, she let out an exasperated breath, shaking her head. "Nothing."

"Maybe he's not here yet," I offered. "Let's wait for a while. Maybe he's having a hard time finding his grammy's house from up in the sky."

Tory shrugged, sitting down in the grass, scanning the skies, waiting.

I sat beside her, eyes flinching at every moving tree branch, falling leaf, and the kids shouting down the street. Life. Neighborhood sounds.

We sat there for thirty minutes before I stood and began to angrily pace. I needed to get back home. Achilles was coming over soon, and I needed to ask him a favor. About the gorillas. Being late wasn't going to help my case.

"You sure he was coming here?" Tory asked.

"How the hell should I know? Raego said they either go for food or somewhere safe. Home."

She just nodded. "Then we keep waiting."

I continued pacing, thinking back on Yahn's interview. He had only been here a few weeks, so I doubted he had gone to his apartment. He hadn't even fully moved in yet. And Greta had lived here for decades, with Yahn visiting throughout his childhood. This *had* to be the safe place he would go to. Where else could he—

I began to laugh. "No fucking way..."

"What?" Tory asked, scanning the sky as if I had seen him.

"I'm going to play a hunch." I held out my hand. She frowned at me before taking it. I Shadow Walked us to a roof in the city. Two taller adjoining buildings butted up against either side of ours, blocking out most of the sun, casting the roof in light shadows.

We were in the warehouse district. Tango music could be heard through the building below.

Because we were standing on top of the building where Yahn attended his dance classes.

But we were alone on the roof, nothing sinister or scaly lurking behind anything. "Worth a shot," I finally complained with a frustrated sigh.

And a rumbling purr answered me.

We both flinched, and Tory whispered, "He's here!"

"Yahn!" I whispered excitedly, grinning as I searched for him. "It's me, Nate! We want to help you." I stared at the brick wall where I had heard the sound, but there was nowhere to hide.

Silence stretched for a few seconds.

Then a section of the wall on the adjoining building shimmered, revealing a very small dragon that hadn't been standing there a moment ago. I shook my head in disbelief as I realized what he had just done. I had never heard of *that* before.

Now visible, he was my size, which was much, much smaller than I had expected the plump Swede to be in dragon form. To my regret, he wasn't brightly colored, and he didn't sparkle. His scales were dark in the dim light, like stone. He snorted, tail nervously lashing back and forth.

I knelt down, holding out my hands with a big, welcoming grin. "Toe-tah-lee awesome! You're, like, invisible and stuff!" I cheered.

The dragon let out a chuffing breath, and then sauntered nimbly away from the wall, mouth open like a dog panting when his owner came home. He even wagged his tail.

Tory stared, mouth open, trying to understand.

Yahn stepped into the light, and his scales flashed brightly, reflecting the sun in a dazzling rainbow of colors as he moved. His horizontal-pupiled eyes were identical to his scales.

"He's fucking… candy-painted," Tory stammered. "Like those gangster cars."

I grinned, nodding as I held up a finger. "And he can blend into the background. Like a chameleon." Tory shook her head in awe, a slow smile splitting her cheeks.

"He's… beautiful."

"Toe-tah-lee," I agreed, laughing as Yahn's tail wagged harder. "Help him shift back. Raego's going to shit when we tell him," I chuckled, shaking my head. "Candy-painted!"

CHAPTER 20

*R*aego hadn't *shit*, as it turned out, but he *had* been stunned speechless. The Reds became very popular with the other dragons, everyone clamoring to find out how they had created such a magnificent dragon. Something none of the dragons had ever heard of before. With an idle comment, I had stated, straight-faced, that it was all attributed to Raego's divine rule.

He had heard me, and returned a very pleased, and thankful smile. I had only done it to appease him, because this had actually all been my fault, and I didn't like owing anyone favors.

After a private talk with Yahn, urging him that everything was going to be okay, and that he probably needed to call Greta, I had left. He had been the opposite of afraid, though.

Because the Diva Swede had come back to a runway and an adoring audience, finding himself the center of attention in Raego's home. A spotlight. Yahn was going to be just fine. But I knew Achilles would be waiting for me at Chateau Falco, so I had Shadow Walked back home.

To find Achilles pounding shots with the other guest I had invited over to the house at the last minute. Ganesh. Who apparently adored absinthe. They hadn't been drunk, but they had drunk enough to get rid of any lingering anger at my tardiness.

I had taken a few moments to tell them the story of Yahn, but since they had never met him, they didn't see the humor in his color scheme. But they had been very impressed at the potential for such abilities. Chameleon scales…

We now stood in a secret hallway beneath Chateau Falco.

Ganesh cleared his throat beside me, eyeing me askance. "Are you sure you want me going in there?" He considered Mallory and Achilles. "Or them?" Ganesh was in his typical form, a giant, reddish-hued elephant-headed man. Kind of like the Minotaur, but less bull. Oh, and he had four thigh-thick arms. He wore a snake-skin belt that had magical healing powers over his thickly woven robes. The belt bore a hatchet on one hip and a noose on the other. One of his hands held a tiny mouse that suddenly crawled over the backs of his knuckles and up his arm to perch on his shoulders. It hissed at me.

I had seen the rodent in a much different perspective the first time. Because the mouse could turn into a horse-sized rodent big and strong enough to carry Ganesh on his back. Because the rodent was his *ride*. Ganesh, or Ganesha, was the Lord of Obstacles in the Hindu pantheon, and his mount, Krauncha, was known as a creature that ate pests – an obstacle to farmers. Imagine a giant, warrior, elephant-headed man riding a rodent, and you'll soon realize that my capacity for surprise was pretty high.

But the world held a lot of surprises for me, regardless. Like candy-painted dragons.

And Ganesh's giant, carnivorous mouse suddenly the size of my fist. Hell, it could even talk! But seeing it now, one would think only, *aww, what a cute little mousey!*

I nodded to Ganesh, scowling briefly at Krauncha. It flicked its tail, and suddenly disappeared in a tiny puff of air. Ganesh rolled his eyes, shrugging at me. I guess I had pissed him off. "I need different perspectives. You're a god." While with the Hatter, I had remembered Shiva's conversation about Makers, and since I didn't know exactly how to call out to Shiva, I had chosen his son, Ganesh. If Shiva knew it, likely Ganesh did as well.

I continued, turning to the Myrmidon. "Achilles, although only a lowly drunken bartender with cankles, knows some gods..." Achilles smirked good-naturedly. He wore tight jeans, military boots, and a *God Save the Queen* t-shirt. But he had crossed out *Queen* with red paint, replacing it with *Grimms*, likely just to annoy me. He was very strong, and in great shape, but he was no beast of a man like my pal, Gunnar.

Achilles was more like one of those smaller CrossFit guys, the ones who do everything with bodyweight. You know they're strong, but they don't look like ridiculous meatheads. That being said, he could react in any situation faster than almost anyone I had ever seen, and watching him fight was a thing of beauty. Perfect precision, both in his offense and defense. Like a snake. His blonde hair was tugged back behind a baseball cap that read *Artemis' Garter*. Which had been the strip club where I first met the weredragons. The building had caught fire and a few people had died. And some dragon hunters had shot me off a roof.

A rough night. But it felt like it had happened a decade ago rather than a few years ago.

I scowled at him. "Are you *trying* to advertise all my past failures?" I asked, motioning towards his outfit. "Never mind. Of course you are." He merely grinned back, tipping his hat.

The two turned to curiously assess Mallory, who grimaced. "And he's my... totally mundane, unassuming bodyguard," I rolled my eyes, my voice dripping with sarcasm.

"Death told me you kept him out of the loop on something earlier today. For... not sharing, right?" Achilles smiled. Mallory muttered under his breath unintelligibly – which wasn't unusual with his thick brogue – but it sounded hostile. Achilles grinned wider, because he smiled at everything. Torture. War. Death. Mayhem. Conflict. Anything unpleasant for others, really.

"Why don't you tell me a little bit about Patroclus," I mouthed off.

His smile shut down like a bank vault, and he shot me an aggressive glare instead.

Ganesh frowned. "Patroclus... I'm unfamiliar..." his eyes grew far away, as if searching his memories. They snapped back to focus a moment later. "Ah, now I remember. You Greeks," he snorted, a soft honk coming from his trunk.

Because Ganesh had an elephant-head. So, he sometimes *honked* that great big trunk of his when he talked. He was dressed casually, which was significantly better than him wearing those ridiculously lethal, serrated blade attachments affixed to his tusks. Like I had seen him wearing a week ago on his way to a match up at the Fight Club.

The one the gorillas had asked to join. A place where all the monsters could cut loose. Even those legends, gods, and beings who were usually prevented from interfering in our world. Because the Fight Club wasn't in our world. Dying there didn't actually kill you. Asterion's Buddhist response to settling disagreements, I guessed. I had been killed there several times, only to arrive back home without any wounds.

I had used this to my advantage a couple times, surprising the dickens out of my enemies and earning quite the reputation. Then I had struck upon the idea that those beings unable to act in our world could do whatever the hell they wanted there, without retribution, because it technically wasn't *in* our world.

I had given the monsters a playground. An arena to fight.

To the death.

And they *loved* me for it.

Especially Ganesh. The peaceful, meditating, doe-eyed elephant-headed god was a different person entirely when in the ring. A straight-up killer.

I wasn't sure if he had any stipulations about not interfering in our world, because I had direct evidence that he *had* interfered a time or two, but regardless, these guys tended to leave our world alone. They were immortals, or the next best thing to it, and didn't want to mess up their situation.

And I have to admit, seeing Death, Ganesh, Achilles, Mallory, Gunnar, Van Helsing, and a dozen others cut loose on each other was downright horrifying – and majestic – to behold.

All because of this punk wizard.

The Vaults, or bank for Freaks, loved me for it, too. Because the receipts from the Fight Club were deposited with them, later used to invest in new bleachers and weapons. Ganesh had even voted to buy a hot dog stand. He fucking loved hot dogs. Or at least Tofu dogs.

I realized everyone was staring at me. Well, not Ganesh. He was hopping from boot to boot chasing the birds carved into the massive wooden door before us. Like a kid at the zoo. Because the birds were *alive*. Or at least *mobile*.

The door was a giant carving of a pond scene, complete with fish, a wolf, birds in the air, and a few other creatures. Occasionally, one of the birds would swoop down to catch a fish. When this happened, another fishling (baby fish) would magically appear at the bottom of the pond. The Circle of Life. I had yet to see the wolf catch one of the birds, but I was sure he had succeeded a time or two. He looked crafty.

I reached out my hand to pet him. I felt his fur ripple underneath my hand, and he growled in appreciation. And like twisting a key, this opened the door.

The door to the Armory. *My* Armory.

A collection of weapons, artifacts, and dangerous magical doodads my parents had acquired and locked away over the years with the help of Pandora.

Yep. *That* Pandora. The one with the box.

She was the custodian of my collection. The collection my parents had deemed too dangerous to fall into the wrong hands. And then, like big stupid idiots, they went and gave me the keys.

I turned to my companions, holding up a hand for them to wait. "Achilles has already been here, and unfortunately, has my trust. But you two," I said to Mallory and Ganesh, "need to swear that you won't ever come here without my express permission – each individual time you need my prior approval." They nodded after sharing glances with each other. "And you will never take anything from the Armory without my direct permission."

Achilles chuckled. "You waited until the doors were open just to force them into this, didn't you?" He laughed harder. "You bastard. Dangling a carrot. Well played." He clapped.

Ganesh didn't look as amused. Not mad. But not amused. I held out a hand, which held an artifact I had once taken from the Armory. A Binder. "Swear it. Now."

Ganesh honked in frustration, but Mallory instantly complied. Once finished, he smiled, looking grateful that I had granted him a brief sliver of my trust by inviting him here.

I arched a brow at Ganesh, who finally complied. "I'm not mad at your lack of trust. I'm disappointed that a god is being forced to swear an oath to a thug wizard." He smiled, but swore an identical oath.

The Binder in my hand forced them to tell the truth, so I had no concern that they were lying to appease me, or using magic to trick me. Listen, it wasn't that I didn't trust them.

But I didn't fully trust them.

The president doesn't share the launch codes to his nuclear *football* either.

An ounce of prevention, and all that.

"Right, let's go take a walk." And I strode into the sandstone walls of the Armory.

CHAPTER 21

My mother squealed in delight, jumping up to her feet. She was an apparition, not entirely physically corporeal, a shade, a wandering soul. My dad grinned at me from the opposite end of the room where he had been reading a book. Death had allowed them to inhabit this place rather than the Underworld, after they had been murdered. Which was just swell. We could touch, but it felt... different. Still, I could hug them again. Which was more than most people ever got.

"How is Indie? You ready for your big day?" she blurted, clapping softly as she grinned.

My heart shrunk two-sizes-too-small, and my face must have matched, because she frowned.

"Nate, what did you do?" she asked in a warning tone. "Never mind. Just go apologize. Right now." And she folded her arms, tapping her foot angrily. "This can wait."

My dad was staring open-mouthed at Ganesh, either purposely avoiding my mother's topic of conversation, or genuinely stunned to see the Hindu god, I wasn't sure.

"Mom, my romantic life can wait. This cannot." Because I had chosen not to share those details about Indie with them... I held out my hand in introduction, pointing at Mr. Nose. "Please welcome Lord Ganesh." I pointed to Mallory. "And an old friend of yours." His eyes were glistening, and his face looked ragged with shame. No doubt feeling guilty for failing them – not saving them from death. My mother and father both smiled at him, pure joy, no accusation on their loving faces. "And my bartender. I forget his name," I said, pointing at—

"Achilles!" Pandora shrieked, bursting into the room and literally launching her whole body at the Greek in an aerial assault. He caught her easily as she wrapped her legs around his waist and hugged him for dear life, burying her neck into his shoulder. Achilles' scarred hand clutched her like a life preserver under her rear, and the other hand petted her hair gently. I heard him let out a deep, pleased murmur.

"Cute," my mom whispered from beside me, watching Achilles and Pandora. She turned to Ganesh and curtsied. My dad was only a heartbeat later, bowing at the waist.

Ganesh grunted, gripping my mother's wrist, and in a very practiced, but odd-looking motion, he kissed the back of her hand, somehow not letting his trunk get in the way. Then he traded grips with my dad, and that just made his day, because he was grinning like a kid in a candy store.

"Hey, I'm right here, too, you know," I grouched.

My mom smiled, mussing up my hair with one hand dismissively. My dad hushed me, grabbing Ganesh's shoulder and leading him away. My mother gave Mallory a great, big hug, and then they also walked away, speaking softly to each other. Achilles and Pandora continued whatever they were doing, some kind of weird Greek monkey hug, or something.

"Hey, minions! I'm right here! I have important things to discuss!"

Achilles grunted and simply carried Pandora away. Ganesh shrugged helplessly at me, while my dad shot me an angry glare over his shoulder, indicating sharply that this was a once in a lifetime opportunity for him to speak with Ganesh. My mom merely scowled at me with her mom vision, and continued speaking with her old friend, Mallory.

"I can't believe this," I muttered.

"We didn't promise to listen to you once we got here!" Achilles called out, and then he walked through a doorway, kicking the door shut behind him. I heard Pandora giggling from behind the thick wood, which sounded suspiciously like a tickle giggle. A *tiggle*.

After a few minutes of standing there, alone, I very pointedly, didn't stomp away.

Or slam a door.

Or anything else melodramatic like cursing, grumbling, or kicking walls as I meandered through my Armory, absently staring at the lethal devices all around me. And considering using them.

On my friends and family.

CHAPTER 22

*I*t had been an hour, and I had marginally cooled off. Taking the time to well and truly get a feel for the Armory. Recently, I had sent Pandora off with a laundry list of things to collect, and she had brought them to me so that I could study them with my lab rats at Grimm Tech. But to be honest, I had wandered around here by myself very little in the past, always under a strictly-guided tour from Pandora. She had never left my side. And the other times I had visited, I had been under a time crunch, visiting only to speak with the guests, not peruse the stockpile.

And what a stockpile it was.

This time, I had no immediate timer. And I had no chaperones.

Which generally allowed me to be more objective. No nagging warnings, no preconceived notions from others to cloud my judgment. Of course, this also increased the risk, but I was made of hearty, wizardly knowledge.

And I was infallible.

"Right," I muttered to myself, impaling the tiny positive-mental-attitude goblin who lived inside the deep, dark, super-black castle fortress of my soul. It was roommates with my silent love for *The Sound of Music* and cat memes.

But I digress.

I passed windows that revealed mountains, and then a few windows later, an ocean, despite being less than a dozen feet apart. I even saw a dark world with hundreds of albinos running around like bioluminescent fish. The Elders. I also saw a white castle on a white island surrounded by frothing white oceans. The Hatter's White World. I stopped looking through windows after that.

My general opinion of the place had also changed. I no longer felt so conservative about the items here. Before, I had treated everything as if it was radioactive and loaded with sexually-transmitted diseases that traveled by sight. But I had seen some darker parts of the world since then. Played with some dangerous items. And squared off against some pretty powerful enemies.

In a way, it was kind of nice to walk around on my own. Without supervision. Or constant chatter. I could do what I wanted. When I wanted. Looking at what I wanted on my own terms without warnings, descriptions, or anything else. I was still cautious, but the danger factor helped clear my head, forcing me to think, rather than rely on someone else warning me if I was about to do something incredibly stupid.

Like touch…

"Don't," Pandora hissed beside me, slapping my forearm away with her palm.

I blinked. Then shook my head as a fog seemed to lift. I took a quick step back from the spear on the wall, staring at it in horror. "What the fuck was that?"

She patted me on the shoulder. "Some of the things can talk. Or override your thoughts. Coerce you. It's why the Armory has a librarian. A custodian. And why you shouldn't walk around unsupervised," she chided.

I scowled at her, studying her cheeks. "Your face is flushed. Did you have a nice… workout?"

Her cheeks flushed a darker color, but she didn't look embarrassed. She just smiled widely at me, neither confirming nor denying. And not acting the least bit ashamed of… whatever the two Greeks had been doing.

"Come. They are ready for you." She studied the room, frowning thoughtfully. "I wonder how you made it this far..."

"What do you mean?"

Pandora shrugged, and clutched my hand in hers, leading me away. "Nothing, really. Just... I must have been more distracted than I thought. I usually know if someone makes it this far."

"Must have been one hell of a distraction, then," I grinned.

She glanced at me. "It was... long overdue."

"Heh. Long."

"Honestly, Nate..." she sighed, letting go of my hand and walking ahead of me.

I followed her, chuckling. At least I had gotten a little payback.

A few minutes later we were back in the room with the balcony. Achilles stood, looking out over a sandy desert.

In a fluffy pink robe. With the Artemis' Garter hat. Like a Greek Hugh Hefner.

"Do you have no decency? This wasn't a booty call, Heel."

He rounded on me, frowning. "Excuse me?"

"Get your head in the game."

"Nate!" my mother shouted. Everyone turned to glare at me.

"You can't be serious!" I shook my head in disbelief. "*I'm* the bad guy here? Do none of you give a shit about anything?" I pointed at Achilles. "The bartender just banged my librarian!"

My mother gasped, glaring at me in full mom mode, and Pandora went from an astonished look to laughing harder than I had ever heard her laugh. But Ganesh saved me from the momster.

"I don't give *shits*," Ganesh said, confused. "That doesn't seem very courteous," he murmured to my father with a frown.

"It's..." my dad tried to shoot me a dark look, but battled a smile as he tried to explain. "A very juvenile piece of slang. He meant that none of us seem to care about his problems."

"Well, wouldn't that just be a terrible existence?" Achilles smirked.

"Zip it, Achilles. Before I put you in high heels and we play dodge the arrow."

He grumbled something under his breath, tightened his bathrobe with an angry yanking motion, and then sat on a couch. Pandora followed, still chuckling, before unabashedly sitting on his lap, squirming inappropriately. "We were *sparring*, Nate…"

"You shouldn't have told him! He would've kept bitching," Achilles smiled.

I blinked at them in disbelief. "Really?" They nodded, grinning like idiots. "Oh."

"Never mind. That look alone is worth it!" Achilles laughed.

I rolled my eyes. "I have a few things to talk with everyone about—"

"Hello," a new voice spoke from a dark corner of the room.

Everyone flinched. But Pandora just sighed, complaining about open doors under her breath.

We turned to see the impossible. Someone had entered the Armory without my approval. Without Pandora's approval. And the level of juice pulsating from that dark section of the room was enough to end us. All of us. If the being so much as passed gas.

This just wasn't my day.

CHAPTER 23

The lighting intensified to reveal a figure on an ornate leather divan. He sat there, in the middle of the couch, legs folded, and four arms displaying various mystic gestures.

Shiva. Destroyer of worlds.

"Father," Ganesh bowed instantly, his trunk sweeping across the floor.

Pandora and Achilles untangled themselves ungracefully, almost falling off the couch before bowing and murmuring a greeting to Lord Shiva.

The interesting part was that my father, mother, and Mallory did not bow, curtsy, or speak. They merely studied the god before them with different looks on their faces. My father looked embarrassed, my mother looked eager to go bake a cake, and Mallory looked… well, cautious.

I frowned at their reactions before turning to Shiva. He didn't seem offended by their lack of interest. "Hey, Sheeves. Where's Toro?"

Shiva turned to me, smirking. "Nandi, you mean."

I shrugged. "They all look the same to me. Has horns, will *moo*."

His eyes tightened, and his bone-white chest seemed to grow momentarily brighter for a moment before fading back to normal.

Around his bright-blue neck hung a set of rosary beads, and twined around the necklace was a living python, tongue flicking out to taste the air. A shining crescent moon centered his forehead, just above a third eye – that creeped me out. It blinked independently from the usual two. And his dreadlocks would shame any Rastafarian.

He turned to Mallory, dismissing me. "Hello, *old friend*." He sniffed the air, and blinked. "You're still *masked?*" His gaze shot to my parents with a curious frown. "What *was* your plan?" he asked himself, tapping his knee impatiently as he studied each of them. "I had hoped to finally discover your schemes…"

The room went deathly silent. I slowly turned, looking from face to face, wondering what was going on. Achilles and Pandora also looked confused. Ganesh looked uncomfortable. Not guilty, but suddenly aware that the topic Shiva was referring to was not common knowledge, and that with his ability to see futures, pasts, and read minds, he suddenly found out a whole lot more than he wanted to know. But my parents and Mallory looked downright sick to their stomachs.

"Not many know. I need to keep it that way. Especially now," Mallory whispered, staring down at his feet.

Shiva nodded slowly. "Yes. I guess there is wisdom in that. But I do have my guesses… I even made a bet with myself. You three have been thick as thieves, and as much as it pains me to admit, I must applaud you. If *I* can't even figure it out, *no one* will. I do wonder *why*, though." His third eye suddenly pulsed with light, on his forehead, directly between the normal ones, as if he was trying to read their minds. He gave up with an annoyed sigh, waving his hand in defeat.

The three victims looked both relieved, and guilty as hell.

"Okay, Mallory just got booted off Team Temple. He is no longer allowed here. You hear that, Pandora?" I snarled.

She rolled her eyes. "Too late for that, Nate. I warned you. Once you grant someone access, they have it. Period. But at least you made them swear an oath. You could always deny him every time he asks," she suggested.

"That." I pointed at her animatedly. "I'm doing that." I glared at

Mallory. His shoulders slumped further at my words alone, because he was still staring at the floor.

"I'll put him on the permanent *no* list, then," Pandora said with an easy shrug.

I rounded on Shiva. "How the hell did you get in here?"

He smirked, pointing at my parents. "They needed a god's help to accumulate so much in such a short time." He held up a slip of paper. "Even though he apparently doesn't trust me implicitly," he said with an accusing frown, indicating Mallory's secret, "your father wrote me a… *Hall Pass* to allow me access. Ad infinitum." He pocketed the slip of paper. Even though he was shirtless, and I didn't see any pockets on his pants. Maybe he stuck it in his crotch, like some women shove their phones in their bras.

I took a deep breath. *Woo-sah*, I murmured silently, calming myself. Ganesh nodded in approval at my gesture. We had been practicing. That, and I had watched *Bad Boys II* recently. But I did shoot another glare at my parents. "You could have told me Divine Intervention was involved in setting up the Armory."

My father opened his mouth to reply, but Shiva interrupted him. "Speaking of Divine Intervention, you caused quite a ruckus at that circus."

I blinked at him. "You *helped* me cause that ruckus. And it was months ago!"

He shrugged. "I may have underestimated time lines. Or miscalculated," he added, glancing at Mallory and my parents.

I stared at him for a second, but I was unable to contain my frustration any longer than that. "What the *hell* are you talking about?" I all but shouted.

He frowned, the crescent on his forehead sparking, despite no light striking it. "We spoke of *killing* your Beast, not *freeing* it. Now it's in a cane. Which is not in your Armory. Because you lost it…" he said in a low tone. "A free agent, so to speak. That and this Ichabod are all anyone is talking about up there," he pointed at the ceiling, likely referring to the gods. This time, only his third eye moved, darting to Mallory for a brief moment.

I broke out in sweats. "Christ."

"No. Not him."

"No, I meant… never mind." My mind raced. "The gods want to use Ichabod?" I asked.

Shiva grunted. "Those already awake are more curious than anything else. They don't hunger for power. They've had enough war in their days. That's a plus for you humans." I let out a relieved breath. "But those sleeping? Yes, I imagine they want to meet the Tiny God. Most definitely. They want *power*. They were put to sleep for a reason. Didn't like to share their toys."

"That… that's better than nothing," I managed. It meant Ichabod had to *want* to wake a god, and that they weren't currently hunting for *him*. "Are those sleeping all bad?" I asked.

"The majority of them, yes. But not all." His third eye grew distant, thinking. "Well, I guess that's relative, isn't it?" He chuckled, slapping his knees with all four palms. "Would you rather be eaten by a bear or mauled by a pack of coyotes? Ha!"

I ignored that pleasant image. "It seems like Ichabod's number one goal is taking out the Syndicate, so maybe we have some time."

Shiva met my eyes with all three of his. "That must be why they took your cane, your Beast," he shook his head, frowning at my naivety. "What man wants only a *taste* of power? Sooner or later, he will want to wake a god. Trust me." And he winked.

Shit. Had I ever heard Ichabod mention waking a god? I didn't think so.

"He really has a hard on for the Syndicate. But what the hell did they do to make him so vengeful?" I asked myself, out loud. I shot a glance at my parents, but saw absolutely no emotion on their faces. Like statues. "You two want to share with the class?" I snarled. They didn't.

"You mean other than the whole imprisoning him with the Grimms for a few hundred years," Ganesh answered, ever unhelpful.

"Ichabod *chose* to do that. He tried to banish them. It's *his* fault he got stuck in his own spell. The Syndicate didn't cause that. This is something different. He's unhinged. Broken."

Shiva frowned at me. "Broken or not, we gods must take the tools provided and…" he flashed us a grin, changing the tone of his voice to that of Tim Gunn from *Project Runway*, "Make it work!"

Achilles clapped. "Flawless."

That's it. I'd had enough. I hit the Greek with a band of air on the mouth, sticking it in place so he couldn't talk. "Children should be seen, not heard," I smiled, anxiously anticipating his reaction. I wanted to let off some steam.

CHAPTER 24

*H*is face turned purple, and if not for Pandora, we would have had a good, old-fashioned, Midwest *rassle* on our hands, which I would have welcomed over this conversation. But she held him back, whispering soothing words to him and easily removing the magical duct tape I had stuck to his mouth.

I turned back to Shiva with a disappointed sigh. "You know, it's alarming what pop culture you find important enough to watch. Deadpool and Project Runway wouldn't have been my first recommendations to get a better understanding of humans."

Ganesh and Shiva shared a look, as if genuinely surprised to hear this. I ignored them.

"Maybe If I can keep Ichabod distracted by the Syndicate, he'll be too busy to think about waking a god. Which may mean I need to help him bring back the Grimms…" The room went dead silent.

"That would be monumentally stupid…" my father finally said. I shut him up with a look.

"Agreed," Shiva said, watching us intently. "You already have one Grimm. How is that working out for you?" he asked snidely.

I sneered back at him. Anyone else would have broken teeth after a comment like that.

But… they didn't call him the *Destroyer of worlds* for nothing.

"Right," I managed, grinding my teeth. "I didn't anticipate my ex-fiancée fleecing me."

My mother gasped, placing a hand over her mouth.

Shiva ignored her. "Should have. She's not the same anymore. The amulet changes people. As does the company she keeps…"

His words hit me, but I was too riled up to give them too much thought. "Yeah. Learned that the hard way. After she tried to kill my friend and rob me blind. Twice. But I don't understand *why*. What the hell could have changed her so dramatically in such a short span of time?" My mother's face was completely white with disbelief.

"Good question," Shiva replied, encouragingly. I waited. He just watched me, then finally sighed, as if giving up on the limited capabilities of my mortal brain. "You should ask her."

"Well, you are *blindingly* helpful. That is such a great idea. I wonder why I haven't thought of that. I should just go up to the woman that wants to murder me and ask her, *how have you been lately? I was just curious why you turned into a psychopath. Want to grab a coffee?*"

"*Murder?*" my mother shouted, a horrified look on her face.

"Feelings," Ganesh offered politely. "I think they like it when you ask about their feelings."

Achilles burst out laughing, and even Mallory let slip a chuckle. My mom didn't look pleased at me ignoring her, or Achilles' laughter. At all.

Shiva snapped the fingers of all four hands, silencing everyone. "You are missing the point. The Grimms are a bad idea. You must hide the Hands of God. That way the Tiny God, or Maker, cannot wake a sleeping god when he finally decides to get around to it. The Grimms – although dangerous – can wait. A vengeful god waking up will *not* wait."

I sighed, stubbornly agreeing. "Hands of God," I murmured, remembering them from the cavern and my previous talk with Shiva. "Are any of them here, in the Armory?"

"No," said Pandora.

Shiva turned to her. "I grow weary of this. I want to speak to… Mallory for a few moments. In private."

Mallory's spine straightened, not with fear. But like a man preparing to walk to the gallows.

"Wait, you're leaving?" I asked, incredulous.

Instead of answering, Shiva clapped all four hands, and the two of them were suddenly gone.

"Damn you, Shiva!" I shouted, waving my fist at the air.

"Unwise," Ganesh murmured. "My father destroys worlds…"

I wanted to roast everyone in the room to barbecue. But I chose tact. "Okay," I said, addressing each face, wanting to take out my anger on someone. "Before anyone else disappears, I want a goddamned answer," I said, eyes fixing on my father. "Why did you really set up the Armory? What gives? I've never gotten a clear answer. And don't tell me it's to *keep the world safe*. I'm beginning to realize that there are always ulterior motives."

"To keep these items out of the hands of his Masters," Ganesh answered, pointing at my dad.

My parents flinched, but didn't speak.

"Yeah, the Academy is a real bunch of assholes," I agreed. "And they have expressed extreme interest in the past about getting access to this place."

No one responded, but I guess there really wasn't much else to add. The Academy sucked. Period. Realizing I wasn't going to get any other answers, I turned to Pandora.

"I need something to keep Tory alert. Something to keep her shifters in line in case she's targeted. We have anything like that here?"

"We have some Moonstone amulets. I'm not sure we have enough for all the students, but as long as they are always near one, none can shift. So just keep the students close together."

I nodded unhappily. Because that would make them easier targets for the Academy. "Do Moonstones work on all shifters?"

She nodded. "I'm glad to see you finally using the items here," she added, smiling.

Achilles leaned forward. "Speaking of, I left my helmet with Pandora a few years ago. After, well… after dinner one night." Her face turned beet red, this time a much more personal flush to her cheeks. "Mind if I check to see if it's here?"

Pandora nodded, speaking quickly. "It is."

Achilles stood, tying his stupid pink robe tighter. "Great, I'll just go grab it really qui—"

"You'll sit your happy ass down, is what you'll do. Unless you want to swear to work for me. I like the hat you're wearing now better anyway."

He glared at me, and I could have sworn I saw fire in his eyes. "It's *mine*."

"Possession. Nine tenths of the law," I smiled. His eyes shot to Pandora, who nodded weakly.

He folded his arms. "Are you really going to deny me what is mine? After all I've done to help you? After New Orleans?" he added with a dark, meaningful grin.

"What happens in New Orleans stays in New Orleans," I reminded him in a warning tone, not wanting to discuss Gunnar's bachelor party fiasco in front of my parents. He smiled wickedly. "Think about it this way, High Heels." His anger was back in an instant. Oh, he didn't like that nickname. Definitely a keeper. *Everything* in here belongs to someone. But now those things belong to *me*. It's not a Lost and Found box. You want it back, you agree to help me. *And* do me a favor," I added, remembering the gorillas.

He actually growled. "I'll think about it. You usually make stupid decisions, and I'd rather not get involved in all of them. I do have a reputation to consider. We'll negotiate."

"No, you'll lick my boots if I ask. And then you'll get your hat back. Or… you won't."

The look on his face was most satisfying.

CHAPTER 25

Pandora took on a lecturing tone, eyes glassy as she interrupted our spat to tell me about the Hands of God and where they could be found.

"The Elders have one, but I recommend against that. I doubt they will like what you've done with their nomads."

I frowned. "Nomads?"

She nodded. "Those who used the Gateway to enter the grounds at Chateau Falco. When they were sent to look for Indie, after she died there."

I leaned forward. "They were originally a hunting party?"

Her gaze focused on me, the glassy look suddenly evaporating. "Yes. Did you not know?"

I scratched the back of my neck idly. "I had heard it, but I didn't think it was their only reason for coming here. I thought they just walked through the Gateway because it was there."

Pandora shook her head. "No. She was cast down into the earth with a Fae seedling. Her death fueled the seedling, birthing the Gateway, granting her to the Elders. But… Death used that power to bring her back. Stealing their sacrifice."

I grunted. "You're saying they wanted to sacrifice her?"

Pandora looked frustrated as she tried to explain. "No, she was *offered* as a sacrifice. I do not know their intentions with her corpse. She belonged to them. But now she is alive. I do not know the Elders opinion on the matter, other than that they need her."

"Okay… that's not ominous. She was just at my house. But the Elders didn't even know she was there."

Pandora shrugged. "They are bonded to Chateau Falco now, and see what the mansion sees." She studied me. "You didn't have her marked as a threat, so they never saw her, because she was not relevant. Many come and go at your house." My parents frowned at mention of the house.

Achilles burst out laughing. "That's what she sai—"

Pandora slapped him in the chest, hard, interrupting his outburst. "Grow up, Myrmidon."

"Sorry," he finally muttered unapologetically, still chuckling to himself.

Ganesh looked truly confused.

Pandora continued as if nothing had happened. "This is merely my best guess. I know so little about the Elders. And even less about your bond with Chateau Falco's Beast."

My dad bolted upright. My mother looked to have stopped breathing. "*What?*" he gasped.

I waved a hand at them. "Tit for Tat. You hold back, I hold back," I growled. There were way too many secrets floating around when it came to me and my friends. It was time to put a stop to it. He looked momentarily angry, ready to reassert his traditional Temple dominance.

But then my mother placed a palm on his hand, shooting him a sad look. "He's right…" My dad finally let out a long sigh, seeming to deflate, looking torn, weary to the bone, and ready to just give up on life. Well, bad choice of words. Give up on spirithood, or whatever.

But he didn't speak. I shared a long look with him, but he just dropped his eyes.

I shook my head, turning back to Pandora. "What *do* you know about the Beast?"

She shrugged. "As much as you." She shot a look at my parents. "The topic never came up."

I didn't need to ask them. I *wouldn't* ask them. They hadn't ever mastered the Beast. But I had been in the cavern. Perhaps I would find my answers there. If not, I would check elsewhere. I no longer felt cozy after hearing so many allusions to secrets regarding my parents. But before they had died, they had chosen to give me the Maker seed... without my knowledge. Which meant that maybe they had a reason.

But I wasn't going to ask.

The ball was in their court. They needed to come clean on their own. Prove their loyalties.

To their son.

"Where are the other Hands?" I asked Pandora. "Wait, how many *are* there?"

"I know of four. One with the Elders. One with the Fae," she shot me a look. "Which I wouldn't advise after your stunt with the Queens."

I grinned absently, nodding. "Good call. Four..." I muttered. "Of course there are four." I shot a glance at Ganesh, and his four arms.

He just shrugged. "Coincidence, I'm sure." I rolled my eyes.

"The Academy has one. And... so does the Syndicate," Pandora continued.

Achilles cursed. Ganesh honked. I just stared.

"Those aren't good options..." I finally admitted.

"How do you feel about robbing the Academy?" my father flashed me a devilish grin.

Despite my feelings, I smiled. "Why not? I'm already on their naughty list. Where is it?"

Pandora met my eyes, watching me intently. "The Library." She swallowed. "In Alexandria."

"Field trip to the lost Alexandrian Library? Hell yeah!" Achilles pumped his fists, which looked absolutely ridiculous in his fluffy pink robe.

"You're telling me that the lost library of Alexandria... isn't lost?" I asked in disbelief. She just fucking smiled.

"I have something that will help..." And she led me away from the group, into the Armory.

CHAPTER 26

I sat in my office, having returned from the Armory an hour ago, thinking criminal thoughts. Robbing the famed Library of Alexandria was going to be dicey. But I could always play the card that I was working in the capacity of one of my other roles. Horseman or ex-Maker – because I still had a teeny seed of the power sitting inside of me for some reason, even though G Ma had told me it couldn't do anything.

But I only needed an excuse if I was *caught*.

I needed to *not* be caught.

But, hell, the Academy had declared war on *me*. My friends. My city. Why should I concern myself with playing nice? Maybe I should rob them blind and leave my fucking business card on the mantle. Take credit for the damn theft. Maybe even steal something else and use it as leverage to call them off my back. Off my friends' backs.

I grew nervous just thinking about that, though. Having them threaten to attack me was one thing, but preemptively attacking *them*? I needed to have brass balls to do something like that.

And I needed a crew. Maybe.

There was always the chance that a one-man job would be easier. Safer.

And I needed to make sure my friends were protected in my absence.

I picked up the phone to call my friends, give them a heads up. That danger might be heading their way. First, I called Othello, to ask her a favor. Next, I called Tory to tell her about the moonstones. But she didn't answer. Maybe she was teaching a class or something.

I called Raego next, because maybe Tory was still there. I wasn't sure if the dragons were in danger or not, but I felt better covering all my bases, just in case. But he was the king of the dragons. The Academy taking him on would start a genuine war. And G Ma's beef was with me, not dragons in general. She wouldn't risk that just to spite me, would she?

"Temple," Raego drawled. "It's like you can hear when your name is spoken…"

"What do you mean?" I asked.

"I just received the most interesting phone call. About you."

"Wait. The Academy… *called* you?" I asked in disbelief. I had been prepared to hear all sorts of hell about Yahn, Tory, and the gorillas. But I hadn't expected this.

He grunted affirmatively. It was hard to tell when Raego was amused or upset. He was… different from most people I knew. I had seen him joking around with the best of us, but I had also seen him calmly command one of his dragons to execute another dragon. He had been drinking a tea, if I remembered correctly. His hands hadn't shaken. Even as the dragon was murdered before him. He simply nodded, and moved to the next task of the day as the other dragons carried out the body.

There was a reason I encouraged Tory to watch over the Reds, and not Raego. I had even made sure that she legally adopted them after their mother, Tory's brief girlfriend, had been killed in our war with the Grimms.

Because Raego was… different. Old Testament. At least when it came to dragon stuff.

"They threatened to call my grandmother, Nate."

I couldn't help it. Out of all the things I had expected, Raego once again surprised me. I burst out laughing. "I need you to back up a minute." I gasped. "They called you to, what, exactly? Talk about my many redeeming features? And somehow that escalated to calling your grandmother? To be honest, I didn't realize you even knew your grandmother." Because his father had been a real son of a bitch, willing to kill Raego for power. Not really a family man.

"You could say that," he muttered drily. "They want you dead. Very dead. They asked me not to help you. In any way. Or else…"

"They would call your grandmother," I finished, not bothering to hide my laughter.

"This isn't a joke, Nate. She's… formidable. A nasty old crone. A real pain in the ass."

"You're the king of the dragons. The Obsidian Son. You're welcome for that, by the way."

"Appreciated," he said. Because I had basically handed him the title when we first met. After he had been forced to kill Peter – now the statue I had earlier seen in his lawn – and I had killed his dad. Kind of. There was a little bit of teamwork involved, but that about summed it up.

"So, what's so bad about Grammy?"

"She's… controlling."

"Raego, I really don't have time for this. I was just calling to give you a heads up about them. I didn't need your help, so don't worry. You're safe from… gram-gram," I burst out laughing.

I heard something shatter on the other end of the line and began laughing even harder. "It's not funny, Nate. She could ruin everything!"

I wiped tears from my eyes. Big bad dragon king was scared of a little old lady. "Calm down. Like I said, I don't need any help. Just lay low. Pretend we're not friends."

"We aren't friends. We're barely business associates," he said flatly.

"Wow. That's cool. Dick," I said.

"Pretty convincing, right?" I could sense him grinning on the other end of the line, and felt relief cascade in. That had actually caught me off guard, thinking he honestly felt that way.

"Very. Just keep that up and gram-gram won't come to make you clean up your room."

"Dick."

"Obliged," I smiled. "Is Tory around?"

"No. She's at the school with the Reds."

"Okay. How's candy-paint doing?"

He let out a contented sigh. "Very well. That really couldn't have gone any better. He is… *toe-tah-lee* excited about being a dragon," Raego chuckled. "And the other dragons couldn't be happier. Thanks for giving me credit."

"Bros," I said.

"No." And he hung up. Bastard.

I let myself laugh a bit more before reaching out to Alucard. He didn't answer either. Probably busy with Tory at the school.

I moved next on the list. Gunnar. The local Alpha werewolf of St. Louis.

The phone rang several times, and I was beginning to grow a bit concerned that he wouldn't answer. Then the line clicked open. "Hey, Cyclops. I just got off the phone with Raego—"

Static, shouting, and gunfire erupted in the background, as if the phone had been on mute for a second.

"What the fuck did you *do*, Nate?" Gunnar shouted, and then the line went dead.

With a suddenly racing heart, I snatched up my satchel, and opened a Gateway on the spot, right into the parking lot at his apartment complex, hoping it was close to the chaos. Raego's banter had lulled me into a false sense of calm. It was raining through the Gateway, so I snatched up my raincoat with an affixed blue scarf from a nearby rack, tugging it on. I had thought it looked cool at the store. Then I slung my satchel around my shoulder.

The soothing sounds of shotguns, the pleasant scent of cordite, fresh rain, and the wails of the dying called out to me, activating my adrenaline, and my magic.

Yep. Right place.

I jumped through, calling out my whips, ready to teach these clowns a lesson.

Whether it was the Academy or the Syndicate.

Two sides of the same coin, if you asked me.

I didn't even realize until too late that Mallory had followed me, lightning spears crackling ominously in his scarred fists. I shot him a look. "This is War," I said, letting him know we weren't friends.

He grinned darkly, and a shadow I had never seen crossed his face as he licked his lips. "How about a little *Panic*, Laddie?" And he let out a large huff of air, dispersing a fog over the parking lot – which was full of wizards flinging bolts of lightning and balls of fire, among other things. Wolves darted here and there in small packs, taking down wizards to the sounds of agonized screams. I didn't see any wolves on the ground, which meant they had been prepared.

Mallory's fog spread like wildfire. Everyone it touched went suddenly ape-shit.

Well, the wizards, anyway. The werewolves merely snuffed at the fog, and resumed their battle, but the wizards were suddenly attacking friend as often as foe.

I blinked at Mallory. "What the hell?"

He just winked, and threw himself into the thick of battle.

CHAPTER 27

With no time to question him, I flung my hand out at the nearest wizard, wrapping up his ankles with my whip. The ice burned his legs, giving him instant frostbite, and knocking him flat on his face. His head rebounded off the wet pavement, and I was pretty sure I had knocked him out cold. Also, fun fact, I did this a millisecond before a werewolf had lunged for his throat.

I had just saved the bastard's life.

Part of me felt relieved at that, but part of me was angry I hadn't been a second slower.

The wolf glowered at me, a familiar black furred beast. Ashley. Gunnar's fiancée.

She bared her fangs at me and then took off to defend her brothers and sisters. I followed her, ready to not be so nice to the next son of a bitch in my path. After all, they had attacked a den of wolves. Their home. Because of me.

They had nothing to do with the situation. Yet their homes had been invaded by a gang of thugs who were intent on harming both those able to protect themselves, and those *unable* to protect themselves. Because fucking *kids* lived here, too.

No more Mr. Nice Guy.

I flung my hand up into the air, calling out to the saturated clouds that filled the rainy evening sky. They immediately darkened, and my pulse dropped from summoning such a doozy without any kind of preparation. The skies roiled and seethed, turning darker, and darker.

I heard a man shout, and felt my spell being attacked. I pretended to focus all my strength on the spell above, but stomped my foot into the ground, hard, splitting my mind into two pieces.

A pillar of asphalt burst from the ground directly beneath the wizard's feet, upper cutting him in the groin with a geological fist. He actually squealed before flying a dozen feet into the air.

And I panted as I released the spell above.

Spears of condensed silver lightning hammered the wet earth like a storm of arrows, each only a few feet long rather than full heavenly bolts from the clouds.

And they only hit magic users. I immediately dove behind the pillar of earth I had used to take out the wizard, and the bolts of electricity hammered into it like blows from Thor's hammer.

Because I hadn't been able to eliminate myself as a target. Lightning was tricky like that. Especially on such a large, wide scale. I had simply painted a target on any magical user in the vicinity. But not the wolves.

Dozens of wizards lay groaning on the ground, impaled through the thigh, arm, shoulder, or hand. I pulled deep from the earth, holding my hands out like I was getting ready to commence an orchestra. A wave of purple smoke rolled over them, putting them all to sleep.

This only worked because they were already dazed, injured, and suffering from whatever the hell Mallory had done to them.

I almost fell over from exhaustion, legs and arms twitching, my whips fainter than they had been a moment ago, and sizzling on the wet earth at my feet as a result of my sharp tremors.

I took a deep breath, trying to clear my head. Whips only, from here on out. Mallory shouted at me from a nearby group of fallen wizards, pointing at his arm where one of the bolts had tagged him, a clean through and through. He was glaring. But I knew he would be fine, because he could heal injuries. Also, he deserved it.

I flashed him a careless grin, and set off to see if there were any more wizards or if the wolves had it all under control.

Luckily, I didn't have far to go, and there were only three wizards still standing amidst a circle of snarling, sputtering wolves. The rain began to fall harder as Gunnar calmly strode up to the ring on two legs, utilizing his ability as an Alpha to appear as a hybrid wolf-man. He wore a singed trench coat – I was entirely confident it was just for the roguish look – as he approached on white-furred giant paws. His boots were gone, but he did wear shredded jorts, like a bad eighties sitcom. They had likely been jeans, and unable to accommodate his massive bulk during the shift, had shredded where necessary. Bits and pieces of soaked fabric decorated the parking lot where the other wolves had also shifted, shredding their clothes.

He rose higher than the other wolves, obviously, because he was on two feet, where the others merely resembled huge Irish Wolfhound-sized beasts. His white-furred wolf-head stared out from his popped collar, and his lone blue eye assessed the wizards before him, who each held a ball of fire in their palms, crackling whenever raindrops struck them. They looked manic around the eyes, probably terrified to find such overwhelming opposition to their sneaky attack.

The soaked wolves instantly parted for their Alpha. I shoved my way through the defensive ring, encouraging the wolves to make room by cracking my whip in the air above their heads. This startled everyone, even the wizards as they sensed another magic user.

"Friendly, here," I managed, trying to sound confident.

Several snarled at me, but they did open a path so that I stood across the ring from Gunnar. Who looked at me with his one, very angry, eye. "You're late," he growled. "But there is still time for dessert." He licked his teeth, eyeing the wizards hungrily. One of them made as if to let lose his ball of fire, but a lightning spear suddenly slammed into the ground, right between his legs, crackling an inch away from his family jewels, and halting his bad idea in its tracks.

Gunnar acknowledged Mallory with a slight dip of his head. Then he took a step forward, unsheathing his long, obsidian black claws. The wolves began to howl, some yipping as they paced back and forth, splashing in puddles, frenzied at the proposition of spilled blood.

"Your lives are forfeit. Make your peace."

He took another step.

Like an idiot, I cracked my whip at his ear.

And the entire pack rounded on me, the newest threat. Gunnar lifted a paw to his ear, revealing a lone drop of blood. The eye that rose to meet mine was not that of my old childhood friend. But a fucking Alpha werewolf beyond reason.

His chest heaved. "You better have a *damn* good reason for doing something so suicidal. Because we like to oblige our guests," he snarled. "Let him pass!" The wolves growled, but backed up a few steps so I could approach the three wizards and one very angry werewolf.

I saw Mallory shaking his head at me, urging me not to do whatever I was about to do.

I ignored him. He had served his purpose. Whatever he had done had caused just enough chaos to prevent any—

"They killed one of the pups," Gunnar snarled, taking an angry step into my personal space. He towered over me by a good foot, dripping water onto my head from his snout. But even without the added height, he was good at looming, and being intimidating.

I let out a resigned breath at his statement, saddened at both the words, and what it implied.

"I'll be the executioner," I whispered, wiping my damp hair back from my forehead.

He shook his head instantly. "No. This is pack business." And he shot a bloodshot eye at the wizards who were trying to look brave. "They all die. To send a message."

I cleared my throat quickly. "Actually, this is on me. I want to make a proposal. Of course, you can do whatever you wish, because this is your territory, and I'm just an uninvited guest. I will abide by your decision, but I hope you at least hear me out…" I said very softly, but very confidently. This tone was important.

Because Gunnar, my childhood friend, wasn't just speaking as my friend. He had a pack of wolves now. And they obeyed dominance. The law of the jungle. He wasn't speaking to a friend. He was speaking to a wizard. Just like the wizards who had attacked, and killed, one of their own. So, I was sure to use words he could relate to.

Because he was in his Alpha form, a hybrid between man and wolf, not fully human. Not fully rational.

He studied me in silence, chest heaving, and the growls and whines began to grow louder, his pack growing angrier. He held up a giant paw, silencing them instantly.

"Peace," he snarled at them, baring his teeth. "I will hear his proposal, and will make my decision afterwards."

He turned to me, and I caught the barest flicker of my friend deep within the monster. He didn't want to kill anyone. Well, a very small part of him didn't want to kill anyone. He had been an FBI agent once, and those morals were still deeply embedded in his core values. But he wasn't just a lone wolf any longer. He was the leader of a pack. A *big* pack. And he couldn't apply only human logic to the situation at hand. He also couldn't allow himself to be just a beast.

So, I had a chance.

"Speak, before I decide myself," he growled in warning, glancing up at the dark clouds.

I took a breath. Then turned to the wizards, my face morphing into a very sinister promise.

"I do not come offering *peace*. I bring the *terror*..." The wolves were utterly silent for a breath, and then they began to grumble in anticipation, realizing I wasn't about to take their prize away. Their vengeance. Their loyal devotion to their fallen child.

The wizards, on the other hand, stared at me with mixed looks of horror, shock, and incredulity. I maintained my smile. I think some of them recognized my phrase. I had said it once before, but more importantly, I had heard a band of brothers use the same phrase.

The Horsemen.

We bring the terror...

A flicker of movement between buildings caught my attention, but I masked my interest by pretending to look up at the darkening sky, only allowing my gaze to briefly settle on the four silhouettes watching the display from a distance. No one else had noticed them, which was kind of surprising, considering I was standing among a pack of monsters who tracked by scent.

I saw Death give me a firm, resolute nod, raindrops splashing against his skull Mask. Then they were gone.

What the hell? Had I called them by saying the phrase?

But none of this showed on my face. Just… a mask. A cool, emotionless mask.

Because I was ready to plant a flag in the blood-soaked earth like an exclamation point.

CHAPTER 28

One of the wizards opened his mouth to speak and I flicked a finger at one of the wolves nearest him. "You dare—" he began.

The wolf – shockingly – obeyed me in an instant, slicing clean through the hamstring of the offending wizard, before cockily trotting back to the circling pack. Gunnar nodded at the wolf, who began panting proudly, blood coating his tongue and teeth. He shook his fur, playfully spraying his fellows with water and blood.

"Like I said. I'm not here for peace. I'm here for war." And, since I really wanted to make a point, and because Death had given me that nod with his brothers, I modified what I had been about to say. "And death. Right here, right now. But I am not heartless. I will allow one of you to survive." The growls grew, and this time not in my favor. I smiled at Gunnar. "Of course, whether the Alpha decides to then let you leave or become a chew toy is *entirely* up to him. Because you *have* performed an act of war. Against an innocent party. In his territory. Against his *family*..." the growls leaned back in my favor, and one of the wizards actually pissed himself.

Gunnar seemed to grin, but I couldn't really tell with his soaked wolf face.

Regardless, it looked downright terrifying to see him flash those long ivory canines.

I turned back to the wizards. "If he lets you live, you will be a messenger. To your brave lords and masters. Those willing to send you on a fool's errand. A suicide mission. While they stay safe in their ivory tower." I let that sink in, allowing silence to build, and their terror to grow to fruition. To ripen. And then rot.

"My message for them is this. You have played with fire. I have tried peace. I have tried understanding. I am finished. I will rain down such pestilence upon your hallowed walls as has never been seen before. I will bring famine to your gates, starving you out, circling your walls with my monsters, so that no food may enter your kitchens. I will murder hope, and birth terror. I will watch every single entrance – magical and non – in and out of the Academy, and..." I took a step forward, face expressionless, staring them in the eyes. Even the wolves were silent now. "I. Will. Eviscerate. Everyone. Slowly." I wiped my hands together, finished, glancing back at Gunnar. "Tell me which ones die. And," I glanced back at the three wizards, then shrugged my shoulders. "If you even want one of them to deliver my message or not."

Gunnar stared at me, a carefully controlled mask, but I could tell that the human part of him was screaming at me. "Why are you taking this stance?"

"The Academy triggered the attack at the Gala yesterday. To try and shut down the school. Because they didn't like me involved with yet more..." I met the eyes of several wolves, "monsters." Their snarls couldn't have been better if they had been rehearsed. I raised my voice to be heard over the din and the falling rain. "They later declared war on me, and all those I care about, because they hold a false belief about my intentions." I shrugged, turning in a circle to address the wolves. "*You* are my family, not *them*. If they won't listen to reason and logic, and instead pursue criminal, cowardly acts of war against me and mine, I *will* respond. They think me a lunatic? A warmonger? A villain?" I leaned in close, tapping one of the wizards hard on the chest. "I'll *show* them a lunatic. And what happens when they fuck with a wizard who is friends with the Horsemen. When they fuck with a man who *rides* with the Horsemen."

The silence was deafening.

I met Gunnar's eye. He woodenly pointed at two of the wizards. I didn't even turn around. I lashed out with my whips, cleanly severing their heads from their bodies.

And a very cold, dark, feeling plunged deep into my chest. I managed not to throw up, convincing myself I had done the right thing. These were not humans. They had killed a kid. And would have killed more without my help. Without Mallory's help. All because they were misguided. But there was no reasoning with them. They were brain-washed by their masters. Killing two in such a horrific, loud way could – hopefully – prevent dozens of more deaths.

I told myself this, but didn't entirely believe it. It didn't change what I had done.

But Gunnar would have been forced to kill all of them if I hadn't intervened. His pack would have demanded it.

I had hopefully saved at least one life today.

And, one small thing I hadn't told anyone, was that I had lifted the sleeping fog right before my speech, allowing the fallen wizards to hear my words, but unable to move or act. The moment I had said my last piece, I had kick-started them. And they had fled.

Any second, the wolves would notice, so wrapped up in my drama that they hadn't even considered the other fallen wizards.

As if on cue, a lone howl tore through the night, and the pack suddenly dispersed, realizing the other captives had escaped. Gunnar growled instinctively, then shot me a thoughtful look. I nodded one time, confident no wolves could see me. He let out a breath, and nodded back.

In thanks.

Both for saving the other lives. And for preventing him from making a decision that would have haunted his pack for generations.

Starting a war.

I turned to the last wizard, piss-pants, then looked at Gunnar. "The wolves are out. Or I'm coming after your families. Like you did today.

I'm tagging in, because this was a criminal act. You might not have known, maybe you weren't given all the details, but that doesn't matter. You fucked up today." He nodded, eyes wild. "Your boss has a beef, tell her to bring it to my house. You know where I live. I'll leave the porchlight on for her."

And I turned on a heel to walk away, glancing over my shoulder to nod at Gunnar. He nodded back, and then barked at the wizard. The survivor Shadow Walked out of there so fast, I almost missed it. Mallory stepped up beside me, muttering under his breath, cursing softly over and over again. I silently opened a Gateway back home and stepped back into my office.

Mallory followed me, then waited. I closed my eyes, speaking directly to the house.

Prepare for war...

The rafters rattled as if the Beast was stretching her muscles. *Yes, Master Temple...* and she sounded entirely too satisfied. I fell into the chair, and began to sob as the realization hit me fully for the first time. I had just committed murder. Mallory grabbed the Macallan, and didn't say a word, pouring drinks instead. I don't remember much after that.

CHAPTER 29

Gunnar found me the next morning. I wasn't sure how long he had been there. But I woke in my study with him sitting across from me, holding a glass of ice water and a bottle of Advil, smiling as he watched me with his one good eye. His other eye socket was covered by the eyepatch he often wore to avoid scaring children to death.

He began shaking the bottle of Advil like a crack dealer would to a junkie in a sleazy alley.

"Wakey, wakey, Horseman."

"Avast, ye landlubber!" I rasped in my best pirate accent. He scowled, and ripped off his eyepatch, tossing it on the couch. My head hurt a bit, but surprisingly, not as much as I would have thought. "I managed not to drink myself to death…" I whispered, clearing my throat. "Damn it."

"Kind of like New Orleans," he smiled, recalling his bachelor party.

That brought up a smile. Well, the good parts made me smile.

Gunnar spoke. "Mallory did some of his voodoo to take off the brunt of the hangover. He said he left a little behind, because you couldn't have a good night without a bad morning."

I grunted, holding out my hand for the painkillers. Gunnar tapped out two Advil, handing me the glass of water. I shook my hand with the pills again. He arched a brow at me, but complied, dumping out one more. "That should be enough for now. No need to be dramatic about a little headache," he said, smiling lightly.

I stared at him, and then lifted up my shirt, twisting to reveal my bruised back from my fight with the shifter gorilla and chimera. Then I held out my palm, peeling back the bandage to show him the oozing brand. His eye widened, and he tapped out another pill.

"Thanks," I rasped, voice a little better. Then I downed the pills and drank.

"Why didn't Mallory heal those when he healed your hangover?"

"Because he knows better," I said cryptically.

Curing a hangover was one thing, but he had likely checked the wound on my palm, and chosen not to touch it, sensing that there was obviously some deep magic involved with it. He also knew that me waking up to healed bruises would only look like sucking up. Because he knew how unhappy I was with him. Even after his assistance last night.

Because we still needed to have a talk.

And he wanted that to be a clean, honest talk, rather than having my mood altered by feeling moderately thankful for him healing an injury of mine.

Which made me think a *little* better of him. He didn't want to sway my opinion.

At least, I think that's what it all meant.

Of course, he could have been so hammered that I was simply lucky he hadn't fried my brain like an egg. Doing magic while drunk was never smart. Then again, I wasn't really sure if he could *get* drunk, or if what he did was magic. Or something else.

Because we hadn't talked. He hadn't told me anything. Yet.

"So, that was fucking insane. Mind filling in the gaps?" Gunnar interrupted my thoughts.

I leaned back in the chair, closing my eyes for a minute. Then I told him. Everything. About my meeting with the Academy. The note from the Syndicate. The cavern. The talk in the Armory. The Hatter and the birthday gift. Even the gorillas and Yahn to lighten the mood.

Everything.

Because, despite our sometimes-rocky relationship, Gunnar had earned a solid place by my side. And, hiding things from him had led to all sorts of issues in the past. Because Gunnar was tenacious. If I didn't tell him outright, he was liable to go find the answers himself.

By any means necessary.

He was *that* kind of loyal. The kind to do something horribly intrusive in order to look out for your well-being. Often to your detriment. He had – several times – gone against my wishes, lied, and outright made things worse for me in order to do something that he thought would help.

He was a wrecking ball.

And I'd rather have the wrecking ball go where I pointed.

He let out a long breath. "I *knew* you and Alucard were hiding something. Fucking gorillas," he laughed lightly. "And a candy-painted dragon," he said, running a hand through his long blonde hair, which was loose today, not tied back in a bun or anything. "Was he the overly colorful one at the Gala?" he asked. I nodded with a faint smile. His beard had been neatly trimmed, and I could tell that he had recently had his hair cut, because the buzzed sides of his head were flawless.

"Shags?" I asked, pointing at his hair, trying to change subjects to his barber.

He nodded absently, still digesting my story. "Can't you just, I don't know, do anything mellow for once in your life?"

I leaned back into the chair, stretching. "This wasn't me, man. I didn't ask for any of this. Well, except for the gorilla thing. But I was just trying to make them stop stalking him, creeping him out," I admitted. "I was at a freaking charity ball, for crying out loud. For your school. For your students. Trying to raise money."

"Let me get this straight. I'm assuming Ichabod is in town, because Indie is here. And they want – more than anything – to take out the Syndicate. Who wants to kill you."

"Don't forget the Academy. They want to kill me, too."

He waved off my comment. "Only two enemies at a time. Are you sure Ichabod is hell bent on this magical whatsit? Maybe he wants to take the Syndicate out by other means, and you could temporarily team up with him." He hesitated. "And talk with Indie…"

I sighed. "I wish. Here's the rub. Even if he didn't want to wake a god and cause all sorts of headaches, I think he wants to steal the Grimms. Bring them back. And Shiva thinks it's only a matter of time before he tries the Sleeping Beauty thing with a god."

Gunnar nodded, staring down at the floor. "Yeah, you're probably right. And he did have Indie steal your cane." He looked up sharply. "You don't think… he's not trying to make her a Maker, right?"

I shrugged, letting out an angry breath. "Who knows? But being a Grimm, she can already harness Maker powers just by being near him. Or, hell, maybe her Grimm stones already hold Maker powers. Other than the time manipulation thing, I don't know what gifts she has."

Gunnar set his forehead in his hands, grumbling. "Okay. Let me think for a minute."

I nodded, climbing unsteadily to my feet. I walked the room a few times, clearing my head, and then knelt down on the ground. Pushup time. I had found it helped wash away hangovers. As horrible of an experience as it was to do pushups while hungover, for whatever reason, it did seem to help me in the long run.

Gunnar watched me, thinking. I ignored him, steadily going through a set of twenty-five, trying not to throw up or let my head fall off.

"Rather than dealing with the two already big problems you have, you blatantly escalated a horrible situation with the Academy."

I growled, breathing heavily. I was exhausted and felt weak. "They were already going to go after you guys. Said so themselves. Before I even mentioned the Syndicate to them. Sure, they might have done it a little more peacefully. Perhaps while you were sleeping."

"Are you serious?" he asked, incredulous. "Would they really have done that?"

I grunted. "I have no idea. They've done some pretty extreme stuff in the past. Like hunting down chimeras. Even the innocent ones. Genocided them."

"That's not a word," he smiled.

"You got my point, didn't you?"

"Still, you can't just make up words. No one will take you seriously."

I settled on my knees, looking up. "I think that wizard last night took me pretty seriously."

His humor evaporated. "Yeah," he admitted in resignation. "We *all* took you pretty seriously after that. You should hear what my wolves are saying about you. You earned some mad street cred." I didn't smile. He shook his head, studying me. "You okay?"

I shrugged. "Does it matter? If I didn't kill them, you would have had to. Even the ones I let sneak away. Then the Academy would have come at you in force. Full-blown war. And likely the other shifters would form an alliance and retaliate. World War Freak." I took a deep breath. "Better to just kill two, and make a big fucking point of the whole damned thing. Fear tactics."

"Like a terrorist."

I nodded in resignation. "Thanks. I feel so much better now."

"I wasn't saying it as a condemnation. Just an observation." He was silent for a time, and I began another set. "You need anything?"

I grunted, finishing up. The last several reps were spectacularly ungraceful. I knelt, panting. That light bit of a workout should not have worn me out so much. I blamed it on the booze.

"I'm going to go shower. Get some grub or something. I'll be down soon. We need to make sure you guys are safe at the apartments. Just in case they come back for you."

Gunnar smiled. "Already taken care of. Raego had been asking me about renting a few apartments for his guys. Spread his forces out in the city. I called him back last night about some sudden openings. They moved in this morning. And they have roommates." He winked.

I laughed. "Well, that's going to surprise the hell out of the Academy if they decide to come and attack again. A sovereign nation's citizen being attacked without reason? Yeah, Raego will call every dragon in the world to meet him in St. Louis." I grinned. "Good call, man."

"You, too."

I frowned. "What do you mean?"

"Letting the other wizards escape while you distracted us with your speech." I nodded slowly. "Also, how long were the Horsemen there?" he asked casually.

I blinked at him. "You *saw* them?"

He grinned, shaking his head. "Smelled 'em. Been around them a few times. Recognizable stink. Like Brimstone."

"The wolves could smell them?"

Gunnar shook his head. "I asked around. Not about the Horsemen, but about the brimstone smell. No one else noticed it. Maybe it's just because I've been around them a few times now." I nodded in relief. The room was silent as I tugged off my shirt, grimacing as the fabric brushed against my bruises and injured hand. "You kind of smell like them, too."

I flinched, practically falling over the table with the shirt still wrapped around my head. "What?" I blurted from beneath the tent of cloth.

"Just a little. Stronger today than usual, but still, just a faint hint."

And my thoughts instantly went to the Mask as I finally tugged the shirt free.

As if reading my thoughts, Gunnar spoke. "Can I see it?"

My arms exploded with goose-flesh. "I don't think that's a very good idea."

He frowned. "Come on. You have a Horseman Mask. I *have* to see it," he pressed.

I shook my head adamantly. "*I* won't even look at it. I *haven't* looked at it. Not the outside, anyway. The thing practically vibrates with power, man. I don't want that. I've already played with enough dangerous artifacts, and only just got rid of my latest Beast. I don't want another one. It stays locked up."

Gunnar let out a frustrated sigh, but he was nodding. "You're probably right. But if you ever change your mind, let me at least *see* it before you go all Biblical on us."

I gave him a very serious look. "I think that if I pick up that Mask, the whole *world* will see it… *as* I go Biblical on them…" I trailed off, feeling disgusted.

Because the Horsemen were not good guys.

They were supposedly the *necessary* guys, but they were tasked with killing off fractions of the entire *world*, for crying out loud. I couldn't do that. Couldn't *be* that.

He was nodding sadly. "Is that why you leaned so heavily on your ties to them during your speech? To scare the hell out of everyone?"

I smiled, nodding. Then I crossed my fingers. "Let's just hope it works." I picked up my shirt, and began heading out of the office. "Now it's time I go wash off that Brimstone smell."

"Okay. I'll be ready downstairs."

I looked over my shoulder to see him following me out the door. "Ready for what? I don't have any plans yet today."

He winked as he brushed past me. Or blinked.

It was hard to tell since he only had one eye.

"We're going to go rob the Academy." And he began to whistle as he made his way to the kitchen. I didn't even bother to argue. If I didn't let him go, he was liable to call G Ma and call her a cotton-headed ninny muffin, or something. Anything to pick a fight and force my hand.

I had a crew. Temple's Two.

CHAPTER 30

I made my way downstairs, freshly changed, and scrubbed clean. Dean had made pancakes and bacon. The smell pulled at me like Pepe Le Pew chasing his unrequited lover, drawing me towards the kitchen.

I walked through the doorway, taking in a deep breath.

"He thought I was banging the librarian! With his mother in the other room, no less!" Achilles roared, laughing his ass off.

Gunnar shook his head in disbelief, then caught my entrance. "You didn't tell me that part, Nate!" he grinned. "What kind of person do you take him for?"

I shrugged, scowling at Achilles. "Love the project car in the driveway." He smiled. Dean growled to himself, muttering choice words.

"Come to pick up your new shoes?" I smiled at Achilles.

He leaned back, crossing his ankles. "No. But I did come to accessorize," he smiled, shoving a large hunk of pancakes into his mouth. He chewed with his mouth open, and I began to notice a twitch in my cheek, because that was a pet peeve of mine.

"You know the agreement. Serve—"

He held up a finger. "Gunnar told me what you're doing today."

I glared at the werewolf, who was suddenly holding his hands up in the air. "He tricked me!"

"Okay, you duped the dumb mutt. What does that have to do with you wanting to check my Lost and Found box?" I asked, venomously.

Gunnar was frowning. I hadn't told him anything about Achilles wanting his helmet. To be honest, I didn't really know what the big deal was. Surely modern technology could provide better protection than an ancient metal helmet. I had never read anything magical about it. Just a helmet. Well made, sure. But still, just a helmet. I had been antagonizing him by telling him he couldn't have it. I honestly couldn't care less.

But since I had started this charade, I couldn't just back down. Or he would think that he could just bully me around again in the future. "The answer is *no*, Achilles. Unless you agree—"

"I'll do you one better. Well, better for me, long term. Better for you, short term."

I closed my mouth, my patience almost gone. Hangovers didn't make for agreeable wizards.

Dean – I hadn't even realized he was in the room – set a full plate on the table, motioning for me to sit. I did. Maybe it would prevent me from shouting as much. I stuffed my mouth with pancakes, motioning for Achilles to continue, managing a pompous, selfless mask.

"I've been to the Library. Know the ins and outs. Where things are kept."

I dropped my fork, and his grin turned wolfish. "Shit."

He leaned forward, rolling his neck back and forth like a bruiser. "I'll be your guide."

I leaned back, thinking furiously. "It's just a library. I can find my way around."

"We," Gunnar corrected.

I nodded. "Yeah. We can find our way around."

Achilles shook his head in amusement. "You have no idea how big this place is, do you? Suffice it to say, fucking huge. It would take you hours. And you'd have wizard guards breathing down your neck the entire time. And whatever else they use for guards. And after your little speech yesterday, I don't think they like you very much." Of course he had heard. He ran a bar.

"But you don't know where the Hand of God is," I argued.

He shrugged. "True, but I know where it *won't* be. Which is a huge asset when you have limited time to search."

"And you want your tinfoil hat in exchange. I don't get it. The helmet isn't magical. You could easily buy a better one these days. Something stronger. Better protection."

Achilles frowned. "It is my helmet. There are many like it. But this one is mine."

I rolled my eyes at the stolen Marines line. "Whatever. I'll get your stupid hat."

He nodded smugly. "And people say you're not that bright."

I threw my fork at him. He caught it, never dropping his grin.

Did I say that Achilles was a badass?

If not... Achilles was a badass. Still, I didn't like being forced into things.

"After careful consideration, I've decided that you may be useful to me. I'll even give you your hat back. On three conditions." He scowled, waiting. "Give a troop of weregorillas access to the Fight Club."

He shrugged. "Already on my docket, so sure," he grinned with a sneer.

Damn it.

"You can't take anything from the Armory unless I agree." He nodded, unconcerned.

"You have to say *please*."

He stood, wiping his hands together. "Please stop being a whiny bitch and get me my hat. Please."

Dean grumbled. Gunnar was smiling. "This is going to be fun. Or terribly stupid. Or both."

"That's the spirit," Achilles slapped him on the back. He turned to me. "Let's go get—"

I hit him with the magical duct tape I had tried in the Armory. "No girlfriend to help you this time," I shot him a satisfied smile. "Right now, I'm going to eat my pancakes. If you're good, and don't speak when the adults are speaking, I'll give you a new hat. How does that sound, my boy?" I made sure my voice was highly animated, like I was speaking with a toddler. Dean coughed, pretending to search for something in the cabinet.

"Dust," he explained without turning around.

Achilles didn't disappoint, glaring at me in silence, not blinking as I ate my pancakes.

I took my time. He finally blinked, unable to even grunt in frustration. But he did exhale very loudly through his nose several times. Gunnar was uncharacteristically very quiet. Dean fumbled around in the cabinets for nothing, the fat liar.

Carl entered the room, clutching my phone as if it were a venomous cobra.

Dean looked ecstatic at the distraction. "Pancakes are ready," he told Carl, grabbing a plate.

Carl cocked his head. "I prefer to feast on the flesh of the unborn."

Gunnar's eye widened and he dropped his fork.

"Eggs. He means eggs," I explained, shaking my head. Fucking Carl…

Carl nodded, not understanding the difference. But he extended his scaled hand, holding out the phone to me. "It is screaming at me. Repeatedly. I think it wants to talk to you." I scrambled to my feet, staring at the screen. Five missed calls from Tory, back-to-back. Then it started ringing again.

I answered immediately, via speakerphone, but didn't even get a chance to speak.

CHAPTER 31

Cries and shouts erupted from the speaker before I heard Tory's voice. "We need help, *now*! I can't fight them off and control the students at the same time!" she shouted over the background noise.

"Who?" But she must have dropped the phone, because I heard a bunch of loud *thuds* and *bangs* as if someone was tapping the speaker with their hand. Then I heard Tory shouting in the distance. I hung up, realizing she couldn't hear me.

"Time to go!" I climbed out of my chair, Gunnar hot on my heels. I looked back to see Achilles pointing at his lips frantically. "But you're so much more fun like this," I said. But before he could throw a fit, I ripped away the spell. He took a big breath, opening his mouth to shout all sorts of nice things at me. "Not now, Heel. My name's Nate, and I'm a dick. I get it."

And I ran down the hall, not even bothering to try and grab my satchel. I hadn't needed it with the wolves. And this time I had Achilles, Carl, and Gunnar. A legendary warrior, a pastey, soul-eating lizard-man, and a handicapped Alpha werewolf.

Still, better than last time. I didn't have time to go find Mallory and explain the situation.

I shouted back at Dean. "Tell Mallory what happened." And I raced out the front door. Instead of a Gateway – since I had used that last time, and I wanted to keep the Academy on their toes – I readied myself to Shadow Walk, holding out my hands suggestively. "Grab me."

Achilles, of course, grabbed me by the hair in a tight fist, smiling innocently.

I ignored his payback and thought about the school, and a likely place to appear. Hell, I hoped she was *at* the school, what with all the damage from the Gala. Then again, only one wall had been damaged, and the school had several classrooms outside of the cafeteria where we had held the Gala.

I imagined one of the classrooms where I had recently taught a precursor to magic to a group of the more advanced students, in order to show them what they might confront in the future.

We appeared in the middle of the classroom, cleanly slicing through several desks as my magic tore through them. Achilles let go of my hair, and I gave him a forceful shove to the chest. He tripped over the desk directly behind his knees, flipping over it to land on his back.

I didn't wait for him to get up as I bolted out of the classroom, looking to pick a fight. Carl and Gunnar ran alongside me, and Achilles cursed, bringing up the rear.

Feral cries from different flavors of monsters rose up in the distance, inside one of the other rooms. I pointed at a few doors, urging everyone to pick one as I latched onto my own choice. There was a good chance that we could find some of the younger kids huddled in a room, likely watched over by the Reds, who had mind-control powers since they were dragons. They often helped Tory control some of the shifters. Like substitute teachers.

But my room was empty.

I heard Gunnar shout out and I followed his voice, bursting into the room, ready to kill.

He stood before a group of a dozen students, and like I had thought, both of the Reds were standing over them, their red eyes in full-blown dragon form, complete with horizontal pupils like a goat. Which sounds weird, but honestly looked kind of cool. And scary. Dragons didn't have the typical snake eyes like many thought.

I shook my head clear of the useless thought, shouted for everyone to lock hands, and then I latched onto both of the Reds, completing the ring. Gunnar stood across from me in the ring, holding hands with two little girls. I nodded, closed my eyes, and focused. I had never Shadow Walked this many at one time, but I needed to get them to safety. Leaving them here under the control of the teenaged dragons wasn't a good plan.

Because they were students as well, and didn't have the strength to keep it up much longer. Especially with a dozen shifters under their influence. In fact, I was surprised they had managed to subdue them at all.

Because these kids were terrified, meaning they were on the verge of shifting.

I ignored several concussive blasts from an adjacent room, realizing Carl and Achilles had not joined me. Not wanting to wait, I ripped us back to Gunnar's apartment complex, assuming it was the safest place in town. All the wolves and a few dragons were already on the premises, guarding their territory, and they could take care of any shifters that lost control.

I staggered, glad to hear Gunnar take control, commanding his wolves to gather up the children. The Reds collapsed into each other, but Ashley was suddenly there, catching Sonya while Gunnar caught Aria. I shot Gunnar a panicked look, regaining my own balance. I needed to get back.

"Go. I'll take care of the kids. Bring the others back. Right here. I'll be sure to clear the area and have shifters on standby!" he shouted over the din of many concerned voices.

I nodded, ripping myself back to the school.

It was oddly silent, and I feared that maybe I was too late.

Then the wall fucking blew inwards, and a body slammed into me. I caught the person, thinking he or she might be one of the students. I got a handful of boob as I staggered, informing my caveman brain that I held one of those elusive creatures known as a *wimmin*. And it definitely wasn't a child. The figure groaned as I turned her around.

Indie stared up at me, eyes wild, confused, and slightly dazed.

CHAPTER 32

I held her for a few seconds, frozen. Then she shoved me back, standing of her own accord. She stared at me from a few feet away. I opened my mouth to ask her what the hell was going on, but she suddenly disappeared.

"What the hell?" I shouted at the empty air instead.

Then I raced through the Indie-shaped hole in the wall, chasing the sounds of fighting.

I saw Tory punch a man in the face, crunching his nose and sending him flying. But not as far as he should have flown, and not as damaged in the face.

Because Tory could literally bend metal, punch through walls, and pick up cars.

But this guy didn't look like any Academy member I had ever seen. He wore hipster jeans, basically leggings, a pair of converse sneakers with the *Avengers* logo on the sides, and a bro tank. He also had an impressive horseshoe mustache.

I stared for a moment at the jarring image before Carl suddenly appeared out of nowhere, ivory blades flashing. The little hipster shit was fast, dodging, ducking, and evading like a ferret. But Carl kept him busy, chasing him out of the room. Tory stood, chest heaving as she guarded a small huddle of older students behind her. She locked eyes with me, relieved.

Which immediately morphed into fright.

I dove to the side just as a desk went sailing right through the spot I had been standing. It hit the ground, bounced, flipped, and flew straight for Tory.

Like Wonder Woman, she punched through it, snarling like a freaking bear. The desk shattered into splinters and metal shards, but the students behind her were unharmed.

I glanced behind me to see Indie panting, having thrown the desk at me.

"Just give me the book, Nate."

"You?" I asked incredulously. "*You* did this?"

She opened her mouth to respond when a black fog flew out of one of the hallways, solidifying right before coming into contact, and decking Indie in the jaw. It was a short, petite, ebony-haired girl. Tory growled murderously, recognizing the woman who had drugged her.

I'll say this. Indie took the surprise punch like a champ, even rolling with it to deflect the force of the blow. Still, it had to hurt like a son of a bitch. The dark-haired girl turned back to fog, and chased after Indie, who was suddenly high-tailing it down the hallway.

Leaving the immediate area enemy-free.

I raced up to Tory, motioning for her to gather up the students. "Let's go. Join hands, kids."

I received several dark scowls, because Tory's students were older. Hell, a few of them might have been my age. But since they had spent a lifetime in the circus, they were wild and savage, only knowing the roar of the crowd, and fights to the death. Beasts in every sense of the word.

I saw the were-gorilla kid I had fought only a day ago. He clutched my chest. "Is Sonya okay? Did you find her? We need to get her to safety!" he looked absolutely panicked.

Which was just damned cute. I managed a quick smile. "She's safe. I'll take you to her. Get everyone to join hands."

And he did. Which was good, because Tory looked about ready to pass out.

As the gorilla kid convinced the more stubborn students to listen, I had a brief second to shout at Tory. "Where's Alucard?"

She stared at me for a moment, eyes distant. I shook her, snapping her back into focus. "He grabbed a couple of the younger kids and vamped out. Fleeing fast as hell. They were too young to even stand a chance," she smiled to herself, no doubt proud of Alucard's decision.

"That's great, Tory. I'm taking you guys to Gunnar. His place is the safest in town."

She nodded, grasping a hand in each palm, completing the circle. Well, except for me. I was reaching out to close it when the black fog hammered into me. Well, it was black fog until a moment before a fist punched me in the gut. Instead of the girl, I saw the features of an old Asian man before I doubled over, flying backwards.

I hit a chalkboard, shattering it with the back of my head.

But at least it broke my fall. Or skull. I stared up, dazed, to see the little Asian man squaring off against gorilla boy. The boy lunged a telegraphed haymaker punch, which the lithe Asian easily evaded, shooting out a left cross to the kids jaw on his way by, using his momentum against him. Gorilla boy went down.

Tory suddenly latched onto the Asian man's collar, and flung him backwards through the hole in the wall. He clipped the drywall on his way through, banging his head, but promptly shifted to his black fog form a moment later, protecting himself from further damage as he disappeared through the opening.

Tory grabbed me, hauling me to my feet. She yanked me over to the circle again, shoving my hands into the moist, clammy hands of two of her students. Then she picked up the unconscious gorilla boy in a fireman's carry, and reached out with both hands to complete the circle, jerking her chin at me to quit slacking off. It looked comical, because Tory was tiny, and gorilla boy was a beefy, football-player-looking guy.

I Shadow Walked us out of the school, dumped everyone into a big pile, and before Tory could argue, I ripped myself back to the room in the school. My mind raced as I tried to discern what the hell was going on.

If Indie wanted my copy of *Through the Looking-Glass*, why had she chosen to attack the school? Unless it was just to draw me out since she had likely discovered she wasn't able to hit up my house anymore.

Then I thought about it again. The hipster hadn't looked like an Academy member. And I had never heard of the black fog spell before. And that dark-haired girl had been the one to drug Tory and leave me that note. Then Mr. Asian had pummeled me for no reason.

"The Syndicate," I growled to myself, stepping over a broken desk as I reentered the hall, searching for any other students. Because whoever was left wouldn't have anyone to prevent them from shifting. Which meant they were just as likely to attack me as the intruders.

Even if all the students were safe, I still needed to save the building and retrieve Carl and Achilles. I looked up to find Indie staring at me from a dozen paces away in the middle of the hallway, panting heavily. Her eyes darted here and there, no doubt looking for the black fog ninja wizards.

"We need to talk," she whispered.

CHAPTER 33

I just stared at her for a breath or two. "I've got a few other things on my plate," I finally spat. But I didn't move. Neither did she. Other than her eyes continuously scanning the hallway for attackers. I could still hear fighting, and although it sounded pretty violent, I didn't hear any animals growling, snarling, biting, or howling.

Maybe we had gotten all the kids out.

And Carl and Achilles were just taking out the rest of the trash. The Syndicate.

Still, I had to be sure. I took a step to follow the sounds of fighting, and was suddenly halted in my tracks by an unseen force. I lifted a very, very angry glare at Indie. My ex-fiancée. The whites of her eyes were black. The eyes of a Grimm. "Really cute, Indie. Just get it over with."

"I'm not going to kill you, Nate. Jesus. Get over yourself."

I blinked at her. That had sounded suspiciously like… the Indie I knew. I opened my mouth, but she interrupted me.

"Don't get ahead of yourself. This isn't some elaborate ruse. My position hasn't changed. And if you knew the whole story, you would be joining up with me rather than continuously getting in our way."

"Our… You. And Ichabod."

She nodded, eyes still flicking about warily. "I need the book, Nate."

"That is *never* going to happen, traitor."

"I don't want to hurt you, Nate." She began walking closer to me, and I was as helpless as a babe under her powers.

"Ichabod's hiding around here somewhere, isn't he? That's why you're able to use the Maker power right now."

Her lips thinned. "No. It's one of my natural gifts, apparently." I opened my mouth to shout out his name anyway, challenging him, because I wasn't sure I believed her. And suddenly I couldn't speak. Because some unseen force was covering my mouth.

Ah, Karma… I could imagine Achilles sitting in one of the desks, laughing at me right now.

"This is important. I *need* the book. Forget about Ichabod for a second," she pleaded, striding closer. Then she was suddenly close enough to touch.

And she didn't let the opportunity pass her by. She latched onto me with a hug I felt deep in my broken heart, a loving fire sewing the two shredded pieces back together with icy-hot thread. I shuddered, which was all I could do. She squeezed me like she once had, a full body hug, arms wrapped around my neck and back as if promising never to let go.

I felt tears falling from my eyes as I shuddered again.

I was so angry with her.

But…

Obviously, I wasn't entirely angry with her. Or else I would have only felt abhorrence.

She pulled back for a moment, tears in her eyes as she whispered. "I miss you so much…"

Even if my mouth hadn't been covered, I wouldn't have been able to speak. My throat hurt. Like when you watch one of those tear-jerker movies, and your jaw and throat suddenly ache out of nowhere as you try to bite back the tears.

Then she kissed me on the lips, twining her hands into my hair in a violent, carnal lust, as if battling with herself. Fighting her urge with tooth and nail.

She pulled back, squeezing my shoulders affectionately, eyes flickering from black to normal as she stared at me, sobbing. "We're trying to destroy them, Nate. They're trying to kill you. We're trying to *end* them. They've done… worse things than you could even imagine…" she trailed off, eyes lost in a silent, unspoken nightmare. But I could tell one thing.

Whatever it was had hit her. Hard.

"Why can't you *see* that?" she begged.

My heart ached for her. To return the kiss. To touch her body. Rekindle our love and figure this out together. I flicked my eyes down at my lips, and her own lips quirked into a very familiar smile as she released her magic.

I struggled with a gravelly throat, almost too emotional to speak. "And why can't you see…" I rasped, "that the ends don't justify the means." I managed. "Let me *help* you."

She cast her eyes down in shame, nodding sadly. "I wish you knew the full story, Nate. Then you would understand," she whispered, lifting her eyes back to meet mine. And I could sense a small difference in her look. The emotion she had displayed was genuine, and was still there, but it wasn't stronger than whatever was compelling her. "I need the book. Please. Just trust me."

I sighed, shaking my head. "It won't do you any good, Indie. It won't take you to him. Not anymore." She blinked at me, frowning. "But even if it did, I… wouldn't give it to you. Not until you explain *why*. What is really going on? What don't I know?"

"As cute as this is," a new voice suddenly spoke up from directly behind Indie, causing her to whirl around in a defensive crouch, releasing her bonds on me. "I'm not really into gushy romance. Or drama." And the black fog jerked towards us fast enough to make the air whistle.

Indie rolled to the side, shouting, "Nate!"

The fog solidified into an older, silver-haired woman the moment before hitting me, and I prepared to meet my maker. *How many of these assholes were here?* I was entirely unprepared to be gently carried a dozen paces away, and carefully set down on my two feet.

Carl burst into the hallway, staring at the two of us, assessing for danger. I just stared at him, then the silver-headed woman standing beside me, and finally, Indie.

Carl followed my gaze, locked eyes with Indie, and stilled as if suddenly frozen. "Mistress," he hissed softly, lowering his blades.

I think everyone frowned at him. I know I did. And Indie, too. Then she flashed a dark, silent threat at the silver-headed woman. She locked eyes with me a moment later, confident that the mysterious woman beside me – who hadn't hurt me, but had protected me from Indie – wasn't going to suddenly attack or kill me. Which to be honest, I wouldn't have been able to stop. I was exhausted in the magic department, still a little rattled from my blow to the head, and I was an emotional dishrag, limp in my very soul.

"This isn't over, Nate," Indie said, her stare darting between me and my temporary companion. "We *will* find one. Especially after my Brothers are here to help." She gave Carl one more glance, as if verifying he wasn't about to attack. Or hump her leg or something, because he was still staring at her.

Then she disappeared. *One what?* I thought to myself, fearing the answer.

"Hello?" the woman beside me asked, voice very loud.

Which startled me. I blinked back. "What?"

"Thought you had zoned out on me. Or cracked your skull harder than I thought." She looked me up and down, eyes briefly darting to Carl, who suddenly looked angry and murderous again. Back to his old self. "Get this straight. We aren't friends. I just can't stand mushy, emotionally manipulative shit like that. Get your head in the game."

Then she disappeared as well.

I stared at the only other person in the hall.

Fucking Carl.

"What the hell, man? *Mistress?*" I asked, ready to kill something or go to sleep.

Before Carl could answer – although he did look embarrassed – Achilles burst into the room.

"I got the last of them a few minutes ago. Little Asian dude. Not sure if he died or just disappeared. But I whipped him good. You guys see that guy in tights with the stache?" he asked, incredulous, shaking his head. "I think he bolted a while ago. What did I miss?"

I just stared at him. "Nothing."

Everything, I thought to myself.

I shook my head, focusing on task. "Did you find any kids?"

Achilles was frowning at the two of us. "No, I think they must have left already. I just saw Skinny Jeans, and The Asian riding their black clouds, but they didn't bother me." He walked closer, studying me. "You look troubled. Did someone die?"

I shook my head, slowly turning in a circle to assess the damage.

There was a lot. I finally settled on Carl, anger building.

Achilles noticed this. "Did you catch Carl eating someone, too? I told him to stop. But at least he stopped the guy from burning the whole place down."

Carl hissed at him, the equivalent of sticking out his tongue at a younger brother for tattling to Daddy about something he had done wrong.

I grabbed Carl by the leather straps of his shirt. "You *ate* someone?"

Carl wilted. "Just a little. He had a face made of fire. Barely a snack. Like crispy bacon."

Achilles grimaced in disgust. I shoved Carl away, muttering darkly. "No more field trips for you, Carl. Let's go."

This time, I opened a Gateway to the apartments. One of the walls collapsed behind us and I sighed in defeat, stepping through. At least nothing was on fire. I needed to make sure everyone was alright. Then go have a talk with Mallory. But first, maybe I would just replay my conversation with Indie, try to gain some perspective.

Not to remember our kiss.

Well, maybe a little…

CHAPTER 34

School was cancelled. Which made Gunnar the best Vice Principal ever. The kids were fine. No injuries, although they had needed to let off some steam, shifting freely and running around in the undeveloped fields behind the apartment complex. Under strict wolf and dragon supervision, of course. Even the weregorilla had no lasting damage.

Tory was rightfully pissed. But she had agreed to swing by Chateau Falco to pick up the Moonstones Pandora had given me. I had given them to Dean in case I was busy. You know, robbing the Academy, or something.

To be honest, everyone was a little pissed. I had waved off Alucard's offer for help, urging him to help Tory instead. Help the students. Keep an eye out. He had agreed, pouting about it.

I had promised to call Gunnar and Achilles when I was ready to leave for Alexandria. Achilles had followed me back to the Armory and I had given him the stupid helmet without a word. Sensing my mood, he hadn't teased me.

Because I couldn't shake my head from thoughts of Indie.

A small part of me wanted to raid the Academy and burn the place to the ground. Or die trying. Anything to avoid the pain of emotions ripping through me. Ripping my partially sewn-up heart back into two pieces. It hurt a whole helluva lot more than it had the first time.

Which had been excruciating.

My head was now officially screwed loose.

I walked through the halls of my mansion, following no pattern, simply wandering. I found myself doing double-takes every time I passed something that may have been a secret door. Because even spaces that didn't appear to be anything special had proven to be extra special.

As in, no one had set foot there in hundreds of years, as far as I could tell.

The house told me things, encouraging me, sensing my pain, and wanting to help. But I was too distracted to pay even the voice any attention. I walked the upper floor, in the hallway where I had first seen Carl out by the pale tree through the mansion's magical windows.

Guardians – griffin and gargoyle statues that guarded my home – prowled the hallways openly, not even bothering to pretend to be stone. Each slowed, dipping a head my way as I approached. I paid them no heed. I felt their ancient eyes assessing me, checking for injury, but the house *shooshed* them, giving me peace.

They were on high alert. Not just because of Indie. But also because of my message to the Academy. I hadn't heard anything back from them, but to be honest, their response might be to drop a magical nuke on my home.

The way the house growled when I thought that made me briefly wonder what would happen as a result. If she could just shrug it off or if something like that could harm her.

I continued on down the stairs, through hallways of paintings, decorations, artifacts, weapons, and art pieces. They were all familiar to me from my childhood. But I paid them no attention this time, other than to idly wonder which of them were secret door handles, or hiding a door, or weapons caches, or a freaking caged demon or something.

Because I had discovered that my 17,000-square-foot mansion – the one that had been in my family for hundreds of years – was much, *much* bigger than I had ever imagined. And that it had more secrets than I ever thought possible.

So, despite everything feeling familiar to me, it felt alien and foreign at the same time. Like I was exploring a vast new territory in the American Colonies, rather than walking through the hallways of an old friend.

After an hour of aimless wandering, I found myself standing at the door I had discovered earlier with Death and Carl. I stared at the tapestry covering the wall, appreciating the forest scene. I even took a few steps to glance out a nearby window, confirming that it was indeed an exterior wall.

I came back to the rug and stared at it again, idly brushing my bandage with my thumb, like your tongue did with a loose tooth. It no longer hurt as badly, although it was still unpleasant.

I felt no magic. No warning. Just an old rug on a wall.

Someone coughed behind me. I didn't flinch, feeling safe in my home since it was on lockdown, merely turning to glance over a shoulder. Mallory stared at me, hands folded behind his back, legs planted firmly on the marble floor. He waited.

I studied him for a few moments, and then turned to face the wall again, not speaking.

I slowly reached out, tugging back the tapestry, and looked back over my shoulder at Mallory. He slowly began to approach, but stopped in his tracks, eyes widening as he stared at the wall. I didn't react, just slowly turned to stare at the rotating rocks.

But, the stones weren't rotating. Instead, they had shifted into a waterfall of sand, spilling down into an unseen grate on the floor. At least, I hadn't seen the grate earlier. The sand continued to fall for a few seconds, and then there was simply nothing between us and a long dark hallway. I kept my face expressionless. Let Mallory think what he would.

And I took a step. The purple torch flared into existence the moment I crossed the barrier.

I heard Mallory gasp behind me, but I ignored it and continued on.

I had nothing to explain to him.

He had some things to explain to *me*.

I continued down the hallway, smirking for the first time in a while as I listened to Mallory curse as he discovered that the torches extinguished behind him just as rapidly as they ignited ahead of me. I didn't tell him that the house had whispered that I could simply keep them all alight if I desired.

Because making people uncomfortable felt good right now. Especially after Indie messing with my head. It was Mallory's turn to come clean. I was pretty sure that was why he had come.

We entered the cavern, and I made my way over to the desk. I sat in the chair, and propped my feet up, leaning back. Mallory stared at our surroundings for a moment before turning back to me, composing himself. I motioned for him to take a look. He didn't walk away, merely swiveled his head, taking everything in. I flicked open the book on the desk, rereading the letter I had found inside, written to Matthias. I didn't recall his name as a Temple, but I had never made it a priority to learn very much about my history. Well, that wasn't true. I had spent quite a bit of time in the Temple Mausoleum at Bellefontaine Cemetery.

But the name *Matthias* didn't ring a bell.

Which meant he hadn't been buried there. Perhaps he had fled back overseas. It wasn't uncommon to find gaps like that in an old family like ours. Often, certain members would find great interest in validating their family trees, tracing back each ancestor and all the things they had accomplished in their lifetimes. Take our Mausoleum, for example. Each member buried there had a statue, a sarcophagus, and a leather-bound book on their life. The Temple Clan had started out that way, like most European royalty.

But it had been a long time since anyone had shared that passion for genealogy.

I had mainly paid attention to the high points. And whatever statues looked particularly cool in the Mausoleum.

So, the name Matthias meant nothing to me. Because I had never seen his statue. Of course, if I had wanted to, I could have checked the family tree in the Mausoleum. That was kept up to date magically, sporting a colored gemstone for each trace of Temple blood in the world. It was how I had found out Ichabod was my ancestor. After counting to five *greats*, I had given up trying to find out exactly what we were in relation to each other. All that mattered to me was that he was a Temple.

I flipped through the book, wanting to find out more about this Matthias, the last occupant of this mysterious room. Ichabod's father. I don't know why. It didn't really matter.

Well, bloodlines didn't matter, anyway.

What *did* matter was his reasons for this room, what the room was, anything about mastering the Beast of the house, and what it meant. Because I had never met anyone who had known—and hadn't known myself—that my house was sentient, and waiting for a new Master Temple to dominate her.

Because the ancient appellation of *Master* had not just been an ego preference. It had apparently meant something, once upon a time. Master Temple was *master* of his house, or, the possessed Beast that masqueraded as a house.

Also, the message had mentioned *Grimm*, capitalized, in the middle of a sentence. Where none of the other words had been unnecessarily capitalized. I set the book on its spine, letting it fall open of its own devising as my eyes roamed to the bookshelf where I had picked up the book that the house had guided me to. *Deus Ex Machina. Fable or Fact?*

Another folded piece of paper fell out of the book, brushing against my fingers. I stared down at it, pondering. This journal also seemed to double as a massive *to do* list, with random bits of paper, scratch notes, even a dried flower and a butterfly wing inside. *Ichabod* was written beside the wing in a child's handwriting, with a crude heart sketched underneath. I smiled absently, reading some of the notes.

Visit mausoleum And Kill rats. Castor Queen meeting. Hide scotch. Body of water accumulating by back shed...

And a bunch of other random notes and reminders. Nothing important. Other than the name *Castor* which had been the correspondent in the original message now sitting beside the book. I idly unfolded the paper that had fallen out as Mallory walked over to one of the bookshelves, perusing the collection.

I scanned the paper quickly, but stopped, jumping back to the top as the tone caught my eye.

Matthias Temple,

We have sorely missed your attendance at recent Academy formal functions. We understand that the Americas are a wild place, full of new magic, but hope that you and your Colonial colleagues can find time to meet with us in the near future. We have much to discuss...

On another note, your recent proposal has been declined. Although we applaud your academic ability to approach problems from a different direction in order to provide a unique solution, your most recent missive has too much potential for dire consequences. We politely advise you that further interference in such matters will bring down the full displeasure of the Academy.

We implore you to continue seeking alternative solutions to the issue at hand, as we are entirely aware of the infestation you face, and would offer our full assistance behind a less-cataclysmic solution.

Warmest regards,

Grand Master Killian

I leaned back, tapping the letter on the table. There was a date on the bottom, but it was smudged with a tea stain. *What were you proposing?* I thought to myself. And what was the problem they were referring to? It was funny to hear that Matthias and his pals seemed too busy to attend bullshit political Academy meetings. Not much had changed in the Temple Clan.

But even more importantly, had he heeded or ignored their warning? Because in old letters like that, they were very precise with their wording, not often exaggerating or embellishing.

A different era.

Which meant they were terrified of whatever he had proposed.

I glanced up to see Mallory watching me. I spoke loud enough to be heard over the waterfall. "How were you able to stop Indie when she broke in? She is a Grimm. With Maker powers."

Mallory didn't answer.

"This is your last chance, Mallory. Things are getting out of control. I've given you enough rope to hang yourself, trusting you with my life.

Things have changed. The game has gotten larger. Or, at least I'm now discovering that it was always much bigger. I need to know."

Without a word, Mallory turned his back on me, approaching the bookshelf.

Part of me wanted to roast him alive for the disrespect, but I saw that he was reaching for a book. I stood anyway, just in case he was about to turn evil on me, revealing he was Lucifer or something equally ridiculous.

His scarred fingers touched the spine of a book, and the torch beside him flared to life.

Then he froze, unmoving. Not removing the book, not placing it back. Just standing there. I would have thought a spell had shut him down or something, but I could see he was still breathing, and I felt no magic. Still, I very cautiously took a few steps closer.

And that's when I saw it.

His shadow. It was not human. At all. He really *was* Lucifer!

The words from my crest whispered in my ears. *Non Serviam...*

CHAPTER 35

Whips of fire exploded from each fist as I prepared to fight the demon king about to erupt from beneath Mallory's skin. Because I had let him inside the cavern, and who knew what dangerous, powerful items were stored here?

But Mallory still didn't move, even hearing my weapons at his back.

Which gave me pause. Not much, but enough to allow him to speak.

"You have no idea how glad I am to finally be rid of that stupid accent," a strange voice spoke from the man that had been Mallory. He still looked the same, well, from the back, because he still faced the bookshelf, hand touching the partially withdrawn book.

And I realized why. He had discerned the purpose of the torches, and that they worked after a book was withdrawn. He had let the torch show me his shadow.

The shadow of a hulking, looming, massive swath of black. Two curled horns extended from a very shaggy silhouette. But Mallory, the man, looked the same.

In fact, the shape kind of reminded me of the *Beauty and the Beast*.

He gently shoved the book back, and the torch winked out. He slowly turned to face me, smiling sadly, still human. "Know my intent was pure," he whispered. And he began to shift.

My pulse raced as – ever so slowly – a monster was sculpted from the man I had known. The man who had worked for my father for years. The man I had shared hundreds of drinks with. The man who had saved me countless times. The man who had killed for me. Defended my friends.

All while holding a big, big secret.

My sense of alarm grew as his legs were replaced by shaggy, cloven hooves, and his chest doubled in size, revealing a tall and lean, almost hunch-backed figure wearing an ancient, tattered shawl and brown leather shorts. His face began to change next, revealing a hairy... beast of a creature. I couldn't quite say what he looked like, because he resembled many different types of animals. Bear, wolf, ox... yet none of these.

And those curled horns were impressive, spiraling on either side of his head like a Princess Leia up-do, before the tips curved out to reveal efficient head-butting weapons.

"Wow, you really are Beast." And I realized he didn't look like any demon I had ever met. And he didn't have wings, so I was betting he wasn't actually Lucifer.

He chuckled, shaking his head. "That's all you've got, boy?" His eyes were a deep golden color, casting a soothing, peaceful sensation on me despite our distance. As if I could sit and stare at him for hours, losing myself in the depths of them.

I stared at him, then glanced down at my whips.

He shook his head, lifting his beefy, calloused palms to me in a *stop* motion. "I have never, and will never, mean you harm. You have my word. On my power. But... I'd like you to guess."

Even though I hadn't been using any magic to bind him to an oath, I felt his magic pulsating around him, binding himself to his words. I snuffed out my whips, folding my arms as I studied him. But... that didn't make any sense.

I said as much. Which made him laugh.

"I thought you were going to be Zeus, or Perun, or some Druidic god. Hell, even Lucifer crossed my mind," I said, pointing at his hooves and horns.

He frowned. "Lucifer? Seriously?" he growled, taking offense. "The other three were my intent. I even stole some items, modified my speech, and went to great lengths to misdirect those around me."

"But the Huntress knew you."

Mallory shook his head. "No, she thought she did. She knew I was an Old One, but she was only guessing about which."

"Old One," I began, thinking furiously. "A god."

He shrugged. "It's all relative. But technically, yes."

"You also mentioned the sea a few times."

"These things are all true. I am… very connected with nature."

"Can I call you Peter?"

He frowned. "Why…" Then he got it, revealing an unintentionally frightening smile. "Oh, well. That might confuse everyone if you suddenly began calling me Peter instead of Mallory. I've never been to Neverland, and am definitely not *Peter* Pan." His bleating laughter sounded like a goat, which brought me a big old smile. "Friends might think you lost your marbles again, calling me the name of your first betrayer."

Part of me flinched at his casual mention of my old friend, Peter. The one who had tried to sell me out to Raego's father. He had enviously chased after magic, in order to be like Gunnar and I, and in the end, it had led him astray. To his death.

"Even then, you were there," I said.

He nodded. "Lying the whole time."

"But *why*? What was so important about your secret? I know plenty of impressive… beings."

He motioned towards one of the concave bowls, where we might sit more comfortably. I nodded, leading him over. He sank much deeper into the cushions than I. Once comfortable, he responded. "It was because of what was to come. You becoming a Maker."

I blinked. "You knew about that ahead of time?"

"I helped your father implement the plan. Because he was under… very intense scrutiny. It was his last hope. He knew his time was limited."

My breath froze. My father had known he was going to die? And for some reason, had deemed it necessary to secretly implant the Maker's seed inside me rather than prevent his death? "What the hell is going on, Mallory?" I chose his human name.

He looked torn, and I began to open my mouth to press, but he held up a hand. "I must be careful here. It is not just about you. Events are in play. Wicked, wild events. You are only hearing the horns of the war that is to come. This isn't just about keeping secrets from you, but about keeping secrets from the *world*, lest they hear." He met my eyes, a sickened look on his beastly visage. "Please understand…"

I let out a breath, recalling that even Shiva hadn't known the truth. "Tell me what you can."

He sighed in relief. "Your father knew events were going to unfold that would lead to his death. Not exactly how, but he knew of three distinct possibilities that all had a high chance of success. He knew this years prior, and spent the remainder of his life building up the Armory, assisting you, bringing Gunnar into his home, hiring me, while also laying many false trails." I stared at him, numb.

"Gunnar was… part of his *plan*?"

Mallory nodded sadly. "It was an added benefit that you two got along. But it would have happened either way. You needed a brother. A conscience. A guardian." He looked about to say more, but halted himself.

"What does that have to do with my old Maker power?" I silently decided to let him talk as much as he was willing to share. I would press him later on details, but right now, I wasn't going to fight him about every revelation, arguing over every point.

"It was your only chance against surviving the Academy's retaliation over the Armory."

I shook my head. "The Armory my dad *created* was ultimately the cause of my *death*?" I asked, combining his two statements. He nodded. "My father acted surprised when he heard about my cursed magic fueling my Maker's ability."

Mallory shrugged. "He was. But only because he didn't know that it would speed everything up, making you stronger faster. That was an added benefit. He knew you would die, but hopefully *not* die if we set things up right," he admitted. "Not everything has gone as well as planned. And many things we didn't foresee have happened." He looked up at the ceiling.

"This room?" I asked, hiding my shock at his revelations.

"Not just this *room*, but the house being *alive*, for one. And that you would Master it. He only knew it was necessary for you to be a Maker to stand up against the forces amassing in the shadows. Not why or how, just that you needed to *be* one."

I shivered. "But I'm no longer a Maker."

Mallory nodded slowly. "Like I said, not everything has gone according to plan. But…" he studied me, smiling softly. "You accomplished many things while a Maker. Perhaps all that you needed to accomplish with the power."

I leaned back in the cushion, which was surprisingly comfortable, and not too dirty after a few hundred years of sitting in a damp room. Then again, they were probably warded just like the books, because I felt no moisture. Otherwise, this entire place would have become one moldy pile of rotten wood.

"Even though it seems opposite, I'm actually very confident that, overall, things are going in our favor."

I frowned at him. "Why did I need a guardian?"

"That was what Shiva was referring to. He thought my intent had been to use you as a Tiny God. To gain power for *myself*. I deterred him from that thought when we spoke privately." He winked at me. "As I had *intended* him to believe. He can't read my mind. This is why I couldn't tell anyone. Not. A. Single. Person. Else, he would have been able to read their thoughts. I don't distrust him. I distrust *all* of them. I guarded your parents' minds as well. To keep the secret." He took a deep breath. "I was put here to keep you safe from the gods, as best as I was able."

"Don't take offense, but why you? You aren't really known for your legendary battle skills. Just your pipes."

"Even gods can change." He grinned at me. "The Dueling Grounds isn't the only place one can cut loose and learn. Although I had to be very discreet about it. I even had to use the nymphs to lure warriors into their glades, where they would teach me to fight in exchange for… carnal pleasures."

I laughed out loud. "You pimped out the nymphs to learn how to fight?"

He smiled. "They definitely didn't mind. And it was necessary."

"Why are you telling me this now? What if someone reads my mind?"

He shrugged. "You didn't really give me a choice. I think we've had enough arguments in front of others that they will continue to assume you don't know the truth. Hopefully, we won't have to play this game much longer. Then again, you are no longer a Maker, so that part of my job is accomplished. The threat of you being gobbled up by a god no longer exists."

"I feel so much better already," I muttered.

"Don't worry. We are far from safe. We need to make sure none of my cousins wake. We can't let Ichabod get a Hand of God."

I nodded agreement as I scratched my stubble. "What's up with the lightning spears?"

He smiled. Like a savage, revealing large, sharp teeth. Not fangs, but more canines than was normal. "I stole them from Zeus. Not as good as his lightning bolts, but better than nothing. He was sleeping, anyway. And it helped my disguise." His voice trailed off, thinking to himself. "Everyone thinks I'm sleeping, too. And they know Zeus is sleeping. They all assume I'm someone I'm not. Some other lightning god. No one would guess that *Pan* – the wild god – was helping the Temples."

I was silent for a few moments as he finally said his true name out loud. "Zeus probably won't like it if Ichabod wakes him up, and he discovers some of his weapons are missing." Mallory grunted. But that would be the least of our worries if Zeus woke up. I climbed out of my chair. "Alright. The way I see it, this doesn't change anything I have to do. Just makes me sleep better. Knowing you aren't secretly trying to kill me or manipulate me."

He nodded, standing. "Never."

I exited the cavern, eyeing the round table thoughtfully on my way by. *Nah...*

I called over my shoulder. "Let's just stick with the angry sailor meat-suit, okay?"

He didn't respond. I turned around to see the old Mallory grinning at me. His clothes were back in place, unlike when shifters transformed. God powers, I guessed. "Aye, Laddie. That'll do. Off to rob the Academy?"

"You better believe it, *Danny boy*." I grinned, feeling surprisingly upbeat and eager. Excited.

Fucking Pan. I had never anticipated that, and realized that I needed to do some research on the old god once things calmed down.

But right now, I had a task to do. I'd heard thieves talk about the thrill of the job.

Must be true. Because I suddenly felt like old times. I was rushing off to nab a magical item to keep it safe from bad guys. The billionaire bookstore thief was back, baby.

CHAPTER 36

We stood in a questionable hotel room outside Phoenix, Arizona, one of those drive up to the door joints located just off the highway. With vibrating beds. Achilles had inserted a few coins, and was laughing with an odd quivering cadence as the bed rocked his world. Gunnar was anxiously awaiting his turn, laughing, reminding me of the fun parts of his bachelor party a few months back. Ashley and Gunnar hadn't gotten married yet, but after the circus, we had all agreed to take a break. Our trip hadn't turned out the way we had hoped, but overall, a fun time.

I rolled my eyes at them, but I did smile.

I had chosen the place because I didn't want anything tying the robbery to me or my house. In case the Academy were somehow able to track my Shadow Walking. I had also considered using a Gateway to a Gateway to a Gateway, all in random places throughout the world, but had decided it was a waste of power.

I had debated even going through with this. I knew the Syndicate would never give Ichabod their Hand of God, and it was equally as unlikely that he would bother the Fae for theirs. The Elders were mine, so they were out. Leaving only the Academy with a Hand of God that Ichabod might try to get his mitts on. And after G Ma telling me about the infestation of spies in her ranks, I wasn't confident of their security. So, we had to steal it. To keep it away from Ichabod.

Mallory stood leaning against the wall, watching Gunnar and Achilles with a wry smile. His role was to sit here, guard the room, and get us the hell out of here when we returned. Or to stay behind and battle any pursuers while we escaped. I had given him a few of my Gateway balls in case anything happened to me – death or unconsciousness – so that everyone could get back home.

But I didn't anticipate that. This would be a stealth operation. If it went FUBAR, our escape plan was predicated on confusion. Let me explain. Per Achilles' request, Mallory had disguised us each as different Asian-looking men and women. It devolved from there.

Mallory was now a large Japanese man holding a Russian Kalashnikov over his Toronto Blue Jays hockey jersey. He had even tacked a dubious looking map of Phoenix on the wall, doodled with red sharpies to mark the most bizarre targets we could come up with.

A table underneath the map was littered with bottles of chemicals, plastic pipes, tools, a box of nails, bullets, knives and a few pistols. I had tossed in a few religious tracts Greta had left on my desk at Chateau Falco. Our discarded boxes of takeout Chinese food sat in the trashcan, and a small pile of bland clothes sat in the corner, looking like obvious stowaway disguises. He had even hung an American flag upside down on the wall, a national distress signal, but most people falsely saw it as an anti-American statement of some kind, which worked for our purposes.

Misdirection.

Every visual cue in the room would momentarily confuse them. Religious Japanese Anarchists? In Phoenix? And that would buy us *time*.

I hoped it was all unnecessary. That we snuck in, nabbed the Hand of God, and fled, patting ourselves on the back as we drank a cold beer at Achilles' bar later. I didn't know what the Hand of God looked like, but Pandora had helped me out in that regard.

She had given me an item that would react to the presence of a Hand of God. This way I wouldn't even have to use magic to find it. Which was good since we would be in a building full of powerful wizards and their monster guards. The sneakier the better.

Achilles and Gunnar were now casually talking about highlights from last week's Fight Club, and debating who might be a good match for the next one, whenever that was. Achilles looked like a nerdy Chinese college student, complete with a black pencil skirt, tan blouse, and glasses. Gunnar was a scrawny Korean thug wearing a tan Adidas jumpsuit with black stripes.

I was an older Asian woman, complete with a cane and a shawl, the matriarchal leader.

We looked ridiculous. A confusing collection of Asian, black-and-tan-clad thieves.

And we all had different vehicles parked in different places around the hotel. We even had our escape routes planned out in case the prototype Gateway balls were actually explosive duds.

Achilles had informed me that the Library was sandstone, so we not only needed to blend into the shadows, but also the walls. Hence the color theme of our garb.

I took a deep, nervous breath

We were about to rob the Academy, the rulers of the wizard world. They considered themselves the police of the magical community. But I saw things a bit differently, now. I was feeling more like they were the Mafia of the magical community. Still, they were big hitters. And my clever idea was to disrespect their boss, declare war on them with a bluff that could make me a casualty during Armageddon, and *then* rob them.

Brilliant, right?

But a very large part of me was overlooking those factors, thinking of only one thing…

I was about to enter the lost Library of Alexandria… Talk about a bibliophile's wet dream.

One, it had been built by Alexander the Great. Everyone had heard of it, debating how much it had impacted and directed the advancement of mankind. A central hub for knowledge, learning, culture, and art. Then it had disappeared. Or been destroyed.

Two, I couldn't even pretend to imagine how many books, artifacts, and whatnot sat on her dusty shelves, waiting to be pillaged.

Which was probably why the Academy had pressed so hard to get my Armory. To add to their already impressive collection.

"We're just going to Shadow Walk in there," Gunnar arched an eyebrow at me, "hoping that our magic slinger doesn't send us directly into anything breakable and priceless. Then we are going to snoop around the largest library in the world and find something – we don't know what it looks like – and then walk out. While avoiding patrols – both magical and non-magical."

I nodded. "We'll be freaky fast." Gunnar didn't look convinced. I pointed at Achilles. "And we'll have a guide." Gunnar's face remained doubtful. "What the hell? You were the one who wanted in on this," I reminded him.

He shrugged. "I'm all about picking a fight, getting some payback. But this mission seems poorly planned. Kind of murders my motivation when I don't see a path to success. Or escape."

"Just tell 'em, Laddie," Mallory chuckled.

"Pandora gave me a magical doodad that will help me sense the HOG." They stared at me, blank expressions on their faces. "Hand of God," I explained. "We need codenames for things. It's what separates us from amateurs."

Achilles stood. "Let's just get this over with."

"Don't sound so cheerful. You were the one who said you could be a big asset, here."

"I just wanted my helmet back."

I stared at him. "You have no idea where it is, do you?"

He shrugged. "I was a little drunk last time I was there," he admitted. He saw the look on my face. "But I'm sure it will be fine. It's a library. How hard could it be?"

I just shook my head in disbelief.

"We're doomed," Gunnar admitted.

I shook my head, this time in argument. "No. We're not. Achilles is a worthless ragamuffin, which is why I reached out to Othello. She found accurate details on what the Library used to look like." I motioned for

Mallory to join us. He did, pulling out a thick, folded piece of paper. He unfolded it and straightened it out on the bed. I pointed at everyone to hold down a corner.

Mallory began to explain, pointing out wings, their historic use, what had been stored where, and anything else that he deemed important. Once finished, Achilles shrugged, muttering. "A thousand-year-old map ain't gonna' help us."

"Aye," Mallory said, unfolding a *second* wad of paper, this one marked up with red ink.

Gunnar and Achilles frowned. "What's this?"

"Othello put some pressure on a few contacts who had sold items to the Academy in the past. Between them, she was able to paint a basic picture of how the place was organized in the last few years. Of course, they could have changed things, but honestly, I doubt it. We're talking about a group of old men and women who like the way things *used* to be. Set in their ways. Also, many of the items probably shouldn't be moved often. So, things are likely as they were. Kept in place. To preserve as much as possible."

Achilles began a slow clap, sloshing his drink on the corner of the map. He looked down, grunted, and wiped it away with his forearm. "This easily eliminates half the place," he said in approval. "How did you get it so fast?"

I studied the map, going over my rough plan in my head, and answered absently. "I spoke to Othello as soon as I heard about the Library. Told her it was important."

Gunnar watched me thoughtfully.

"The wizard banged the hacker," Achilles nudged Gunnar's elbow, flicking his head my way as if I couldn't hear him.

I rolled with his assumption of a physical meet, rather than our phone call. "No. We just did a few yoga routines. Like you and Pandora."

Gunnar burst out laughing. "Is that what they called it in Greece?"

"We didn't... it wasn't..." he turned his back, and walked into the living room. "I'll be ready whenever you two are finished primping."

I smiled at Gunnar, bumped fists with him, and then folded up the papers.

Mallory took them, silently wishing me luck with his eyes. I pretended to be annoyed and rolled my eyes. "We still need to have that talk, Mallory. I haven't forgotten."

He dropped his gaze, sighing, maintaining the ruse of his identity.

I turned to the others. They had been watching us. "Okay. Our plan is to go in quick and quiet. Use Pandora's amulet to find the HOG, then sneak the hell out of there. Remember, try not to kill, and try not to let them realize *what* you are. If they find three dead bodies with claw marks, or spear wounds, or fireballs burned through them, it won't take them long to realize who was really behind the theft." Gunnar growled defiantly, but I held up a finger. "I know you want revenge, but just remember our goal. We've got more important things on our plate right now. Your vengeance won't matter if Ichabod gets the HOG."

He finally nodded.

"Sneaky, sneaky, sneaky," I murmured, tightening the straps of the small backpack on my shoulders. I turned away from them, waiting for them to place their hands on my shoulders.

I discreetly slid my hand under my shirt as I touched something inside one of those tourist satchels people use to stow passports and cash when traveling. I hadn't told anyone about it. Then I Shadow Walked us into a discreet wing of the lost Library of Alexandria.

CHAPTER 37

We appeared in a darkened corner of an alcove behind a thick shelf bursting with scrolls and parchments. I motioned for everyone to stay low. We couldn't see much of the Library from our vantage point, but I felt a vast open space around us, like an auditorium. Which meant echoes.

But something was wrong.

"I swear it! *Library of Alexandria* has been said at least ten times by Freaks in the last twelve hours," a man argued. *Shit.* That had been us, speaking the name of our target. I hadn't even *thought* about that. Pounding footsteps came closer, a lot of them, until a group of six wizards stood not a dozen feet away on the other side of our shelf. I could see their boots, but not their faces because we were crouched low. I was simply thankful that they hadn't sensed our arrival.

I kept my finger on the item in my satchel, my Horseman Mask. I had channeled my power through it to Shadow Walk us here, hopefully fucking with their wards.

"Breaches all around," a breathless voice suddenly gasped, the sound echoing loudly.

Then a fire and light show abruptly ignited the air from beyond our shelf, concussive booms and roars of flame that cast light all around the dim Library. "What the bloody hell is *that?*" the first wizard shouted over the noise.

"I *told* you. We've been breached. We're under attack. At least three different points. All on the other side of the Library!" the breathless wizard argued. Two pairs of feet departed at a run.

There was a pregnant pause, and I held my breath. *Shit.*

Achilles and Gunnar were slapping at my ankles, no doubt encouraging me to get us the hell out of here. But the amulet Pandora had given me was growing very warm. We were fucking *close* if it was reacting so strongly. But we couldn't move with the wizards right next to us.

And it seemed someone else had decided to crash the Library.

Ichabod. I was suddenly glad I had decided to act on this crazy plan.

"I don't recognize you, boy," the first wizard said softly, and I heard a sharp intake of breath from the other wizards. "What is the code phrase?" he asked in a low tone.

The breathless voice didn't even hesitate. "We bring the terror."

The first wizard grunted. "Too many new faces. Need to discuss that with the Grand Master."

"I'll leave that up to you. I'm new here. But we need to call down the other guards. The animals. Use them to scent out the thieves."

"It's that Temple bastard," the first wizard growled.

Another voice spoke up. "Didn't pick up his flavor anywhere. The Grand Master shared it with us – the silver color that tastes like fennel." He took a big whiff, and sighed. "Nothing like that here right now."

I froze, fingers still on the Mask. They had codified my flavor of magic? Silver and fennel? What the hell was that all about? They could see magic specifically by color? And smell?

Gunnar squeezed my ankle again, but I tugged my leg free, missing part of the conversation.

"He's behind it. Somehow. Some way. We'll hang him by his ankles, soon."

"With all due respect, Sir, we need to do something about *this* right *now*. Can we put Temple on hold?"

"Right. Judson, Walsh, round up the shifters and go—"

Screams and explosions erupted from across the room. Then shouting, and the sound of many breaking things. "Go, go, go!" the first wizard shouted.

The sound of two pairs of racing footsteps faded, leaving only two pairs of boots now.

"Hold on a moment, boy," the first wizard said, his tone darkening. "Shift just changed ten minutes ago. That code phrase you gave was for the previous shift—"

A sudden concussive *thump* of power rattled the shelf, and I heard a body drop. "You should have left well enough alone, old man" an entirely different female voice said. A familiar voice…

What the hell? One of the attackers was here masquerading as a guard?

"It's… relatively safe for you to come out, now, Temple," the same voice said softly. "And your two goons." For some reason, it didn't startle me to hear she knew I had been hiding behind the shelf. Perhaps it was the adrenaline pounding through my blood.

But Gunnar was practically yanking my boot off. I shook him away, glancing back at the pair to silently tell them to be ready for a scrap. Their eyes were wide, ready to fight to the death, but wondering why the hell I was entertaining this strange thief. We had been *made*, after all.

I withdrew the Mask – which still resembled a coin, but now a plain American Silver Dollar – from my satchel and slowly stood, hiding it between two of my fingers.

Gunfire now combined with the screams, animal howls, explosions, the steady *whoomp* of fire, and the sounds of death. Something the size of a city bus roared, and my forearms burst out in gooseflesh.

"Any minute now…" the voice urged. And I stepped around the shelf, ready to incinerate or join forces. Whatever would get me the damn HOG.

CHAPTER 38

The silver-haired woman from the attack at Tory's school stood before me, her eyes quickly assessing me for threats. She must have found me lacking, because her eyes immediately darted back to the sounds of battle behind us. Horns vibrated the air, some type of alarm system. I actually saw figures dashing about in the distance.

Because it looked like we were standing in an amphitheater. The place was enormous.

Trees, ponds, open balconies, shelves climbing up into the five-story range – like my cavern – and cozy reading areas. Massive tables for studying the rolls of parchments. Sandstone walls and marble columns held up a giant mosaic roof with depictions of Alexander the Great in his various war campaigns. Mesmerizing statues marked turns in the walkways, all Greek-era gods, heroes, and monsters. I even saw one of Achilles with an arrow through his heel. The place was breathtaking…

The woman snapped her fingers to get my attention. My amulet was hot to the touch against my chest. I had to be standing right on top of the HOG. I kept my eyes trained on the woman before me, wondering her role in this, and not wanting to betray my interest in the shelf behind me. Maybe I could talk with her, knock her out, nab the HOG off the shelf, and then Shadow Walk out of here before anyone even knew we had entered.

To be honest, the arrival of more thieves concerned me greatly, but… it could also end up being incredibly useful. Distraction.

"You need to get the fuck out of here. You don't know what you're doing."

I blinked at her. "But masquerading as a guard is clever and smart?" I asked, nudging the body of the wizard at my feet. He was still breathing. Which meant she hadn't killed him. "Who the hell are you, anyway? You haven't tried to kill me. Yet. Just like earlier today at the school. Almost like you want to talk to me or something." I studied her. "Was it my eyelashes that made you fall madly in love with me? I hear they do that. But I don't go for cougars."

She flashed me an amused smile. She wasn't old, but she wasn't young, either. *Experienced* was the best word I could come up with. "I'm going to pretend I'm not staring at an ancient Chinese matriarch." *Damn*, she was good. "I've bedded real men before, Temple. Sorry, but you don't make the cut. Save me from trust-fund billionaires."

"Don't forget the eyelashes," I added.

"Right. You almost make the cut. Because of the eyelashes." She studied me up and down, then her head jerked to the side and she cursed. "Time for you to get gone, if you're smart." Then she disappeared.

I didn't waste a second, turning to quickly scan the shelves behind me.

"Nate," Achilles whispered from directly in front of me, peering through the shelf, having shoved aside a roll of papers as tall as him. I almost pissed myself as I saw the pair of eyes reflecting the fires behind me.

"Get down!" I hissed, tearing through boxes and glancing down at my amulet after a few seconds of fruitless searching. And I froze.

The amulet was stone cold again.

Which meant…

Son of a bitch. The *woman* had the HOG. That was why my amulet had reacted so strongly. I rounded on my heels, planning to knock her out cold and steal it before any—

And I came face-to-face with a dozen angry wizards glaring at me. They stared from me to the body by my feet. I pointed at the ground. "That wasn't me," I began, but they interrupted.

"Bind her. Whoever she is. We'll get the answers we need out of her. Find out how long she's been working with Temple." It took me a moment to remember that they didn't see me as Nate Temple. They only saw my disguise.

And the wizards began to advance.

I shouted something vaguely Asian and threw my backpack at them, diving to the side. Bars of air reached out to me, but I sliced through them, still touching my Mask in an effort to keep up my disguise. If we were caught, they would get my friends, me, my Mask, and find out exactly who I was.

And they wouldn't be gentle.

I heard them cursing as I rolled behind the shelf, because they didn't want to damage any artifacts. My eyes widened to find Achilles and Gunnar simply gone.

And that's when they hit me. Hammering me with power from a dozen different wizards, flattening me into the ground like a pancake. I couldn't even move. I released my power, but kept the coin hidden between my fingers. I would keep it hidden as long as possible, and if necessary, cause a scene and hide it in a random bookshelf or something.

Hands grabbed me, pulling me to my feet as a heavy blanket of magic fell over my shoulders, blocking me from tapping into my power. I really wished I had worn my cuffs again. But knowing where I was going, I had assumed that they would be useless. After all, I had used them against the Academy a few days ago, and wearing them now would have given away who I was.

If I had gotten in a fight, and their magic had slipped off me, they would have instantly known who I was. So, I had relied on the Mask.

To my detriment.

And the mysterious silver-haired woman had beaten me to the HOG. My friends were gone.

I was goose-stepped back up to the line of wizards, where I received the most hateful, murderous looks I had received in a long while.

Two of them were Justices. Luckily, the Grand Master wasn't here.

"She's no terrorist. It's a disguise. It's fixed to her so I can't remove it. Wild magic. I don't recognize it."

"She doesn't have anything on her," another wizard growled, tearing through my backpack.

"Who *are* you?" I recognized the voice. It was the first wizard. They had awoken him. "You're not the one who attacked me…" he frowned.

"See?" I pointed at him eagerly. "Proof!"

"How many of you are there?" he snarled.

I glanced from side to side, pretending to be scared, but really hoping to find Achilles and Gunnar hiding somewhere else. But I saw no one. I turned back to the wizard. "I was trying to check out a book."

They didn't find that funny. "Take her to the Stone. We'll bleed it out of her. Let's g—"

"Look out!" one of the other wizards shouted, pointing up into the air. Spears of black, shifting clouds, zipped through the lofty air-space, like a flock of birds sometimes did, forming unique, shifting, mercurial geometric shapes.

There were three of them.

"What are they?" the first wizard growled.

"Dementors," I said loudly. They turned to face me. "Or Death Eaters," I frowned. "I can never remember which one is which." I knew from first-hand experience that the Academy hadn't discovered the world of Harry Potter. At least none of the ones I had met.

The first wizard took a step closer. "And are these Death Eaters with your crew? These Dementors?" he asked, tone dripping with warning. "Because we aren't scared of Death Eaters or Dementors." From his tone, I could tell he had no idea what *Harry Potter* was, and that he was trying to intimidate me, which made it all the funnier. "We are the *Law*. We are the *Academ—*"

One of the black-fog shapes slammed into his back, knocking him into the shelf.

It began to wobble, tilt, and then fall. He struggled on all fours, staring up at the collapsing shelf in horror. Two more of the blurs hammered into the remaining wizards, darting in and out like sharks or wolves. Circling back before they could recover, and suddenly my ward was gone.

I set my hands on the mask, ready to Shadow Walk to a different corner of the Library, shouting out Asian-sounding syllables in an effort to get the attention of Achilles and Gunnar.

I opened my mouth to shout again, and one of the black-fog shapes hammered into me, shifting into the silver-haired matron right before contact. She struck me like a tackle, and I prepared to introduce my skull to the falling shelf, then experience thousands of years of history pummeling me to death.

But I felt nothing of the sort.

Instead, I felt the cool night breeze brushing my cheeks, blowing my hair in wild disarray. I opened my eyes to see that we were very high above the ground.

Because we were standing on a freaking Aqueduct, one I had seen on tourist brochures before. The Aqueduct of Segovia in Spain. City streets below us buzzed with activity, busses, taxis, and tourists milling about like insects. But I was high enough up that they didn't see me.

I froze, ready for a fight. The woman was nowhere to be found, but I heard her voice on the breeze. "Your… friends are safe at home. But you are still in danger. And I'm too tired to take you home. Babysitting is so exhausting. Honestly, it's like you've never done this before. I don't know why everyone is so scared of you. Falling for a rookie mistake, of all things."

"It's very brave to talk to me while hiding. Show yourself," I demanded, wondering what the hell rookie mistake she was talking about. "Who *are* you?"

"We're not friends. I just hate those assholes," her voice whispered in my ears. I spun, trying to catch a glimpse of her, but all I saw was more wind.

"You have two of them now," I pleaded, confident she was part of the Syndicate. "Just keep them the hell away from Ichabod."

There was a stunned, pregnant silence. Then her voice called out from a different direction. "You are being hunted. Run away, little rabbit. Run away…"

I felt her voice fade away to nothing, leaving me all alone.

I growled to myself, ready to Shadow Walk back home. I had tried. At least Ichabod didn't get it.

A flash of light and sparks erupted behind me, which I caught in my peripheral vision before a tight fist gripped the back of my coat, yanking me through the Gateway that had appeared directly behind me.

Almost as if they had known where I was, or something.

You are being hunted, little rabbit… the memory of the voice taunted me.

CHAPTER 39

I felt cold magic wash over me, and instantly knew I was no longer a cross-dressing Asian grandmother, just Nate Temple again. Hands patted me down in a dark room, slapping my chest angrily. They took my amulet, whoever *they* were, but they hadn't found the coin I had tucked into my pocket. My Mask. I hadn't yet been able to see my abductors, the room cloaked in shadows.

"Where is it?" a familiar voice demanded from the darkness.

I blinked. No…

"Black damn, boy. You rose holy hell in there and didn't even get it?" he shouted. "My, how far the apple falls from the tree…" he shoved me away, turning his back, and the area slowly illuminated as if someone had turned up a dimmer switch.

I stumbled, but just stared, my vision beginning to pulse with rage.

Ichabod turned to sit down in a chair, glaring at me. Indie stood beside him, shaking her head, face grave. And I realized how they had been able to remove my disguise. Makers.

"If it isn't two of my favorite people," I began, taking an angry step forward.

Ichabod grunted, turning to Indie with a shrug. He held up the amulet. "Fat lot of good this will do us. Looks like we'll need to escalate your phase now. They can help us retrieve it." He didn't sound happy about this, but he did sound resolved.

"You two were in the Library," I said in disbelief.

They turned to look at me in unison, as if surprised I had spoken. Then they began to talk softly, under their breath, ignoring me.

I snapped my fingers. "Hey! What the fuck are you two planning? And what were you after?" I asked, feigning ignorance, hoping I was wrong.

Indie turned cool eyes on me. "You know what we were after. But someone beat us all to it."

"You're going all-in," I growled in disgust. "To wake a god and doom us all. Because the Syndicate hurt your feelings," I spat. Ichabod's shoulders tightened, but he ignored me.

They resumed their conversation. "How the hell did you even know about the Library? How did you know where I was?" I shouted, ready to explode. I stood no chance against the two.

Indie's eyes immediately darted away, but Ichabod chuckled, pulling something from his pocket. It was a few strands of hair, glinting in the dim light. I stared, momentarily confused, and then shot a sharp look at Indie.

"You…" I whispered. "When we kissed…"

"Spit it out, boy," Ichabod smiled. "She took some of your hair."

I ignored him, continuing to glare at Indie in disbelief. We had kissed. I had believed her. Kind of. At least with the kiss. That it had been genuine. Not enough to change her mind, but that at least some small part of her was still there.

But… she had merely used the moment to steal my hair. To track me. To the Library. I found that I was shaking. And I was ready to do something very, very stupid. My fingers slowly began to reach for the coin in my pocket. *Let's see what a Horseman can do*, I thought to myself. "What next?" I rasped.

Ichabod stood, frowning at my hand as it moved. "There will be no need for that." I found myself suddenly frozen, unable to move. He calmly walked up to me, reached inside my pocket, and tried to grab the coin.

A flash of light followed by wails and screams of agony from the pits of hell filled the room, and Ichabod went flying. We all coughed at the sudden smell of smoke and Brimstone.

Indie took over, freezing me in place again just before I could touch the coin. I snarled at her, but she merely stared at my pocket with a frown. "What just happened?" she coughed, glancing down at Ichabod. She didn't go to help him.

Which made a small part of me happy.

He cursed as he climbed to his feet. He stared at me for a long silence, then at my pocket, thinking. Then a very sinister smile split his unshaven cheeks. "Didn't expect that. I won't even ask what it is, but I caught a sense of what it can *do* before it zapped me to high-heaven…" His smile stretched wider, as he turned to Indie, who was avoiding my glare. "I do believe that my descendant just gave us the answer to our problem…" He pointed, indicating the coin – Mask – in my pocket.

I blinked. "What the hell are you talking about?" I growled.

He brushed off his hands, smiling at Indie. "Prepare to meet your Brothers, my girl. Nate, here, is going to take us to Rumpelstiltskin, like a good little boy…" his grin was wolfish, and I suddenly felt sick to my stomach.

I struggled, knowing it was useless.

"I will do no such thing."

"Ah, but you will. Or we will immediately go slaughter your friends. All of them. Right now. We'll even let you watch."

Indie looked sick to her stomach, but didn't argue with him.

"I don't know where he is," I argued.

"Nice try. He's with your Hatter. Right, Indie?" he asked, turning to her. Her lips tightened, and her eyes closed for a moment before she let out a weak nod.

"It's for the greater good, Nate. Please, trust me…" she said.

"Hate sells," I said absently. Then I looked up. "Hitler sounded very similar. Had a lot of fans." I let a small, humorless smile onto my face. I felt cold. Emotionless. "Not too many friends, but he did like his pets, though. Sucker for animals, Hitler was." And I very pointedly glanced at Ichabod, then Indie. I turned back to him after a pointed silence. "On an unrelated note, have you ever considered a mustache? Not the curly kind, but a small, square patch just above your lips? I think it might suit—"

He waved a hand, silencing me with power. "Enough. We leave immediately. One way or another. To murder your friends, or to retrieve Rumpelstiltskin. Your call." He folded his arms. "I'll wait for an answer." He released the magic that had sealed my lips closed.

What was it with all these clowns threatening my friends? But they were right. It was my weakness. The way to break me. I let out a frustrated breath. "Let's go make a deal with Silver Tongue," I whispered, defeated, damning them both to hell.

I wasn't really sure how to use the Mask, or if there was a way for me to warn the Hatter ahead of time, but I had no choice. I already had the Academy and Syndicate trying to kill all of my friends. I couldn't defend them against another sociopath.

I would just have to let the Grimms into the Hatter's realm, and hope he took out the trash.

I hid the smile that burned inside me. Maybe this would be fun…

I touched the Mask, focusing on the White World, just as Ichabod and Indie touched my shoulders. With a peal of thunder, we were gone.

CHAPTER 40

I found myself sitting on the Hatter's nice white leather couch, wearing a swanky white cotton suit. We were alone. Ichabod jerked his head from one side to another, a globe of force hovering in his palm, ready to defend himself. His face was ice, and he wore a crisp black suit, a black silk dress shirt, and black leather loafers. He looked surprised at the sudden change of clothing, shooting me a calculating look. I frowned back, but more at the color of his clothes. Seeing no immediate threat, he released the orb of power in his palms.

I glanced over at Indie to find her staring down at her silver cocktail dress, complete with a black frilly bottom, and a black, low-necked, lace-trimmed top, drawing the eye to her impressive décolletage. *Silver and black...* I thought to myself.

I grunted, openly feasting my eyes on her chest. "I'll miss those," I muttered with a lewd, dismissive sneer. As one would when recalling a lowly one-night stand. "But I'm sure I'll find better later. Should never buy the first car on the lot." I turned away, but not before hearing her sharp, wounded intake of breath.

Cry me a river.

I glanced back at her, furrowing my brow mockingly. "Crocodile tears will get you nowhere. You're used goods. Maybe one of the

Grimms will have fun playing with you before they tear the stones out of your arm." I leaned closer, whispering softly. "I hope they take their time."

Her face was a thunderhead of both outrage, and guilt.

"You have *no* idea what is going on, Nate…" she hissed. "If you did…"

"If I did, *what*?" I growled, panting.

Ichabod snapped his fingers before Indie could answer. "He comes. Put on your most welcoming smiles." He glanced over his shoulder at me. "In case you were wondering, I've set allies in play. If they don't hear from me in the next few hours, they are to destroy every brick and stone in St. Louis. Starting with your friends' properties, of course."

"You wouldn't dare," I growled, hearing heavy boots approaching. If Ichabod was telling the truth, I needed to warn the Hatter not to kill him on sight. Then again, if the Hatter put them in place, maybe I could whisk back home and protect them while Ichabod and Indie got a tour of the guest rooms.

Maybe I would even let this whole Grimm thing play out. Bring them all over so that Indie and Ichabod would have roommates with Rumpelstiltskin. I could only imagine what kind of shit show that would be. The Grimms, their old boss, their de-facto new boss and Sister Grimm, and their old prisoner, Ichabod.

Ho' boy.

I flicked a discreet glance down at Indie's forearm to the stones embedded deep in the flesh. With them and Rumpelstiltskin here, I wasn't sure what needed to happen next. Rumps had seemed in no shape to do anything magical the last time I had seen him.

A whipped dog.

Would Ichabod or Indie need to take control somehow?

But I didn't really care. Because after my most recent talk with the Hatter, I was very, *very* excited to see how this played out. Because he wanted guests, and Ichabod and Indie wanted to bring some guests here.

Or, hell, perhaps the Hatter would just annihilate both of them the first second he saw them. Trespassers. I would give him an innocent, helpless look, and maybe that would be it. Solve my problem with Ichabod and Indie once and for all.

I wasn't sure how I felt about Indie dying right next to me, though.

Sure, I was angry, furious, and if she had attacked me directly, I probably wouldn't have held back in killing her myself. But she was about to face a creature that could end her with a thought.

And she had no idea.

And I would be sitting right next to her when it happened.

Part of me wondered what she had been talking about when she had said that I knew nothing of what was really going on.

But I was saved from this thought as the door opened, and the Mad Hatter strode in, not remotely surprised to see me sitting on the couch. He also didn't seem surprised to find me with guests, as if his power had informed him that I wasn't alone. I shot him my planned look of desperation, trying to let him know that this was entirely against my will.

Because Ichabod had zipped my lips shut again, the crusty shit-stain.

The Hatter spent a second assessing me, reading my face, and then his gaze flicked to Indie and the stones on her arm. He grunted almost imperceptibly before his eyes drifted to Ichabod, who had been standing off to the side, near the bookshelf. He studied his clothes first, a thoughtful frown painting his features. Then his eyes lifted to Ichabod's face.

The Hatter froze as if suddenly receiving a blow to the gut.

My eyes flicked to Ichabod nervously. Had he been strong enough to stop the Hatter somehow? In his own home?

But Ichabod looked poleaxed as well, as if some force had simultaneously nut-tapped both of them. His face flipped through a whole list of emotions that made no sense to me.

I rounded on the Hatter, feeling that ward over my lips had suddenly disappeared as a result of Ichabod's shock. "Kill them! Now!" I shouted at the top of my lungs. "They kidnapped me—"

The Hatter just flicked a hand at me as if throwing a fireball, not even turning to look in my direction. I flinched, expecting to be incinerated, but nothing happened. It had been an instinctive reaction, ordering me to *be silent*.

Then I saw. He was staring at Ichabod with the same wash of emotions as he was receiving.

The room was dead silent for a full ten seconds. Then...

"Father?" Ichabod whispered.

And a single tear fell down the Hatter's cheeks, splashing into his beard. Indie and I slowly turned to stare at one other. She wore the same stunned look of surprise I felt. She hadn't known. Hell, it looked like *they* hadn't known either.

"My son..." the Hatter rasped. And then he was pounding towards Ichabod, but not in an attack. To squeeze him into his big, burly chest in the most impressive display of grief and love I had ever seen between two men.

I just shook my head, my world shattering to a million pieces.

What the hell was I going to do now?

CHAPTER 41

They hugged, cried, laughed, and the Hatter mussed his son's hair. Indie was sobbing openly. Not because she was so overjoyed for Ichabod, but because the literal waves of emotion in the room were overwhelming. Hell, I hated Ichabod for what he planned to do, and even I felt my throat tighten.

After a few giant pats on the back that seemed to jostle Ichabod's eyeballs, the Hatter grasped him by the shoulders, forcing him back a few steps, studying him from head to toe.

"I don't understand," he whispered.

Ichabod shivered, eyes red. "I tried to stop them, Father. I did. But I didn't know my way into the Sanctorum. I couldn't find it."

The Hatter dropped his gaze, taking a deep breath. "It has been so long, my son. So long…" his voice trailed away, taking in the walls of his prison, staring out the window, an angry look growing on his face. "Sit. What would you like to drink?" he asked everyone, trying to compose himself.

But I suddenly found myself floating in a hazy fog, as if my spirit was hovering above the group. Indie still sobbed beside me, and I saw my face. Utterly blank.

I had read that letter in the cavern. Written to Ichabod's father, Matthias Temple.

Matthias was... the *Hatter*. And he was... my ancestor.

And he hadn't ever told me.

My mind tracked back as the two spoke softly to one another. Part of me watched this, but the majority of my brain was racing through my Memory Palace, recalling every conversation I had shared with either of the men before me, trying to see how I had missed this fact.

The cavern had only opened after I became the true Master of Chateau Falco, dominating the Beast inside with my Maker powers. But Ichabod had seemed horrified when he learned of it. That the house had bonded to me. But he hadn't *said* anything.

And as an adult, the cavern had never let him into her most sacred library. His father's old office. *Why?*

I cleared my throat, back in my body, surprised to find I was holding a drink and that my mouth tasted like absinthe. I didn't remember receiving it, drinking it, or swallowing it. And the pain of the fire didn't even hurt enough to faze me. Judging by the sensation, I had taken a very liberal gulp. Indie coughed, apparently having done the same.

"What... the hell is going on?" I turned... to Matthias. "You never told me we were related."

He looked guilty, nodding to himself. "I didn't think it would matter. I can't leave, and I didn't want a new friend to become only a friend of obligation. You liked me for... me. I didn't want to taint it by you being forced to feel a connection with me because of our blood."

I stared at him, leaning forward. "You *knew*... this whole time. I've shared everything with you..."

Matthias nodded sadly. "Yes."

I turned to Ichabod. "But... you *knew* about the Hatter..."

Ichabod wouldn't meet my eyes as he answered. "I knew of the Hatter... but not that he was..." he trailed off, eyes finally flashing to me. He looked sick to his stomach, his shock temporarily overwhelming his hatred of me.

The Hatter locked eyes with me. "This is the one you lost," he said, pointing at Indie. I nodded, remembering our earlier conversation, when I had tried to obscurely warn him about Ichabod's plans.

That plan was now officially blown to hell.

"And this is the one wanting to destroy the Syndicate," he said, pointing at Ichabod. Again, I nodded, ignoring the thoughtful looks the two shot me. Matthias Temple grunted. "They seem fine to me," he said harshly, before turning back to Ichabod. "Tell him. He needs to know."

Ichabod studied me with a frown for a moment, no doubt wondering what his father had been referring to, but pleased that he had somehow come out on top.

I poured more of the milky absinthe into my glass. This might be my last drink before I became Rumpelstiltskin's new roommate. I even filled Indie's glass without bothering to ask if she was drinking something different. She didn't even flinch. Just began to drink greedily.

Part of me realized that she hadn't appeared to have any issues with her powers lately. No loss of control. Her training with Ichabod must have gone well. Not that it mattered now.

Ichabod began speaking in a lecturing tone. "My father was in charge of the American Makers. Descended from those first sent over. We were unaware that the Grimms had followed us here to these shores. They began to plague us. Murdering each new creature that they discovered, because America was an unexplored continent, complete with new… Freaks, unlike those found in our homelands overseas." He took a drink.

"After time, it became obvious that there were more than we had thought, and that two brothers – Jacob and Wilhelm – had taken charge, direct bloodlines from the original Grimms. Full bloods." His eyes finally turned to Indie and I. Me, because I had killed them. She, because she now wore Jacob's stones in her arm. "But you know about them already…" He said, eyes flicking to Matthias, who nodded slowly. What were they so nervous about?

"My father fought tirelessly. I was just a boy, but in time I became old enough to understand that it was not going well. My father beseeched the Academy for assistance on a plan to take out the Grimms once and for all. The American gods were wild, untamed, and in that, he thought he had found an opportunity to... cleanse the world of the Grimms. But the Academy denied help."

And I had seen reference to that. In the letter from the cavern. Matthias had... wanted to do the same thing Ichabod hungered for. To wake a god. I shivered, horrified.

"He... grew more distant after that," Ichabod whispered, not meeting Matthias' eyes. But I saw his face. They were pained, troubled, and guilty. An absent father's eyes. "My father grew prone to fits of anger, rage, and... madness. Utter disregard for his fellow Makers and the Academy wizards. He was desperate to make this world safer, so sought to gain more power from his Beast. The Maker's Beast. I did what most boys do. I rebelled. Temple tradition," he smiled sadly. "My father sought out the assistance of a small group of other Makers and wizards in the Americas. Those less blindly submissive to the Academy. Those who had suffered under their... alliance." He lifted his eyes to mine. "These men and women were his last hope..."

Indie fidgeted uncomfortably. Whether at knowing this had all been done as a result of the Grimms – of which she was one – or because she knew part of this story. But Ichabod never looked away from me.

I spoke up. "Who was Castor Queen?"

And the Hatter's face abruptly turned red with rage. Ichabod shot me an incredulous look, no doubt wondering where I had gotten the name, but quickly jumped up to calm down his father. I stared, dumbfounded, wondering what I had done. The letter I saw had been *friendly* between the two! Matthias was shouting incoherently, and Ichabod was speaking softly to him, holding his arms down, trying to cool him off.

"Let me finish, Father! Then we'll talk about that bastard, Castor Queen..." This, for some reason, worked, although Matthias' face remained red, and he was breathing fast and hard, staring down at his boots, muttering under his breath. I shared a look with Indie. *Good lord...*

"My father," Ichabod continued, "formed a group of like-minded men and women. They called themselves... the Syndicate. And my father led them. With his friend... Castor Queen."

I blinked, unable to comprehend. Matthias was actually growling now.

Ichabod met my eyes, nodding at whatever emotion he saw on my face. I just felt numb, and had no idea what he saw. "They worked together for a time, bringing peace where the Academy wouldn't aid them. But… the Grimms were too powerful, and they grew desperate."

Matthias' face was stone, carefully composed rage at the memory, no longer muttering.

"Then my father came up with his plan to wake a god, notifying both the Syndicate and the Academy. His solution to the Grimms…" He cleared his throat, nodding at his father compassionately. "But he was betrayed. By his long-time friend, Castor Queen. The Syndicate – in conjunction with the Academy – *banished* him. Declared him a madman, a monster, unfit to occupy his seat in the Americas lest he doom them all. His partners, and his friends. Abandoned. Him. Because, little did my father know, Castor Queen had teamed up with the Brothers Grimm. To use them as a weapon for power, to take the Americas for himself, free from the Academy. To take the Syndicate from my father. And I was suddenly an orphan, running for my life…"

CHAPTER 42

No one spoke. Matthias and Ichabod both took long drinks from their glasses. They locked eyes, and nodded at each other with sad smiles of understanding, unconditional love. Peace.

I was in shock. For many reasons. The Syndicate had been around for that long?

Matthias had started it, and was later betrayed by his best friend.

Ichabod had been orphaned. He must have later come back to Chateau Falco, wondering why he couldn't enter the cavern, or Sanctorum, as he had called it. He had then made it his life's purpose to take out the Grimms. To take out the Syndicate for their betrayal.

But had instead been kidnapped, taken by his nemesis.

"If you never entered the... Sanctorum, how did you learn any of this?" I asked softly.

A queasy look passed across his face. "The Grimms were very... arrogant after my capture. They taunted me with this tale for... hundreds of years, trying to break me. They almost did."

I shivered involuntarily, but Matthias spoke up.

"I had truly become lost in myself, with my Beast. I sought information anywhere I could find it, and my Beast... obliged. Chateau Falco never forgave me for that. Jealousy, perhaps."

I stared at him, eager. "You were the last Master Temple," I began, thinking furiously. I turned to Ichabod. "And because of your father's... *choices*," I winced apologetically at the Hatter, but he merely shrugged off my concern, "the house didn't submit to you."

Ichabod shrugged uncomfortably. "I thought it had merely been a boy's fancy. Imagining that my home could talk to my father. That maybe he truly *had* been mad."

His last word hit me like a rock, and I suddenly shook my head. "Wait… that doesn't make sense…" I turned to Matthias. "Why did you adopt that name? You aren't the Mad Hatter. He's just a character in a book… A book written long after your banishment."

Matthias nodded sadly. "Like I said, I had crossed into madness. Then was secretly banished here. But one friend visited me often. The only one before you." He looked up at me. "Death."

I stared in disbelief, not following his answer.

"He knew how much I missed the world, so he brought me books. Stories. To help me cope in my life of solitude. But in my madness, I became particularly… obsessed with your Lewis Carroll. Especially his Mad Hatter. I lived vicariously through those books, reading them hundreds of times. I *became* him, in a way…" he trailed off, silence filling the room for a few long seconds. "Death stopped bringing me books after that. But he did make it so that I could communicate with him via a paired copy of the book." He smiled at me. "The one you have."

My head felt ready to explode. Death had owned the book before me? And he had never said anything. But why had he given it away? And how had the ogres gotten their hands on it? Secrets upon secrets upon secrets.

Matthias stared sadly at his trappings. His prison. "Castor and his crew sent me here. To this place. I refused to help him, calling him a Black Hat for his evil plan to work with the Grimms. In response, he told me he would show me the punishment for being a White Hat in a world of Silvers and Blacks." He held out his hands, indicating this white world around us. "I discovered his betrayal too late. The Academy never knew the truth, just helped Castor Queen subdue me, believing his lies about my dangerous intents. Castor Queen did the rest… He used me as a scapegoat for his true crime – of taking over the Brothers Grimm. Using them as a sword to clear away his enemies."

I barely heard Ichabod whisper. "I never knew the details of that part, just that he had betrayed you, not what he had done with you after the trial… I tried to avenge you, Father…" Matthias nodded compassionately.

I let out a deep breath, downing more of my drink. I was definitely feeling buzzed. "This is un-fucking-believable…" I whispered.

Matthias shot me a glare. "Watch your tone, my boy… This isn't easy on any of us, if you missed that…" he warned, idly picking up his violin. Ichabod's face crumpled at the sight.

"You… still play?" he asked softly.

Matthias didn't answer, he just began to play a haunting tone, closing his eyes.

Indie and Ichabod both let out soft sobs. I just shook my head, unable to share their emotions as my mind raced with what – the hell – was going to happen next?

Ichabod wanted to wake a god and bring the Grimms back, and judging by the looks of it, his father would do anything to make up for their shattered past. Because a father would do anything for his son…

Especially when that son only wanted to avenge him.

CHAPTER 43

*I*ndie clapped softly once Matthias finished. Ichabod had a nostalgic look on his face as Matthias gently set the violin down.

I recalled the instruments I had seen in the cavern, wondering if one of them had been Matthias' treasured violin.

A new thought hit me.

"What's up with the round tabl—"

Ichabod spoke over me. "Father, I need your help…"

Matthias, obviously, chose to focus on his son rather than me. Indie shot me a condescending glare at interrupting their mending relationship.

I just wanted to know if that damn round table in the cavern had once seated some knights.

But my fanboy interests were not shared by the group.

"Whatever you need, my son," Matthias finally replied.

"Whoa, whoa, whoa. Maybe you don't agree before you hear what he wants. Because he wants to bring the Grimms back, Gramps. Great Gramps, or whatever the hell you two are," I said. "You know, the ones who fucked up your lives? Two wrongs don't make a right."

Ichabod nodded, fire coming back into his face. "Yes. Nate is right. I will use them to hunt down the Syndicate." He pointed at Indie, the stones embedded in her arm. "She has bonded with Jacob Grimm's amulet in such a way that they will *have* to obey her." Ichabod leaned closer, whispering urgently, conspiratorially. "Use the Syndicate's own weapon against them. Salt the earth. *Destroy* them. In your name. In the name of *all* Temples…" he rasped. "Full circle."

Indie fidgeted uncomfortably, but didn't speak.

I frowned at her, but she shook her head almost imperceptibly, mouthing *later*.

Which made me frown harder, but the other two Temples hadn't noticed, so intent on their plan, considering the possibility of revenge after so long.

Matthias turned to me, scratching his beard. "What say you, my boy?"

Ichabod looked ready to rip my heart out if I said one thing out of line. He even drew a finger across his throat, but Matthias held up a hand. "Do not threaten your descendant, Icky," he admonished.

I burst out laughing. "Oh, boy. Icky?" I mimicked writing it down on my thigh, and putting it in my pocket. I smiled at him.

"*Join* us, Nate. The Syndicate is your enemy. You've been battling alongside me this whole time while pretending to be against me," Ichabod pleaded.

"And I've done a pretty damn good job of pissing them off without the help of a god!" I shouted, panting, my vision pulsing red.

Ichabod scoffed. "You've pissed off their underlings. Not *them*!"

I shrugged. "Still. Pretty easy. No god required." I folded my arms stubbornly.

Ichabod leaned forward, reaching towards his hip with a manic grin. "But all of your successes were with the aid of *this*."

And he withdrew my old eagle-headed cane handle. It shifted into a full-length cane sword, tip thumping into the floor, and it seemed to vibrate on a molecular level. Ichabod looked pained as he held it, and Matthias instinctively growled, scratching at his arms as he stared down at it. As if they could sense my Beast trapped inside. And I abruptly realized I could, too. Not an uncomfortable feeling like they were experiencing, but more of a pleasant, *hello*, from an old pal.

Because my old Beast seemed to be alive and well, sitting inside my old cane.

I stared at it, and then slowly turned to Indie with a hostile glare. "Thanks for that."

She looked both ashamed and outraged. Although I wasn't sure if the shame was about her jealously trying to kill Othello – who had been giving me an innocent back rub at the time – or for stealing from me.

But I saw the outrage. And that simple emotion alone helped me ignore her crocodile tears. Because one small part of her was still defensive. Which meant she was dead to me. I grunted, dismissing her as I turned back to Ichabod.

"So, you stole my cane. Why?"

"Because we may need it for bargaining power."

I was shaking my head. "Not going to happen. I freed him."

Matthias burst to his feet, looking horrified. "WHAT?" he roared, startling all of us. He stared down at the cane as if it was a ten-foot-tall fire-breathing cobra.

"Calm down. He's innocent."

"Oh, the *hell* he is!" Matthias roared.

Ichabod was simply shaking his head at me, looking amazed at how incredibly naive I was.

"Do one of you want to tell me why it's so deadly? I mean, look at it. It's almost about to murder each of us. Any minute now…" I whispered theatrically, as nothing at all happened.

I felt a purr of satisfaction from the cane.

Ichabod glared at me. "He's no danger to you. Not directly. But the world… that's a different story. These…" he shot a look of disdain down at the cane, "Beasts were chained to Makers for a reason." He pointed at Matthias. "Look at what his Beast did to him? And he was a Maker like the world had rarely seen before." Matthias cast his eyes down, nodding. Ichabod waited for this look before continuing, face guilty, but adamant. "It brought a man like this, a *Temple*, to his knees. Turning him into the Mad Hatter. But even before that, it broke him. Changed him," Ichabod whispered, face haunted, reliving his last childhood memories of his father.

Matthias nodded vehemently. "He speaks the truth. The last one that… broke free, or was granted freedom… was banished to the opposite end of the world. A team of Makers, wizards, witches, shifters, and Fae could barely restrain her…" he stared at me, very intently.

He finally took a step closer, pointing a finger at me. "Chateau Falco…" he breathed.

I just blinked. "Narnia?" I said. "But… she seems so nice…"

CHAPTER 44

Matthias looked as if I had hit him in the head with a ball-peen hammer. "Narnia?" he finally whispered in a baffled tone. "What the devil are you talking about?"

I shrugged. "I gave her a name, rather than saying, *hey, house,* all the time."

Matthias threw his hands up in the air, about ready to explode. "We do not name the murderous, world-ending Beasts restrained by generations and nations of magic."

I shrugged at him. "Why not?"

He growled under his breath, pacing. "Because she already has a name. *Falco*, you fucking idiot child," he roared, turning his back on me as he panted. I opened my mouth to defend myself, but he suddenly spun, pointing a finger at me, and I found myself floating a foot off the ground, held by my throat by an unseen force. "And not only have you tried to change her name, weakening her bond, but you may have freed *another* Beast upon the world!" he shouted. I began to choke, and he threw out a hand. I dropped to the couch, gasping as I clutched my throat.

In that moment, for some obtuse reason, I decided to never call my house *Narnia* again.

After a few tense moments, he let out several deep breaths. "It must stay here. Where it can do little harm. I'm collateral damage. Used goods. It can't escape this place."

"If," I began, throat raspy, "It's so dangerous, why hasn't it escaped the cane?" I managed.

Ichabod shrugged. "I don't know. This is why we took it from you. Because freeing your Beast, and leaving it in a home that embodies *another* Beast could have cataclysmic reactions. What if they had *mated?*" Matthias rounded on his son, looking horrified that he hadn't considered the same thought.

"What?" I declared, incredulous. "You thought my cane and house were going to get it on?"

Ichabod shivered, studying his father. "I had heard stories of a Beast trapped in a house, but I had no idea it was *our* house. I had long ago decided that my father saying he could speak to the house was a condition of his madness, since it had never spoken to *me…*" He shook his head, dismissing the personal revelation as he turned back to me. "But when I saw that you had dominated Chateau Falco, and that it obeyed you, all became clear. I knew only that you had your Beast, and your cane," he winked, reminding me of our conversation when I had first told him about it, "and that you had dominated Chateau Falco. But when we fought at the Circus, imagine my surprise to see you no longer had your Beast, and that you were once again a wizard." He shrugged. "Not knowing what else to do, and fearing the worst, I sent Indie to retrieve the cane, assuming the house would sense me if I tried myself. I couldn't risk two Beasts, one free, one chained, so close together."

I frowned in thought, reaching out for the Beast to hear his side of the story.

Ichabod yanked the cane away, sheathing it in a cocoon of magic I could not penetrate. Matthias grunted in approval, and then shot me a very, very disappointed stare.

"You don't want to hear his side of the story?" I asked, incredulous. "Why he hasn't escaped if he's so dangerous?"

Ichabod frowned. "I believe he can only escape if you *let* him escape, since *you* freed him. But you never completed the break. You broke him from *you*, but didn't quite *free* him from his prison. Which brings up an interesting dilemma…" Matthias frowned, thinking Maker thoughts. Then he gasped.

"He's a free agent."

Ichabod nodded slowly. "My fear exactly."

I'd heard Shiva say the same. I waved my hands. "Excuse me, what the hell does that mean?"

Indie spoke up. "It means someone can take him, bond him, and become a Maker."

I frowned, unsure what to say to that.

"Why didn't you just *tell* me all of this, Indie?" I whispered suddenly. "I would have listened. You didn't have to betray me. Rob me. Attack my friends. Go fucking crazy."

She stared at me for a good long while, her face darkening. "If you knew half of what the Syndicate has done, you would side with us in an instant."

"So, tell me!" I threw my hands in the air. "And, no. I wouldn't. I would help you destroy them, but we don't have to call back the Grimms, or wake a god to do so. We just need to join forces. Hell, I have the Armory! We can—"

"Exactly," she growled.

Which brought me up short. I blinked at her. "Exactly, what?"

Ichabod chuckled, leaning back in his chair as he motioned for her to continue. She nodded back resolutely, then turned to face me, folding her hands in her lap.

"Who built the Armory?"

I frowned. "You know that. My father."

She nodded. "Who did your father work for?"

I rolled my eyes. "Himself. Always himself."

"Not the Academy?" she asked. But she didn't seem to truly care. Almost as if we had had this conversation before, and she was just reminding me of bullet points.

"Not really. He hated the Academy. Feared what they were doing. He considered himself a lone wolf, not that he let them know the depth of his hatred," I said, leaning closer. "Look. Get to the point. We've done this dance enough times for me to know when you're baiting me," I smiled softly. Not in humor at the situation, but at the faded memory of when conversations like this with her had been pleasant.

Because we had been on the same side.

"Do you know anyone else who hates the Academy?"

I rose my hand. "Um. Me. I do."

She nodded in faint amusement. "Who else?"

I frowned, thinking. Who didn't hate them? They had become a useless group of old men and women hiding in safety, declaring their judgments from a distance, and shaping the world to their benefit.

Not unlike...

I blinked, rounding on her. "The Syndicate?" I asked.

She nodded slowly, waiting.

I waited. "Okay..." I urged. "I really suck at these games, you know."

She locked eyes with me, taking a deep breath. Not sympathetic, but resolute. "Your father... worked for the Syndicate."

And my heart stopped for a beat. Then it double-timed to make up for it, and I latched onto every iota of power I could, ready to obliterate her very existence.

Something hit me, and I shut down. Magically, rationally, physically, and emotionally.

And I found myself in a very, very dark place.

CHAPTER 45

I woke up to – more or less – the same scene. Ichabod enjoyed my pain. Immensely, because I found him watching me like a sociopathic kid with a magnifying glass had just discovered a nest of ants.

I squirmed uncomfortably, feeling as if part of my soul had died down. "It's okay. I won't murder all of you just yet…" I said softly.

Matthias laughed softly, not at the situation, but at my comment. I shot him a look and he lifted his fist. "Temples are made of stronger stuff."

I waved him off, and he froze, staring at my hand. I frowned, then remembered it was my bandaged hand with the brand. Our family crest. The bandage had come loose at some point.

He slowly lifted his palm to show me a weathered scar of the same crest.

I turned to Ichabod with a dark smile. "Team Temple rocks. Where's yours, Icky?"

Matthias grumbled. "I will not have my sons fighting. Or great-great-great-grandson fighting my son." He finally sighed. "Temple will not fight Temple. We have enough enemies."

"In point of fact, Temple *will* fight Temple if Icky doesn't jump off the crazy train sometime soon. I won't let him wake a god. You should know. You tried, and it broke you."

Matthias nodded. "But from what you tell me, these are different times. And we have a Maker in the family again. I can tell him what I did wrong. And you could always take back your Beast," he offered casually.

I threw my hands in the air. "No. Not going to happen. I got rid of it for a reason—"

And the room grew silent until Matthias finished my statement. "Because you didn't want to end up like me..." he said softly, nodding without disdain. "Understandable." His gaze grew distant, and even Ichabod shifted his gaze away from me for a time.

I continued to pretend Indie did not exist.

She had known this information – whether true or not – but rather than telling me, she had kept it close. Attacked me. All she would have had to do was tell me—

"That never would have worked, Nate, and you know it," she whispered. "The second I would have said something bad about the notoriously righteous Temple clan, you would have shut down. Told me I was brainwashed. That the Grimms were controlling me. That Ichabod was controlling me." She leaned forward. "When it was really *you* being controlled... by your own father."

She didn't say this with malice, but with the cold, unrelenting eyes of truth.

She genuinely believed it. And she was one smart cookie. It was why I had hired her, and ultimately, proposed to her. She was made of rare stuff. Having been a Regular her entire life, she had desired to weather the storm and join my magical world, even though I had pushed her away for so long, not wanting her to get hurt.

But then she had gotten a big dose of power, and that power had changed her. Corrupted her.

And in the end, she had hurt *me*, the big bad wizard.

I shook my head, not replying, refusing to believe her words. She was simply a mouthpiece for Ichabod. I listened as Matthias spoke. "Now you know that it wasn't just me being cracked that landed me here. It was political. Castor Queen wanted the Grimms. I wanted to destroy them. The moment I reached out to the Academy, Castor knew, and set everything in motion."

I thumbed my lip, reaching back for my drink. I took a big sip, then tapped the glass idly as I watched him. "You're telling me that the Syndicate were originally the good guys?"

Matthias dropped his gaze. "The *better* guys, maybe," he admitted.

I took another drink as Ichabod picked back up on his join-or-die spiel. "The Syndicate has been poisoned. Almost immediately after my father created them. And that poison has grown deep into the roots. The trunk is rotten, and after what they've done to our family, I can't see how you don't want to end them."

"I gave a speech today," I said, swirling my glass.

Ichabod and Indie frowned. Matthias leaned closer, watching me. "I adore speeches."

I frowned at him, wondering if he was pulling my leg, but he just stared. And I remembered that he came from a time where a speech was a big event. Men spent months, years, drafting a speech. Because it was their only means of communicating with the masses. Especially in the American Colonies. They had to nail it. Right then. Right there.

"Mine was really just a threat."

Ichabod rolled his eyes. "If you're trying to impress or scare me, do get on with it, so that I can show you my previously-prepared mock fear, and we can move on to the real fucking issue."

"Language," Matthias warned in a fatherly tone.

Surprisingly, it worked.

I shook my head at Ichabod's comment. "I threatened to bring the Academy war. I might have hinted – just a little – that I would use my Horseman mantle to mete out justice if they didn't play nice." I held out the coin from my pocket, showing Ichabod and Indie. The room was silent. I let it build, taking another small sip before pocketing the coin again. "I meant every word. They crossed a line. They think I'm working with the Syndicate to doom the world somehow." And I suddenly wondered if the Academy had suspected my father of the same thing. But I couldn't take Indie's words on faith. Not anymore. My face didn't show this thought as I continued. "That I'm building an army to challenge them."

Ichabod's eyes gleamed with anticipation, no doubt imagining me bringing that to the table.

I met his eyes. "The Syndicate hates me. They seem to hate quite a few of us Freaks, or at least they make their riches off of the backs of our misery," I said to Ichabod, referring to the circus, among other things. "Anyway, I told you that to say this. My threat to the Academy equally applies to the Syndicate."

Ichabod clapped. "That's the spirit—"

I held up a finger. "But we will not wake a goddamn god to do it," I added.

He laughed out loud. "You're willing to abuse a power that hasn't even been entirely granted to you," he pointed at my pocket, "and call out the Riders to clean up your enemies, and you believe this is more noble than waking up a god?" He shook his head in disbelief. "Own it, boy. I am. My plan will *end* their scourge."

"A scourge that your own father strengthened," Indie added in a soft tone.

I snapped at her. "What proof do you have?" I pointed at Ichabod angrily. "Him? Really?"

She sighed, as if entertaining a toddler's hissy fit. "Drop the Temple Tantrum, Nate. If you won't believe us, why don't you ask him yourself?" she snapped right back.

"It's so nice to have the family together again, isn't it?" Matthias grinned softly at the three angry Freaks in his home. "But perhaps we should focus on what we can agree on…"

"Rumpelstiltskin," Indie leaned forward.

Matthias shot me an uneasy look. I shook my head, and saw Ichabod make a motion out of the corner of my eye. He drew a finger across his throat, reminding me of my friends.

Shit.

Matthias pleaded with me. "Perhaps their plan has merit… Have you at least considered it?"

I let out a loud breath. "Of course I've considered it. And it only took me two seconds to realize how terrible of an idea it is." I pointed at Indie. "Despite her progressed control, she doesn't stand a chance leading them. This isn't anything personal, Indie," I growled as she began to argue. "They have been Grimms their entire lives, and have been locked away for hundreds of years. They are more animal than man. Nothing like the Grimms Matthias had in his day. They. Want. Vengeance. Or did you forget that fact after, you know, they killed you to get to me?"

I was panting, and hadn't realized I had been pounding the table with my fist to enunciate each word.

Before anyone could argue, I pressed on. "Ichabod fucking lived with them over there. He *knows* what they're like."

Ichabod nodded in agreement. "That is why we must *use* them. They are animals that we can use to our *advantage*. In combination with your menagerie of Shifters, my Beast, a God, your Horsemen, Chateau Falco, and the stones *embedded* in her damn arm that can control the Grimms, we actually stand a chance to *end* the Syndicate. Once and for all. Free the world from their control. Their madness. Their corruption." He locked eyes with Indie, giving her a confident smile. "I *trained* her, Nate. Not just to master her abilities, but how to master *them*. *All* of them. She can do it, boy. Give her some credit."

I shrugged. "You want us to sell our souls to beat them. Just like Castor Queen sold his soul to get rid of Matthias." I folded my arms. "Sins of our fathers… Not with my help."

Matthias had been silent, watching us go back and forth with a pensive look, and I hoped that name-dropping his nemesis would put him firmly on my side.

"I think I must agree with my son on this one, Nate." My hope died. By fire. Then firing squad. "Nothing personal. But after hundreds of years, they are likely deeply entrenched in every major facet of the supernatural world. It will take this level of fortitude and dedication to break them." He studied Ichabod. "You truly trust she can manage them?"

He nodded confidently. "She can. And if she has any issues, I will be there to support her."

"Because you did *so* well against them last time. I remember a pretty necklace they gave you. Not a necklace, but some word I can't recall. It rhymed with *leash*," I said, frowning in thought.

His eyes were livid, and if Matthias hadn't lifted a hand to stop him, that might have been my last breath.

"Boys," he warned. Ichabod actually wilted a bit, but shot me a nasty look first. Then he cleared his throat. "Silver Tongue. You have visitors," he bellowed, snapping his fingers.

The man instantly appeared before us.

Indie and Ichabod both gasped in horror.

"Holy Hell..." Indie whispered.

"This wasn't my idea," I told him with a sad frown. Which made him all sorts of terrified.

He actually peed himself. I realized in that moment that I had a gift for causing this.

Matthias grimaced at the smell. "You are to be handed off to new jailers. You may remember the name *Ichabod* from your misspent youth. Ichabod Temple, my *son*. He needs something from you, and it would please me for you to provide it to him. Promptly. No deals. In fact, this *is* your deal. I will no longer punish you for hurting my grandson, Nate."

Rumpelstiltskin peed himself even more at mention of Ichabod, his wary eyes flicking back and forth to Indie, myself, and finally Ichabod. He looked sickened, haunted, and... messy.

"I'm not sitting next to him," I offered, wondering what the hell I could do to stop this.

"I don't understand," he rasped, as if not having spoken in a few months. Which was likely.

"It is not your place to understand, Silver Tongue. Only to obey," Ichabod spoke softly, eyes twinkling. "Any act of betrayal will subject you to my own displeasure. And I'll do my best to live up to my father's oh-so-high standards," he grinned wickedly, glancing at Matthias.

Rumpelstiltskin's eyes widened, not having realized that he had been summoned into the middle of a family drama. Or at least not having connected it yet. But working for the Syndicate, it was entirely likely that he had known of their relation.

Ichabod handed the cane handle to his father. "Hold onto this for me. A pledge that one day I will return to free you from this hellhole. Once I have avenged our family." He shot me an ugly look as he said it, implying that I had dishonored our name.

Matthias unhappily took the cane, with two fingers, and then shoved it in a white bone box I hadn't seen. Then he locked it with an ivory key I also hadn't seen. Then the box simply disappeared, and he quickly brushed his hands on his pants. Then he nodded, a very hopeful smile on his face as he stared at his son.

Papa Temple had just made it abundantly clear he would do anything for his son.

Even end the world.

Anything to get his freedom and family back. Anything to attain vengeance on Castor Queen. My stomach felt like a bowl of rancid, flammable oil as I stood, turning my back on them. I had tried. And failed. The Grimms were coming back.

CHAPTER 46

I paced in the cavern, walking the length of the room, hoping that the waterfall would calm me down. We had left the Hatter—

Matthias, I corrected myself. *Matthias Temple*.

And although he had shot me many uneasy looks, he had ultimately sided with his son.

Rumps – unsurprisingly – needed some time to recuperate, and rather than keeping me around to kill Dark Team Temple's mood, they had seen no reason to deny my departure. They had what they wanted. They didn't think I could do anything to stop them. They were going to get the Grimms back, and then rob the Syndicate of their HOGs. And wake a god.

At least I had convinced them that they had to call back the Grimms on my property, beneath the tree, stressing that it would lend her credit in their eyes. They would sense the final resting place of their fallen Brothers. Where Indie had been rebirthed as a Grimm, and where a giant, fucking, impressive alien tree towered hundreds of feet in the air.

I wasn't sure if it really mattered, but I felt better with the resources I had here.

I let out an angry breath, startling Mallory, who had made it back from Phoenix very concerned. Because we hadn't ever showed back up at the hotel. Achilles and Gunnar had been magically dropped off at his bar, and had immediately called Dean. But Dean and Mallory hadn't heard from me. Since time with the Hatter moved at a different pace than my world, it wasn't long before I showed back up, startling Dean and Mallory.

My disappearance had taken a bit of explaining, and Dean had called Gunnar to fill him in.

Which meant it was late when I grabbed Mallory by the arm and led him here, to the cavern.

Pan, not *Mallory*.

Was anyone truly who they had pretended to be? Who I had *known* them to be? It seemed everyone was wearing a mask of some kind. That thought made me acutely aware of my own Mask in my pocket, still shaped like a Silver Dollar. I had yet to truly look at its true form – the face of the Mask – not wanting to tempt myself. Or soil my pants.

But no matter how many times I had told myself I would lock it away in the Armory, it still sat in my pocket. Because I didn't want to let it out of my sight.

And…

My father was in the Armory.

The one who had allegedly been working for the Syndicate for the last few years prior to his murder. Making the Armory off limits now. Out of principle. Because stowing it there would mean I would need to confront him, and I wasn't ready for that. With all the secrets and lies, it was hard not to entertain Indie's claim, even though the larger part of me denied it outright.

But part of me still wanted to kill him.

Even though he was already dead.

He had never told me about the Syndicate, good or bad. And with all the craziness going on lately, he'd had ample time to do so. Any one of the times I had entered the Armory to share my problems with them or Pandora, for example.

But he hadn't.

Which either meant it was all a lie – like I hoped – or that he had known how I would react, and hadn't dared add on to my already dire problems. Or he hoped I would never discover it.

"Pan," I called out. I heard him hurrying my way, not running, but politely and obediently obeying. He was a freaking god, but he still acted like my batman. My bodyguard. I had found out what – who – he truly was, and it had been more or less painless. Because I had spent time around him, seen him act. If he had wanted to abuse me as a Maker, make me his pet, he could have done so many times. Any time I had been injured. But he had simply patched me up, put me back on my feet, and joined my side to go back into the fight.

Actions speak loudly, folks.

Still... This whole thing had started with him and my father, and if my father was Darth Vader... Pan could be as well, or he was about to hear one hell of a surprise...

He reached my side, no longer bothering to hide his true form since we were secluded in the mysterious cavern – or *Sanctorum*, as Ichabod had named it – and no one else could enter here. I had caught him up to date on my failed theft of the HOG, how the black-fog woman had saved me. I assumed she was with the Syndicate, because her partner in crime had drugged Tory and left that note. Then attacked us at the school.

A new thought hit me. Had she known my father? Had she... *worked* for him? Was that why she had saved me? Because she had been his employee? If so, why hadn't I gotten any recruitment letters? It was pretty obvious to the world that I was anti-Academy. Shouldn't the Syndicate have approached me before things went so far south?

I shook my head. My father was innocent. He had to be.

I focused on the god, the wild one. The horned god. Pan.

"You seem... pensive," he said.

"Wary."

"Weary?"

I shook my head. "No. Untrusting."

He nodded carefully, his wicked horns glinting in the purple torchlight. "Anything I can do to appease your mistrust?" he asked.

I was silent for a few moments, thinking. "I... don't distrust *you*, Pan.

But I'm beginning to fear that *no one* has been up front with me lately, nefariously so..."

He sucked in a small breath, seeming relieved that I wasn't referring to him. But this was about to stress the bounds of our relationship. Find out who he really worked for.

I met his eyes. "You worked for my father for a long time. Drove him around, protected him. I would say that he trusted you more than almost anyone. After all, he sought you out in order to help me down the road, correct?"

Mallory nodded, betraying nothing on his weathered face.

"Who was he, really? What did you think of him?"

Mallory hesitated, thinking. "This sounds like a loaded question..."

I shook my head. "I need an answer. Why did he do what he did every day? You were around him the most."

"He spent a fair amount of time around your mother, too," he chuckled.

I didn't laugh, not even wanting to consider *her*, and whether she had also been a member of the Syndicate.

He caught my mood, and frowned, studying me. "He wanted to do what was best for the Freaks. Always. Above all. He would go to great lengths to make sure they were taken care of when the Academy wouldn't do what needed to be done."

I nodded slowly, glancing away for a moment, struggling against my next question. I finally took a deep breath and turned back to him. "Are you a member of the Syndicate?" I asked, ready to defend myself.

Mallory guffawed. "No, boy. I'm a god. We don't do *clubs*. I'm just a bodyguard for your family. A protector to help you on your path."

I slowly let out my breath, grateful for at least that much. "Was my father involved with the Syndicate?" I whispered.

Dead silence met me. I slowly moved my hand closer to my pocket, just in case.

He watched me, completely still. "Perhaps this is something you should ask him..."

My pulse began to race. "You realize that your evasive answer *is* an answer, right?"

Mallory slowly nodded. "Aye, but there is more to the sto—"

"Motherfucker!" I shouted, throwing my hands up into the air. Lightning hammered into the ceiling, enough force to blast a hole through the roof. It was instinctive, primal, not cognitively decided. My rage simply took over for a heartbeat.

Chateau Falco growled in disapproval.

"Can it, Beast!" I shouted, letting loose another volley into the ceiling.

Chateau Falco grumbled in response, but grew quiet. The lightning died, and where I expected to see a hole in the roof, I only saw the same old pretty constellation-like gems. Warded. I grunted angrily. I couldn't even throw a proper Temple Tantrum. Part of me almost smiled at Indie saying that. She had often teased me about it in the past.

But so many things had changed since then.

I turned to see Mallory on the tips of his hooves, ready to flee or defend himself from me. Not defend and kill, but prevent me from harming him or… myself. Genuine sadness filled his eyes, and I could tell he wanted to say so much more.

He opened his mouth to speak, and then closed it, waiting for me. I nodded at him, waving a dismissive hand. "Go on," I muttered.

"I will tell you whatever you want, honestly, truth in every detail, pulling no punches…" he began. "However, I would prefer you speak to him about his choices. I don't like to talk about people when they aren't here to defend themselves. You deserve answers to your questions, but I shouldn't have to pay the price for those answers." He waited until I finally gave him a resigned nod. "That being said, all you need do is ask, and I will answer… Because I don't work for him any longer. Truth be told, I only worked for *him* so that I could one day work for *you*…" I could feel the honesty in his tone.

A small part of me reached out to that comment like a lifeline. I needed it in that moment, because I was in a very dark place. Loyalty.

"I need you to promise me something. When I talk to you, am I really speaking with someone else? As in, are your loyalties for me trumped by any other god, being, or group?"

He shook his head, and I let out a soft breath of relief.

"If I speak to you, what is said is never to leave your lips. Ever. Even if my life is in danger as a result. Not until I'm dead and buried for a decade. Can you accept this?"

Mallory let out a hungry grin. "It was always that way, Master Temple," he whispered. "But I'll do you one better. Since you have enough drama for several reality TV shows," he said sadly. And a vortex of golden light suddenly surrounded him. He used his horns to slice open his palm, drawing blood. Looking closely, I could see that his blood was flecked with flashes of silver and gold and light. Crimson, still, but like a sparkling, royal crimson.

And he swore an oath to serve me. Period. Only me. Not Zeus. Odin, or any other god. Not Shiva, Ganesh, or the Big G. Only me, Nate Temple. *Master* Nate Temple. No matter what happened, who it betrayed, who it hurt, he was mine. The end. "I brand this oath to my bones."

As he finished speaking, the words wrapped around him, swirling like a mini cyclone, and then they hammered into his flesh, and judging by the look of true pain on his face, it seemed to *literally* brand his bones.

A burning stench even permeated him for a moment, and his skin looked red and tender to the touch. He took a deep, shaky breath, and then met my eyes, waiting.

"Where do you hide my Macallan?" I asked, miming a spell of supreme, untamable power with wild hand flourishes, as if he could no longer deny my authority.

He grunted. "Wasn't part of the contract," he winked. I scowled at him and he began to laugh. "I'll tell you this. I'm the wild god." And he leaned forward with a clever glint in his eyes. "I will always know where to find the *good stuff*. Be right back, boy."

I laughed, rolling my eyes as he disappeared. I made my way to the fireplace in the center of the main area in the cavern. I lit the fire with my magic, not bothering to see if there was some magical switch to do so, and leaned back into a chair, thinking furiously.

He appeared a moment later with a wooden tray, seemingly carved from the oldest tree I had ever seen. The tray held a glorious bottle of the fifty-year-old Macallan, two Gurkha Black Dragon cigars, and two wooden cups – looking as if carved from the same source as the tray.

"Come now, boy. You can tell your bartender your troubles…" he grinned, pouring me a glass. And I shared my thoughts, what I possibly planned to do.

His eyes widened as I spoke, but he didn't laugh at me, knowing my penchant for wild plans that always seemed to go my way. Or at least a little bit my way. We spoke for a very long time, and although we didn't get hammered drunk, it was an… interesting walk back to my rooms. I briefly remember commanding one of the griffin Guardians to fly me to my bed.

He didn't. But I think several did escort me back, like the Secret Service did for the President.

CHAPTER 47

I sensed someone standing near me as I lay in bed. I instantly rolled off, struck the nightstand with my nose, and fell on my back, knocking the wind out of me. "Here comes an ass whipping," I wheezed to the intruder.

"Master Temple," Dean's voice sounded urgent. "You have a visitor. And you smell like a used bar rag."

Not an attack. Just Dean, my butler. "Well, you take the usual precautions, and I'll go take a quick shower."

Dean walked around the bed to stare down at me. "She is outside the Gates, and refuses to proceed further. She instead demands that you meet her."

I blinked. "Demands?" I growled in disbelief.

Dean nodded slowly, his face ashen. "Mallory has her in his crosshairs, but advised me to tell you he shouldn't shoot." Dean saw the flash of anger on my face. "He thought it… unwise."

"Bloody terrible idea, more like it," Mallory's gruff squawked on the radio on Dean's hip.

I climbed to my feet. "Who the hell thinks they can show up to *my* house, stand at *my* gates, and demand *me* to come out?" I asked, genuinely stunned at the ego. "Is it Van Helsing? Doesn't want another sniper round to mess up his shirt?" Then I remembered. "Wait. You said *she*."

Dean just nodded. "If you would please meet me at the front door when you are refreshed, Master Temple. I believe all will be clear momentarily."

I grumbled at his back as he departed, slapping my cheeks, wondering what time it was. It felt like I had only just fallen asleep, but I'd had a trying few days behind me. Regardless, I knew that Indie and Ichabod were going to attempt to open the gateway to the Dark Realm with the Brothers Grimm tonight. Mallory and I had spent a few midnight hours in the cavern, discussing plans, how we could stop them, how we could get the Hand of God back from the Syndicate. Hell, *if* we should get the Hand of God back from the Syndicate.

After all, if they had it, Ichabod wasn't likely to get it.

Not without my help.

It looked like me laying around after this Grimm ordeal, maybe catching a movie and taking a nap, could likely solve all my problems. Causing a stalemate.

But I knew my luck, and as if the universe was reminding me, some random stranger now stood outside my gates. Demanding things. Maybe it was Indie, trying to talk to me without Ichabod present, but not being able to come inside the walls. I entered the bathroom, slapped some water on my cheeks, wiped on some deodorant, and fidgeted with my hair.

Then I summoned Carl as I strode down the hallway towards the stairs. He appeared beside me a moment later, following a pace back, waiting for my command.

"I think we have an unwanted guest at the gates. I want you to keep your eyes out. Don't act unless shit goes sideways, but be ready to interfere if necessary."

Carl's thin reptilian lips tightened hungrily as he nodded.

"And no eating them this time," I warned. His smile vanished, replaced by a darker, smoldering hunger. "Don't get hangry on me. I have enough going on."

"Yes, Master Temple," he said obediently, but I could definitely feel him biting his tongue.

Because he was an Elder, and they fed on souls. His kind had been banished by a tag-team of every supernatural nation in existence.

Now that I thought about it, there had been a lot of banishing going on in the past several hundred years. When those alive deemed it prudent to simply put a lid on the problem rather than eliminating the problem. Which just meant some lucky SOB like me got to deal with it later when they broke out.

We reached the front door – which had been replaced numerous times – to find Dean standing there, waiting. He pulled open the door, and extended a hand for us to exit. "Be ready," I whispered to him as I walked past.

Chateau Falco heard me as well, and I felt a sudden *thrum* of energy emanating from her walls, whether defensive or offensive, I didn't know. But the house would be fine. I gathered that much. Dean rubbed his arms idly, studying me. I shook my head and patted the door frame. "Wasn't me," I smiled as I walked out.

And because Dean was the butler to a pretentious once-billionaire asshole, he had a car waiting for me. An ivory-colored Bentley that gleamed in the sun as if cream had literally just been poured into a mold. Carl murmured appreciatively, and I grinned, glancing back over my shoulder. Dean wore a self-satisfied smirk. He loved his job. A vicarious asshole.

The wheels gleamed in the sunlight like molten chrome, and the engine purred softly, idling. I turned to Carl, assessing him, and then shook my head. He frowned. "I was thinking you might disappear against the color, but you're pastier."

His face had no reaction. Which either meant he didn't get it, or didn't find it funny.

Must be the former.

I climbed inside, motioning him to open the passenger door. Sure, most billionaires had drivers, but Carl wasn't really chauffeur quality, and Mallory was busy with a sniper rifle on the roof. So, with a great sigh of disdain, I settled in behind the wheel, putting on my airs at such a task being so beneath me. Because this mystery guest likely expected to see that.

Carl grunted from beside me, rubbing his claws idly on the seats. Then he took a very deep whiff through his nose holes, blue eyes closing in ecstasy. "Calfskin. Delicious. I can almost still hear the echoes of their dying screams as they were sacrificed to furnish your luxury," he commented casually, literally just speaking his mind.

I stared at him for a very long moment. "Just when I think you can't get any creepier, Carl...," I finally said, and shifted the car into gear.

He nodded absently, taking it as a compliment.

And I drove down the driveway, watching the trees zip by on either side like a tunnel.

We neared the gate, and I slowly came to a stop. I stared at the person on the opposite side of the ancient gate through my windshield. I hadn't expected *her*. In fact, I kind of wanted to turn the car around. I sat there long enough that even Carl shot me a questioning look.

"Are we playing a game, or are you trying to anger her?" he asked, genuinely curious.

I smiled. "Good idea." And I began fiddling with the stereo as I rolled down my window. I accessed the playlist stored in the car – courtesy of Dean – and cranked up Jet's *Ice Cold Bitch* as loud as I could. I sat there, listening to the opening riff, letting the guitar intro roll over me.

Carl clapped his hands over his ear holes at the explosion of sound. I snickered and rolled the rest of the windows down. Then the sunroof. I studied the interior of the car for a few moments, then glanced at my *guest*, unsatisfied. I held up a finger for her to hold on a moment.

I shifted the car into reverse, backed up a few feet, and then pulled forward again, turning the wheels so that the side of my car now faced the gates. I parked and climbed out, leaving my door wide open. Then I opened the driver's side backseat door – which was different from most cars. The hinges were near the back, rather than the center of the car. This was designed so that the driver could open his boss's door with minimal fuss, rather than having to waste a few seconds taking two additional steps to reach the door handle.

The things that money could buy...

This effectively created a cone of sound cast directly at her, blaring the chorus of the song, now. *Cold Hard Bitch, just a kiss on the lips...*

I smiled and waved at her. "Good—" I looked up at the sky, realizing the sun was directly above us, "afternoon," I finished. "To what do I owe the pleasure?"

She studied me from beyond the gate, and then she took a big old *whiff*. I frowned as she let out a frustrated growl. Her eyes tracked to the sign I had recently installed. A great wooden piece that said *Beware of* – but a giant claw or bite mark obliterated whatever the sign had been warning against. "It wasn't you," G Ma hissed, turning back to me.

"That wasn't creepy." I looked at Carl pointedly. "And I know creepy." He nodded back politely. I both loved and hated Carl for little things like that. It was hard to upset him.

I turned back to G Ma. "What were you checking me for?" But I knew. She wanted to see who had robbed her, but since I had masked my powers with my... Mask, she couldn't pinpoint the flavor of magic at the scene of the crime. The silver light and licorice-type smell I apparently gave off. I was suddenly very glad that I hadn't taken the coin with me downstairs. I had hidden it in a secret compartment in my room that I was sure even Dean didn't know of.

She turned to Carl and sniffed him, too. He sniffed right back, eyes rolling back into his head. *"Delightful,"* he breathed. "You've experienced so many years of pain and loss I could lick away... Mind if I have a nibble?" He grinned through inky black teeth.

She stepped back in surprise, and then seemed to take him in for the first time, as if suddenly recognizing him. Her eyes locked onto mine. I grinned. "What have you done?" she whispered.

"Creepy Elder Carl, meet senile Wizard G Ma," I chuckled.

"You ignorant fool!" she spat, furious.

I shrugged. "That obviously isn't what you came here for. Did you just come to get a whiff of Eau de Nate? Or are you ready to skip the foreplay? I've got things to do, right, Carl?"

He grunted affirmatively.

Her outrage was a physical presence, seeming to make the air suddenly heavier. But almost as soon as it began, the air lightened again. She blinked in disbelief, staring from Carl to me, and then to the mansion perched on the slight hill behind us. I guess my house hadn't liked her magic, even if it had been just a reaction of her emotions.

I let my smile grow wider, turning into a yawn. I shrugged, motioning for her to proceed.

Her gaze lingered on the home thoughtfully, but she finally dismissed it. "You have declared war on the Academy, murdering two—"

"Technically, it's not murder when you are defending yourself from an act of war. They actually call that a *casualty*. Right, Carl?"

"Yes, Master Temple. My brothers even use the bones of these casualties to create new weapons. Circle of Life. Better for everyone."

G Ma's face was a disgusted mask, but I managed to keep the sickened feeling that hit my stomach off of my face as I motioned for her to continue. *Fucking Carl…*

She composed herself, deciding to simply ignore Carl. "You believe that your various friends, powers, and upbringing allows you to behave in such a manner. But you forget. You are a wizard again," her smile was back, and it dripped venom. "Such wizardly disagreements are not handled by War, but by a Duel… between the parties involved. You and I."

She slipped a thick, folded letter through the gate, then turned on a heel, taking a few steps away. Carl handed me the piece of paper after checking it for traps. I read it, and my stomach dropped out of my nether regions. I looked up to see a Gateway opening before her, but I cleared my throat to stop her.

"I'll have to reschedule."

"Then I will have to destroy your city and all known associates. With the help of my own Allies. Nasty group of monsters." She smiled. "You're not the only one with friends, Temple."

"Listen. It's not that I'm changing my mind, it's that I have something to do tonight."

"Be there or don't. That is your prerogative. I'll be waiting at the…" she sneered in mockery, "Fight Club."

"Wait, first of all, that isn't a thing."

She rolled her eyes. "Secrets don't apply to me. I can discover anything."

"Okay, let's pretend there is a secret Fight Club. What are the terms?"

"Winner takes all," she laughed.

"And the loser?" I pressed.

"*He* will be forced not to retaliate against the winner, and to let them handle their business unmolested."

"Or *she*," I corrected, glaring. She nodded with a slight condescending smile. I tapped the card in my hand, thinking furiously. "Okay. I'll see you there. You know how to get there?"

She rolled her eyes. "King Midas and I go way back," she chuckled huskily. "Way, *way*, back," she hinted suggestively. Gross.

"Right. See you there, I guess. Any particular rules?" I asked, wondering how the hell I was going to make this work. I was supposed to be here, to somehow thwart Indie when she attempted to bring back the Grimms, and that meant I would need to resolve this little wrestling match quickly. Very quickly. Against the strongest wizard in the world. And I couldn't let her win or I would be effectively neutered to protect my friends.

She shrugged, unconcerned. "Bring your toys. And your Second, if you require one. I'll be prepared for either eventuality." She took one step through the Gateway before she hesitated, turning to look at me over her shoulder. "Just know that by participating, you are agreeing to the consequences. Winner takes all. Loser and his… or *her* minions may not impede the winner for one week after the Duel."

I nodded, gritting my teeth as the car blared *Cold Hard Bitch* one last time. "See you in a few hours."

But she was already gone.

CHAPTER 48

I stood in the field, growling under my breath, glancing down at my watch repeatedly. It had taken me a few hours to get everything ready, but here we were. Punctual.

"I don't actually have to do anything, do I? I'm kind of tired," Raego said, idly extending his claws to inspect them in the fading sunlight. Only his arms were in dragon form, the rest human. His scales were an inky, glistening black. His dark hair blew in the wind, and his loose white shirt whipped back and forth revealing his well-muscled chest. He wore tight tan khakis tucked into his stupid mid-shin boots. He was much more pleasant when away from his dragons.

But he looked like a goddamned pirate.

"Don't worry. I think it will just be me. But if she has a Second, you may have to entertain him. Or her…" I added, frowning.

He shrugged. "As long as they aren't too much trouble," he murmured.

"A little professionalism would be swell. I gave you a candy-painted lizard."

He sighed, arching his back as he stretched. "It's the Dueling Grounds. We can't really die there. You *die* a horrible death, and wake up in your beautiful mansion," he shrugged.

I scowled. "It's not the dying that concerns me. It's the fact that she wants to take St. Louis for the Academy. Maybe open a chapter here. Start bossing you guys around. Maybe even declare you a threat and hunt you."

He growled, face partially shifting to that of a dragon, as dark puffs of vapor curled around his snout. Then he was back to human form. Still sporting his claws, though. "I'm not a fan of that part."

"Then get your head out of your scaly sphincter."

Out of nowhere, Asterion, the Minotaur, was standing before us. He wore a grave expression.

I smiled at him, glad to see his stupid bull face. "Hey, how have you—"

"We wait for the challenger. No speaking, please," he said in a very clipped tone.

I blinked. "You're not allowed to talk with me?"

His features cracked slightly. "It would be improper to fraternize with a contender."

Raego burst out laughing.

I took a step towards the Minotaur, and he instantly drew one boot back into a better fighting position. I halted. "Whoa. I'm not going to attack you, Asterion. What's going on here? It's just two people duking it out." I glanced at Raego. "Okay, maybe four if the JV Team gets involved."

Asterion blinked in surprise, but he recovered quickly. "Your Second will definitely be *involved*," he said curtly.

Raego's ears perked up at that. "I thought I was the backup dancer if they chose to chicken out…" he said in a dark tone.

Asterion shook his head. "The challenger will bring a Second, making it two on two."

"I don't think that's how it works. I've read about these things," I began, but the Minotaur's glare stopped me cold.

"You've read storybooks, old accounts." He took a step forward, not aggressive, but full of authority. "This is *my* place. Midas and I make the rules. And this is how it will be."

I held up my hands. "Okay. Calm down. If that's how you want it, that's how we'll play it. I've just never heard of a Duel going down like that," I said lightly, trying to calm him down. He seemed highly stressed. Anxious. Uneasy. "What's really going on, Asteri—"

"I am here, Asterion," a new voice said from behind me. I whirled to see G Ma standing mere paces away. She wore tan robes, without adornment, and she looked different. She *felt* different. I couldn't really place it precisely, but something was off. I tacked it to her likely having a talisman or artifact of some kind on her person. Something to tip the scales in her favor.

But that was fine. Like a good Boy Scout, I had come prepared as well.

Then I saw the figure behind her and blinked.

But that was nothing compared to what Raego did.

He was suddenly a full-blown black dragon, baring his giant fangs at the newcomer, puffing black fog from his nostrils as he glared at…

A little old lady.

She shook her purse at Raego. "Don't you *dare* take that tone with me, boy," she warned.

His voice was more beast than man as his eyes locked onto G Ma, the Grand Master of the Academy, who was smiling broadly. "You asked my *grandmother* to be your Second?!" He roared, emitting an outraged burst of black fire-smoke at the sky.

But the little old lady answered instead. "When a dear friend tells me that my grandson is acting up, I tend to listen. I've got a few things to remind you about manners, it seems." She scowled like every grandma could, and Raego suddenly shifted back into human form, muttering under his breath as he stood there, naked. The grandmother looked him up and down, appalled at his impropriety as she leaned closer to G Ma, whispering loud enough for all to hear. "He used to do that as a boy. Always running around with his wee little dangly flying free."

"Grandma!" Raego hissed.

The old women chuckled knowingly before turning back to us.

Asterion cleared his throat, and pulled back an invisible curtain.

The roar of a very large crowd rolled over us, and I heard a very familiar voice urging them on with a megaphone.

"Wizard versus wizard! Dragon versus dragon! I know this wasn't our previously scheduled fight, but let me assure you, this one will go down in the books... The matrons want to teach their progeny a lesson..."

"Fucking Achilles!" I snarled, rounding on Asterion, who looked guilty. "I didn't know it was Fight Night!" I argued. "How many people are here?" I all but shouted. I had thought we would have some privacy, not an arena.

He shifted from foot to foot, motioning me further inside, where the crowd was shouting even louder now. "All of them," he said honestly.

Grandma Dragon complained behind me. "Raego, be a good boy and help your grandmother across this shit-infested field. Honestly, you were raised better than this." I turned in disbelief to see Raego with his arm around her shoulder, assisting her through the field, pointing out fresh patties for her to avoid. He even clutched her purse in one hand. He wouldn't meet my eyes. I grumbled under my breath, and her beady little eyes locked on to me. "But perhaps it's just the company you keep," she added.

"Yes, grandmother," Raego mumbled.

"Fucking great," I snarled, shooting one last hateful look at G Ma before I strode past Asterion and into the Dueling Grounds. Her laughter followed me inside the ring, somehow overpowering the riot of cheers and shouts.

CHAPTER 49

We stood face-to-face in the center of the ring, stands of people surrounding us, hooting, hollering, and drinking. The bookie made his rounds, but I didn't check to see the odds. I needed a clear head.

I had recognized many faces, even the gorillas, who nodded at me with big smiles of appreciation. Ganesh sat beside Achilles and Shiva, who was eagerly devouring a bag of grapes. Ganesh didn't look pleased, and judging by his battle armor, I must have taken his moment of glory with this unasked-for duel.

With two little old ladies.

I saw Cain smirking at me – the Biblically-famous, world's first murderer, of his brother, Abel – and remembered his promise to make me pay for a comment I'd once made – telling one of the Horsemen about not being *able to part with my cane*. He hadn't found the joke funny.

After Cain's look, I tuned out the crowd, focusing instead on the two old ladies before me. I addressed G Ma. "How did you know I would ask Raego to be my Second?"

Duelists were typically allowed to exchange words prior to the fight, and Asterion seemed open to allowing this, even though he had changed the rule about Seconds.

Then again, with the crowd present, and the fact that we had interrupted their scheduled Fight Night, I could understand why. These warriors wanted a show. And with theirs taken away from them, it was up to me to provide them with an alternative.

Which I was more than ready to do right about now. To use it as an outlet to unleash all my pent-up anger from the last few days in one nuclear explosion.

She shrugged at me. "Wasn't that hard to anticipate. I didn't think you would bring your dog, because he's too busy guarding the violent horde of monsters in that school of yours. What better Second is there? A sovereign ruler of a supernatural nation." She shrugged. "That being said, I would have asked Gertrude to help anyway. She's quite… formidable," G Ma laughed, glancing pointedly at Raego, who was idly kicking the dirt with his toes, not meeting his grandmother's judging look.

"Stop that, you big baby," I growled at him.

He looked up at me, face desperate. "She's my grandmother, Nate. I can't beat up my grandmother. She used to box my ears. And make me cookies." His eyes flicked her way. "And she has a temper. She's so controlling—"

I strode up to him and slapped him across the face with my open palm. "Get your shit together, man!" His eyes latched onto me, infinite pools of darkness as I awoke his anger. "No real harm can come to her here. Just pretend it's a dream where you can finally stand up to her. You're the *king* of the freaking dragons, man. Act like it. Technically, she's *your* subject! I don't have time to change diapers!" I hissed, turning my back on him.

He called over my shoulder softly. "Either way, we lose, Nate. We either beat up two old women, or we get beat up by two old women," he muttered, sounding depressed.

I sighed. "My pride can take that. Just not the ultimate consequences. We have to win, so I can stop the Academy from—"

G Ma cleared her throat. I turned to her, frowning. "Point of clarity. I am no longer the Grand Master of the Academy. I swore-off my title prior to delivering you the invitation to our Duel."

My heart stopped. And her smile grew. "You…"

She nodded. "Quite right. Did you really think the Academy would risk getting involved? Committing to possibly ignore your crimes. Based on the outcome of a silly duel?" She shook her head in amusement. "I am acting as a mere member of the Academy, trying to prevent a child from throwing a temper tantrum that could harm all of us. And thus, I have no minions."

"But you said—"

"The loser of the duel must not interfere with the winner's actions for a one-week period. I am not a title-holding member of the Academy. Just one very old, very strong, stubborn wizard."

I took a deep breath, thinking. "You're just a wizard right now. Who leads the Academy in your stead?"

"They don't discuss issues like that with the rank-and-file wizards, but I think it's safe to say they will vote on a new leader. Tonight. After the results of our duel are known."

Which probably meant that she would be reinstated if she won, but not if she lost.

I was about to take her title away. I wasn't sure how I felt about that. Sure, she was a big stinky asshole, but what about the next guy? Would he or she be a bigger, stinkier asshole?

She was the monster I knew.

"Opponents, prepare to face—" Asterion began.

"Wait! I have something to say," I interjected, a sudden thought coming to mind.

Asterion frowned, shooting a quick glance at Achilles, who had leaned forward with interest. "That's not part of the Duel…"

"Sure it is. The whole point of this," and I lifted my voice for all to hear, "is to produce a show. An outlet for your bloodlust, right?" I shouted at the crowd. They roared in response. I glanced at Asterion and then Achilles, hoping they let me proceed. Achilles looked amused.

"I don't see the harm in it," he shouted out.

G Ma began to protest, but I held up a hand. "You can have a speech, too. But let me finish. I hate it when persistent, nagging old women try to tell me what to do, speak over me, think they know everything."

Again, I said this loud enough for all to hear, and the crowd loved me for it.

I took a few steps, holding up my hands as I spun in a slow circle. "You came here for your regular Fight Night," I pointed a finger back at G Ma. "But she took that from you. Still, I can promise you a good show. Maybe even better than your regularly scheduled event." I winked.

Their laughter and applause thundered across the clearing. I squinted at the perpetual sunset, glancing at the flickering torches ringing the Dueling Grounds behind the bleachers.

"Chaos, carnage, and blood, you will get," I smiled broadly. "You've all fought in the ring. Earned your stripes, or your arrows for loose lips." Many chuckled at that, because one wasn't supposed to talk about Fight Club, and was used as target practice for one month if they broke this sacred oath. "You *know* me. I've earned my stripes, too. I helped set this place up with Midas and Asterion. Despite losing to that old man that one time," I shrugged in embarrassment, "you know that I have the… gift to entertain, and typically bring more than asked for. Just look at my real-world hobbies…" Murmurs filled the crowd in a hushed, but persistent buzz as the audience briefly shared clipped tales about my life with each other. I let it build for a minute, and then die down, knowing I had their complete attention now. "That being said," I began, "There is at least one person in the crowd who doesn't belong." I leaned forward. "*Find them.*"

The crowd went silent, and then they roared in outrage, overshadowing G Ma's sudden arguments. I smiled over my shoulder at her. "Nice try," I mouthed. For the Academy to vote on a new leader, they would have to immediately know the outcome of the fight. Because they were very strict about their rules. Waiting for her to appear back in her bed after she lost would make them seem weak. But making a decision on a new leader a moment before the outcome was known to the public would make their decision seem legitimate.

I had gambled, hoping to take that away from her.

Because for the Academy to know, someone had to be spying on our little party here.

It turned into a witch hunt, and in a clearing full of experienced, hardened killers, they were very efficient. Also, they all knew each other, because they had spent the last few months watching each other fight and die.

One white-haired, portly gentleman was soon shoved into the ring, face red as he panted. I took a few steps closer, shaking my head sadly, recognizing him from the Gala. "Tsk, tsk, tsk," I murmured, circling him like a shark. The crowd began stomping their feet in unison, a slow, steady, thunderous drumbeat.

"I-I was only doing as told," he argued, suddenly terrified. I wasn't sure he knew the specifics of the place, but either way, this was going to be fun.

"You should know that when you bring a sword to the big boys' table, they all have swords, too," I grinned menacingly.

I turned my back on him, finding Achilles. He nodded at me, grinning like a wolf, and the look in his eyes was impressed, and thankful. *Set an example.* That was his thing.

I turned back to the fat, old wizard, shrugged, and then snapped my fingers at Raego. He instantly shifted to a huge black dragon, and roared, sending a cloud of black smoke straight at the wizard's chest. He flung up his hands in defense, but as the smoke washed over him, he froze into an obsidian statue, still holding his hands out protectively, a mask of horror on his face.

I stepped closer and reached out a hand. I tapped his chest with a fingernail, loud enough for all to hear.

Once.

Twice.

Then I called Stone Skin around my fist, and gave him a theatrical right cross to the chest.

He exploded into a billion tiny fragments of obsidian wizard.

"Nice," Raego commented.

I dusted off my hands, bowed to the crowd, Achilles, Asterion, and then to G Ma.

"Oh. Did you have anything you wanted to say?" I asked gently. "I didn't mean to take so much time with my little speech."

The smile that split my cheeks was entirely genuine as fury overtook her.

She shook her head, lips tightening.

Asterion cleared his throat. "Duelists, prepare. Cage match. Whatever you have on your person is allowed. On the count of *three*. ONE… TWO… THREE!"

CHAPTER 50

*G*Ma shrieked, using her aged vocal chords to shatter my ear drums, and it was definitely magically enhanced. Because it made me stumble.

Which had been her point. She leveled a finger at me almost simultaneously.

But I'd already been reaching into my pocket, and quickly threw up the small glass bead right as a fiery spear flew my way, dripping liquid fire onto the ground as it screamed through the air. My small, tiny glass bead zipped over to the projectile as if magnetically attracted.

But it wasn't magnetic. If anything, it was magic-etic, latching onto any significant power coming towards the last person who touched the bead – in this case, *me*.

One of my little defensive prototypes from Grimm Tech. To be honest, I didn't even have to throw it. It would have worked just as well from my pocket, although it would have ripped through the fabric, or burned through it, catching my pants on fire and giving me third-degree burns. We hadn't solved that little glitch yet.

The bead *ate* the spear, turning it into a tiny little puff of ash.

I laughed out loud, only to find a dozen new fiery spears suddenly screaming my way, like an invading army storming the gates of a besieged castle. I desperately reached into my pocket to cast the rest of the beads up in the air, hoping I had enough. They were prototypes, so I had brought what I could when I had raided Grimm Tech after first hearing about the Duel.

I dove to the side, lashing out with my elemental whips at the last second. A firecracker sound ensued mid-air as the beads ate her spears, but several did land where I had been standing, charring the earth in great, big, explosive divots.

My whip latched onto her ankle, and I yanked as hard as I could, not letting go. She gasped as the pain of unbearable ice squeezed her ankles, and then again as she was suddenly jerked my way. I met her face with my Stone Skin fist, shattering her jaw. Her face wobbled, and her eyes began to roll back into her head as she fell, and her hand came into contact with the earth. But then she was suddenly gone. I looked up to find her standing a dozen feet away, dazed.

Wow. Shadow Walking while almost knocked unconscious? That was impressive.

It only took her a second to recover, taking a deep calming breath as a golden orb illuminated the interior of her stomach. Her jaw hung loosely, but the golden orb suddenly flashed from her stomach throughout her body, like I was seeing an MRI of her insides. The golden light touched her face, almost blinding me as it pulsed. I covered my eyes, scrambling to my feet.

I took a few lateral steps, getting out of her immediate attention as I reassessed. Her face was completely healed, but she still looked dizzy, which gave me a minute to check on my partner.

Naked Raego and his grandmother simply stared at each other from six paces away.

Neither moved, advancing or retreating, but stared at each other, horizontal-pupiled dragon eyes glaring with fire. Raego's eyes were black, making it impossible to tell where he was looking since it was just a shining ebony wall across his sclera.

His grandmother had startling blue and gold-flecked eyes, which I had never seen before. I had only seen solid-colored eyes – red, green, blue, silver, black – up until Yahn, anyway.

But a mix? Nope. I could only imagine what she would look like when in dragon form.

But, of course, that wasn't happening. Because the lazy lizards just stared at each other.

"Do something!" I shouted at Raego as my eyes flicked back to G Ma. She was rolling her hands together, striding my way with confident, angry steps, a ball of nebulous green power forming. Brief flashes of electricity illuminated the interior of the orb, like she had trapped lightning in a ball.

Raego gasped as his hand suddenly shifted into a long black claw. I was momentarily relieved to see him actually doing something, until I saw his face. It was strained, angry, and desperate. Then I got it.

They were battling in their heads. Trying to force the other to shift.

And I had never seen anyone stand a chance against Raego, because he was the prophesied Obsidian Son, the ultimate shifter dragon.

So, grandma Raego was either incredibly powerful or Raego wasn't giving it his best.

I continued shuffling until Raego's grandmother was directly between G Ma and I. "Raego, come *on*! She's a little old lady! She's still holding her purse, for crying out loud. *Try!*"

He gritted his teeth, snarling, but not meeting my eyes as his other hand exploded into a claw. "She's... four... hundred... years... old," he hissed.

That stopped me short. I had no idea dragons could live that long. But I was saved from an academic conversation as G Ma flung her ball at me – but grandma Raego still stood between us, smiling at her grandson with a triumphant grin.

Little old bitty was about to get zapped by friendly-fire.

But the orb went straight through her without harm, and it was suddenly all I could do to defend myself. I threw my arms into a crossing motion over my chest, activating the spelled bracers I wore under my shirt. The orb struck, and rather than killing me, sent me cartwheeling across the clearing.

I skidded on my back, spitting out a mouthful of dirt I had gotten at some point on my journey. The bracers fell off, burned out. I crab-walked backwards as G Ma continued to advance. "Grandma, what psychotic ideals you have," I quipped, climbing to my feet.

"All the better to kill you with. I regret this won't be permanent—"

But I was suddenly gone, Shadow Walking to the opposite end of the ring. I flung my hand down, and a loud *cracking* sound erupted at my feet. Then I instantly Shadow Walked to another random location, copying the *cracking* sound. None of these were lethal. Just sounds.

I did this six more times, catching her whirling my way with each one, tracking the sounds.

I did it one last time, but the instant before materializing, I silently flung my hand out across the clearing. There was a small delay before the cracking sound erupted where I had pointed, and G Ma whirled towards it to find only empty air where I should have been standing.

Because she didn't know I was instead standing directly behind her. I had hoped she would rely on her familiarity with the *cracking* sounds over her sight. And I had been right.

I used my Stone Skin right hand to hammer the back of her knees, knocking her to the ground with a jarring blow that may have cracked cartilage, leaving her kneeling before me and still facing away from me.

Without hesitation, I swung my other hand to hit her in the throat with the web of flesh between thumb and forefinger, hammering her windpipe. I continued my momentum, spinning in a clockwise full circle as I swung my leg high above my head, casting Stone Skin around my boot. At the apex of the arc, I swung it down in an axe-kick motion I had learned from Achilles.

She was still kneeling, clutching her throat as she gasped for air when the blow struck her neck, hammering her down into the earth. I prepared one last fatal blow to end this farce. I needed to get to Indie stat, to stop her from waking the Grimms. Put a fork in it.

But grandma Raego suddenly lashed out with her wings, striking me with a claw in the face, knocking me clear so that my execution blow sliced through the earth only inches away from G Ma's head. I turned, wiping the small gash on my cheek to find a majestic beast, a blue and gold scaled dragon, flesh like old stone, and multiple horns forming a fanned crest above her head.

Raego grunted triumphantly, having won their pointless battle of wills.

"This is to the *death*, Raego. Stop. Fucking. *Playing!*" I shouted. He nodded, and burst into his own impressive inky black dragon form, scales like polished black glass. The grandma spat flame at the ground before them, drawing a line. It was a combination of liquid blue and yellow fire, like napalm, and I could feel the heat across the ring as she lifted her wings, folding them up into a massive wall behind her, trebling the look of her size, which was already impressive. Like a peacock fanning his tail.

Raego snarled, drawing his own line of black smoke in the earth before him. His eyes briefly flicked my way, and he jerked his neck back, lids widening as he looked behind me.

I didn't have time to react as something hammered into me, burning, scalding, and shredding my clothes. Like a thousand razor blades coated in liquid nitrogen and acid.

I flew through the air, directly between the dragons, landing on my wounded back, gasping.

I found myself staring up at grandma Raego, who was licking her long, stained, ivory fangs with a thin, red tongue. She smelled like cats and excessive perfume. I saw her purse dangling from a spine on her armored back as Raego roared, hoping to distract her long enough to save me. Her jaws opened and her teeth lashed out as fast as a cobra.

To gobble me up.

CHAPTER 51

I had subconsciously grabbed the coin in my pocket, willing to do anything to win. Time seemed to slow, but I think that was a common feeling when you were about to die.

I *had* to win.

Sure, if I died, I would find myself in bed, get up, walk it off, and head over to meet Indie and her gang of sociopaths, hoping to stop them.

But I wouldn't be able to interfere as the Academy picked apart my friends. Gunnar, Tory, her students, the Reds, Raego and his dragons, and anyone else I loved. For one week. Which would be long enough for the Academy to destroy them all.

I was magically tapped. At least for half an hour or so. My magic typically regenerated pretty fast, but I had slept little, eaten less, and pretty much drank only alcohol for the last few days, so I wasn't optimistic.

But my hand held a coin.

A Silver Dollar.

Would it help? What were the consequences? I knew G Ma would recognize the scent from the Library. But it was a powerful artifact, full of power of its own, as Matthias had told me.

But it was *also* a Horseman Mask, and there was the rub.

I had used it already… kind of. And nothing had happened.

But the only way the Mask was going to save me this time was if I donned it.

Slapped it right against my rosy cheeks.

I noticed that grandma Raego's head hadn't moved any closer, and it snapped me out of my thoughts. I looked around, and found no one moving.

Well, except for four shadowy figures steadily approaching me. No one paid them any heed, both the crowd and contenders frozen like statues. My old friend knelt beside me, wincing after he pulled me up into a sitting position and assessed my back.

He met my eyes. "It's bad."

I blinked. "Did you stop time or is there a Grimm here?" But I knew better. His brothers stood a few paces away, watching me from beneath their hoods.

Death shook his head. "This is a moment of choice. You didn't have all the knowledge necessary before to make an objective decision." He flicked his head at my hand.

I pulled out the coin, not looking at it. He gazed at it with wonder, eyes momentarily distant, and… eager. I closed my fingers, not tapping into the power. He nodded back. I wanted to shout at him for not telling me about the book, his past with Matthias, him creating the Mad Hatter.

But this wasn't the time or place for that.

"Tough call…" he offered.

"I put this on, and I'm a Horseman. I won't be able to help my friends the way I need to. So, I'll win this fight, but not be able to do anything."

He smirked. "It will heal you. But you could still get your ass kicked by these two old gals. Even *with* the Mask. You are untrained," he admitted. "The mask amplifies what you *are*, it doesn't *make* you into something you are not. That's why we are *chosen* in the first place."

I frowned down at it. "Other than possibly still getting my ass kicked, the rest was true, right? I won't be able to help them. Damned if

I do, damned if I don't," I repeated his quote from a few days ago in Chateau Falco.

A wisp of a smile flittered across his face. And for the first time, it registered with me that none of them were wearing their masks. He studied me thoughtfully. He even took a second to glance back at his brothers. After a silent exchange, they each nodded once in encouragement. "We do not know. Perhaps wearing the Mask only this one time will not make you a Horseman. We're also at the Dueling Grounds, not the mortal realm…" he shrugged. "Who knows?"

My mouth fell open. "You're shitting me…"

He shook his head, sitting down himself. He was a tall guy, and he was now sitting pretty close to the dragon's open mouth. A small drip of saliva had built on the tip of one tooth, ready to drop and land on his shoulder. He looked at the drop, and casually placed his palm against the offending tooth. Like clay, her entire head slowly pivoted until it was out of his way, and she was no longer looming over me, but was instead a foot away from me so that her bite would strike only earth.

Death unconcernedly wiped his hand idly on his robe of black cobwebs. "As I was saying, when I was offered my Mask, I was immediately given the *choice* by an Agent of Heaven and an Agent of Hell. I was the first, so it had to happen that way. I accepted, asking only that I complete my vengeance first." He held out a small bone in his fist, rubbing it nostalgically with his thumb.

A carving made from the bone of his son. I had found it for him. What felt like a decade ago.

I shivered at the thought of him just carrying it around. Morbid and macabre to the extreme.

Then again, he *was* Death.

Still, it felt akin to Jesus carrying around a crucifix or a crown of thorns as a keychain.

"I chose to accept." He indicated his brothers with a casual motion of his hand. "They each received different summons. War actually wore his Mask quite often before he was recruited." He shrugged. "Well, several times, anyway."

"I can put on the Mask… But what will it do to me? What will it *allow* me to do?"

Death shrugged. "No one ever asked my opinion about a Fifth Horseman," his eyes were distant as he answered, not telling me the full truth. Before I could press, he met my eyes again. "At some point, probably a very obvious point, you will know when donning the Mask is final, and what that would entail. At that moment, you may even still be given the opportunity to decline." His face morphed into a grin. "I'm sure there will be… consequences for sampling the cookies, but not buying anything," he added drily. He scanned the clearing. "Any longer and our talk could negatively affect those present. Are you ready?" he asked, anxious to hear my answer.

I reached into my pocket, withdrew a small object and placed it in the dirt directly before the dragon's mouth. Then I slowly met Death's curious frown, and winked.

With an echoing laugh, he was gone.

Grandma Raego's jaws slammed down, snapping closed on the tiny object and a mouthful of dirt before her.

This left me a foot away from her very startled eyes, seeing that I was suddenly not immediately before her, and that she was the one who had moved.

"A kiss from me to you…" I whispered as I flicked her in the eyeball with my fingernail. I rolled away as she recoiled in pain. She started to open her jaws to spit out the mouthful of dirt, but I cast a tiny spell into the object clinging to her teeth.

An explosion blew off her snout. Right the hell off.

It sent her reeling and screaming with horrifying, pained animal sounds as blood and burnt flesh rained down around me. I jumped to my feet, and although Raego looked horrified, he shouted, "Purse!" as he slapped his flank urgently with his claws. I frowned for a moment, and then realized that if he had been in human form, he would have been patting his pants pocket.

Where I had gifted him a few of my prototypes ahead of the fight.

I turned to the still screaming Gertrude to see her purse dangling from her back, still stuck to one of her spines. I smiled wickedly, sending out a flash of power at the dangling handbag.

"A woman's never far from her purse," I murmured.

The tiny jolt of power exploded like a small supernova, a ring of force erupting outwards from her in a perfect circle, sending everyone crashing to their knees. Except me. A ring of black thorns had formed around my feet, and I realized I was still holding the coin in my fist.

But it was no longer a coin. I was cupping my Mask. That buzzed with power in my hands.

I turned towards G Ma, and as slow as an exotic dancer removing an article of clothing, I placed the crystal Mask over my face. It latched onto my skin like a dozen tiny fairy hands, and the unpleasant buzzing sensation ceased. It still felt unpleasant for a moment, but differently unpleasant. Because it was shifting and adjusting to the contours of my face. It didn't hurt.

In fact, a cooling sensation rolled over my entire body, washing away all of my injuries.

And if I hadn't seen the bed of crystals on the interior, I would have told you it had been made of crisp, untouched velvet, so seamless was the space between my face and the mask.

A carnivorous horse neighed from beyond the ring, and I stared through the mask – flickers of reflective fog now decorating my peripheral vision – as black bolts of lightning pounded the earth outside the torches, into the wild, untamed void that existed beyond the Dueling Grounds. Thunder crackled and growled across the skies, shaking the bed of thorns at my feet.

Grimm, my unicorn, strode out from the dark void beyond the protective ring of torches, his black peacock mane flaring out to display brilliant crimson orbs on the edge of each feather. Silver and white sparks crackled around his hooves as he strode up to the ring. He licked the tips of his long, razor sharp teeth, but of course, he didn't enter the arena itself.

Because that would have been cheating. His display was purely an intimidation factor. He did perform an odd kneeling motion in my direction. I dipped my head back, ignoring the silver fog at the edges of my vision.

The crowd had been silent, but at the sight of the unicorn and my Mask, they began to *roar*.

I slowly turned to acknowledge them, and as I did, whichever section I faced died down to hushed, awed, possibly terrified whispers, only to rise back up like a Leviathan as my gaze continued on. Like the opposite of the *wave* they did in sports stadiums.

The gorillas looked particularly speechless, likely doubting their decision to join Fight Club.

I turned to face G Ma. Her face was ashen, and she was shaking her head in disbelief.

"You... It was you at the Library..." she whispered, stunned. "You have no idea what—"

"KNEEL!" I commanded, and the thunder boomed above me like an exclamation point.

She obeyed. Immediately. Instinctively. Not as if she had chosen to do so, but as if her body had just reacted to my tone. And the thunder.

A deep *gong* boomed, an ominous, warning sound. It faded away almost instantly, and I frowned at Achilles and Asterion, wondering if that was a new addition to signify the end of a fight. They looked just as startled, so I played it off.

Raego prowled up beside me, refusing to meet my gaze, but willing to stand beside me.

"Submit," I commanded the old wizard.

"Kill me, as is your due," she said, staring up at my Mask with awed horror.

I shook my head. "I will either torture you for hours, or you can submit. Your choice. I *will* have your submission, one way or the other."

She frowned, shaking. "Duels are to the death. It would be... disrespectful to draw it out."

I shook my head. "The monsters here just want to see violence. They won't mind. You have three seconds to decide." And I began counting out with my fingers, glaring down at her.

She finally caved as my third finger began to unfold, shouting out her submission. I glanced back at Asterion, who turned to Achilles. The legendary Greek warrior studied the scene before him for a few moments, considering, then let out a slow nod. "Terms?" he called out. "If you refuse to kill her, and she accepts, you must issue new terms. Then I will call off the Duel."

I blinked behind my Mask, elated. I couldn't have asked for a better response.

I turned to G Ma. "You will obey Raego here until sunrise. Neither dying, or winning our duel. This will force the Academy to act. Without their spy, they will not know the outcome, and must decide accordingly." Her eyes grew wild. This was not at all what she had hoped for.

Even though she had been willing to lose everything to beat me, she hadn't considered that I could actually win, or that I would be able to – or decide to – tap into my Horseman powers.

Or whatever this was.

I hadn't felt anyone speaking to me, commanding me to obey the Ten Commandments, or to defend the innocent. And I heard no chorus of uplifting trumpets.

Just that deep, ominous *gonging* sound.

"Please. Kill me. You are meddling in events that could destroy the world…" she begged.

I shook my head. "That is a result of *your* meddling in events that *are* destroying my world. My *friends*. My *home*." She dropped her head, trying to find a way out.

"What do you want?" she whispered, defeated.

I bent down, and used a finger to lift her chin. "To work together against a common enemy."

She didn't meet my gaze, but she spat on the earth. "You mean your *allies*. You intend to mislead me, delivering us straight into the arms of this reborn Syndicate. I would rather die."

I sighed. "I know you don't like me. At all. I don't like you either, so you can trust that I'm telling you the truth. Otherwise I could have just killed you and taken away your control of the Academy." She hesitated at that, so I pressed on. "Help me stop the last Maker, so he doesn't wake a god. Through this, I'll prove to you that I'm not a part of this Syndicate."

Her eyes widened in absolute horror at mention of waking a god. "I-I can't trust your words. By taking out the Maker, you are benefiting the Syndicate," she finally stammered, still reeling from hearing Ichabod's plans.

I nodded slowly. "This is true. But it is better than the alternative. We will deal with the Syndicate after this mess. One problem at a time. The Syndicate has been around for a long time now." She began to argue, but I snapped my fingers, silencing her. "I have objective proof of this. I don't care whether you believe me or not. It doesn't change the facts." I paused, letting my words sink in. "I promise you that I'll have a long talk with the Syndicate afterwards..." I growled, menacingly. Part of it was because an image of my father flashed before my eyes.

A member of the Syndicate.

"I agree," she rasped.

"Not so fast. That was condition number one," I said softly. "You will swear the following on your power." She froze, waiting. "You will reclaim your title of Grand Master of the Academy. With that authority, you agree to leave me and mine alone. Forever. St. Louis is off limits to the Academy – unless you have my direct permission beforehand. Or if there is objective agreement that someone has performed a crime. Not a crew of judges from the Academy, but a panel that includes other supernatural factions – of both our choosing."

She cowered before me, nodding in horror, out-politicked.

"Secondly, you will meet with me at my request, the moment I request it, without delay, and you will actually *listen* to what I have to say. You will treat me as a nation unto myself, granted all the respect and courtesies you do the other supernatural nations. Not an enemy. Not an ally. Both of those choices will evolve as a result of future discussions. Just like any other nation. Innocent until proven guilty. An equal. St. Louis is my nation as far as you are concerned." I glanced at Raego. "Obviously, I'm not seeking to rule over any of the supernatural groups here. But I do consider myself the unofficial policeman of this town." Raego nodded in agreement, and gratitude.

There was a pregnant silence. "I… agree," she whispered.

"Swear it on your power as a wizard."

Her head dropped further, but she complied.

"Now, run along to the Academy, and reclaim the title you pretended to sacrifice. Failure to succeed will result in a dinner party with my Brothers," I said, tapping my Mask pointedly. "Only *after* this success will you inform the Academy of our *agreement*. Text me when you have completed these tasks."

Her shoulders sank lower with each word. "I swear this on my power…" and I felt her do it.

I stepped back. "I think we're all done here," I said to the crowd. "I've got a date with a Grimm," I said loud enough for all to hear. The crowd simply watched me depart, no longer cheering or clapping, just watching in stunned silence. My terms would change their lives.

Forever.

Raego didn't speak as we left. He didn't speak on the way home either. He did say, "Good night," when I dropped him off, though.

I had taken the Mask off immediately upon leaving the Dueling Grounds, and it sat in my pocket, a very normal, plain-looking Silver Dollar.

But my thoughts were not normal, plain, or confident.

They were terrified.

CHAPTER 52

*E*verything was ready, despite my errand to the Fight Club. Thanks to Mallory – Pan.

Elders crouched unseen in the distance, evening sun limning their hiding spots as they watched, waited to receive our guests. I had lowered the defenses of the house, allowing Dark Team Temple to at least enter the grounds, but not allowing them access to Chateau Falco itself.

Falco hadn't been pleased about it, even knocking a painting down when I asked.

Still, Carl and company had set up a defensive perimeter around the property just in case things went badly. And the house, or Beast, had dampened all magic in the surrounding area, except for my gang, of course, which consisted of Carl and Gunnar. Mallory also crouched on the roof, his trusty sniper rifle locked, ready, and loaded, likely staring at us even now. I had wanted to keep Mallory as far away from them as possible, in case anyone managed to discover his secret now that he had shared it with me. He was a wild card, and I needed everyone to think that I knew nothing of his origins. I couldn't risk Icky boldly telling me in front of others that he knew the truth, because then the others would know that I knew. I needed that Ace up my sleeve.

Just in case. The point was, if the Grimms wanted war, we would bring it. But I was hoping it never reached that point.

Entirely by accident, I had found a long white hair on my sleeve when Ichabod and Indie had abducted me. I had covered it, making sure to keep it in my pocket, not knowing *how* it could be helpful, but knowing that it *would* be helpful at some point.

The trio of evil appeared directly before us, having Shadow Walked. They studied me, Gunnar, and Carl with curiosity. Three versus three, as agreed upon earlier. They scanned our surroundings warily, but with the mansion behind me dampening their powers, they were unable to sense anything amiss. Because if they were close enough for Indie to tap into their powers, it would be pretty fucking obvious they were outnumbered, and we would have a Grimm on our hands who could match each of us toe-to-toe.

Still, Icky was a Maker, and I had tried my hand against him twice. Losing horribly once on his terms, beating him once on my own terms. Only time would tell how the cards would fall in round three.

But they didn't know about the dozen wolves, dragons, Alucard, Tory and her shifters, or the other Elders lurking in the labyrinth and wooded grounds, close enough to be dangerous if necessary, distant enough to be unseen and unnoticed.

As the trio assessed the potential threat, I studied Rumpelstiltskin – Silver Tongue. The man who had been around for generations, gaining personal power by making deals with supernatural beings in order to grant them their greatest desires.

For the small price of... *something*. Often a life of servitude to his masters, the Syndicate.

My father's face flashed before me again, but I waved it away immediately, focusing on my breathing like Ganesh had been teaching me. I was crap at meditation, surprisingly. Well, I was good at meditating, but not at actually accomplishing anything cool through meditation. Like he had when he had disappeared my pants, or had the knot tying and untying contest with Asterion.

Eventually, I might master the whole Astral Projection thing – traveling outside your body to witness events across the world, all without having to risk harm to your body. Then again, certain adept people could notice your wandering spirit watching them, and trap you.

I'll put it plainly. Your spirit is meant to stay inside your body for a reason. Flesh is armor. Without flesh, you are unprotected, and an especially talented person could do some pretty serious damage to your soul before you got it back. If they *let* you have it back...

They could also simply hold your soul until your body died, or you became a vegetable.

Creepy stuff, right?

I didn't play around with it yet. Not anywhere dangerous at least. I had tried on Mallory and Dean several times. Later bringing up conversations that I should have no knowledge of.

I'll be honest. My sole purpose with risking to attempt Astral Projection had been to finally discover the location of my Macallan that Mallory always managed to keep hidden from me.

I never found my answer, but it had been worth a shot, and I got some practice out of it.

Ichabod was studying Carl, who was studying Indie, who was intently studying the tree, none aware of the other's interest.

I studied Rumpelstiltskin.

He had once been the enforcer, the lieutenant, the politician in charge of the Grimms.

But that had ended when he tried meddling with me and mine.

His face was a mask of leathery, worn, deep scars, all of them different demeaning names, marked on him for life. I idly wondered how they had been inflicted – with tool, or with thought via Matthias Temple's Maker power – but quickly shifted my focus. I didn't want to know.

He also looked worn. Haggard. Spent. Defeated. Ashamed.

I must have been staring pretty intently, because his eyes briefly flicked in my direction. I winked before he could look away. His lips parted instinctively, but he immediately slammed his gaze back to the ground as Ichabod took a step forward. I could tell my action had startled, confused, and given him a small taste of hope.

While also giving him a small flicker of fear. Because my wink could have meant anything at all. That I was going to enjoy his torment, that I was going to send him back to Matthias, that I had some brilliant plan to take him away so that I could spend decades torturing him myself, or that I was going to kick his scrawny ass through the Gateway into the Dark Realm.

He began to shake as the possibilities grew in his mind.

Perfect...

Ichabod took a step forward, clearing his throat. He nodded at Gunnar, "Wolf king," he said in a clear voice. I wasn't sure how that title kept getting tossed around, but I had heard several people refer to him that way. "Why are you here?"

I answered instead, like we had arranged beforehand. Well, not entirely like we had planned.

"We agreed to have equal representation. And his tricks amuse me," I said, grinning.

Ichabod grew still, as if ready for a trap. He turned from me to Gunnar, wary.

I tossed a forearm-sized stick at Gunnar. It struck him in the shoulder and fell to the ground. He didn't move, other than to glance down at it with furrowed brow, and then shoot me a sharp disapproving look.

I sighed is disappointment, then cupped my mouth as if imparting a secret to Ichabod. But I whispered it loud enough for everyone to hear. And I cupped my mouth the wrong way so Gunnar could obviously hear me. "He was much better at it when he had both eyes."

Ichabod just stared at me. He shook his head, then addressed Carl openly. "Elder. Carl, if I recall..." he said in a polite, but questioning tone.

Carl stared back at him, face emotionless.

"Carl's still working on his people skills. He's more of a non-megalomaniac lover. Don't be offended," I drawled. "Can we just get this over with? I don't want this to happen, I told you why it was a bad idea, I got outvoted. You made an agreement that you would leave my city alone if I complied. Carl and Gunnar are my witnesses to that promise."

Ichabod nodded slowly. "Yes, yes. Leave us alone, and I'll leave you alone. Neither of us wants to be here, so let's be finished."

I gave a curt nod, biting my tongue. The moment he turned his back, I gripped the hair in my fingers, snapping it in two as I mentally cast a previously-planned spell. In the same exact instant, I used a light tendril of additional magic to retrieve the stick I had hit Gunnar with.

Because I knew using my magic would set off an alarm bell with Ichabod and Indie.

As expected, they both whirled, fists up to protect themselves from whatever I had been about to cast at them.

I frowned back, glancing down at the stick. "I was just going to try the fetch thing again, guys…" I could see Indie studying me with a calculating gaze, trying to bite back a laugh, but also wary of my tricks. Because she knew me so well.

I dropped the stick with a regretful expulsion of breath. "It's okay, Gunnar. We'll try again later," I said, ignoring his one-eyed glare. "Who's a good boy?" I asked in an animated voice. "*Gunnar* is. Yes, he *is*!"

Ichabod cursed. "No more magic. Next time I'll react first, ask questions later."

I shrugged. "Whatever you say, Icky. I'll just be a good boy and sit at the kiddie table with my friends. Can we talk? Please?"

His face darkened, and he turned his back again. "Quietly," he snapped. Indie stared up at the tree, and Carl was practically salivating as he watched her. I whispered angrily to him, jostling his shoulder. "You can't eat the Grimm, Carl. Close your mouth. You're drooling."

He flinched, as if I had woken him from a nap. But he did drop his gaze and take a breath. Then he casually scanned our surroundings, after checking that Ichabod and Indie were not paying any attention to us.

"Christ!" Gunnar whispered. "His face looks like a circumcision gone bad."

I nodded absently. "Like Rumpled Foreskin…" Gunnar barked out a sudden laugh, and Ichabod shot us a warning glare. I mouthed *sorry* to him. He shook his head, turning back.

"What is the plan, Nate?" Gunnar murmured. "You can't honestly be okay with allowing him to let them through. If Indie can't control them, they won't care about any promises you made with Ichabod. Because, remember, they will recall having Ichabod on a leash for the last several hundred years, so I don't think they're particularly scared of him."

I nodded, not speaking as the trio conversed with Rumpelstiltskin.

"We're going to watch. See how this plays out..." I replied softly, keeping my magic ready, but not touching it. I tried finding that calm place inside of me. The one that I had been so successful at finding when I had dominated my Beast, trapping it inside my cane. But I was unsuccessful this time. For obvious reasons.

Things were pretty dicey at the moment. Lot of moving pieces. I could barely keep up.

If people would at least just be who they said they were, I would feel a whole lot better about everything. But, no. They all had to choose different masks, personas to wear.

My own Mask was in my pocket. Along with the Fae Cuffs that nullified magic used against me. I wasn't wearing them yet, not wanting to give away my advantage too early, but I had them, ready to accessorize.

I heard Rumps clearly as I focused, blocking out all other sensations.

"It's not that fucking easy. When he took me, he also negated all my contracts. When I planned to do it last time, I was juiced up on hundreds of years' worth of deals. Now, I have none to my name, and I've been in... convalescence for the past few months."

"That's your problem. We could always arrange a visit with my father," Ichabod warned.

"No! I just want you to know the facts. This could very likely kill me. Or not even work."

"For your sake, it *better* work..." Ichabod growled.

Rumps sagged his head, taking in a deep breath. When he looked back up, his eyes were different. No longer terrified. Well, not *as* terrified. Madness still danced there, but it was momentarily subdued.

"Look at it this way, Rumps," I called out. "You're getting exactly what you wanted a year ago. Your old band back together." Then I frowned. "Well, not *exactly* what you wanted, I guess. Since Indie is going to take them from you." Then I pretended to think – fast, because Ichabod looked about ready to have a bowel movement from sheer outrage. "Of course, once they're free, back home, they might have some questions for you. Like, *why did you take so long to save us?* And *why are you passing us off to a new boss? A female* boss, at that." I tapped my lips. "Just idle speculation. Please continue."

Ichabod grabbed Rumps by the collar, shoving him closer to the tree. "There is power here. I can sense it. Use it to make up for your shortcomings," he snarled, as if disgusted to touch him.

Carl spoke up out of nowhere. "You cannot touch my sacred wood."

"Mother of God," Gunnar wheezed, chuckling lightly.

Ichabod turned, surprised, not getting the double entendre. "Nate and I have an agreement."

Carl shook his head. "This has nothing to do with Master Temple." And, *man*, did it rankle Ichabod to hear Carl refer to me as that. I would have to buy him a new shirt. Or let him eat someone. Just a little. "Silver Tongue," he cocked his head sideways at me, silently questioning if he had used the correct name. I nodded, and he resumed. "Won't be *able* to touch my wood," Carl clarified. "It doesn't belong to Master Temple. It merely resides here. Even he could not command it so." And although the double-entendres were raining down, making it hard for me to keep a straight face, I was pretty sure he was lying. Because I had tapped his… wood before. Of course, that had been a confusing time where I had been dominating both my house and Carl, after taking a vision quest with my Beast under… Carl's sacred wood – the Gateway to the other Elders.

But maybe my timing had just been superb.

Or Carl was learning how to lie.

Rumps suddenly grunted in surprise, drawing everyone's attention. "He's right. I can't tap into his wood…" he shot us an angry glare. "Tree," he amended.

Indie frowned, studying Carl. Gunnar simply smiled, beefy arms folded.

Then she took a step closer to Carl, looking very respectful, beautiful, and polite as she asked in an overly serious tone, "Carl, may *Silver Tongue* and I tap your sacred wood?"

There was absolutely no hesitation. "Yes, Mistress."

My jaw fell open, and Ichabod grinned triumphantly.

As they turned back to the tree, I smacked Carl on the shoulder. "What the hell, Carl?"

He shrugged. "She smells nice."

Gunnar coughed into his fist, but I could tell he was smiling at Carl's response.

"You and I are going to have a long talk about the dangers of the opposite sex. And the things that are more important, and less creepy, than liking someone's *smell*."

Rumps focused back on the tree, sighing as it began to glow brighter. Not strong, but definitely brighter, as if someone had juiced up the tree sap with glow-sticks. I felt the power building, and the mansion behind me growled in response. She wasn't pleased, but some part of what Carl said must have been true. Because she sure wasn't preventing it from happening.

Rumps spread his hands, one palm resting on the Grimm stones embedded into the flesh of Indie's forearm. She watched, transfixed.

"I'll be able to do this on my own?" she whispered. He nodded absently.

"With the stones from Jacob's amulet bonded to your flesh, and the inherent abilities you now possess, yes," he admitted. That simple statement from a terrified prisoner made me realize that Indie had been telling the truth. She could use her Maker power. Even without Ichabod.

Indie watched his every move like a good student. She would be able to do this on her own soon. Which couldn't be good. But a Gateway suddenly appeared, revealing a gaping maw of darkness so complete that it made the color black look as bright and cheerful as a unicorn shitting a rainbow.

CHAPTER 53

Any minute now, an army of Grimms was about to pour through the void and onto my lawn. Gunnar dropped his arms, looking suddenly tense as he shot me a worried look.

Why wasn't she here yet? I thought to myself, growing anxious.

Then we all heard it. The angry sounds of a mob in the distance. I just stared, transfixed, eyes flicking from Rumps to the void, back and forth like a metronome, listening to the shouts.

An eternity passed before a silhouette materialized on the other side of the void, assessing this bright new world. The shouting behind him abruptly ceased. Our world was likely blinding. Especially at sunset. After spending hundreds of years locked away in a lightless world, it would literally hurt him to step through into our world. But I had already considered that.

"Silver Tongue, old friend. It's been so *long*," a gravelly voice spoke from the vague form.

"We were unable to locate you, Grimm."

The figure grunted in acknowledgment. "I can sense Jacob's amulet, but it feels different. He left us a time ago, promising the moon." He paused dramatically. "But I haven't seen any moon yet, and I don't see one now. Just our old lord and master – face mauled – and Jacob's amulet, but *not* Jacob's amulet..." The figure shifted, as if taking a step closer, but still not stepping through. "And what have we *here?*" he bellowed, chuckling. "Ichabod Temple! Jacob's old dog! How have *you* been, my boy? I've got another leash for you. It seems you misplaced yours."

"*Leash!*" I said loudly. "That was the word I was looking for earlier, Icky."

He ignored me. "Much has changed, Helmut..." he answered. "Come see for yourself."

The shadow had a name.

"Helmut Grimm?" I burst out laughing.

"Looks like someone woke up ready to die," Helmut growled menacingly, his shadow seeming to shift to an aggressive stance, but it was hard to tell from the void.

"Come on out, hat-head. I've got something for you," I teased.

"Did you have to *immediately* piss him off?" Gunnar growled, furred claws bursting out.

With a swift motion, Helmut darted through the opening.

He stood before us in a ready fighting stance, crossbow aimed my way.

I waved at him, then put my hands in my pocket innocently.

He squinted, practically blind, but that crossbow still aimed true. He wore a collection of dark canvas-type clothing, bands of fabric crossing his frame as if he had used – and reused – any kind of fabric he could find for clothing. He was barefoot, feet muddy, and I could bet his soles were as hard as stone. Because his boots had likely worn away years ago.

Hundreds of years ago.

He continued to squint in my direction, thick, unkempt, whitish blonde beard resting against his chest. His eyes were crystal blue, and his long curly hair matched the beard. Not grey, but a faded blonde. I wondered if this was a result of lack of sunlight, because his skin was alabaster.

I tossed him something without warning.

He squeezed the trigger of his crossbow, releasing the bolt, the moment I moved. But I had anticipated it, and had also thrown up a single glass bead while tossing him his gift. Because I had accidentally found out that the beads didn't just work on magical attacks.

The bead ate the bolt in a slight *puff*, and he caught my projectile in a fist.

He glanced down to find a pair of expensive Ray Ban sunglasses. He frowned down at them, then looked back at me, still squinting.

I put on my own pair of sunglasses, and looked up at the fading light. Then I turned back to him, smiling like a good host. "Might help with the bright light," I said with a shrug. "I teased you to get you to step out of the darkness," I admitted with a guilty grin.

He didn't speak, just continued staring. Then he replied in a gruff tone, as if not having spoken the words for quite some time. "Thank you…" And he put them on, instantly making him look like a dystopian version of Billy Gibbons or Dusty Hill from *ZZ Top*.

"No big deal." I pointed at Ichabod. "I'm his descendant. I don't like him very much, and am completely open to you collaring him." I leaned forward in a mock whisper. "But I'm not allowed to interfere, so I'll just keep quiet over here." I shoved my hands back in my pockets and began to idly whistle, kicking dirt with the toe of my shoes.

I saw a smirk split Helmut's features – again, the first in probably a very long while.

Ichabod glared daggers at me, turning to address Helmut. "We have much to discuss, and even more to plan. I should also add that he," Ichabod pointed at me, "killed Jacob, Wilhelm, and all the others." Helmut's face hardened, no longer smirking as he slowly turned to reassess me, but Ichabod continued. "Gather your Brother—"

And Rumpelstiltskin suddenly let out a muffled grunt, disappearing right from under us all. *Finally*, I thought to myself, putting on a feigned mask of startled surprise and wariness, hands out of my pockets as if ready for an attack. The Gateway had immediately winked shut, effectively trapping Helmut Grimm in our world, and leaving his Brothers behind.

The only sign that something magical had happened had been a faint flicker of black fog, a silhouette latching onto Rumpelstiltskin, and then they both disappeared.

Without hesitation, Ichabod latched onto Indie and Helmut, and Shadow Walked away as fast as they could, but not before shooting me a furious glare.

He saw only my marvelous performance of surprise and fear as I scanned the area around us. Carl and Gunnar had instantly done the same, but their reactions had been genuine.

The black fog reappeared a few moments later, sans Rumpelstiltskin. It materialized to reveal the silver-haired woman I had already met. I flung up a hand, stalling Carl and Gunnar.

She dipped her head, shooting a wary smile at each of them before her gaze settled on me. "That was a bold move. How did you know I'd take the bait?"

I shrugged. "More like *hoped*."

Her eyebrow rose. "That's an ironic choice of words..." she said, studying me.

I felt suddenly self-conscious. Did she know about my Mask? My alias as the Horseman of Hope? I didn't think so, but I didn't want to press her on it. That wasn't relevant right now.

"I thought you would want to at least discover who was knocking on your door. Once you did that, I was confident you would seize the opportunity to take back your... old employee. You seemed pretty intent on visiting a Library yesterday, so I assumed you would be equally interested in taking another of Ichabod's toys away."

"We have only two of four..." she replied cryptically.

I smiled. "They're up to speed," I pointed thumbs at my two friends.

I frowned at her thoughtfully, glancing at her feet, behind her, then meeting her eyes. "I heard once that you guys leave trails of embers and sparks. Even saw it once with Rumps." Her eyes crinkled with amusement at that. "But I don't seem to see that anymore."

She nodded. "Too many people heard about it. We fixed it."

"Oh. Sucks for us, eh?" I said.

She nodded, bringing the conversation back to the HOGs. "Do *you* have any?"

"Not that I know of. My goal was to keep them as far away from him as possible."

She nodded, a pleased smile splitting her tough cheeks. "That is good. I would hate to have to resort to violence. Still, to be safe, I'm going to check the house."

I shook my head. "Not an option, but thank you for asking."

Her smile evaporated. She watched me thoughtfully, then gave a single nod. "We'll get back to that part in a minute. How were you able to get my attention?"

I smiled. "Took a page from the bitch who tricked me at the school," I said, touching my hair. "At the Library. When you saved us."

She cursed under her breath, hand idly reaching for her hair. "I normally tie it back. Rookie mistake." Her hand dropped, and she glanced at Gunnar and Carl, studying them from head to toe, then doing the same to me. "Smart, but what if my intent had been to simply kill you all?"

I shifted my gaze behind her. Her shoulders tightened as she took a lateral step, fearing an immediate attack as she flung up her arms. A dozen armed monsters stood ten paces away, and two more just like them boxed her in on the other sides, Tory leading one, and Alucard the other. Her only way out was through me, or one of the walls of shifters and Freaks. No one spoke. A dragon roared in the skies, blocked from view by the massive tree.

"This isn't a threat. I don't mean you any harm… tonight. This was my answer to your question. I was prepared for any eventuality. Consider this a temporary peace offering. The enemy of my enemy is my friend."

She turned back to me, much more uncomfortable now. "Impressive. I didn't hear a thing."

Gunnar grunted. A dismissive sound at her compliment, basically saying, *of course you didn't. They're mine.* Well, the wolves anyway. But Alucard and Tory looked bloodthirsty.

I glared at Gunnar for good measure, but it was his bad side, so he probably didn't even notice. Then again, I spotted the beginning of a smirk splitting his bearded cheeks, so perhaps he knew damn well I was glaring at him.

I turned back to… "What's your name?" I asked.

She casually withdrew a cigar, lighting it. Gunnar let out an incredulous snort. "You smoke cigars, lady?" he chuckled, grinning.

She frowned at him, but continued lighting, taking a few puffs, considering my question.

But I had forgotten all about my question, my eyes transfixed on the cigar in her fingers. "That's a Gurkha Black Dragon," I whispered.

She met my eyes, approving of my attention to detail, I think. It was a calculating look. "I do. My old boss gave me a box of them. Never was a smoker, but these things?" she waved the cigar in the air, it's powerful scent wafting my way, making my knees threaten to give out. "Can change a girl's mind." The only other person I knew who could afford them had been…

My father.

And Indie's accusation about my father working for the Syndicate threatened to destroy me. After speaking with Pan, I had harbored the notion that maybe my dad had succumbed to them against his will. Extorted. Like the Grimms. But this woman had attacked Tory's school. And she had obviously worked for my father. My mind literally went blank for a moment.

"You look peaked, so let's make this quick," the woman said, watching me thoughtfully. "My name is not important. I must think on your… offer. You sure about not giving me a tour?" I nodded firmly. "Hmm… That makes this complicated," she said thoughtfully. After a few moments, she continued. "You may consider yourself no threat to us for the time being. *Allies* is a very strong word, but you've been moved to the *don't kill on sight, not necessarily an enemy* category. It's a transitional stage. You can either go back, or, *very* unlikely, you proceed to the ally group." She turned her head to look at where the Gateway had been. "Looks like we missed one. Bummer, since their inclusion back into the fold would only make my life easier. Give me time to do my nails," she added thoughtfully, sounding very serious. I realized that she didn't really talk like someone of her age should. "But at least we have Silver Tongue back, if slightly… used."

I forced a smile on my face, blocking all thoughts of my father from my mind with a neat meditation trick I had learned to control. I plastered a guilty grin on my face instead. "At least he's not dead... Might help with the whole *ally* thing, right?"

"Perhaps. Perhaps not," she said bluntly, sounding like it wasn't up to her. I glanced at Gunnar, sensing him about to speak. I had time to see his eye widen in surprise as he stared at the woman, and I jumped back a step, fearing she had chosen to attack the second I turned my head.

But she was simply *gone*. Only a phone sat on the ground where she had stood. I scooped it up, and found a single phone number in the contacts. Likely a direct line to her.

Gunnar growled, turning his unspoken question on me. "Does she work for..." he trailed off, confused, but not wanting to say it out loud.

I nodded, pocketing the phone. "The Syndicate. It's okay. I know three syllables is stretching the limits of your barking capability. I love you anyway." I felt testy, anger growing inside me.

He just shook his head, whether at my answer or my jibe, I didn't know. Didn't care.

I clapped a few times, signaling everyone to gather round. "Phase two, gang," I called out. "Let me catch you up to speed..." Alucard traded grips with Gunnar, and Tory murmured encouraging words to several of her students. The wolves needed no hand-holding.

As I spoke, I made my own plans. It was time for a daddy-son date.

CHAPTER 54

I kicked the door open. After I had gently petted the wolf carving. I wasn't cruel to animals. Unless it was Gunnar.

So, as the door to the Armory began to open, I gave the giant door a swift kick. It crashed into the wall with a loud bang, and I heard several voices cry out in alarm. I strode through the halls, clutching two sealed packages in my fist, trying not to squeeze them, incinerate them, and annihilate the ashes.

My power curled inside me like a snake, slithering in agitation, ready to strike.

My mother burst into the hallway, a defensive glare on her face that abruptly shifted to stunned silence, her mouth clicking closed. I pointed vaguely off to the right, dismissing her with a silent, unquestionable demand. "I'll deal with you momentarily. I'm here to speak to my dear-old-dad," I growled.

Her face went blank, likely in understanding of exactly what I was doing here, but wise enough to not voice it in case she was wrong. I did notice her eyes dart to the packages in my fist. A tell. Because without a word, she dipped her head sadly, and retreated in the direction I had commanded.

Which allowed me to see Pandora, who had been standing behind her, watching the scene with cool eyes. "Remember the time I showed you Achilles and his wrath?" she asked softly.

Which caught me entirely off guard. "I don't have time for a trip down memory lane."

She nodded in understanding. "I sense change in the air."

"Not change. Retribution," I growled. "Punishment. Closure."

She watched me sadly. "Know that, like most things, his actions served multiple purposes. Those relevant to the *then* and those relevant to the *now*," she spoke softly.

"How nice. Did you want a trophy for single-handedly changing my mind?" I directed my eyes to the walls, tables, and shelves around us, all lined with items considered unbelievably dangerous. "Or did my father give you enough of those already? On behalf of the Syndicate."

Her lips tightened. Not in anger, but in acknowledgment of a well-delivered blow. "One must control one's anger. Passion should never rule reason. *Let not the sun set on your rage.*"

I smiled hungrily. "*I don't go to sleep angry,*" I said. "*I stay awake and plot my revenge...*"

"*Holding onto anger is like grasping a hot coal with the intent of throwing it at someone else; you are the one who gets burned.*"

"Cute. Buddha. Did my father give *him* a hall pass, too? Like all the other gods I'm discovering he was drinking buddies with?" I shrugged. "At least you can take comfort in the fact that I can't kill an already dead man. Shame," I shrugged, maintaining my smile.

"All is not as it seems. Listen, and take heed of his response. *Patience is a virtue.*"

"While we're reciting fortune cookies, I guess I'll toss another in. *Beware the fury of a patient man,*" I said, taking a step forward, jutting out my jaw. "And I've been infinitely patient."

She nodded, giving me a few moments to calm down. Which only stirred my anger to new levels. Condescension was not a good position to take with me. Ever, but especially now.

"Ichabod Temple speaks much the same way, and you claim to despise him for his actions. He is willing to do whatever it takes to achieve revenge against the Syndicate. You judge him for his actions, but his motivations you applaud? While at the same time harboring hatred in your heart for a man you think worked with the Syndicate?" She watched me, face expressionless, not judging, not demeaning, but speaking rhetorically. "Contradictions cannot exist, Master Temple. Not in part. Not in whole. You cannot hate someone willing to destroy the Syndicate, while also hating someone for allegedly being part of the Syndicate." She dipped her head politely, and walked away, calling over her shoulder before she left. "He's waiting for you. I set out drinks."

And I stood alone in the hallway, panting, the wrappers crinkling in my fist. I took a deep, deep breath, and tried to regain control of my emotions, even closing my eyes. I envisioned a small strip of silk, focusing on its vibrant colors, and seeing each individual thread in the weave. Then I mentally tied a simple knot, which felt as difficult as lifting a car.

My heart rate was increasing, so I took slower, deeper breaths, forcing my calmness back.

The image of the silk knot resettled.

Then I tied another knot, slowly, carefully, controlled.

It was easier. Not *easy*, but *easier*.

I watched my creation in my mind, proud of myself. I had never been able to achieve this with Ganesh without distractions sneaking in. I knew I was still a long way off from tying forty knots or more, and even further off from mentally sharing the same silken cord with another person, taking turns to tie knots. Still, it was a huge accomplishment, and I was proud of myself.

Somehow, I knew that if I opened my eyes I would see a real silken strip of cloth before me with two neat little knots in the center.

But I didn't open my eyes to check. Instead...

Well, I incinerated my creation, funneling as much of my white-hot rage as possible into the destructive act, seeing my father's face in the flames.

I opened my eyes to see a small pile of ash at my feet.

I felt much more stable. I think.

I suddenly realized I wasn't alone. Death had just exited my father's room. He wasn't wearing his Mask, he was just like when I had first met him in Achilles' bar.

"I need to speak with you."

"That's nice. I'm a little busy," I said, shoving past him. "Might have someone coming your way soon. New tenant."

"That is what I need to speak with you about," he frowned.

I stopped in my tracks, turning to face him. "Excuse me?"

"Your parents. They cannot stay here. Not much longer. Your time with them is limited. Very much so."

Which made me angry. How dare he...

Wait a minute...

That wasn't very rational. I had just told him I was planning on sending them back to the Underworld, in an expression of my anger.

But now that he said the very same thing for different reasons... I was suddenly *angry* with him? Pandora's words repeated in my mind, and I sagged my head. "Contradictions. Double standards," I spoke quietly. "I'm being irrational. Ridiculous, even."

Death said nothing. I lifted my head to find him watching me cautiously. "It serves me no pleasure to inform you of this. But it is best done like taking off a Band-Aid. Short. Quick. Less painful." I opened my mouth to argue, remembering my words to my mother only moments ago, and an ocean of vile shame and putrid guilt rolled over me. My mouth clicked closed. He nodded in understanding. After all, he was Death. Kind of his wheelhouse.

"It was always temporary, wasn't it?" I finally whispered, knowing the answer.

"Yes. And with gods on the rise, and... other recent events, I must secure the borders..." I knew what he meant by *other events*, the Silver Dollar that was figuratively burning a hole in my pocket. He nodded, glancing down at my pants pointedly.

"How very... Trump of you."

He winced. "Poor choice of words. My apologies."

"How long do I have?"

"Not long. I would say your goodbyes quickly." He reached out a hand, face full of pain. "I wish it were otherwise, but I gave you more than most. Knowing that it would make this moment all the more unbearable... It was worth it, to give my Brother more time to spend with them."

I met his eyes. "I guess I'll forgive you for the Hatter thing. For not telling me..." He dipped his head in thanks, releasing my hand. He opened his mouth to say something, closed it, tried again, and then simply cleared his throat as a single tear fell down his cheeks. Then he was gone.

Now, seeing Death spill a tear over the deceased was one to make even the heartiest of men feel a sniffle. This, all by itself, killed my anger like a doused flame.

Minutes ago, I had wanted my father to pay for his crimes. His lies. Now, I had the unique experience of knowing that he was going back to the Underworld.

I wasn't sure what that entailed – Heaven, Hell, whatever – but it changed my perspective when nothing else could have.

I was still angry, disappointed, but no longer raging. I called out my mother's name.

But she didn't respond. I let out a soft, horrible breath, eyes burning.

I tried one more time. "You raised me better than that. And... you can't be that mad at me. You're made of sterner stuff, *devil woman*," I said, smiling sadly as I used the phrase my father often teased her with. "You're a Temple..." I smiled softly, speaking more for my own sake. "I love you, mom, even though I don't understand what you did... Deep down, I love you. I was just..." I smiled wider, "having a Temple tantrum."

She slipped from the shadows, face a hot, wet mess.

I boldly prepared myself to withstand the Mom-ocalypse.

Without a word, she rushed at me, latching onto me to squeeze me as hard as she was able, her fingers like claws digging into my back. Her sobs rocked me, shaking my body as she clutched me like a life raft in a raging sea of storms.

Her *love* hit me, pouring into my injured soul like a flash flood.

I breathed in, and imagined the smell of freshly cut grass, something I always attributed to her. Because one of my fondest traditions with her had been us lounging on a blanket in the sunshine as we picnicked after my first day back to school each year.

Her cleaning my scraped knee as a boy, giving it a magical healing kiss – mom magic, that unconditional, invincible, unrelenting, *real magic* – before handing me back my wooden play sword as she said, face utterly serious, *you're not going to let the evil dragon get away with this*, and shooing me back outside to play.

To vanquish my enemies. More memories of our shared moments stabbed into me, twisted me raw, and filled me with pain. The pain of unconditional love.

Because I now realized that this fountain of love was about to be taken from me.

After an eternity, she finally released her grip, stepping back to instead squeeze my arms.

Her eyes were bloodshot, and her face quivered with tears, but she was smiling under it all. "You were the best magic we ever made, Nate…" She let out a soft, whimpering laugh, wiped her cheeks, and said, "Make us proud. Follow your heart…" and she gently shoved me towards the door to my father. Then she slipped away on silent feet. But her sobs pounded into my heart.

I stood for a moment, hand resting on the door, studying the grain of the wood. I wondered exactly what I wanted from my father, knowing the future of his upcoming, final journey.

I glanced down at the two packages in my fist, and a small, painful smile split my cheeks.

Perfect…

CHAPTER 55

My father sat before me, waiting with solemn acceptance in his eyes. He had poured two drinks that sat on a nearby table. They smelled strong.

Good.

I watched him for a moment, remembering all the moments just like this when I had entered his study at Chateau Falco.

As a child – covered in mud from head to toe and standing beside a small, stubborn, white wolf who was equally caked in filth – eager to share our adventures of the day…

From my first real fight with Gunnar, both of us yelling over the other, while my father calmly watched, face masking the amusement he later explained he had felt…

My first broken heart in middle school, when he had first let me have a small taste of his adult drink, which I had immediately spat out in disgust…

Sharing my course load and class curriculum during my first Christmas break back from College, and telling him about a fascinating young woman in my Russian Studies course…

My plans to open a bookstore, with him analyzing my projections, challenging my ideas, finally coming to a conclusion on our loan terms, because he didn't do charity to family or friends…

The moment I handed him my last payment on the loan – hard-earned money. The first such money I truly felt was all mine, and not inherited...

These memories, and many more, flew through my mind like a movie montage, and in almost every single instance, I had found him in his study, drinking his Macallan, and...

I approached him now, and silently handed him one of the packages.

His face lit up like a child at Christmas, but not just for the item, but as if he had just relived those same moments, and the memories were solidified with the act of handing him...

"A Gurkha Black Dragon..." he whispered reverently, smiling softly at the cigar.

I didn't dare risk speaking, so simply nodded, and then took a seat.

He opened the cigar sleeve, and withdrew the aromatic cigar, drawing it to his nose for a big whiff down the length. His eyes closed, and he hummed his approval.

I opened mine, clipped the edges with a cigar cutter from my pocket, and lit the tip with a small, steady, ball of magical flame, puffing for a few moments.

I handed it to him, exchanged it for his cigar, and then repeated the process until we were both puffing contentedly, a cloud of smoke shifting like an amoeba above our heads. I reached for my drink and took a long, sensational pull. "Fucking Macallan," I smiled, shaking my head.

My father chuckled softly. "I stashed some here long ago, because Mallory always hid it."

I smiled. "From you too?" I didn't challenge him on Mallory. That didn't matter right now.

He was typically a confident, powerful, demanding man. But right now, I sensed his anxiety. He must have known my original intent in coming here, but he had also been speaking with Death, so likely already knew about his imminent departure.

"Tell me a story..." I said softly. "I just met a woman who enjoyed these cigars. Picked up the taste from her old boss..." I paused. "Know any stories like that?"

I didn't sound angry, and I realized... I *wasn't* angry anymore. Who was I to judge? I had made plenty of bad calls. And, like every son, I had just learned that my father wasn't perfect.

I couldn't begin to imagine molding a tiny human for twenty years into the best version of myself, and that man someday later coming back to me to judge me on my shortcomings. But I imagined it would be… humiliating and painful. Soul-deep painful. Agonizing. Shameful.

He had let out a long sigh at my words, taking some time to gather his thoughts. "I deserve your anger. Don't bury it. Bad for the soul, your mother says."

"As are cigars!" her voice called out from beyond the door, and I burst out laughing.

She had been spying on us, pressing her ear to the door.

"Begone, devil woman!" My father bellowed, grinning like a fool. We heard her shriek playfully, the sound growing further away and turning into overjoyed laughter.

"She always knew how to make us laugh…" I smiled.

My father nodded, chuckling. We both seemed to gravitate towards staring out over the balcony that overlooked the sand-swept plains of wherever the hell this part of the Armory was. I remembered the different landscapes I had seen through the windows – different worlds – despite being only a few feet apart.

All in all, we handled it like brave men. Drinking, smoking, and avoiding any chance of touchy-feely moments. Two cold, powerful men. Family. A naturally occurring Testoster-zone.

"Remember your birthday on the boat? When we talked about extreme measures?"

I nodded, recalling that it was the first time I had heard mention of his Pandora Protocol, which I discovered – many years later – to be this Armory. After he and my mother had been killed for it. By a rogue Academy member trying to gain access to it.

"Around that time, I was… presented with a dilemma." His voice was rough, and he took a long drink, clearing his throat. "The Academy was threatening to take something that they shouldn't take. Straight robbery. *For the good of the world*, they said. Which they believed justified their actions. This artifact was to be taken from an upstanding family – who had provided decades of loyal service to the Academy – that had recently declined to sell the artifact to the Academy. The family had no intent to use this artifact. It was merely a family possession that they desired to keep where it belonged. Period. They weren't even a powerful bloodline."

I found myself interested, because he had rarely shared details on his professional life, instead, fascinated to hear about my own childish adventures with Gunnar. "Go on," I said.

"I fought for them, tried to make the Academy see reason. They didn't need this artifact. And if they *did* need this artifact so badly, *why*? Because the only use for such an item would have resulted in great ripples in the world, harming many magical beings. Or at least, the equivalent of amassing nuclear weapons while stating *we don't want to use them, we promise.*" I remembered G Ma's almost identical comment to me a few days ago. "This did not put me in their good favors, and I soon found myself blocked from any discussions. Discussions that were open to all members of the Academy. Especially members with a name as distinguished as our own. I found out that day that the Academy had become outright political. No longer pretending to be otherwise. They were after power."

"That's typically the case. Whether openly or in the dark. Power is always the goal…"

My dad nodded. "I know, but they had played me well in my life, keeping those topics buried too deeply for me to see. This situation had caught everyone by surprise, because most didn't refuse the Academy. It gained attention like a wildfire, revealing a dark, slumbering monster that none but those at the top had ever known existed within our ranks. Soon a feeling of *if you're not with us, you're against us* permeated the very air in the halls of the Academy. Fear."

I waited, taking a few deep pulls on the cigar, enjoying the taste, and the time with my dad.

"I was… approached. A group within the Academy feared the official stance, and their own safety. I met with them, secretly, with masks, so none may betray another. They seemed virgin, fresh, and I'll admit… *exciting.*"

I nodded, understanding his position. "We ultimately decided to take the item first, use our resources, knowledge, and abilities to get items like this before the Academy could. I ran this operation." He held out his hands, indicating the Armory. "And was quite successful." He took a few moments to enjoy his cigar and a few sips of his drink. I refilled us, waiting, his story helping me relieve myself of those monstrous emotional tentacles my mother had magically ensnared me with.

"I soon learned the error of my ways. The group I had met was part of something larger, and had existed for many, *many* years. The Syndicate," he whispered, finally saying the name out loud. "And now that they had me dead to rights, with proof that I had taken these items ahead of the Academy, they attempted to blackmail me." He met my eyes. "By harming you and your mother. Did you ever wonder why the Academy tried so hard to get you to go to their schools? Although they are hungry to enlist, they usually don't try *that* hard. I believe it was really plants for the Syndicate, but I fought them tooth and nail, researching like a mad man, trying to build up Temple Industries, fortifying the Armory, barring it from entry for all but a select few. I hunted gods, monsters, made deals with devils to keep you, your mother, and this Armory safe. Because *those* monsters were better than the Syndicate, who wanted all the items I had stolen."

I had to remind myself to breathe. "Then you were murdered."

He nodded, tapping his chest with a faint grin. "Was going to happen sooner or later. They were getting desperate. It's why I gave you the Maker's gift, to try and give you a fighting chance, because in my adventures, I found reference to a prophecy long thought dead. It's why I hired Mallory, worked with Shiva, and many others. This was your only option to survive what is to come."

I shivered. "But I ruined that…"

He sighed. "Perhaps. But all is not lost. Many different branches to success sprouted from the fact that you merely *inherited* the power. Nothing was said about a Maker having to be present at the war, just that you needed to *become* a Maker to survive long enough to see it."

"That can't… listen. Prophecies aren't real," I argued.

He shrugged. "Possibly. Then again, you're still breathing, and despite setbacks, the whole world knows your name right now. You must have shown them that Temple charm." He winked.

I smiled softly, nodding. "Yeah…"

"Listen. You dominated an unknown Beast possessing your home, befriended the Four Horsemen, gave a licking to the Grimms, worked with Elders, slapped down the Syndicate, and even batted down the most powerful of the Fae… I think you're doing just fine."

I let out a frustrated breath. "That was all luck. And friends. And none of that matters if Ichabod wakes up a god."

"Gods have been awake before. Really depends on which god he's bringing back." He leveled a fatherly stare on me. "And where you stand when the cards fall…"

Before I had a chance to press him on the prophecy, Mallory burst into the room, panting as if having run several miles to find me.

I jumped to my feet, nerves suddenly feeling like live wires. "What happened?"

"Ichabod…" he gasped. "He's at the gates. You never put the defenses back online!"

Shit. I hadn't reinstituted the wards keeping my enemies out. I tried now, mentally reaching out to Chateau Falco, but heard no response. Was it because I was in the Armory?

I jumped out of my chair, but my father's words made me hesitate. "Talk to him. Try to let him know that not all of the Syndicate is poison. Much like the Academy. And tell him that I would have liked to meet him, maybe I could have even talked him off the ledge."

I nodded, not feeling too optimistic about the result. "We still have time. We'll pick this up later, Dad," I said, forcing a smile. I hoped I wasn't lying.

"Liar," he grinned. "Get over here. Death waits on no man."

Like two men on the gallows, we embraced. No words. Just physical touch.

It's a powerful thing. I felt my anger, my rage, my sadness pulled away, and in its place, was a roaring bonfire of hope. My dad had given me the tools I needed to become the greatest form of myself.

Arete.

The rest was up to me.

"We wanted you to have the world, Nate. Make it a better place," he whispered in my ear.

Then he shoved me away, taking a few giant puffs of his cigar. I did the same.

Mallory grabbed the bottle, raising it for a toast. We smiled back at the wild god, raising our glasses. A sensation seemed to bloom to life in that small space, like a budding flower. A band of brotherhood – immortal, indomitable, steadfast, and resolute. We drank from our glasses while Mallory liberally guzzled the bottle.

Then Mallory and I began to run.

"Bring the terror, Nate! Memento Mori!" my father shouted as we fled the room.

And power seemed to roar up inside me in response, fire suddenly doused with gasoline.

CHAPTER 56

I stood on the opposite side of the gate, the Bentley idling behind me in a soft purr, staring out at my ancestor. He was dressed in a casual navy suit with a crisp white dress shirt. The foreboding gate extended high above his head, parallel bars of old Damascus Steel bridging from one old stone pillar to another, the words *Chateau Falco* looked haunting, a warning, a promise.

I glanced down at my phone as I received a text from a contact I had created, *meddling old wench*. It said two words: *it's done*. So, she was the head dame of the Academy again. I pocketed my phone, smiling to myself. It was early, only an hour after I had last seen him. But he didn't look the same now. Something was different.

Ichabod appraised the *Beware of...* partially-destroyed sign with a chuckle. Then he met my gaze. He smiled politely, as if extending an olive branch.

"Do you eat food?" he asked me.

I frowned. "Well, of course I eat food."

"Let's grab dinner and talk. Under truce. Away from… everything," he waved a hand, encompassing our surroundings.

"You mean away from my protections."

He sighed. "Your wards are down. If I meant you harm, you would already be harmed."

I frowned, opening my mouth to argue, but he forestalled me, raising a palm. "That was not a threat. I understand our interactions have been... unnecessarily tense. I want to dine with my descendant, break bread, talk, and leave on good terms, hopefully."

"I'm not joining your posse."

He shrugged. "All I ask is that you join me for the length of a meal with an open mind. After that, you can leave with the hatred in your heart intact, if that is what you wish." He paused, waiting. "Although, I really hope that isn't the result. Come," he called, "you have my word that I will not harm you." He didn't swear it on his power, but he came from a time when his word had been his handshake, and I could tell, even though I didn't like it, that he was being sincere.

What did he have to gain here?

But I nodded, tossing the keys to Mallory. "Be back soon. Watch the house."

And I Shadow Walked through the gate rather than bothering to open it. His shoulders tightened at my sudden use of magic, but relaxed after seeing I had just been too lazy to go through the laborious process of buzzing Dean to open the gates. We climbed into his Cadillac Escalade, a new model, completely chromed out with all the bells and whistles, but I didn't acknowledge this. I just sat patiently, waiting for the other shoe to drop as he carefully drove through town, a pleased, relaxed look on his face.

~

We sat in a relatively quiet steak house, a table well-apart from any other guests, in the back corner near a window overlooking the city from five stories up. I had been here before. Frequently. With Indie. It had been our spot. A familiar face appeared, our usual waiter.

"Mr. Piper," I smiled. "It's been a while."

He nodded, concealing his grin from his coworkers. "It's John, Master Temple. I hope you've been well."

"Cut the bullshit, John," I said, leaning forward. "Did you get the girl or not? The one..." my eyes flicked to Ichabod, who was watching with sincere interest, "that Indie and I helped you snatch. The one you claimed was *out of your league.*" It was difficult to keep the happiness on my face after mentioning Indie, but surprisingly, Ichabod shot me a saddened look, recognizing my pain, and not gloating over it. Which was just... weird.

"With you two lovebirds as my inspiration for what lay in store for me, I wasn't going to accept anything less than a *yes*. You two gave me hope." He grinned. Stab, twist, rip. My mouth tasted like ashes.

"You got a date?" I managed to maintain my smile.

"I got a *ring*," he corrected smugly.

I jumped up to shake his hand, speaking without thinking. "Wait till I tell... Indie." I said, smile still plastered on my face, but it felt cracked, about to slip. I noticed a chef glaring at John. "Do me a favor, John. My guest and I desire a little privacy, and even less attention tonight. But I'm proud of you. We'll grab drinks soon. You can tell... me all about it."

John caught my tone, reverting back to professionalism, nodding at my request for privacy.

Ichabod ordered an expensive bottle of *Opus One*, and we each ordered a Filet Mignon, chef's choice on every detail. John brought the wine back out a few minutes later, filled our glasses, and departed without a word.

I buried the talk of Indie, and studied Ichabod in the dim lighting. He had cleaned up. Trimmed his beard, cut his hair, and he struck a rather dashing figure. I idly wondered if I would carry any of his features when I was his... well, when I was older. I doubted I would make it to seventy, let alone four-hundred-and-seventy, or whatever he was.

I had seen Ichabod in almost every type of emotion. Shame, guilt, fear, anger, and righteousness. But I had never really seen him calm. I had seen him in a good mood, but I had never seen him look so relaxed, which began to set off all sorts of alarm bells in my head.

He lifted his glass. "To fathers, our role models, our aspirations to greatness," he toasted.

I smiled, unable to stop myself, because his words were genuine, and heartfelt.

"I could ask how you've been, how you like your wine, about the Sanctorum, and a list of other things that would waste time, and leave you on edge, waiting for the other shoe to drop, so I'll just cut to the chase. If that works for you?" he asked, taking another sip of his wine, eyes lidded as he hummed his appreciation.

I nodded. "That would be preferable," I replied. As politely as possible.

"I have acquired a Hand of God." He leaned forward, smiling lightly. "No thanks to you," he chuckled. But he didn't appear to be boasting. I had seen him boasting. He was genuinely amused. Not amused that I had failed, but simply amused, as if I had said a funny, casual joke.

"Oh," was all I could manage, my mind reeling. Who had he stolen it from? But it didn't really matter. Water under the bridge. He had a HOG... he snapped me out of my fears.

"I regret our current situation," he spoke softly, swirling his glass, watching the wine whirl.

"You mean that I don't want to be part of your evil plan?" Here it was. The Ichabod I knew.

He let out a sigh, frustrated, but not at me, at my words. "No, I regret that I didn't take the time to get to know you before embarking on my quest for vengeance." He lifted pained eyes to mine, and my breath tightened in my chest.

It was like I was talking to a stranger. And I instantly flashed back to another dinner, when a Grimm had used his powers to imposter Indie. Was this really Ichabod?

But... the man before me had mentioned things Ichabod would never have told Helmut Grimm. And no matter how good Indie was, I knew it couldn't be her. I would have sensed some flicker of reaction upon seeing our old friend, John Piper. Especially at his good news, which was pretty much solely accredited to Indie's love advice.

So, this really was Ichabod, but not the Ichabod I knew. He interrupted my thoughts.

"Long ago, I risked my life to destroy the group of friends that I knew betrayed my father. And I failed. I was captured," he said, face a mask of grief. "All I wanted was to avenge him. Punish Castor Queen. Destroy the Grimms. But I trapped myself with them, thinking I would be clever enough to escape. Hubris," he muttered, taking another drink.

"I've never had that problem," I admitted with a sarcastic grin. He smiled back.

"But you know all of that. What I'm trying to say is that I spent *centuries* building, growing, and feeding my anger, trapped in a leash held by my enemies. So, I was a bit… wild when I escaped. Feed your beast long enough, and you soon realize it may be calling more shots than you intend." He winked at me. "Free advice."

"I think I already know something about that," I admitted.

He smiled, leaning back. "Here I was, back in the land of the living, released by my very descendent. And what do I do? I flee. To go back to war. Back to what I knew. Living like a feral animal. And never once considering the importance of reconnecting with my only living relative. The last living Temple. Even though you had just been through hell as well. A hell that I had caused, as a leashed dog in their servitude. Even worse, they hated Temples because of *my* actions so long ago. They hated *you* because of *me*. But I took no responsibility for that, or care for your pain. Like a good soldier, I just went back to war. I think they call it PTSD now…"

I studied him, part of me still waiting for the old Ichabod to return, but also surprisingly interested in this new version of the man I thought I had known. My ancestor. I wasn't sold or anything, but I was more open to listening now. "I'm pretty sure they would have found a reason to hate me with or without your transgressions against them," I smiled.

He chuckled, nodding. "Likely. You do have my stubborn streak. They don't like those."

"Then why bring them *back*?" I asked, not as an attack, but truly not understanding.

He sighed. "A necessary evil. The Syndicate knows I'm back, and knows I'm gunning for them, even if they might not have the knowledge of why…" he met my eyes. "About their crimes against my father. I'm sure that was done *off the books*, as they say."

I waited, because he hadn't answered the question.

"I need soldiers, to protect me, but also to help me fuel my plans. Being around me will give them Maker powers, for those who don't already possess such natural gifts. Doing the spell on my own would leave me weakened, and no one wants that. No one even wants me to continue pursuing this, refusing to even believe that the Syndicate is *real*, let alone that they're pulling the strings behind the curtain," he admitted, a touch of anger in his features. But he quenched it instantly, taking another drink of his wine, and refilling our glasses.

I hadn't even realized I had almost finished mine.

"What if you lose control of them?" I countered.

He met my eyes, nodding. "That's one thing I'm here about. Indie can control them, but... she has fled." My heart stopped at the truth in his eyes. "I don't know where she is. And, if you hadn't noticed, she's a little... unbalanced."

"But that is your *fault*! You brain-washed her," I whispered, anger rising back to the surface, but remembering to keep my tone low. *Indie had fled? Good lord...*

He shook his head sadly. "I assure you, I did not."

I leaned back, refusing to believe him. "That... can't be possible. She has changed too much in too short a time. That's not natural. Something had to have happened."

"Something *did* happen, but I swore an oath not to divulge any details." He leaned forward slowly, an eager gleam in his eyes. "Know that I would if I could. But. I. Cannot. Speak. Of. It." He drew out each word, emphasizing them. "But I'm hoping you can find out for yourself. Go. Speak with her," he pleaded.

I growled to myself, punching my palm with my other fist in frustration. "She won't *listen*."

"I fear you're right. But there is no telling what she may do on her own. I *can* say this. Her hatred for the Syndicate almost surpasses my own."

I frowned, wanting to scream, force him to tell me. But I sat in my seat, shaking subtly with unspent tension. I needed to hit something. Blow something up. I took a deep breath, meeting his eyes. "I understand your hatred, but there has to be a better way. I've shown you a better way."

He studied me. "I spent hundreds of years in darkness so complete that I couldn't even *remember* natural light. Only torches, and even those were few and far between – a luxury. I pondered this, planned, debated, schemed." His eyes were distant, cold, merciless. "I came to no other conclusion. My father was right. Only a god could dig them out of their holes, reveal their true identities." He leaned forward. "Those we trust the most have the potential of hurting us the most. Some of our most trusted friends, those like Castor Queen, who brought me candies to a dinner at Chateau Falco only *days* before betraying us to the Academy. I would have bet that the devil himself couldn't have broken that man." He locked eyes with me. "And my father was the *Founder*. One of *them*. Even *he* didn't see it coming."

I shivered involuntarily, wondering if I was reliving their lives, that one of my friends was about to stab me in the back, destroying all that I had built. All that I had saved. Conspiracy. Even the Academy hadn't believed me.

"The Syndicate haven't had their enforcers, their Grimms, and that is the only thing that has saved you since your parents were murdered." He took a deep pull from his drink. "Until now, that is. Because they have Rumpelstiltskin back. Who knows what tricks he has up his sleeves? And now Indie is gone. It is not good. It is potentially *fatal*. No matter where you stand."

He didn't sound as if he was condemning me, even though he had every right to. Because I *had* handed Rumpelstiltskin off to the Syndicate. Whether he knew that part or not, I wasn't certain. I had aided them, even though I hated them for everything they had done, both to me and my friends. To the world. But, like my father, I had knowingly chosen to assist them.

Ah, I love it when judgment comes around, full circle.

CHAPTER 57

*I*chabod nodded at me. "Even though I have every right to be, I am not angry with you. I take responsibility. Rather than sitting you down, like now, and explaining the full story, I chose to pursue it on my own. You did what all Temples have always done. Tried to do the right thing."

I nodded. "Trying doesn't mean succeeding. I'm beginning to learn that." And I took a gamble. "You know my father worked for them. But did you know it wasn't by choice? That he was extorted? They promised to harm my mother if he didn't comply. Harm me. He was also just trying to do the right thing," I said softly.

He nodded in understanding. "It's how they work. The path to hell is paved with good intentions…" he recited. Again, not a judgment of my father, just an observation. "They *must* be eradicated. Waking a god is the only path to success. A god can end them all with one swift action, no matter where they hide."

I sighed, holding up my palm. "That's what scares me. The ability and power to eradicate an entire group of people with one thought. Who is to say this god won't do the same to you. To me. To anyone? It's too much power. Power corrupts, but absolute power—"

"Corrupts absolutely," he finished, smiling sadly in agreement. "I know. But consider this…" Our waiter, John, approached with two steaming steaks, and Ichabod requested another bottle of wine. I was famished, and dug into my steak immediately. The marbled meat practically melted on my tongue, and was just the right side of rare. I saw Ichabod's eyes momentarily close as he took his first bite, murmuring his approval.

"It took me a while to be able to stomach such rich food after I came back," he said, neatly tucking into his steak. We finished our meal in silence, John pouring our drinks with the new bottle, then leaving. We were both lost in thought until we completed our meal, shoving away the plates. John retrieved them, bowing as he left.

"You were saying," I prompted.

"These gods… They were once here, in our very world, correct?" I nodded. "And yet they didn't destroy it."

I frowned. "Well, I'm sure some of them would have wanted to, but the others stopped them. Checks and balances."

He nodded enthusiastically, as if I had hit the nail on the head. "I'm not looking to bring a vengeful, human-hating god back. That wouldn't go well for any of us. After all, my goal is to punish the guilty, not harm the innocent. If I simply wanted the world to end in ruin, I would let the Syndicate have their way, find a quiet home in a quiet corner of the world, and a woman to keep me company. Try to build a library like my father once had. Maybe even get into the book acquisition business," he teased, grinning.

"Fat chance, old man," I said, smiling lightly.

He held up his hands in defeat, grinning. "Maybe work *for* you, rather than trying to compete with you, then. Spend some time reconnecting with my family…" he said, practically a whisper.

I smiled, but the thought was dashed almost immediately. "But you'll be working for a god."

He leaned back, thinking. "Perhaps. But like I said, I don't intend to bring back a vengeful god. Just a *god*. Perhaps even a nurturing god. One who can help heal this broken world…" He watched me, gauging my reaction. Before I could reply, his eyes lit up. "How about this? You give me a list of gods you *don't* want woken up. Then a list of gods you would be okay with. Like I said, I'm not trying to start Armageddon, or Ragnarok. I simply want to punish the wicked. Those who have attempted, and largely succeeded, in enslaving us for so long."

And I began to wonder. What if he was right? What if Shiva was lying, playing a game of his own, jealously hoarding our world for himself? What if we could wake a god, one willing to help heal the cancer of the Syndicate. Not for pain and war, but because they were a slow, lethal poison in our world. A healing god of some flavor.

And an icy chill raced down my spine. A mix of fear, and... hope.

Could he be right? Or was he playing me?

Or was he simply speaking to a relative, admitting his failures, and wanting to rejoin the family? I had met the Hatter. He was a good guy. Dangerous, sure. But everyone I knew was dangerous. The Hatter was a bit cracked now, but had started the Syndicate to prevent the Academy from becoming too powerful. He had lost control of his creation because he had underestimated the greed of his friend, Castor Queen. Queen had wanted power. And had been willing to do anything to get it. Because thus was the nature of man. Not all men, but as a collective, we were pretty violent little creatures. Power-hungry, greedy. Good, sweet, and kind, too. But it only took a few bad apples to ruin a barrel.

But a god? Other than the famed Olympians – who were known far and wide for their pettiness – most gods seemed above such ambitions. After all, they already had power.

"I don't know," I said honestly, thinking furiously at all the possibilities.

He nodded. "I understand. It is a big decision. But consider this. You've been sleeping for centuries, millennia. You suddenly wake up and want to play..." he met my eyes. "Would you immediately go out and light all your toys on fire?" He held up his hands. "I know some would, but that's why I give you the option. Choose whomever you want. We will discuss and debate, of course. I may have knowledge that you don't, and vice versa, but together, I'm confident we can come up with a god who is suitable to the task, and not malicious."

I took a sip of my drink, considering the positives and the negatives.

"Despite our past interactions, and the way I portrayed myself. I am not a bad person. Quite the opposite. I want to punish bad people. I've crossed lines, done things I regret… But they were all in hopes of avenging my father. You once did the same thing, from what Indie has told me." I frowned, but he wasn't looking at me. He took a deep breath, as if debating speaking further. "I also made a Blood Debt. Against the Syndicate," he added in a very soft voice. "And ironically, both yours and mine were related to them, although you didn't know it at the time. I cannot change my course. The power used in my Blood Debt will not *allow* it…"

I just stared, everything suddenly making much more sense. He *had* to finish this.

Because Blood Debts were no joke. His drive and ambition suddenly made a lot of sense.

He set his napkin down, and propped his forearms on the table. "I will proceed in one day. Tomorrow night. Sunset. You can help me, even pick the god. Or, we can continue on as we were. At odds," he said softly, a torn look on his face. "I truly hope that is not the case."

"I'll need to think on this," I said, going back and forth in my mind. "My father wanted me to tell you that not all of the Syndicate were bad. Some were like him… Like your father."

Ichabod nodded in understanding. "They will be given opportunity to repeal and repent, as it were. I won't blindly execute." He leaned forward, face serious. "But I will require *proof*. Many will lie, scheme, cheat, and manipulate to save their hides. Much as an atheist will pray on his death bed. This is a den of vipers, and we must tread carefully. I have no desire to harm an innocent man. But they will need to prove their innocence, and a god will be able to see through the lies." He brushed off his hands, ending the conversation. "Shall I drive you home?"

I shook my head. "Thank you, but I'm going to take a walk. Clear my head."

"Understandable. Tomorrow. Sunset. Beneath the Arch," he said. "I'll be available prior if you wish to speak with me." He turned to go, but paused. "Oh, and if you manage to locate Indie, please let me know. I will do this with or without her, but I'm concerned that she may cause herself harm." He glanced back, meeting my eyes. "Or those close to her."

I nodded absently, swirling the last of my drink as he paid for dinner and left the restaurant.

I spent a good thirty minutes going over every option, back and forth, playing devil's advocate against myself. I finally downed my drink with a growl.

I needed objectivity, and after the meeting with my parents, then Ichabod, I didn't have it.

What does every lone man do when they need to rejuvenate?

I called my dog.

CHAPTER 58

Gunnar blinked at me several times, shaking his head. "That is some seriously heavy stuff," he said, resting his face in his upturned palms, then slowly sliding his fingers through his long, blonde hair. He still wore no man bun, for which I was eternally grateful. Maybe it had finally gone out of style.

I nodded back at him. "Right?"

"And this all happened last night? Over dinner?" I nodded. I had called Gunnar last night, telling him to meet me in the morning. Then I had guzzled several glasses of water, and gotten some much-needed sleep, waking up early to eat a big breakfast. I wanted to be juiced up and ready to go when shit hit the fan. Since I now definitively knew the feces were a-flying.

After breakfast, I had found the mutt on my doorstep, like any faithful hound. Gunnar leaned back in the chair now, lifting the front two legs off the ground as he propped his boots onto the ancient, priceless table, amazed as he stared out at the incredible surroundings.

"Really?" I motioned towards his feet.

"Yes," he replied, not looking at me, eye still tracking the Sanctorum.

I flicked my finger, flipping the front of the chair up so that he crashed to the ground on his back in a loud gust of air. I didn't let the chair fall though. He sat there for a moment, and then began to laugh, resting his hands on his large chest. He then pointed up at the ceiling.

"Your favorite. Like a ceiling of glitter."

I rolled my eyes, and grasped his hand, pulling him to his feet. "Let's walk. We need to work on your *heel*." He merely shook his head, matching my stride. I pointedly glanced down at his boots, acknowledging him with positive reinforcement. "Good boy. Good heel."

He punched me in the arm, lightly for him, but still jarring to me. After a few moments of silence, walking through the center of the massive cavern of books, artifacts, and statues, he spoke up. "Can I finally see it?" he asked excitedly.

I smiled, pulling the Silver Dollar from my pocket. I flipped it on my thumb in a high arc. He shot out a hand to catch it, and an invisible bolt of lightning struck him from on high, along with the now familiar wails of the damned, sending him flipping over a small couch before rolling into one of the shelves. I burst out laughing, having forgotten what it had done to Ichabod.

He groaned, climbing to his feet as he shot me a scowl. "You did that on purpose."

I laughed harder, shaking my head. "No, but I should have remembered. The same thing happened to Ichabod. I honestly forgot." I scratched my beard idly. "But if I *had* remembered, I would have done the exact same thing," I admitted, scooping up the coin from the ground.

"Put it on. I want to see what it looks like."

I shook my head, shoving the coin into my pocket. "No way, man. One time was enough."

He pondered me. "Then why are you still carrying it around?"

I opened my mouth, then let it close. "Just in case, I guess," I said, hoping to change subjects.

He grunted, and rejoined me on our walk. It was fun to watch him, because rather like a new puppy, his eye darted from item to item, up, down, left, right – sensory overload. I had made him swear an oath never to share, talk about, or repeat anything about the very existence of this place. Even to Ashley. He hadn't liked that last part, but memories of my conversation with Ichabod, that the Syndicate was known to find weaknesses and exploit that person into working for them, any one of my friends could be more than they appeared. Even if they didn't want to be.

Everything the Syndicate touched turned to poison. Inciting fear. Both in those working for them, and those working against them. Another point in Ichabod's favor.

But then Shiva had warned me how terrible it could be to wake a god... unless he was lying.

It was one of the main reasons I had wanted no part of my Maker's power. Well, that and it would have been taken from me regardless if I had missed my deadline against the Beast Master.

Fucking curses. Get you every time. Twice, in my case.

"Why aren't you talking with your dad? Mom?" Gunnar asked, having to contort his head much more than most to view the entire cavern. Because he only had one eye to see it with.

"We said our goodbyes. It was... good. About as good as I could ask for. Anything else would have just tarnished it. It's possible that I would have simply stayed there with them until they left, always wanting more, torturing myself and them. Death was right. Clean break is best."

Gunnar nodded in understanding, but he did shoot a sympathetic look my way.

"Plus, I'm trying to avoid my emotions right now. Sitting with them wouldn't help. I need to be objective. I don't have too long to make a decision."

"And you're still convinced it was all a setup? This big secret life plan thing? That you're not just reading too much into your father's comments?"

I shook my head. "Mallory confirmed it." Then I paused, looking at him. "Even you."

"What?" he frowned, slowing down to look at me.

"Your... adoption," I pointed at the rune on his wrist, the one that meant *family*. "Everything. He said I needed a protector. And you came along..."

He was dead silent for a minute, because I hadn't shared that particular piece of information with him when I told him the situation. "Your telling me that your parents had something to do with me being an orphan?" his voice was very low.

I shook my head quickly. "I'm not saying that at all. My father – from some old book, or a conversation with some… being – learned that I would need a protector. Two, actually. Mallory and you. He hired Mallory, and found you. I'm not sure if he picked you because we were friends, or if he somehow helped us become friends. All I know is that our friendship was initiated for a purpose. Good thing we get along, eh?"

"Speak for yourself," he muttered, a faint grin on his face. But I could tell he was troubled.

He opened his mouth, lifting his hands up at the room around us, a dozen questions in his eye. And then the walls began to rumble ominously, and a tingling, unpleasant feeling suddenly dug into the base of my neck. Not physical, but a sensation that something was very, very wrong.

"We need to go. Now!" I shouted, turning to sprint back the way we had come. Gunnar raced behind me, boots pounding into the floor. I veered off into the hallway, torches bursting to light in rapid *pops*, extinguishing behind me just as fast so that it sounded like an ominous staccato drumbeat, urging us on, faster. Gunnar was nipping at my heels to stay within the light as we burst back through the opening into Chateau Falco.

I heard the wall sealing behind us, hiding the doorway, but I was too stunned by the rest of the house to pay it any mind.

It was almost quivering with rage, like a low, earthly growl.

If it had been an animal, it would have been snarling.

Gunnar instantly shifted into his wolf form, an explosion of fabric confetti raining down on us. I shot him a look, and nodded. He tore off down the hallway, sniffing the air as he ran.

I chased him, wondering what the hell was going on.

With a curse, I realized that I had forgotten to turn the security back on. I tried to do so as I ran, but felt a very strong resistance pushing against me, which was what was infuriating Chateau Falco.

Because someone was already here. Either a lot of someones, or one very *powerful* someone.

CHAPTER 59

I pelted after Gunnar as he burst through the open door leading outside. Mallory was on the roof, shooting down towards the tree, judging from the concussive *booms* that echoed across the morning landscape as I continued running towards the action. But whatever he was aiming at wasn't being hit, because all I heard were explosive *clanging* sounds coming from the direction of the tree. Some kind of shield or something.

But it was loud.

A dragon roared, illuminating the sky with flame. Wolves snarled and yelped. Blade struck blade in thunderous blows. At least Tory and Alucard had taken the students home to rest, because this sounded like full-blown war.

Then I saw them around the base of the tree. Indie, with her eyes closed, holding out her hands intently, and the air warping slowly before her as she tried to open the Gateway to the land of the Grimms.

Helmut Grimm still wore his sunglasses as he fought both dragon and wolf with a large sword, not seeming to break a sweat. Then he abandoned his sword in favor of shifting to match the wolves and dragon. Predator on predator.

The air began to grow darker before Indie, and Ashley lunged to tackle her just as I reached striking distance. But Gunnar was faster. He struck his fiancée mid-air, sending them both tumbling into Indie, knocking her from her feet, and ruining her Gateway. Gunnar's white-furred wolf form landed on top of Ashley's smaller, wiry black wolf-form, fangs gently resting against her throat. She whimpered in submission, but didn't sound pleased. But Gunnar knew I was undecided on Indie, that I wanted to talk to her, find out what the hell had turned her psychotic.

Indie jumped to her feet, eyes black orbs, hands outstretched like claws. In fact, they suddenly *became* claws as she glared first at the wolves, and then me. Which would make this all the more difficult. Two Grimms against a few wolves, Carl, and…

I blinked. The Reds! They must have snuck away from Tory's watchful eye.

The teenaged were-dragons darted back and forth before Helmut, long, graceful necks flicking sinuously at the Grimm, trying to take a quick bite out of him. But he was now a larger red dragon. I shot a pleading look at Carl before turning back to Indie.

She still had her claws outstretched at her hips, and she took an aggressive step my way, shouting, "How dare you work with them! The Syndicate are EVIL!" and she threw a bar of white fire directly at me. I barely avoided it, diving to the side at the last second. I had seen that once before. Because it had almost killed my friend, Othello. I met her eyes, shocked she would resort to such lethality so soon, and I saw a panicked look in her eyes, as if she was afraid of what she had just done. Just like she had when she had thrown the spell at Othello. She had crossed a line.

"I'm not working with *anyone!*" I shouted, drawing her attention back to me. I couldn't have her attacking Gunnar and Ashley, who were only just now getting to their feet. I shook my head, eyes darting to Gunnar. He got the hint, and circled around to help against Helmut, leaving Indie and I to face each other.

Another bullet struck an invisible dome around us with a loud *pinging* sound, and Indie's dark eyes angrily darted up to where Mallory was likely perched on the roof. I had no idea if she could do anything about him from here, or even see him, but I wasn't going to let her try. I called on my whips, fire this time. I cracked one twice above her head, showering her with sparks.

Her black-eyed gaze shot my way, and her lips pulled back with fury. "I will have my revenge, Nate. The Syndicate will burn…" she promised. "And all those who aid them."

Ashley was not an obedient puppy.

Because, out of nowhere, she was suddenly airborne again, sailing straight at Indie's back. I hadn't even seen her circle around, and Indie had no idea. From my position, I could do nothing to prevent it.

I opened my mouth to shout a warning, but I let out a strange squawk instead.

Because Carl was suddenly between them, calmly kicking Ashley away before she could make contact. Without pausing, he flicked out a hand, and lightly tapped Indie on the spine.

She crumpled like a wet noodle, unconscious or dead, I wasn't sure.

I stared incredulously. Carl acknowledged me with a wary bow before turning to Ashley who was clawing back to her feet. He bowed to her as well, ignoring the feral look in her eyes.

"My apologies, wolf. I thought it better not to maim Master Temple's fiancée." He glanced at me, eyes hopeful that I would agree. "Despite their recent… relationship struggles. Love conquers all, as they say…" he added as if asking a question, cocking his head like a lizard.

I nodded back, unsure how else to respond. "Thank you…"

But it was a good move, because up until that moment, I had been very concerned about Carl. He had displayed odd affinities for Indie, as a result of her ties to his tree. I wasn't sure if he saw her as a comrade, or worshipped the ground she walked on, but he had just proven that he was firmly on my side.

I heard Helmut struggling behind me, and whirled, having forgotten all about him. The Reds had him subdued, laying on top of him, and Gunnar had the Grimm's throat in his jaws. I approached slowly until Helmut was staring at me from out of his red dragon eyes. "Shift back. Now. Indie is down. Your next choice could determine her fate," I said, my voice cold.

He continued to stare at me, but he must have remembered that the only way to get his brothers back was with Indie. He needed her. In an instant, he was back to human form, naked and hairy. The Reds shifted back, as did Gunnar.

Which left an interesting display of tangled naked people at my feet. Gunnar stepped back, grinning suddenly. "This job," he chuckled.

Because Sonya and Aria were suddenly naked and sprawled across the groin and chest area of a much older man. Like we had just caught them after the act of a very intense… studying session with their professor.

Helmut grinned, glancing down. "That's nice…" he growled.

Sonya and Aria jumped back, glaring down at the Grimm, who only laughed harder at their embarrassment. I tugged off my shirt and threw it at them. "Share," I said, realizing it wasn't that big of a shirt. "Go get inside and get some clothes."

Sonya shook her head, throwing the shirt on the ground as she shot a hateful glare at Helmut. "Like I would ever get with such a hairy old man," she spat, arrogantly placing her hands on her hips. But her eyes *had* assessed his package. Aria shrugged, and tossed on the shirt. It was long enough to just barely cover her rear, and Helmut grumbled his approval.

Out of nowhere, Gunnar kicked him in the freaking head.

Hard enough to knock him out. I turned to him in disbelief. He jerked his head over my shoulder, where Ashley was striding up to the group, naked as the day is long. "I didn't want him taking a peek at my girl," he said flatly.

Aria nodded matter of factly, and Ashley, having heard his comment, gave him the most adoring smile I had seen from her lately. Then she began to kiss him, very intensely.

Sonya cocked her head, studying them, and began a slow clap.

Which brought the two wolves up short, panting lightly, but still clinging to each other.

I turned to Carl. "Take them to the dungeons. You and Mallory are on guard duty."

Gunnar cleared his throat. "Is that a good idea?"

I frowned back at him. "You two obviously need to get a room. The Reds will kill Helmut if he opens his mouth, and I've got some things to do."

Gunnar rolled his eyes. "I meant," he dropped his voice, "because Carl has expressed some unique interests in Indie lately."

I nodded, turning back to Carl. "Swear that you will not let her escape."

"Always, Master Temple. I follow you." And despite his recent actions, I felt the sincerity.

I nodded back. "Gunnar, take the hairy one to Mallory. Unless you want to take him to the dungeon yourself. Have a little talk with him about wandering eyes…"

Gunnar growled back at me as I walked away, unhappy with his situation, but I heard Ashley talking him down and offering to help. Which perked him right the hell up, refusing to let her touch the vile, naked man. I smiled as I walked away. Letting Carl pick up Indie.

But I did glance over my shoulder, verifying that he did as I had told.

I trusted him, but it never hurt to verify.

CHAPTER 60

I had told Gunnar to get his people ready an hour before sunset, just in case. I had also called Tory, telling her to get her students to safety. She had politely informed me that Raego had offered to babysit the students, and that they would be spending some time with Yahn… and the moonstone amulets. I had grinned, telling her when to be at my house. I had sent the Reds home to talk to Raego, letting him know of the situation.

I had a few missed calls. One of them from Van Helsing, but he would have to wait.

I called back the other missed call. "Yeah?" a gruff voice answered.

"Returning your call."

Achilles grunted, recognizing my voice. "That was one hell of a show…" I could hear him grinning, practically drooling on the other end. He lived for the fight. "You still… you know. Nate?" he asked.

I rolled my eyes. "The one and only. No change, which is surprising." He was referring to my Mask. And me becoming a Horseman. As far as I knew, I wasn't one. No obvious signs that I had been recruited to the God Squad. "You haven't seen anything yet. Things might get dicey here, soon. You bored?"

"I don't have plans. Was thinking of shutting the bar down early anyway. What did I miss?"

I took a deep breath, and gave him the big picture. He listened intently, pausing me to ask a few questions, but generally, listening.

He was quiet for a very long time, until I thought he may have been disconnected.

"Hello?" I asked.

"Yeah. Just thinking." I heard him making a drink, ice cubes tinkling, then he took a big sip. "If there's one thing I've learned in my many years, man-child, you should almost always go after the broad."

"I have her here in my dungeon, actually."

He chuckled. "Not very conducive to a romantic encounter. Unless… she's into that."

I sighed, wondering how I could get Indie to calm down enough to have a real conversation.

"Just an opinion. I made the mistake of abandoning the girl once. For revenge." Then he laughed. "Isn't that ironic… Seems everyone is hunting for revenge, and for once, I'm the smartest man in the world."

"That can't last long," I smiled. "Bring your minions."

"With pleasure…" he purred, verifying the meeting time.

I disconnected the call, scrolling up to call Van Helsing back.

I jumped to my feet with a shout as the flip-phone in my pocket began to blare a pop jingle on full blast. *"I just met you, and this is crazy. But here's my number, so call me maybe."* My heart raced, but I answered it, willing to do anything to end the stupid song.

"Cute, Cindy," I growled.

"Thought it appropriate. Wait, who is Cindy?" she asked, confused.

"Cindy. Syndicate. Kind of rhymes," I answered. "You never told me your name, so…"

"Whatever. Listen. Ichabod has a Hand of God. Silver Tongue told us. And we can't locate those in our possession. They seem to have been misplaced."

I sighed. "I heard… I had a chat with Ichabod last night," I admitted, cursing to myself.

"You *met* with him!" Cindy shouted into the phone. "Are you trying to get yourself killed?"

"It was under truce," I replied testily. "I think we need to have a sit-down meeting. I'm not sure how your organization works, but bring some decision makers. I think we need to have a family meeting."

"Family meeting…" she repeated. "We're not meeting with Ichabod. We're not suicidal."

"No… *your* family, not mine."

She paused for a few moments. "That is very interesting. And what makes you think our 'holier than thou' siblings would deign grace us with their presence?"

"Leave that up to me. They owe me a favor."

"Hmmm… White flag and all that?"

"Yes, a shut-down Ichabod discussion. Then a fight. The rest stays on the shelf."

"I don't think you're clever enough to arrange that. They won't listen. They're very talented at the not listening thing," she said caustically.

I took a deep breath, because this next part was risky. If the Academy learned I was housing the Grimms, they might not be able to help themselves, wanting to kill them immediately. If the Syndicate found out I had the Grimms in my dungeon, they would take them and disappear, no question about it.

"The two Grimms abandoned Ichabod. She wants to bring back the rest. And she doesn't need Rumps any longer to do so. Judging from my brief conversation with the newest Grimm, I don't think they're drinking the Syndicate's Kool-Aid any longer. They feel betrayed. And their new boss is not beholden to you."

"Yet," she corrected.

"True, but I'll do you one better. She's hell-bent on destroying you guys for some reason."

The line went very quiet, and I realized she knew something.

"Which is only going to help her recruit…" I let that comment draw out for a few silent seconds. "Why don't you tell me why she hates you. You know something. Maybe I can help."

"When do you want to meet?" she said instead, avoiding the question.

"An hour before sunset. Ichabod is moving forward at sunset. This gives us time to plan, talk, strategize."

"Where?" she asked tersely.

"Chateau Falco."

"No. Too much protection there. You could shut us all down."

"Yes," I argued. "But if I really wanted to shut you down, I wouldn't need the house." She laughed out loud at that. "It's also the only place the Academy will agree to, *because* of its protections. Keeping them safe from *you*. Two, I have some more Gurkhas…" I smiled.

"Sold to the man with the Gurkhas," she replied, amused, but I caught the momentary pause before she had replied.

"Not-so-subliminal conversations, we were having," I said in my best Yoda impersonation.

"I don't know what you're talking about, weirdo." And she hung up. Maybe the age-gap had killed my comment. Then again, I'd never heard an older woman like her say *weirdo*.

I let out a breath as Sir Muffle Paws jumped onto my desk, landing beside a book. He looked at it, deeming it worthy of his bulk for the duration of a nap. He stepped onto it, performed three precise circles, and then promptly lay down, purring contentedly. I smiled absently, picking a new number on my phone as I set Cindy's phone down.

She answered on the first ring. "Yes?" she said in a clipped tone.

"Remember that new club I told you about? We're meeting." I gave her the time and place.

There was a very long pause. "We're all going to die, aren't we?" she asked.

I wasn't sure if she was being literal, or making a joke. "No. We're going to behave like adults. Drink. Talk. Discuss our common goal. No history. Then we fight him." I gave her a quick rundown on the situation, hearing her breathing grow faster on the other end. Not afraid, but definitely stressed.

"How many do you need?"

"All you can trust."

She paused. "You realize that this provides me an excellent opportunity to possibly ferret out some double agents. If I invite them, and they can't show, they can be added to a list for me to later look into."

I sighed, understanding her position, but not having any time to care. "Do what you will. But you come in peace. Or you will leave in pieces."

She grunted instinctively, then cut it short, remembering who she was talking to, and our new positions. "I see," she corrected. "We will see you soon."

"Wait," I urged before she could hang up. "For the meeting, only bring yourself and one other. I want to make sure we're all on equal footing. If they bring one, only you come in. If they bring two, you have a backup. Have the rest on standby for sunset at the Arch."

"And if they bring an army to the meeting?"

"I doubt they would, because they don't want to expose how many of them there truly are. And you would notice if a large chunk of your Academy was suddenly unavailable." She murmured agreement. "Also, if they bring more than two, they wait outside. If they bring one, your backup waits outside."

"Smart," she said approvingly. Then she hung up after a hasty good bye, not waiting for my response. It sounded more rushed than disrespectful, as if she suddenly had a thousand things to arrange beforehand.

But even if she had been being petty, I didn't really care. Let her have her small victory.

As long as it got her wrinkly ass here in time.

I tried calling Van back, but he didn't answer, so I sat back in my chair, planning, scheming, trying to count three steps ahead of the upcoming battle as I idly watched Sir Muffle Paws doze away on my copy of *Through the Looking-Glass*, dreaming sweet dreams, not a care in the world.

CHAPTER 61

I had primped and preened, dressed in a tee with a casual sports jacket and jeans. I wore new boots, and had even trimmed up my beard a little, throwing on a bit of product to tame my wild hair. I looked and smelled fresh. But I stood on the other side of the door, not moving. Terrified. Anxious. Eager. Desperate. Angry. Hurt. Heartbroken.

Because all that separated me from Indie was the wooden door leading to the dungeons.

With a long sigh, I pulled open the door, and took a step inside, masking my emotions behind a calm, cool, and collected façade.

The face of my father.

The face of a Temple.

Carl was already standing; no doubt having noticed me lurking outside for ten minutes. He dipped his head, and glanced over at the first cell. Indie sat on a wooden stool, facing the wall, but at least her back wasn't pointed my way. Her hair was messy, and her clothes were stained and ripped in a few places, but she wasn't bleeding anywhere, and looked unharmed.

"Has she said anything?" I asked.

Carl shook his head. "Not a word." He pointed over his shoulder, past a second set of doors. "Helmut is down there with Mallory. He didn't want them talking to each other." Carl looked uneasy, anxious as his eyes darted to Indie.

I frowned. "What's wrong, Carl?"

He turned back to me. "Have you seen my brothers?"

"They are guarding the grounds, like they have been for the past few days."

He nodded, tension fading from his face. "Okay. I haven't had time to check in on them, what with spending so much time with you at the mansion."

I smiled. "It's okay. Juggling tasks is part of being a good leader. You'll get the hang of it."

Carl nodded. "Very unusual for us. We stay close. Like a pack. Makes my skin itch not being near them for such a long spell."

I put my arm around his shoulder. "I'll get you back with them soon. Maybe rotate one of them out for you here."

Carl suddenly stared out at one of the tiny fist-sized windows, distracted. A moment later, an owl flew by, a feather landing on the outer edge of the window. Carl let out a relieved breath, shooting me a sickly grimace. "Thought I heard something out there."

I felt a little uneasy. Was being away from his people that much of a drain on him? I really knew nothing about the Elders. This whole time I had been treating them like I would any other human. But maybe I was wrong. Maybe he shared traits with werewolves, needing to be part of something bigger.

"I'll get the hang of it. Just adjusting. No need to rotate me out, Master Temple."

I watched him for a few moments. He watched me right back, unblinking, which was one of his many creepy traits. Especially with his albino scaled lizard-like face. "Just let me know if you change your mind. She can't get out of here on her own, and can't use her powers here in the dungeon due to the wards, but I want to make sure we have a guard here at all times, just in case."

"Yes, Master Temple. I will let you know."

I stepped past him, closer to Indie. She didn't move. Not even her eyes. She just continued staring at the wall, as if in a trance. But her breathing was regular, and as I tapped on the bars of the cell, her body shifted minutely, letting me know she was purposely ignoring me.

"Indie," I breathed. "Talk to me. I need to understand."

She didn't reply.

"What happened? Why did you leave Ichabod? Why didn't you come to me sooner? Why block me out? What did he do to you?"

She let out a soft grunt of disdain.

"I want to help."

"Then let me out of this cage so I can go destroy the Syndicate," she said, voice monotone, not shifting her gaze in the slightest.

"Not until you tell me what happened."

Her lips tightened. "What's the old saying? Like father, like son?"

Which lit me up like a bonfire. "Who the *hell* do you think you are? You think you're the only one who has ever experienced *pain*?" I roared. "Boo-fucking-hoo. You got an owie, and now the world needs to burn. Poor little Indie. Got killed, came back from the dead for a second chance, but that still wasn't good enough for her highness. Got a buffet of power dumped into her lap, and ran away to train with a stranger rather than her fiancé. Scraped her knee, and decided to become a full-fledged terrorist. Not asking her fiancé – who hadn't heard from her in *months* – for help, but put his entire city at risk as she had her temper tantrum. Even after I came in and saved the day, like I *always* do…"

She didn't reply, which only compounded my anger. My pain. My broken heart.

"Your pride just couldn't take it. The spotlight wasn't on the once brilliant, once beautiful, bookstore manager I fell in love with." I slapped my palm into the bar to enunciate each of my next words. "And. You. Threw. A. Fit," I snarled, vision blurring, the entire cell seen through a red haze. "Then you almost killed my friend. *Your* friend. And stole from me," I seethed. "But *that* wasn't enough for Princess Prissy Pants, either. You had to attack a school of innocent, struggling kids." I dropped my voice into a dark hiss. "I have a theory on that. You can't stand that they are strong where you are weak. They overcome. You submit, masking your weaknesses behind a wall of excuses and finger-pointing. You're not the woman I knew. You're a coward."

I turned my back on her, taking deep, shaking breaths. Carl stared at me, amazed at my outburst. I saw Mallory standing in the open doorway, eyes wide in stunned silence.

I heard a small sob, and slowly turned.

Two tear drops rolled down the face of the woman I had once loved.

But she still sat with her back straight, eyes pools of tears, doing her best not to cry. The sob had been an involuntary escape of the river of emotions roaring through her.

And I felt like shit.

Kind of.

"An *owie*," she whispered, repeating one word from my soapbox speech. She let out a humorless chuckle of disbelief, sucking it back in immediately. "Leave. Now."

I did.

Before I exploded with the anger and guilt warring to consume my soul.

Carl and Mallory watched me leave, not uttering a word.

CHAPTER 62

I sat in the fully-stocked living room near the front entrance, waiting on my guests to arrive: the Academy and the Syndicate, Gunnar, Tory and Alucard, Mallory – maintaining his guise as my bodyguard – and Achilles. I heard a car pull up, and Dean stuck his head in to warn me.

But I was already on my feet, walking towards the doorway. I patted the head of one of the Guardians on my way by. Dozens of them now moved freely throughout the house, a display of power, but also for my protection. They would keep this meeting from turning into a bloodbath.

Dean opened the door before anyone knocked, welcoming them to my home as a guest.

Which was important. Because *Guestright* would also act as an added benefit. If they accepted the offer to enter as a guest, then harmed someone, they would have to sacrifice – not permanently – a significant chunk of power as retribution. Until they were able to rectify their grievance against the host. Leaving them weaker for the other guests to pounce on. The house was quiet, acting as any other house, but the Guardians each paused to study the newcomers.

G Ma stood at the door, an older gentleman behind her. He looked frail, but his eyes were deep with knowledge and power. I didn't know him by looks, but imagined he held some important title in the bureaucratic machine that was now the Academy. Maybe even the person who would have taken G Ma's place if she hadn't submitted to me in the Fight Club.

G Ma nodded at me politely after accepting Dean's invitation. She turned to speak over her shoulder. "Please wait outside. It seems I am the first one to arrive. Children these days don't understand punctuality," she added, smiling sweetly at me.

I didn't rise to the bait as I led her into the room. Mallory was suddenly present, offering her refreshments. He had uncorked several bottles of nice wine and a few pitchers of ice water, as well as bringing out a large tray of tiny sandwiches. She accepted some wine, and sat back in one of the couches, idly watching the two Guardians wrestling with each other before the lit fireplace. "No need to dawdle. I'll be fine while you gather the other guests," she spoke to me without looking.

I smiled, and came back to the foyer just as Gunnar and Ashley entered. Gunnar wore his catchy eyepatch, which made me smile even wider. He grimaced in response, turning to Dean, who had politely squeezed his upper arm in greeting. He did the same for Ashley. The two werewolves wore *family* runes tied to the Temple Clan, and were not considered guests, but extensions of *me*. They joined G Ma in the other room, pouring drinks and sitting across from her. Light conversation flowed, and I turned back to the entrance, waiting.

So far, so good, I thought.

The nameless silver-haired Syndicate member appeared in my driveway out of thin air. No car or anything. Then again, I hadn't been able to turn the defenses back on because of this meeting. Because technically, almost everyone coming was some sort of enemy.

The Guardians had become very alert, but then again, maybe that was a result of the shocked squeal of alarm G Ma's partner wizard had emitted upon turning to find the Syndicate member suddenly standing behind him. Interesting… The wizard hadn't sensed her using magic, but she had obviously used some form of magic to get here. I hadn't even given it any thought, because I had seen her do wizard stuff, so had just assumed she was a wizard. But perhaps she was also more. I could tell she was no Maker, thank the gods, but she was… something.

I noticed the conversation in the other room had suddenly grown quiet at the sound of the wizard shrieking outside. I quickly darted through the open door to prevent a potential attack as I heard Dean say behind me, "Welcome, Miss…"

But I didn't hear her reply as I met G Ma's concerned look. "He's okay. Just startled. She came alone."

"Yes, didn't want to cause a panic," Cindy replied from directly behind me, making my shoulders tighten. "Is that hunk of metal outside an expensive art piece? Something only a trust-fund brat could appreciate?" she teased.

"Creepy factor of eleven," I said, turning to shake her hand, ignoring her quip. Her silver hair was pulled back in a bun, and she wore dark pants and a shirt, the better to fight in, I guessed. She accepted my handshake awkwardly, and I motioned for Mallory to grab her a drink. Which was important.

Giving someone a drink, or anything to hold, reduced their cognitive functions by a small margin, giving them one more thing to consciously consider. So, if things went sideways, whether they knew it or not, I would possibly have an extra iota of time to react. Also, sandwiches, to give them *two* somethings to worry about. Gunnar and Ashley had scarfed both their snacks and food, subtly proving that it wasn't poisoned, while also drawing attention to the familiar preconceived notions people held about werewolves being unsophisticated.

But they had actually eaten fast so that they would have their hands free if shit went down. We had rehearsed this with everyone after events a while back when Gunnar had royally fucked up with a guest, putting me in a pickle. A curse, to be precise.

I realized that G Ma and Cindy were staring at each other like two strange cats in an alley. "Do I need to get a squirt bottle or something?" I asked, smiling softly.

They turned their glares on me for a moment, then realizing they had acted in concert, quickly averted their eyes, both taking a seat. "Is this everyone?" G Ma asked impatiently.

"Can't have a party without me," Achilles called out cheerfully, entering the room, tugging Asterion and Ganesh behind him. Which caught G Ma and Cindy *entirely* off guard. I hadn't known he was bringing the two with him, either, but I was suddenly pleased with his initiative.

"Lord Ganesh, and Asterion, the Minotaur." I pointed at Achilles. "And my bartender."

G Ma and Cindy seemed to have barely heard me, openly staring at the trio.

Another few seconds added to the reaction factor, I thought to myself, knowing that everyone would be a little less interested in throwing down with these three in the room.

Tory slipped past Asterion, who was shifting uncomfortably from foot to foot under the attention of G Ma and Cindy. Ganesh waved from over his shoulder, his ears rippling out of habit. Alucard trailed Tory, a smooth smile on his face. He also wore sunglasses, a bro-tank, swim trunks, and flip flops. A statement. The sun was his friend. Porcushine.

They waved at me, but shifted their smiles to blank stares at G Ma and Cindy.

"You crashed my party," Tory said with false pep in her voice. "We'll talk about that. Soon. But not right now. Because I respect Nate." And then she flashed them a dazzling smile, but her eyes shifted bright green for a few seconds, reminding them she was more than just a pretty face.

The two older women tensed at this, again, like angry cats.

Then their eyes latched onto Alucard. He smiled at them, faintly revealing his fangs. Enough for them to notice, but not enough to appear threatening.

"Vampire," G Ma growled.

"Master Vampire," Cindy corrected.

"*Daywalker* Master Vampire," Alucard grinned, taking off his sunglasses. "But you can just call me Sunshine."

I bit back my grin. "Meet Alucard. The humblest man… *monster* I know."

"Obliged," he drawled, turning on his Southern charm.

"Converse!" I clapped my hands. "Break the ice. This is a truce. I'll be right back."

I had tried calling a few others, but hadn't heard back yet. I approached Dean. "Master Temple," he smiled, pleased to be doing something in his typical capacity for once.

"I think this is all of us, but be ready for any additional guests." I began to turn away, but he caught my arm.

"There is someone waiting out back by the kitchens. I didn't want him alarming the others."

I frowned. "Who?"

"One of Carl's... associates," he said. "I didn't understand his name, but I doubt I would have been able to repeat it if I had," he admitted.

I nodded, remembering Carl trying to tell me his real name once. I had given up and settled on *Carl*. "Okay. Speaking of the Elders, I think we need to be more... considerate. We've been treating them like humans, and I'm beginning to realize that they really aren't like us. Maybe get to know them a bit, give them some freedom, ask what they need. That kind of thing."

He nodded, thinking. "That is very... wise of you. This is my specialty. I will think on it."

I clapped him on the back. "Good. Keep them from killing each other until I get back," I called over my shoulder, jogging towards the kitchens.

Not looking first, I opened the sliding door, and gasped to find one of the Elders only a few inches from the glass, waiting patiently with his hands behind his back. He took a step back, frowning, as if unsure of his offense.

"It's okay. You just startled me," I said, smiling politely.

He looked slightly relieved, and nodded. "I spoke to... Carl," the word sounded alien on his tongue. "And he requested that he be given a few minutes to check on us. I offered to switch with him, but he told me to speak with you first."

I smiled, nodding. "That is fine. Give him all the time he needs. Thank you for being such a great help around here. I truly appreciate it."

He shot me a sickly smile, but I reminded myself that they were unused to being civil. Those were human things. Dogs and monsters didn't say *thank you*. They just didn't eat you if you hadn't displeased them. The Elder turned and left. "Try not to scare the wizard out front!" I yelled. He waved his hand, acknowledging he had heard me, but he didn't slow down.

I jogged back to the living room, ready to do something important, give a rousing speech that would leave everyone shouting, *Nate! Nate! Nate... You're toe-tah-lee awesome and stuff!*

Where was Yahn when you needed a cheer squad?

CHAPTER 63

Instead, I entered to find everyone yelling at each other, and a desperate looking Dean waving his hands in the air like a madman.

I touched the doorframe with a hand, and called out to Chateau Falco.

She answered with a loud *thump* that made the walls shake and the chandelier suddenly begin swinging to and fro. Everyone halted, staring up at the ceiling, but they were all powerful practitioners of one sort or another, and knew that the sound hadn't been caused by something falling down on an upper floor.

Because the very air tingled as if lightning was about to strike.

I cleared my throat, and they all turned to face me, various shades of astonishment and fear in their eyes. Except for my friends. They knew about Chateau Falco already. Although they did look a little guilty at not stopping the arguing themselves before the house had to do the dirty work for them.

"I think everyone needs to calm down, enjoy their refreshments, and celebrate their similarities, not display their differences," I spoke clearly, politely, but sternly. "The house doesn't tolerate rudeness from her *guests.*" I was sure to enunciate the last word, reminding them of the situation, of their agreement.

Everyone composed themselves, shooting quick, guilty glances about the room.

I took a seat on a vacant chair, eyes roving from person to person with faint, thankful nods for their acceptance in joining me here today. Dean approached on silent feet to hand me a drink. I took a sip, and began to speak as he quietly left the room. All eyes riveted on me. "Here's where we stand…"

And I very carefully laid out the situation. Indie had gone rogue and wanted to free the Grimms. Ichabod wanted to wake a god. I left out such trivial details as, *I tried to rob the Academy*, or *I kicked G Ma's ass at the Fight Club*, or *the Mad Hatter is my relative and agrees with Ichabod*, or that *I'm currently holding the Grimms captive in my dungeon.*

Just the relevant facts.

They listened in rapt attention, many of them aware of different aspects that I was omitting, but since they didn't know what parts everyone else knew, they were all content to feel like the smartest kid in the class. Ahead of the group. Like I favored them over others. I caught many discreet nods, winks, and conspiratorial grins during my diatribe, but I didn't acknowledge any.

"I'm not sure if this is part of some larger goal. Two different goals. Different phases of the same goal. A distraction…" I trailed off. "All I know is that they each hate the Syndicate."

G Ma spoke up. "On that we can agree," she breathed.

Cindy smiled too sweetly at G Ma. "I must profess my agreement with bringing back the Grimms. Makes my life so much easier not to handle all the dirty work. Of course, I would have to kill this Indie to take them back. I wouldn't want anyone trying to sweep up our sloppy seconds." Her eyes locked on G Ma.

Without warning, and saving us from the cat fight, Inky and Barbie, two sprite representatives of the Fae who always managed to interrupt at the worst possible moments, suddenly burst into the room. I scowled at Dean, but he merely stared at them, shaking his head. They zipped over to Tory, hovering near her ear, whispering something to her that I couldn't catch.

Barbie was a stunningly beautiful silver sprite who disagreed with clothing, and she could appear as whatever she wanted to be. For example, a werewolf, a fully-sized human, anything. I wasn't sure if it was illusion or magic, but I had seen her do it numerous times. She was a nympho-sprite as well, gaining her power from sex.

Don't ask.

Inky, on the other hand, was an ebony-colored matronly sprite, and I wasn't entirely sure what abilities she had. All I knew was that when the two showed up, I started to get a headache.

Tory listened intently, then frowned at them. They looked agitated, nervous, and angry.

Tory turned to us. "The Fae are concerned. They sense change in the air. They want me to tell you that *theirs is safe*. And desire to know *who failed*." The sprites nodded their agreement.

They were talking about the HOGs, which made G Ma quietly angry.

I glanced at Cindy, who looked murderous. "We are still trying to find ours." G Ma, although startled to hear the news, also bore a slightly satisfied expression on her face at Cindy's failure.

"I think it's safe to say it was theirs. But we're going to stop them," I told the silver sprite.

"See that you do." Then they zipped back out the door. Everyone was silent for a moment.

"See? This is productive. We all have reasons for agreeing to stop Indie and Ichabod. But I think we can agree on the most important thing – no one wants an angry god to come back with a Maker in his pocket. Even a nice one." Until I said it out loud, I hadn't even been sure I was in agreement with this. But I wasn't a fan of a supreme being walking in and telling us how to live our lives. Everyone seemed to agree, but the Minotaur was silent.

"Who are the likely candidates?" Gunnar asked, drawing my attention away.

I pointed at Mallory, who handed me a dossier as if waiting to do so. G Ma frowned at that.

I tossed it on the table. "These are the potential sleeping gods. At least those we could discover. My father had gathered this list long ago. Not for these purposes, but more of a compendium for the gods. All of them. Consider this the consequences if we fail. A motivation of sorts," I added drily. "We have less than an hour before we need to be at the Arch. Make your arrangements so your reinforcements will be ready and waiting by sunset."

Everyone nodded, pulling phones to their ears or typing texts.

I stood beside Mallory, not speaking, letting them discuss amongst themselves. I sipped my drink, replaying my argument with Indie. Mallory nudged my elbow, looking at the clock. It had been fifteen minutes, and everyone was pouring through the papers on the desk, discussing and debating with each other.

Putting the situation into harsh perspective.

I had already read the list. Had spent hours reading over it, discussing it with Mallory. He hadn't necessarily been sold by Ichabod's offer, but he did see potential merit in it. "Is this the right call?" I asked him softly.

He shrugged. "There are right calls, and right calls. If it means anything, I would have done the same." He smiled. "But that could just mean we're both wrong," he admitted.

I sighed, watching them look at the lists. I had been concerned I would find Odin's name on the list, what with the ravens seen hanging out in my tree lately, like a bad foreshadow. But Odin was already awake, and had been for some time, apparently. Still, his ravens were on my crest...

As they discussed and debated, sharing what they knew of the gods on the list, one voice was surprisingly silent. Ganesh. I walked over to him, smiling. "Glad you came."

He met my eyes with a faint smile. "You took my moment of glory at the Fight Club. Wanted to stretch my legs a bit." I smiled, nodding.

"What do you think?" I finally asked him.

He shook his head discreetly, and whispered, "Don't do it."

And I felt an icy orb hit me in the stomach at his tone. *Don't do what?* I thought to myself.

"What do you think, Lord Ganesh?" G Ma asked, watching us skeptically. He gave me one last look and then walked over to the table, sharing what he knew with a somber voice.

I pondered his comment, letting them discuss. When I looked up, I saw Asterion watching me thoughtfully. He gave me a slow nod, and then jumped back into the conversation. I frowned at his back, growing frustrated as I turned away.

To find Achilles watching me. He mouthed one word. *Indie.* And then he tossed me a bundle of fabric. I opened it to see his *God save the Grimms* tee from our meeting in the Armory. I met his eyes. "I washed it," he said.

I turned around and walked up to the bar, refilling my drink in a shaking fist.

Ganesh, Asterion, and Achilles all had conflicting advice, it seemed. I had literally no idea which decision was right. They all had *potential* positives, and *definite* negatives.

And I had been avoiding another topic of concern. The Hatter still had my cane. The one with my Beast. I needed to get that back once all this was finished. Bury it deep. Lock it away in the Armory or something. And if I stood against Ichabod, how in the hell was I going to look the Hatter in the face and politely ask him to give me back my cane. *Oh, yeah. I stopped Ichabod. Your long-lost son. Can I have my cane back now?*

Because if Ichabod and I met on the field of battle, one of us would die.

I looked at my watch, surprised that time was almost up. We had ten minutes to get there. I could Shadow Walk any stragglers, or make a Gateway, but still, it was time to get ready for the dance. "It's time."

G Ma suddenly spoke. "Just a moment. Stopping Ichabod is important. No argument. We will battle him and prevail." She snorted confidently, indicating the room full of extremely powerful people. "But we are neglecting to discuss the other problem. That of the Grimms."

I cleared my throat. "They aren't a concern. Trust—"

Dean burst into the room, a frantic look on his face. He stared at me, mouth opening several times, choosing his words carefully. "Carl has been injured," he said warily.

I blinked. "What? How? Did he fall down?"

Dean was shaking his head, looking frustrated as his eyes darted back and forth to the guests in the room and me, trying to get me to understand something he wasn't speaking out loud. "No, he's… where he was earlier when you spoke with him."

My heart stopped, darting to Mallory, who suddenly looked very, very concerned. Confusion overtook me, overwhelmed by too many moving parts, too many enemies. "He asked me if he could switch with Carl. That Carl had asked him to…" I trailed off, momentarily dumbfounded.

Mallory growled. "Carl told me he wouldn't dare switch places with them. That something felt wrong."

"They escaped," I said, locking eyes with Dean. He nodded adamantly.

"Who escaped?" G Ma demanded.

Cindy looked me in the eyes, assessing, then they flashed in revelation. "His lady love. He had her captive this whole time, the naughty boy!" she turned to the group. "The Grimms!"

CHAPTER 64

The room devolved into panic, everyone shouting over one another, until the house began to rumble and groan, silencing them all.

"Okay. New strategy. We still have to go stop Ichabod. But now we also have to stop Indie." I looked up to find everyone staring at me. "We have to split up."

The room was silent.

Before anyone could argue, I made the decision, wrapping myself in a void of cold, analytical action. My emotions were a danger now. "The Academy and the Syndicate will confront Ichabod. You are the most powerful, the only ones able to stop him, a Maker."

The two women – enemies of each other – locked eyes, and after a very tense moment or two, nodded. They even shook hands.

"We need at least one magic user here to hold-off Indie. The rest will be shifters. Overwhelming odds. Because it's not just her, but Helmut and the Elders."

"A bloodbath," Achilles grinned. "You don't bloody disappoint, Temple. Not at all." And he was suddenly holding his helmet, and a spear butt hammered into the ground in his other fist. He donned his helmet, and Cindy – the silver-haired whatever she was – appraised him like a wildcat studying a lamb.

She really *was* a cougar.

I clapped my hands. "Go! Shoo! Time is a-wasting!"

G Ma and Cindy were the first out of the room, the rest followed me as I jogged towards the front door. Dean caught my arm, pulling me back with surprising strength. Everyone jogged past me, congregating in the driveway, scanning the grounds, searching for Indie. I noticed Sir Muffle Paws watching me from the hallway, twitching his tail back and forth. He lifted his chin disdainfully, and then turned his back on me, strutting down the hallway, away from the mangy humans.

He was much nicer when he slept. Most other times he looked like he wanted to eat your face, but he was kind of cute when sleeping. Like earlier, in my office when he had been sleeping on the book, *Through the Looking-Glass*, while I made phone—

I froze, eyes darting back to him, but he was gone.

He had been sleeping on my book.

The one I had spelled.

The one that should have zapped the ever-living hell out of him on contact.

Yet I had watched him touch it, and even go to sleep on it.

Dean shook me again, harder, physically shaking away my alarm. "Master Temple! Are you even listening?" He was shoving a pistol into my hands, urging me to take it. My fingers closed around it, and I looked back up at him. He grabbed me by the cheeks, staring into my eyes. "Pull. The. Trigger." Then he shoved me out the door, closing it behind me. And I knew exactly who he meant for me to shoot.

Indie.

I stumbled down the steps to find Achilles, Ganesh, Asterion, Gunnar, Ashley, Tory and Alucard watching me. They looked at the pistol in my hands, and their faces grew somber. Achilles shook his head very slowly so that no one else could see.

I didn't consciously know why, but I flung off my jacket and tore off my shirt, replacing it with the one Achilles had given me. Tory rolled her eyes, but Achilles nodded in approval. I shoved the pistol in the back of my pants, but I knew if I was going to use any gun, I was going to use my abracadabra gun. Magic. I silently commanded the Guardians to protect Chateau Falco, since the wards were still down, and there was an unknown force preventing me from bringing them back online.

Indie.

I ran, and my monsters followed.

~

WE REACHED THE TREE, but no one was there. Not a Grimm or Elder in sight.

"Where else could she have gone?" I hissed out loud, wondering why the Elders had freed her in the first place.

Then it hit me.

The Elders had been searching for her for a long time, thinking her the key to their freedom. The fact that she had died there, and been brought back had prevented them from feeding on her. Only Carl and a few dozen of his friends had made it over. Kind of like the Grimms. Limited.

They were trying to break free.

But Indie had goals of her own, and wouldn't be afraid to murder all of them to get her way.

But there were no dead Elders on the ground. Which meant they had agreed on something.

The Hand of God. Pandora had mentioned that the Elders had one. Indie must have made a deal of some kind, like *Give me the Hand of God and I'll free you.*

To be honest, it was a twofer. She could possibly get not only an army of Grimms, but *another* army that the world had decided to banish hundreds – if not thousands – of years ago.

"We might need more fighters," I said out loud, suddenly very nervous.

"What are you talking about, Nate?" Tory asked, eyes darting around the grounds as if I had seen something they hadn't. "I could get the students. Do you want me to call Raego? You think we need them?" she asked in a nervous whisper

I turned to face her, to face everyone. "No. We don't have time for that. Indie's here. Now. In the tree, I think." I shouted at the top of my lungs, not seeing Mallory with the group. "Mallory! We're going to need you down here. NOW!" My rushed breathing was terrifying everyone.

Gunnar gripped me. "Nate, calm down. What is going on?"

"I think she made a deal. Free her, and she'll free them. *All* of them. The Elders."

"I thought they wanted to *kill her and eat her*," Gunnar argued.

I nodded. "That's what they initially thought, but she's a Grimm with the power of a Maker. She can do a lot of things. And she's been training with Ichabod. She could do it. If she can open a Gateway for the Grimms, she can open a Gateway for the Elders. They don't need to eat her. She'll open the door *for* them. And I bet you she asked for their Hand of God as a bonus. I think this whole damn thing has been a ruse. Or a series of unfortunate events. Or a power-play."

Gunnar turned to look at the tree. "Which means we have two armies coming our way."

"Worst case scenario," I agreed.

Tory was already on the phone, as was Achilles. Alucard looked thirsty.

For blood.

I glanced back at Ganesh to see he had taken the time to fix long, curved, wickedly-serrated blades to his tusks, a good four or five feet each, arcing out away from his body. His eyes were black orbs, and his ears were tucked back slightly, like a dog when they were in a scrap. His shoulders also bunched forward, and his upper two arms held bone axes, his lower two hands some kind of wicked spiked device over his knuckles.

Brass knuckles?

I shivered at the sight. He was a nightmare.

Then there was Asterion. He had ripped off his traditional robes, wearing only cotton pants that were tied tightly just above his knees, the ribbons blowing freely in the wind like Macho Man Randy Savage from those wrestling events. Matching ribbons were also tied around his biceps, and the tips of his horns had foot-long trident attachments, looking like rough, unfinished steel, blacker than coal. The runes on his nose ring pulsed with golden light, casting a reflection back on his eyes so that it looked like his glare pulsated with golden power. He snorted, shaking his head and squeezing his fists until I heard the knuckles pop. The Minotaur didn't want a weapon. He *was* the weapon.

He met my eyes. "Just like the bachelor party," he grinned.

He must have been thinking of a different bachelor party, because although things had gone sideways at Gunnar's weekend bash, it hadn't ended in a full-blown war. But I nodded anyway.

Two dozen black-clad men suddenly raced towards us as if out of nowhere.

"Have they been here the whole time?" I asked Achilles incredulously, recognizing his Myrmidons, the legendary sackers of Troy.

He shook his head. "I had them on standby. Outside the gates. Didn't want to spook the Elders guarding your walls," he shrugged. He watched me as his men gathered around him. None spoke, focused on only their spears and shields. White painted stripes splashed down their helm and chest, as if someone had dipped their hand in paint and simply wiped it from top to bottom. It wasn't neat. It wasn't perfect. But it looked haunting.

I avoided Achilles' stare, knowing he was reading me, wondering what I would do about Indie. But I was pretty sure that our relationship had changed to *it's complicated...*

As if on cue, the giant pale tree suddenly began to glow, brighter and brighter at a steady rate, and then it began to pulse. And a wide opening slowly materialized at the base.

"Get ready," I said as wolves began to howl on the edges of my property.

Dragons roared in the skies, but they sounded miles away, more like distant thunder.

Still, I pretended it was dragons. That way I could also pretend we weren't all about to die.

CHAPTER 65

Thunder and lightning flashed in the distance, in the direction of the St. Louis Arch. The rumbles were delayed, hitting our ears the moment Indie stepped out of the tree, holding a small object in one hand. Her eyes locked onto us, then my shirt.

And she hesitated, frowning, mouth open to speak, but no words coming out.

Before she could formulate a sentence, a contingent of both Grimms and Elders rushed out of the opening behind her, gathering on either side, and glaring at the small army before them.

The wolves howled, closer, and the familiar roar of dragons echoed them, also closer now.

I looked up to try and find them, but it was impossible with the setting sun. Two dark specks fluttered out from the tree, flapping as they fled the impending war.

Ravens.

The Myrmidons rattled their spears against their shields, and then just began launching them at everyone but Indie, without an ounce of shame at the surprise attack. The enemy broke rank, and raced towards us, blades of bone and steel clashing against Greek metal. Wolves began pouring over the landscape in the distance, darting around bushes as they raced our way, and the familiar explosion of fabric signaled the shifters beside me taking form. Battle form.

Gunnar shook his ruff beside me, and let out a long, drawn out howl, calling his pack to war. They responded, running faster, and howling their support. Then he was suddenly in the thick of it, knocking over one Elder, dodging another's blade, and then darting back to rip half the face off of the downed Elder. Then he moved on, targeting anyone on the sidelines that attempted to pick off any stragglers in the Myrmidon's steady formation of advancing shield and spear.

Ashley – also in wolf form – darted between the Myrmidons like a wraith, hamstringing Elders and Grimms alike as they were distracted by the flashing spears and shields, the cacophony of sound as they stomped closer to the middle, a congested pit of sweat, shouting, bodies, and screams.

Both of pain and joy.

"Crazy bastards," I muttered under my breath.

Alucard and Tory stood side-by side, grinning as a trio of Grimms ran straight at them. Alucard suddenly zipped ahead, leaving a trail of light in his wake before punching straight through a Grimm's chest. He reappeared beside Tory, his blood-soaked hand gripping a heart. He gave it a long lick, then tossed it on the ground, before taking a bow towards the two remaining Grimms, who had stopped short in stunned disbelief.

Tory didn't waste a second, her eyes pulsing green as the earth exploded around them with pale roots that trapped their feet, before continuing up their bodies to encase them in two wooden cages. She held up a hand, and then clenched her fist.

They were crushed, screaming the entire time, not even having a second to defend themselves. Looked like Tory and Alucard had remembered a few things from their previous scrap with the Grimms. Namely, kill first, ask questions never. Then they moved on, hunting out new enemies.

Ganesh let out a great tremendous *honk* of his trunk from behind me right as the Minotaur let out a horrifying roar that was a mix between the angriest bull you had ever seen, and a dinosaur.

Then they barreled into the fray, running past me. I heard someone running up behind me and whirled, whips in my fists, but it was only Mallory, panicked, furious eyes taking in the sounds of war. I lowered my hands, not extinguishing the whips. "Can you do something to help? Like you did at the apartments?"

"Casting everyone into a battle frenzy is dangerous when they're already bloodthirsty."

"But I saw them attacking themselves last time. Can't you just hit the bad guys so that they attack anything they see, hopefully each other?"

Mallory nodded. "It will give me away…"

"Then make a grand entrance, goat boy," I grinned. His response was to explode into a devil on cloven, razor-sharp hooves, standing a good eight feet tall. His arms were wiry, but corded with well-developed muscle. No bruiser like Ganesh and Asterion, but a scrapper. His fists were stained, and I momentarily thought it was blood, only to decide it more resembled the color of wine. The party god had wine hands.

From the waist down he was a swath of matted fur, not clean, and not pretty, but as if he had just spent a decade on an island by himself with only a volleyball to talk to. His hair was wild, and his ribbed horns caught the glow of the moon. He held two clubs in his fist, covered in moss and fungus, but I saw jagged tips sprouting through the growth, and realized they were living vines of thorns that seemed to writhe and flex like a nest of snakes.

He wore a necklace with a small set of pipes on his chest. With a nod, he held it to his lips and blew out a jaunty little tune, frantically pointing his finger at his targets while he did so.

It hit them like a light blast of water, making the targets stumble in surprise, and then shake their heads from the annoying sound in their ears. Then they looked up, and their eyes were pits of madness. They each tore after whoever was closest to them, friend or foe. Two even went at Indie, who suddenly found herself fighting for her life against creatures she had just liberated.

She destroyed them without much effort, eyes flashing black, but looked suddenly fearful, not understanding the situation.

It may sound like we could handily win this.

But that's because I hadn't mentioned that while all this was going down, *more of them kept escaping the tree.*

"Pan! Close that tree! Do some nature stuff or something!"

He glared down at me, eyes glowing like liquid gold, his lips pulled back into a perpetual snarl. I took a step back until I realized that was just what his face looked like. A hangry face. I pointed urgently, and he followed my motion, with a resolute nod. Then he freaking jumped over the crowd of warriors to land beside Indie, batting her aside like a weed.

"Hey, asshole! That's my fiancée!" I shouted on instinct, then frowned for a half-second as I realized what I had said, before tearing off after her, darting through the battle with my whips. I caught a stray Elder, yanking his legs out from under him so that he fell to his back, and was immediately stabbed by a spear. My other whip flashed out around a Grimm's neck, and as I yanked, I felt no resistance, because my whip was now roaring with a never-before-used white fire, and had instantly vaporized the Grimms flesh. I glanced down at my other whip, covered in plain fire. Then I made it match the white fire, so that both charred and scorched the earth as they sat coiled beside my feet.

I had no idea what power it was, or what element I was tapping into, but I didn't care. But it made me very consciously aware of the coin in my pocket, wondering if they were connected. I dared not actually don the Mask, for fear of the Grimms copying me, creating dozens of Horsemen to fight off. I shivered at the thought.

Instead, I twirled the whips over my head like a helicopter, clearing room, satisfied with the exclamations of pain and burnt hair and flesh as the fire tore through anything biological.

I saw Ganesh honk his trunk at me, indicating a charred stripe across his back where I had hit him. But he was soon preoccupied, squaring off against two very wild looking Grimms. Well, they all looked wild – long, matted hair, greasy skin, and pale as ghosts. I suddenly realized that all the bad guys had pasty skin, both Grimms and Elders.

"Death to the Whiteys!" I shouted as I scanned the area for Indie.

Whether to kill her or save her, I wasn't sure. But I knew I had to stop her first.

The two Grimms smiled at Ganesh, holding out their arms dramatically to attempt to shift into what they thought was a four-armed elephant shifter. Their looks of surprise were soothing to my soul, right before Ganesh lunged forward, impaling each of them on one of his bladed tusks. He reached out with his unarmed hands, and pulled them closer, down the length of the swords, and their agonized screams almost made me lose the contents of my stomach. Then Ganesh punched them each in the face with enough force to dislodge them from the blades. Their amulets hung from his bladed tusks, trophies of war.

And he stomped on, looking for more toy soldiers to dismember.

I ran through a sudden opening, quickly skidding on my knees to barely dodge friendly fire as one of the Myrmidons flashed out with his spear, catching a jumping Elder in the throat. I climbed to my feet, continuing my run, but almost immediately tripped over three dead bodies, landing face first onto an Elder that looked alarmingly similar to Carl. I flinched, jerking my eyes away, only to see an Elder sneaking up on one of the Myrmidons who had broken rank. I swung my hand behind me, and then brought it crashing forward until my fist pounded the earth. My whip screamed through the air, white sparks of fire cascading down around me, burning through the bodies I lay on, and then it cleanly sliced through the Elder like a hot knife through butter.

The Myrmidon spun, staring at the two halves of the Elder for a moment from beneath his helm. He glanced at my whips, followed them back to me, and then nodded in thanks. A sword abruptly tore through the front of his chest from his back, extinguishing the life from his eyes. The Grimm behind him didn't even smile in satisfaction, his eyes locking hungrily onto me.

Helmut Grimm. And he had trimmed his beard into a perfect square, which looked absolutely stupid. He'd also found new clothes. Nothing fancy, but better than the homeless look I'd first seen him in. He now wore jeans and a long-sleeved shirt. And cowboy boots.

I climbed to my feet, snapping the tips of my whips on the ground in an alternating cracking sound, taunting him as I stared at him, hungry to avenge the murdered Greek. Helmut took one look at my whips, frowned, and then his sword was suddenly coated with a similar white flame. He was too astonished to even notice Achilles sneak up behind him and kick him square in the back, sending his sword flying. The white fire disappeared from the blade, and it was soon trampled under by a trio of Elders trying to fend off the rolling pack of wolves nipping at them in coordinated strikes.

I glanced up as something moved in my peripheral vision, only to see a tiny girl falling from the sky, and two dragons urgently flapping their wings to get away from the chaos, because two other red dragons exploded from the swarm of bodies – Grimms – launching up into the sky to fight off the two invading red dragons. My friends. I cursed under my breath as the small girl landed beside me, because I recognized her, and instantly knew who the two red dragons were.

The Reds. Sonya and Aria. Teenagers. And now they were fighting for their lives, up in the sky where I couldn't reach them, against the same monsters that had killed their mother.

The blonde teenaged girl stood from her crouch, the ground a crater around her. Camilla. She was smiling as she shouted, "Heard you needed some air support!" And then she hunched over for a second, and her clothes exploded into tatters, releasing a chimera where the cute girl had been. The cobra that was her tail arched up over her back, spraying venom at some attackers I couldn't see because she stood in my way. I heard a triumphant shout behind me, and dove to the side, narrowly avoiding a big ass battle-axe that buried itself in the dirt where I had been standing. The Grimm heaved, trying to pull it free, then let it go, grinning down at me as I scurried back on all fours, trying to find a safe spot to climb to my feet and use my whips. The man held up two palms, balls of identical white fire like my whips roiling in the air.

But before he could launch them at me, he was suddenly sprayed with a fine green mist, and I watched as his skin instantly began to melt and bubble. Then a bar of fire as thick as my torso struck him, incinerating him before he had a chance to scream. I turned to see the lion-head on the chimera's chest cough once, extinguishing the flame that had poured out from her mouth. The cobra tail swayed back and forth behind his back, scanning the scene. Then the goat head bleated, nodding at me, and the chimera charged off on all fours into the thickest of the battle.

I climbed to my feet, careful not to trip again as I ran, searching for Indie. Explosions roared up from the earth on either side of me as I moved, and I distinctly heard the sound of blade on blade as I raced past Achilles and Helmut, going head to head, moving like shadows and snakes, dodging, striking, and laughing.

Having the times of their lives.

CHAPTER 66

I slashed more bodies than I could count; yet there were still so *many* of them. The warriors were instinctively shifting the tides of battle because they were sick and tired of tripping over the corpses – and were now relocating close to where Pan – *Mallory* – had thrown Indie.

I saw Elders fighting Elders, Grimms fighting Elders, Grimms against Grimms, even three red dragons up in the sky fighting one, which meant one of them had been hit by Pan's blast of bloodlust, or Panic, and the Reds had gained a temporary new ally.

The chaos made things a hell of a lot easier for me as I slipped through the crowd. I didn't want to waste any more power than necessary, because I needed to stop Indie, who had access to a Maker's power, way stronger than my own, but I was the only spell-slinger available.

I caught sight of Pan desperately clawing at the door, swinging his club at a few Elders and Grimms that tried to dart out between his legs, like he was playing whack-a-mole, but there were too many moles, and he couldn't focus on closing the door as they continued to pour out.

"Myrmidons, protect Pan! Help him close the damn door!" I shouted as a trio thundered past me. They nodded in acknowledgment and shifted course, heading his way.

I turned to see Indie standing before me, a stone pyramid in one fist, and bleeding from a cut on her head. She stood uncomfortably, as if either her legs or her side had been injured, and she was putting all her weight on the one leg.

She stared at me, eyes gripping my soul, eyes I had fantasized waking up to every morning. Eyes I had imagined saying *good night* to every time I went to bed.

She glanced at my shirt, a small amused smirk emerging on her face.

"God save the Grimms?" she asked, eyes taking in the war around us. Then she looked back at me. "Or just one Grimm?" she asked, as she slowly began sauntering closer, whips of white fire erupting from her fists, just like mine. She didn't necessarily have to hold them, as they were just extensions of her hands. So, she didn't let go of the strange pyramid-shaped stone.

Which looked very familiar to me for some reason.

She glanced down at the whips with interest, cracking them to either side of her for a moment. Then she slowly lifted her eyes to mine. "Nice upgrade."

"Indie, you can stop this. All of this. Let me help you. Let me tell you the truth!" I shouted, desperate. She just stared back, but she had stopped advancing. Then her face became angry again as two wolves lunged at her.

With a flick of her wrist, they died instantly, the white whips ripping them in half. She lifted her hands until a large dome of magic surrounded us. Well, us, Helmut, and Achilles, who seemed not to notice, too entranced with their own fight, which had moved to spear on spear.

Indie cleared her throat. "There, that's better."

And she began to walk closer, slamming her whips to the ground beside her, shaking the earth as she neared me.

"Indie, for the last time, STOP! I don't want this!"

"Mama has an owie. Won't you kiss it and make it better?" She cooed in a playful tone, pouting her lips. But her eyes weren't playful.

Not at all.

I flung my hand out, whipping the white fire towards her face. Her eyes momentarily flashed in surprise that I had attacked first, but I saw them shift to anticipation an instant later as she brought her own whip up to block.

Our whips touched. We... crossed swords.

And we both went flying in opposite directions, our whips extinguishing instantly.

I tumbled and rolled on my ass, banging my head against the head of some dead dude, making me see stars.

But as I opened my eyes, I was very thankful for the blow. Because it had slowed me down. Because I was only a hair's width away from my nose piercing the dome of power Indie had thrown up around us, and it thrummed with deadly electricity, my hair standing on end in warning. I saw through the dome as I yanked my head back. Several bodies littered the ground, still breathing, but eyes wild. No doubt electrocuted as they tried to break through the dome.

I scooted back and climbed to my feet, just as someone backed into me, knocking me down again. I rolled away, fearing it had been Indie, only to feel a boot slam down, trying to squish my melon, missing me by inches. Helmut cast an angry glare down at me from his missed strike, but Achilles unleashed on him, keeping him busy. He had simply tried a crime of opportunity as I flew into their path.

"Get your head in the game, Temple!" Achilles snarled in a strained voice from beneath his helm, but he didn't look at me. I found my hand resting on an odd shaped hunk of rock, and without looking, I picked it up as I stood, eyes locking on Indie.

She was on all fours, scrambling across the ground, looking for something, but she was moving oddly. Then I saw it. She was missing one of her hands, leaving just a nub behind.

"Indie!" I yelled, hurling the rock the moment before I had called out her name, reacting on instinct, and hating myself for it.

She jerked her neck in my direction, trying to see what magic I would throw at her so she could respond in kind and not have another white power explosion.

Heh.

And the rock struck her right in the temple, knocking her to the ground as she fell on her side. The rock landed right in front of her face, and she stared vacantly at it, stunned. The dome of power disappeared with a static popping sound, and the sounds of battle grew instantly louder.

I ignored this, focused only on the fact that I saw her chest rise and fall.

I let out a breath of relief. She was still alive.

I hadn't killed her.

As I ran towards her, my eyes settled on the lucky stone I had thrown.

It was shaped like a pyramid. My projectile had been the stone I saw her holding earlier. The Hand of God. And I suddenly remembered where I had seen one very similar to it.

In the Temple Mausoleum. The statue of my mother had been holding one just like it.

But I didn't have time to think on that, because Indie's eyes had refocused, latching onto it, and her shaking hand was slowly reaching towards it, but as if she was having trouble using it.

"Closed!" I heard Pan bleat in the distance. I scanned my surroundings, hoping I wasn't about to be overrun now that the dome of protection was down, and the Grimms saw their new boss wounded. A rally.

But I gasped to see most of the enemy down. Ashley limped, two paws injured, and a heavy gash decorated her side, but Gunnar prowled beside her, guarding her from the few survivors.

Everyone was wounded, I realized, as my gaze made a full, quick circle. But the dome was no longer a concern, because a ring of Greek steel blocked anyone from coming my way. Achilles even had Helmut on his knees, a spear pierced through his shoulder, and a sword to his neck, keeping him still. Helmut looked to be in severe pain, but he stared defiantly at Achilles, and Achilles stared right back, neither moving.

But I couldn't worry about any of that right now. I turned back to Indie, slowly raising my hands in a peaceful gesture as I approached. I didn't want her trying to kill me out of self-defense, thinking I was rushing to kill her.

"None of this is what you think. What he *let* you think," I whispered, close enough for her to hear me, wondering if Ichabod had truly set all this up, taking me out to dinner to simply cause me enough doubt to give him enough time to act. To put Indie in place to sabotage me, knowing my wards had been down at the house. To get a HOG from the Elders.

Or Indie had gone rogue, deciding to wake a god herself. And the result had just been a string of coincidences. But none of that really mattered right now.

I met her eyes as her surviving hand continued crawling across the earth in fitful jerks, trying to grasp the pyramid. She even used her nub to help support her questing arm. But I wasn't worried about the stone right now. She couldn't use it, or she would have done so in the beginning. She just needed to get it to Ichabod. And he was a little preoccupied at the moment, judging by the explosions still booming near the Arch.

But why did he need two HOGs? He already had one. Unless... he'd been lying... And Rumps had been lying. Cindy Syndicate hadn't actually confirmed that they had indeed lost any of their two HOGs... And the Fae had said theirs was safe. Which meant the Fae had sensed the Elder's HOG switching hands almost instantly, and had sent the sprites to warn me... It had just taken Dean too long to warn me about Indie's escape. Enough time to let her do all this.

"What happened to the woman I loved?" I pleaded, slowly advancing, unable to kill her without an answer.

Her gaze locked onto me, right as her hand touched the pyramid. The stone began to glow, infusing her with strength as she shivered in response. Shit. I should have worried about the stone. Then she slowly began to sit up, never looking away from me.

And I saw that her eyes were filled with tears.

Power roared through her, giving her enough strength to climb to her feet, although not healing her hand. The sounds of battle were gone, everyone watching, but I caught flashes of light and peals of thunder in the distance.

In the direction of the Arch.

Then she gave me my answer, as everyone watched.

CHAPTER 67

She spoke through a dry throat, full of both internal and external pain, despite the stone partially healing her.

"She fell in love with a magical boy. A boy fast on his way to becoming a glorious, splendid man. She lost her life, and was brought back as a Freak, because the boy had loved her enough to convince Death himself to save her. The boy hadn't even needed to ask, because Death was his brother…" she whispered, eyes never leaving mine as a vortex of light slowly began to coalesce above her head.

"Indie, stop," I whispered, white whip erupting into existence at my side.

She paid it no mind as she continued to speak, the power building above her. "War came, and she discovered that her new enemies wanted vengeance. After a small victory, she went off to train, to come back to her beloved and help him fight back the storm. While away—" she paused, letting out an unintentional sob, opening her mouth to continue, but no sound coming out.

Tears painted my cheeks, distorting my vision, and what remained of my heart felt like it was slowly burning away to nothing, and the whip in my fist grew stronger, more powerful, wilder as my raging emotions fed it, nurtured it, urging me to kill this woman I had once loved.

Indie shook her head angrily, wiping away her tears with her mostly cauterized bloody nub, painting her cheeks crimson. "While away, her mother was… brutally murdered," she finally managed.

And I fell to my knees.

She watched me without mercy, nodding slowly as the power began to grow above her, shooting bars of light up into the sky. Thunder and lightning responded from above a suddenly thick blanket of clouds above us. Angry, darkening clouds.

"A sticky note found on her chest said *love you #Syndicate*," she whispered.

A sticky note. Just like the one I had found at the Gala. From Cindy.

"Her mentor carried her through this crisis, and became her ally against a common enemy. The boy she once loved wanted to save the world with half measures. Second guessing himself at every turn. Because he thought he knew pain…"

"Indie," I rasped. "None of this will change that," I tried, but she cut me short.

"Now the girl is lost in a dangerous world full of monsters, hungry only to avenge her mother. She has lost the ability to ever love again…"

The tears openly falling down her cheeks mixed with the blood, forming a curtain of red, as if she was crying blood. I heard Helmut let out a soft sob behind me, as if against his will, and as I risked a glance, I saw that even Achilles was staring, dumbfounded at Indie.

"But the story isn't over," Indie continued, a haunted smile on her face. "The girl chose to wake a god to make everything right." She slowly lifted her eyes to the light show above her, calling out, "Goodbye, magical loverboy."

And the world exploded in a flash of light so bright I thought I had been blinded.

CHAPTER 68

I crawled around on the ground, wiping my eyes, trying to see, not remembering falling. My vision slowly came back, but the world was dark, where before it had been brightly lit by Indie and the pyramid stone.

The Hand of God.

The sun had finally set, to be replaced by a very bright moon and a thin veil of clouds. I heard others cursing, mumbling, and trying to gather themselves as my vision came back. Indie was gone, just a black ring where she had been standing. I turned my head to find Achilles kneeling, his spear stuck in the ground. Helmut Grimm was gone.

In fact, as I looked around, I realized that none of our enemies were standing.

Had we killed them all?

"They just fucking *disappeared*? *All* of them?" Pan, was shouting, running from person to person, seemingly not affected by the explosion of power. Which made sense. He was a god. And he seemed to be right. No living enemies were present.

Ganesh openly stared at Pan. "My father would have lost his bet," he muttered to himself, but loud enough for me to hear.

I frowned, scanning those standing. We had lost several wolves, but everyone was injured to one degree or another. Pan now hurriedly ran from person to person, healing them. Ganesh, body coated in gore, did likewise, calmly murmuring to each person as he placed his belt on them.

Because he had a snakeskin belt that healed things. From almost any injury.

I hoped.

Ashley jumped up from beneath Ganesh's bulk, naked and eyes wild with the temporary high of Ganesh's healing belt, but I knew she would crash like a sack of bricks soon. She rolled her hands in amazement, no longer broken, or whatever they had been.

I heard Pan softly blowing his pipes as he knelt over Sonya, who had a fucking hole in her chest. I ran her way, frantic, only to see her jump to her feet as Pan moved on to the next one. Aria clutched her tightly, relieved to have her dragon sister back. Camilla rubbed Sonya's back with a bloodied hand, murmuring softly. I heard one of the Myrmidons grunt in approval at the display of young, pretty flesh.

I threw a bar of air, knocking him on his ass and into the tree.

"Just be thankful Tory didn't hear you, Myrmidon," I growled at his incredulous look.

"Didn't hear what?" Tory groaned, climbing to her feet with Alucard's help. They were both liberally coated in blood, and although looking exhausted, didn't appear injured.

"Nate just took care of some business for me," the vampire snarled, glaring at the offending Greek. Achilles burst out laughing, shaking his head as he helped the soldier to his feet. I continued searching, to make sure everyone was alright, but no one would meet my eyes. Instantly casting their gaze down at the ground rather than look at me.

"What gives?" I muttered under my breath, satisfied that everyone was more or less okay.

"Please…" a voice on the ground whispered in agony. I turned to see an Elder writhing in pain at my feet. "Merc—"

Achilles calmly lunged his spear into the Elder's open mouth while softly answering me. "They just saw you ripped to shreds, emotionally. And the god thing," he said, idly scratching his forearm before yanking his spear out. This casual, subtle motion almost made me vomit.

I saw Charon – the Boatman to the River Styx, in the Underworld – calmly paddling from body to body on the other side of the battlefield. He already had a full boat of dead souls, and despite drinking a can of cheap beer through his sewn-up lips – splashing it all over his face in the process – I heard pieces of a dirty limerick floating across the air from his direction. I nodded at him, and then turned away. He had a long night ahead of him.

"We need to gather up all the Grimm amulets," I said absently, more reminding myself.

Alucard and Tory nodded, not meeting my eyes, and began to collect them.

I shook my head, wondering how Indie had done it. I had thought only Ichabod could wake a god, but perhaps with enough Grimms in the mix, she had been strong enough to get it done. Regardless, it didn't really matter *how* anymore.

But since she wasn't really a Maker, a Tiny God, had she succeeded? Had she woken one of the sleeping gods? If so, they would instantly find Ichabod – if he was still alive – and make him his or her tool. But more importantly, which god had she woken up?

A car pulled up, and the oddest assortment of people climbed out, carrying balloons and gifts wrapped in bright, shining paper. I stared at them, not comprehending the bright colors.

Van Helsing, Baba Yaga, and the Huntress. Baba's creepy, hulking house followed behind her, a living creature that wore robes, had a giant bird skull for a head, and walked on chicken feet. It was both a house, and a creature, bigger on the inside than it seemed on the outside.

I blinked, suddenly very interested in comparing notes with her about sentient houses…

But they interrupted my thought as they began to sing in loud, unsynchronized tones. "Happy Birthday to *you*, Happy birthday to—"

They stopped, dropping the gifts as they suddenly noticed the carnage. The dead bodies.

"What in the living *fuck?*" Van Helsing belted out, hands reaching for the crossbow on his back. The Huntress held two knives in her fists, eyes darting around wildly. Baba's familiar lurked behind her as a green orb of power suddenly coalesced above the witch's palms, illuminating her homely face.

Before anyone could answer, a Gateway ripped open a dozen feet away, and G Ma and Cindy jumped through, leaving behind a large group of other wizards I could see opening Gateways of their own. The Arch stood in the distance, and I saw quite a few fires.

"We did it! We stopped hi—" G Ma began.

"Holy shit balls," Cindy blurted out, interrupting her, stunned at the number of bodies surrounding us. Which, again, was not a phrase I would have expected an older woman to use. The birthday party crowd had crept closer, and had their weapons trained on the two older women suddenly appearing out of a Gateway.

G Ma scanned the area. "Two Grimms did *this?*" she whispered, horrified.

But before I could answer, and rip Cindy to shreds for murdering Indie's mother, a low, deep horn broke up our reunion, sounding as if it could have been heard across the world. I felt my skin tremble and my stomach quivered uneasily.

Achilles, Asterion, and the Myrmidons disappeared as if they had never been there, which startled the hell out of everyone, thinking they had just been taken out from under our noses by Indie or Ichabod.

The horn wailed one more time, and then all was silent.

The sky suddenly broiled with thunder and lightning, flickering red flashes behind almost-black clouds that had appeared out of nowhere, shifting and moving like stirred cotton candy.

I heard a *glug, glug, glug* sound behind me and turned to see Pan, now looking like Mallory, drinking straight from a bottle of Macallan. Everyone turned to him as he polished off the entire bottle, like that guy in *Animal House*. He let out a very loud burp behind a fist, and hurled the bottle at the tree where it shattered. He turned to meet my eyes. "The Greeks are going to war…"

Dean was running our way, panting as he held out Sir Muffle Paws as if to get rid of him.

This wasn't the most bizarre thing I could have imagined right now.

But everyone else turned to watch, staring as Dean finally reached me, extending the cat in shaking arms. The cat was forty pounds, after all. "Master Temple, the cat—"

"Please do not refer to me as *the cat*," Sir Muffle Paws corrected.

I shouted, jumping backwards, having been focusing on Dean, not the cat.

I stared as Dean set him down on the ground. Sir Muffle Paws climbed on top of a Grimm's chest, right beside a very gory wound, and licked his paws a few times, preening. Then he began batting the amulet around the Grimm's neck playfully for a few seconds. He instantly grew bored, and looked up at me, and the eyes I saw were not the same eyes I had ever seen in that filthy feline's head. I remembered how he had sat on the book I had spelled, but it was a very distant thought now. Because he spoke.

"Idiots everywhere," he chastised, eyes shining like liquid gold. "Did you need me to lay it all out for you, boy?"

"That cat can fucking talk," Van Helsing stated dumbly.

I opened my mouth, but twin *cawing* sounds erupted from right above me. I threw my hands in the air, expecting an aerial assault, when two sets of claws hit my shoulders, biting into my flesh. They didn't move, and I winced, slowly turning my head to see two ravens perched on my shoulders. They were staring up at the crackling sky.

"Ya done fucked up, kid," one of the ravens said.

"The Allfather won't like this," the other replied from my opposite shoulder.

Everyone's heads darted from one to the other like watching a ping pong match, faces incredulous, and mouths open.

"Not one bit," the first one replied.

"Nevermore?" the second one asked, staring out at my friends.

"Too much," the first raven replied.

Before I lost what little sanity I had remaining, I shook them from my shoulders, darting free from any talking animals, scowling at each of the three from a safe distance as the ravens settled on the ground beside Sir Muffle Paws, bowing politely to one another. The ravens were huge, if that mattered.

"Is *anyone* who or what they *say* they are?" I shouted, having reached my limit for surprises.

Everyone was silent for a few seconds.

"I am," Van Helsing said softly. "I'm Van Helsing, and I came here for a surprise Birthday Party. With the girls. Right, Dean?"

I turned to Dean, who looked suddenly embarrassed. "I… planned it long ago. I lost track of time with all the…" he motioned at the ground. "Whatever this is," he finally said, looking sick to his stomach. The Huntress and Baba murmured their agreement about a party and stated their names.

Instead of listening, and possibly murdering everyone out of sheer frustration, I reached into my pocket and grasped the coin.

"Dean, Pan. Get everyone inside. Feed them. Clothe them. Give them a room. Everyone needs to sleep here tonight. And they need to get anyone they care about behind my walls. Chateau Falco just became our castle."

"Why do you say that like you won't be here?" Gunnar growled anxiously, walking towards me as if to physically prevent me from leaving.

"Because I have something I need to do. Right now." And I closed my eyes, Shadow Walking to a door inside Chateau Falco. The house rumbled in a low steady growl, not pausing to take a breath, so to speak.

I stood before the door to the Armory.

Pandora was Greek, and all the Greeks near the tree had disappeared.

The carving on the door in front of me still moved like normal. I let out a sigh of relief. I searched for the wolf, not seeing him at first. Then I spotted him, hiding behind the tree, shaking. He ducked out of sight, and since it was a two-dimensional carving, this prevented me from petting him.

SHAYNE SILVERS

From opening the door.

I pounded on it, but no one answered. "Shit."

I stood in silence, terrified at the compounding nightmares building in my mind. The Greeks, with one of their gods and an Armory at their disposal. Had Death gotten my parents out in time?

Seeing no other option, I desperately gripped the coin in my pocket, closing my eyes as I pulled power through it. Wind whistled in my ears a moment later, and I opened my eyes.

I stood on a mountain that overlooked a burning St. Louis. A campfire crackled behind me.

I turned to find four cloaked creatures – much larger than normal men – sitting by the fire.

"Brothers," I began in a low tone. "I might need your help…"

My black-feathered unicorn, Grimm, neighed, suddenly standing beside me, pawing the ground with a razor-sharp hoof, sparks of white light charring the earth.

The four hooded figures – wearing their horrifying Masks this time – leaned forward with hungry anticipation…

DON'T FORGET! VIP's get early access to all sorts of Temple-Verse goodies, including signed copies, private giveaways, and advance notice of future projects. AND A FREE NOVELLA! Click the image or join here: www.shaynesilvers.com/l/219800

*Nate Temple returns in the hilarious novella, **DADDY DUTY.** Nate and Alucard are put in charge of babysitting the Reds - but the girls sneak out to meet a boy at a Johnson Beaver concert instead. A herd of tribal centaurs and a coven of bloodthirsty vampires later, Nate and Alucard realize they aren't cut out for this Daddy hobby...*
*Turn the page for a sample! Or **get the book ONLINE!***

TEASER: DADDY DUTY (TEMPLE #6.5)

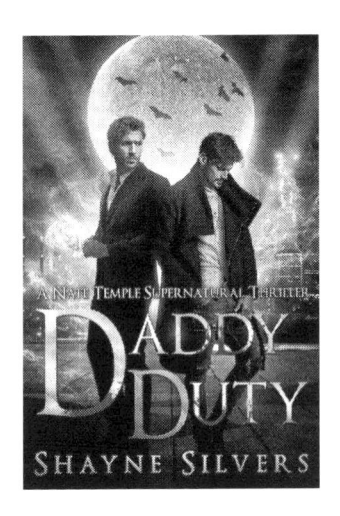

I dove for cover behind a dented, filthy trashcan as a storm of arrows sailed just over my shoulder to hammer into the brick wall, showering me with grit and dust.

"Find the wizard! I want Nate Temple's head!" a baritone voice bellowed.

That last sentence, and the steady drumroll of clattering hooves splashing through the large puddles of the alley behind me, urged me back up to my feet to resume my sprint. The echoes made the sound more ominous to me, like a reenactment of the stampede that killed Mufasa in *Lion King* with those damned water buffaloes or whatever they were called. Those hairy cow things. Hungry snorting and outraged neighs accompanied the sound of hooves, pressing me onward as effectively as a cattle prod.

I rounded a corner, almost slipping in a puddle, in hopes that making turns would give me a few more precious seconds of breathing room.

Because, like *rock* beats *scissors*, centaurs beat wizards every time in a straight-shot race.

Good thing I was a dirty cheat. Because the puddle had just given me an idea.

At the next turn, I flung my hand down at the ground, drawing out the heat from the water to turn several large puddles into thick sheets of patchy, black ice. My vision wavered and I stumbled a bit, even at such a small use of my power. Wizards could do some pretty cool stuff.

But I had used up a lot of power in the last hour, trying to keep my ticker ticking.

"Heh," I muttered to myself, as I took a deep breath and continued running, flipping open the top of the satchel at my hip to check that the book was still there. The book that had started this whole mess. It was tucked neatly inside, and I didn't spot anyone immediately behind me.

I needed to get *gone*. But first, I had to find my way out of this maze of alleys. Then, I would worry about finding the parking lot where I'd left my car. I pelted on further, huffing and puffing as I sprinted for all I was worth, shooting quick glances over my shoulder in a nervous twitch looking for my pursuers. I didn't know how many of the monsters were after me, but it didn't really matter. All it would take was one lucky shot with those damned arrows and I would be a wizard kabob.

I turned to check ahead of me, and abruptly skidded to a halt, panting.

"Shit."

A chain-link fence rose before me, bisecting the alley, and blocking my one path to freedom.

I heard the triumphant shouts of my pursuers, much closer now, and whirled around just as the first of them came into view, rounding the last corner before the damned fence.

The centaur was a mashup of horse and human – a horse body with a human torso rising up in place of the horse's head. The horse part of the monster resembled one of those shaggy Clydesdales from the *Budweiser* commercials. Thick, shaggy, brown hair covered the majority of his body, but from his huge waffle-iron-sized hooves to his knees it was a dirty white. Same with his chest. Then again, *chest* was using the term loosely.

Because just above the white patch of fur rose a tanned, heavily muscled humanoid torso, covered in a coarse mat of wiry chest hair like steel wool.

Beneath the hair looked to be a six pack on top of a six pack. And his arms looked as thick as my thighs. His face resembled that of a retired MMA fighter, full of lumps, scar tissue, and a harsh, almost caveman-like chiseled skull structure.

But the hair on his head momentarily took my breath away...

It glistened like a *Vidal Sassoon* commercial as a rare beam of sunlight pierced a section of the alley. Time slowed, and I imagined Norah Jones singing *Come away with* me...

The centaur was aiming his bow at me, grinning hungrily. And, since I was transfixed by his beautiful hair and the soothing sounds of Norah Jones in my head, I didn't move.

Lucky for me, he was too busy celebrating a successful hunt to watch his feet. His hooves.

His mad trot got the better of him the moment his hooves struck a patch of the invisible ice, and his momentum and bulk prevented him from stopping. His hooves buckled as they briefly skidded across solid ground again. And then his fetlock snapped the moment they hit the next ice patch. He cried out in pain, flipped, rolled, and then slammed into a dumpster, denting it. Several bags of trash – piled higher than the recommended limit of the dumpster – disgorged their contents all over his luxurious mane in sickening wet smacks and splashes.

Which sharply concluded Norah Jones' solo in my mind.

The next two centaurs were too close to do anything differently. They skidded, slipped, skated, tripped over each other, and then finally crashed into the first wailing centaur, hammering him further into the metal dumpster and the wet, goopy pile of trash. The damp air was suddenly saturated with an eye-watering stench of rot and decay that I could actually taste on my tongue. The sharp popping of more breaking bones made me feel a tad guilty. Horses had weak ankles, or fetlocks, and although their injury was beneficial for my immediate survival, I didn't feel very good about myself.

After all, they weren't the bad guys.

I was the bad guy.

I had stolen their book.

The next centaur proved to be wiser, and launched his powerfully-muscled frame over the ice patch, landing safely on the other side, where he continued to gallop straight at me without pause. I might have shrieked in a very masculine, intimidating tone before throwing my body up the chain-link fence. I scrambled to reach the top, and seriously considered tossing some fireballs blindly behind me, but I could feel the warning signs in my body. I was just about spent in the magic department. I had used quite a bit of magic over the last hour, and didn't want to risk knocking myself out cold by overexerting myself.

When it came to magic, I was powerful, but not limitless. So, I threw my skinny ass up the fence, careful that my bag didn't get caught up in the rusted metal protrusions.

I had almost reached the top when an arrow sliced clean through the strap on my satchel. I felt the book's weight obeying gravity and shot out a hand to snatch some part of the bag, but was too late. The single peal of a deep conch horn echoed in the alley, followed a heartbeat later by a dozen more identical calls from various points all around me. From different alleys.

The bag splashed into a puddle at the base of the fence as the centaur skidded on his hooves, snorting and growling at me. Instead of dropping for the book, I scrambled like a monkey, moving laterally across the fence, closer to the brick wall of the alley. I heard the creaking of the centaur drawing back his bowstring to pierce me with an arrow, point-blank.

"Time to die, Nate Temple…" he growled.

With a great huff, I launched myself off the fence, twisting in mid-air. A big swath of the metal tore loose from the brick wall right below me, jarred free by my sudden motion. A heartbeat later, only the bottom of my boots struck the side of the building, feet tucked tightly against my body so that I was momentarily horizontal to the ground and upside down.

I immediately lunged out like I was trying to break the world record for box jumps. I heard the centaur's bow string *snap*, and felt the arrow graze my thigh as I catapulted off the wall, both fists outstretched in a *Superman* pose as I flew sideways off the wall.

The centaur barely had time to grunt before my fists connected with his thick jaw, backed by my entire bodyweight, and perhaps a last-second, tiny boost of magic I may or may not have added to my fists…

Get your copy of DADDY DUTY online today!

*Turn the page to read a sample of **UNCHAINED** - Feathers and Fire Series Book 1, or **BUY ONLINE**. Callie Penrose is a wizard in Kansas City, MO who hunts monsters for the Vatican. She meets Nate Temple, and things devolve from there…*

(Note: Callie appears in the Temple-verse after Nate's book 6, TINY GODS… Full chronology of all books in the Temple Universe shown on the 'Books by Shayne Silvers' page.)

TRY: UNCHAINED (FEATHERS AND FIRE #1)

The rain pelted my hair, plastering loose strands of it to my forehead as I panted, eyes darting from tree to tree, terrified of each shifting branch, splash of water, and whistle of wind slipping through the nightscape around us. But... I was somewhat *excited*, too.

Somewhat.

"Easy, girl. All will be well," the big man creeping just ahead of me, murmured.

"You said we were going to get ice cream!" I hissed at him, failing to compose myself, but careful to keep my voice low and my eyes alert. "I'm not ready for this!" I had been trained to fight, with my hands, with weapons, and with my magic. But I had never taken an active role in a hunt before. I'd always been the getaway driver for my mentor.

The man grunted, grey eyes scanning the trees as he slipped through the tall grass. "And did we not get ice cream before coming here? Because I think I see some in your hair."

"You know what I mean, Roland. You tricked me." I checked the tips of my loose hair, saw nothing, and scowled at his back.

"The Lord does not give us a greater burden than we can shoulder."

I muttered dark things under my breath, wiping the water from my eyes. Again. My new shirt was going to be ruined. Silk never fared well in the rain. My choice of shoes wasn't much better. Boots, yes, but distressed, *fashionable* boots. Not work boots designed for the rain and mud. Definitely not monster hunting boots for our evening excursion through one of Kansas City's wooded parks. I realized I was forcibly distracting myself, keeping my mind busy with mundane thoughts to avoid my very real anxiety. Because whenever I grew nervous, an imagined nightmare always—

A church looming before me. Rain pouring down. Night sky and a glowing moon overhead. I was all alone. Crying on the cold, stone steps, and infant in a cardboard box—

I forced the nightmare away, breathing heavily. "You know I hate it when you talk like that," I whispered to him, trying to regain my composure. I wasn't angry with him, but was growing increasingly uncomfortable with our situation after my brief flashback of fear.

"Doesn't mean it shouldn't be said," he said kindly. "I think we're close. Be alert. Remember your training. Banish your fears. I am here. And the Lord is here. He always is."

So, he had noticed my sudden anxiety. "Maybe I should just go back to the car. I know I've trained, but I really don't think—"

A shape of fur, fangs, and claws launched from the shadows towards me, cutting off my words as it snarled, thirsty for my blood.

And my nightmare slipped back into my thoughts like a veiled assassin, a wraith hoping to hold me still for the monster to eat. I froze, unable to move. Twin sticks of power abruptly erupted into being in my clenched fists, but my fear swamped me with that stupid nightmare, the sticks held at my side, useless to save me.

Right before the beast's claws reached me, it grunted as something batted it from the air, sending it flying sideways. It struck a tree with another grunt and an angry whine of pain.

I fell to my knees right into a puddle, arms shaking, breathing fast.

My sticks crackled in the rain like live cattle prods, except their entire length was the electrical section — at least to anyone other than me. I could hold them without pain.

Magic was a part of me, coursing through my veins whether I wanted it or not, and Roland had spent many years teaching me how to master it. But I had never been able to fully master the nightmare inside me, and in moments of fear, it always won, overriding my training.

The fact that I had resorted to weapons — like the ones he had trained me with — rather than a burst of flame, was startling. It was good in the fact that my body's reflexes knew enough to call up a defense even without my direct command, but bad in the fact that it was the worst form of defense for the situation presented. I could have very easily done as Roland did, and hurt it from a distance. But I hadn't. Because of my stupid block.

Roland placed a calloused palm on my shoulder, and I flinched. "Easy, see? I am here." But he did frown at my choice of weapons, the reprimand silent but loud in my mind. I let out a shaky breath, forcing my fear back down. It was all in my head, but still, it wasn't easy. Fear could be like that.

I focused on Roland's implied lesson. Close combat weapons — even magically-powered ones — were for last resorts. I averted my eyes in very real shame. I knew these things. He didn't even need to tell me them. But when that damned nightmare caught hold of me, all my training went out the window. It haunted me like a shadow, waiting for moments just like this, as if trying to kill me. A form of psychological suicide? But it was why I constantly refused to join Roland on his hunts.

He knew about it. And although he was trying to help me overcome that fear, he never pressed too hard.

Rain continued to sizzle as it struck my batons. I didn't let them go, using them as a totem to build my confidence back up. I slowly lifted my eyes to nod at him as I climbed back to my feet.

That's when I saw the second set of eyes in the shadows, right before they flew out of the darkness towards Roland's back. I threw one of my batons and missed, but that pretty much let Roland know that an unfriendly was behind him. Either that or I had just failed to murder my mentor at point-blank range. He whirled to confront the monster, expecting another aerial assault as he unleashed a ball of fire that splashed over the tree at chest height, washing the trunk in blue flames. But this monster was tricky. It hadn't planned on tackling Roland, but had merely jumped out of the darkness to get closer, no doubt learning from its fallen comrade, who still lay unmoving against the tree behind me.

His coat shone like midnight clouds with hints of lightning flashing in the depths of thick, wiry fur. The coat of dew dotting his fur reflected the moonlight, giving him a faint sheen as if covered in fresh oil. He was tall, easily hip height at the shoulder, and barrel chested, his rump much leaner than the rest of his body. He — I assumed male from the long, thick mane around his neck — had a very long snout, much longer and wider than any werewolf I had ever seen. Amazingly, and beyond my control, I realized he was beautiful.

But most of the natural world's lethal hunters were beautiful.

He landed in a wet puddle a pace in front of Roland, juked to the right, and then to the left, racing past the big man, biting into his hamstrings on his way by.

A wash of anger rolled over me at seeing my mentor injured, dousing my fear, and I swung my baton down as hard as I could. It struck the beast in the rump as it tried to dart back to cover — a typical wolf tactic. My blow singed his hair and shattered bone. The creature collapsed into a puddle of mud with a yelp, instinctively snapping his jaws over his shoulder to bite whatever had hit him.

I let him. But mostly out of dumb luck as I heard Roland hiss in pain, falling to the ground.

The monster's jaws clamped around my baton, and there was an immediate explosion of teeth and blood that sent him flying several feet away into the tall brush, yipping, screaming, and staggering. Before he slipped out of sight, I noticed that his lower jaw was simply *gone*, from the contact of his saliva on my electrified magical batons. Then he managed to limp into the woods with more pitiful yowls, but I had no mind to chase him. Roland — that titan of a man, my mentor — was hurt. I could smell copper in the air, and knew we had to get out of here. Fast. Because we had anticipated only one of the monsters. But there had been two of them, and they hadn't been the run-of-the-mill werewolves we had been warned about. If there were two, perhaps there were more. And they were evidently the prehistoric cousin of any werewolf I had ever seen or read about.

Roland hissed again as he stared down at his leg, growling with both pain and anger. My eyes darted back to the first monster, wary of another attack. It *almost* looked like a werewolf, but bigger. Much bigger. He didn't move, but I saw he was breathing. He had a notch in his right ear and a jagged scar on his long snout. Part of me wanted to go over to him and torture him. Slowly. Use his pain to finally drown my nightmare, my fear. The fear that had caused Roland's injury. My lack of inner-strength had not only put me in danger, but had hurt my mentor, my friend.

I shivered, forcing the thought away. That was *cold*. Not me. Sure, I was no stranger to fighting, but that had always been in a ring. Practicing. Sparring. Never life or death.

But I suddenly realized something very dark about myself in the chill, rainy night. Although I was terrified, I felt a deep ocean of anger manifest inside me, wanting only to dispense justice as I saw fit. To use that rage to battle my own demons. As if feeding one would starve the other, reminding me of the Cherokee Indian Legend Roland had once told me.

An old Cherokee man was teaching his grandson about life. "A fight is going on inside me," he told the boy. *"It is a terrible fight between two wolves. One is evil — he is anger, envy, sorrow, regret, greed, arrogance, self-pity, guilt, resentment, inferiority, lies, false pride, superiority, and ego." After a few moments to make sure he had the boy's undivided attention, he continued.*

"The other wolf is good — he is joy, peace, love, hope, serenity, humility, kindness, benevolence, empathy, generosity, truth, compassion, and faith. The same fight is going on inside of you, boy, and inside of every other person, too."

The grandson thought about this for a few minutes before replying. "Which wolf will win?"

The old Cherokee man simply said, "The one you feed, boy. The one you feed..."

And I felt like feeding one of my wolves today, by killing this one…

∼

Get the full book ONLINE!

∼

Turn the page to read a sample of **WHISKEY GINGER** *- Phantom Queen Diaries Book 1, or* **BUY ONLINE**. *Quinn MacKenna is a black magic arms dealer from Boston, and her bark is almost as bad as her bite.*

(Note: Full chronology of all books in the Temple Verse shown on the 'Books in the Temple Verse' page.)

TRY: WHISKEY GINGER (PHANTOM QUEEN DIARIES # 1)

The pasty guitarist hunched forward, thrust a rolled-up wad of paper deep into one nostril, and snorted a line of blood crystals—frozen hemoglobin that I'd smuggled over in a refrigerated canister—with the uncanny grace of a drug addict. He sat back, fangs gleaming, and pawed at his nose. "That's some bodacious shit. Hey, bros," he said, glancing at his fellow band members, "come hit this shit before it melts."

He fetched one of the backstage passes hanging nearby, pried the plastic badge from its lanyard, and used it to split up the crystals, murmuring something in an accent that reminded me of California. Not *the* California, but you know, Cali-foh-nia—the land of beaches, babes, and bros. I retrieved a toothpick from my pocket and punched it through its thin wrapper. "So," I asked no one in particular, "now that ye have the product, who's payin'?"

Another band member stepped out of the shadows to my left, and I don't mean that figuratively, either—the fucker literally stepped out of the shadows. I scowled at him, but hid my surprise, nonchalantly rolling the toothpick from one side of my mouth to the other.

The rest of the band gathered around the dressing room table, following the guitarist's lead by preparing their own snorting utensils—tattered magazine covers, mostly. Typically, you'd do this sort of thing with a dollar-bill, maybe even a Benjamin if you were flush. But fangers like this lot couldn't touch cash directly—in God We Trust and all that. Of course, I didn't really understand why sucking blood the old-fashioned way had suddenly gone out of style. More of a rush, maybe?

"It lasts longer," the vampire next to me explained, catching my mildly curious expression. "It's especially good for shows and stuff. Makes us look, like, less—"

"Creepy?" I offered, my Irish brogue lilting just enough to make it a question.

"Pale," he finished, frowning.

I shrugged. "Listen, I've got places to be," I said, holding out my hand.

"I'm sure you do," he replied, smiling. "Tell you what, why don't you, like, hang around for a bit? Once that wears off," he dipped his head toward the bloody powder smeared across the table's surface, "we may need a pick-me-up." He rested his hand on my arm and our gazes locked.

I blinked, realized what he was trying to pull, and rolled my eyes. His widened in surprise, then shock as I yanked out my toothpick and shoved it through his hand.

"Motherfuck—"

"I want what we agreed on," I declared. "Now. No tricks."

The rest of the band saw what happened and rose faster than I could blink. They circled me, their grins feral…they might have even seemed intimidating if it weren't for the fact that they each had a case of the sniffles—I had to work extra hard not to think about what it felt like to have someone else's blood dripping down my nasal cavity.

I held up a hand.

"Can I ask ye gentlemen a question before we get started?" I asked. "Do ye even *have* what I asked for?"

Two of the band members exchanged looks and shrugged. The guitarist, however, glanced back towards the dressing room, where a brown paper bag sat next to a case full of makeup. He caught me looking and bared his teeth, his fangs stretching until it looked like it would be uncomfortable for him to close his mouth without piercing his own lip.

"Follow-up question," I said, eyeing the vampire I'd stabbed as he gingerly withdrew the toothpick from his hand and flung it across the room with a snarl. "Do ye do each other's make-up? Since, ye know, ye can't use mirrors?"

I was genuinely curious.

The guitarist grunted. "Mike, we have to go on soon."

"Wait a minute. Mike?" I turned to the snarling vampire with a frown. "What happened to *The Vampire Prospero*?" I glanced at the numerous fliers in the dressing room, most of which depicted the band members wading through blood, with Mike in the lead, each one titled *The Vampire Prospero* in *Rocky Horror Picture Show* font. Come to think of it…Mike did look a little like Tim Curry in all that leather and lace.

I was about to comment on the resemblance when Mike spoke up, "Alright, change of plans, bros. We're gonna drain this bitch before the show. We'll look totally—"

"Creepy?" I offered, again.

"Kill her."

Get the full book ONLINE!

MAKE A DIFFERENCE

Reviews are the most powerful tools in my arsenal when it comes to getting attention for my books. Much as I'd like to, I don't have the financial muscle of a New York publisher.

But I do have something much more powerful and effective than that, and it's something that those publishers would kill to get their hands on.

A committed and loyal bunch of readers.

Honest reviews of my books help bring them to the attention of other readers.

If you've enjoyed this book, I would be very grateful if you could spend just five minutes leaving a review (it can be as short as you like) on my book's Amazon page.

Thank you very much in advance.

ACKNOWLEDGMENTS

First, I would like to thank my beta-readers, TEAM TEMPLE, those individuals who spent hours of their time to read, and re-re-read Nate's story. Your dark, twisted, cunning sense of humor makes me feel right at home…

I would also like to thank you, the reader. I hope you enjoyed reading *TINY GODS* as much as I enjoyed writing it. Be sure to check out the two crossover series in the Temple Verse: The **Feathers and Fire Series** and the **Phantom Queen Diaries**.

And last, but definitely not least, I thank my wife, Lexy. Without your support, none of this would have been possible.

BOOKS IN THE TEMPLE VERSE

CHRONOLOGY: *All stories in the TempleVerse are shown in chronological order on the following page*

NATE TEMPLE SERIES

FAIRY TALE - FREE prequel novella #0 for my subscribers

OBSIDIAN SON

BLOOD DEBTS

GRIMM

SILVER TONGUE

BEAST MASTER

BEERLYMPIAN (Novella #5.5 in the 'LAST CALL' anthology)

TINY GODS

DADDY DUTY (Novella #6.5)

WILD SIDE

WAR HAMMER

NINE SOULS

HORSEMAN

LEGEND

KNIGHTMARE (TEMPLE #12) — COMING SOON...

FEATHERS AND FIRE SERIES

(Also set in the TempleVerse)

UNCHAINED

RAGE

WHISPERS

ANGEL'S ROAR

MOTHERLUCKER (Novella #4.5 in the 'LAST CALL' anthology)

SINNER

BLACK SHEEP

GODLESS (FEATHERS #7) — COMING SOON…

PHANTOM QUEEN DIARIES

(Also set in the Temple Universe)

COLLINS (Prequel novella #0 in the 'LAST CALL' anthology)

WHISKEY GINGER

COSMOPOLITAN

OLD FASHIONED

MOTHERLUCKER (Novella #3.5 in the 'LAST CALL' anthology)

DARK AND STORMY

MOSCOW MULE

WITCHES BREW

SALTY DOG

CHRONOLOGICAL ORDER: TEMPLE VERSE

FAIRY TALE (TEMPLE PREQUEL)

OBSIDIAN SON (TEMPLE 1)

BLOOD DEBTS (TEMPLE 2)

GRIMM (TEMPLE 3)

SILVER TONGUE (TEMPLE 4)

BEAST MASTER (TEMPLE 5)

BEERLYMPIAN (TEMPLE 5.5)

TINY GODS (TEMPLE 6)

DADDY DUTY (TEMPLE NOVELLA 6.5)

UNCHAINED (FEATHERS… 1)

RAGE (FEATHERS… 2)

WILD SIDE (TEMPLE 7)

WAR HAMMER (TEMPLE 8)

WHISPERS (FEATHERS… 3)

COLLINS (PHANTOM 0)

WHISKEY GINGER (PHANTOM… 1)

NINE SOULS (TEMPLE 9)

COSMOPOLITAN (PHANTOM… 2)

ANGEL'S ROAR (FEATHERS… 4)

MOTHERLUCKER (FEATHERS 4.5, PHANTOM 3.5)

OLD FASHIONED (PHANTOM…3)

HORSEMAN (TEMPLE 10)

DARK AND STORMY (PHANTOM… 4)

MOSCOW MULE (PHANTOM…5)

SINNER (FEATHERS…5)

WITCHES BREW (PHANTOM…6)

LEGEND (TEMPLE…11)

SALTY DOG (PHANTOM…7)

BLACK SHEEP (FEATHERS…6)

GODLESS (FEATHERS…7)

KNIGHTMARE (TEMPLE 12)

ABOUT SHAYNE SILVERS

Shayne is a man of mystery and power, whose power is exceeded only by his mystery...

He currently writes the Amazon Bestselling **Nate Temple** Series, which features a foul-mouthed wizard from St. Louis. He rides a blood-thirsty unicorn, drinks with Achilles, and is pals with the Four Horsemen.

He also writes the Amazon Bestselling **Feathers and Fire** Series—a second series in the Temple Verse. The story follows a rookie spell-slinger named Callie Penrose who works for the Vatican in Kansas City. Her problem? Hell seems to know more about her past than she does.

He coauthors **The Phantom Queen Diaries**—a third series set in The Temple Verse—with Cameron O'Connell. The story follows Quinn MacKenna, a mouthy black magic arms dealer in Boston. All she wants? A round-trip ticket to the Fae realm...and maybe a drink on the house.

Shayne holds two high-ranking black belts, and can be found writing in a coffee shop, cackling madly into his computer screen while pounding shots of espresso. He's hard at work on the newest books in the Temple Verse—You can find updates on new releases or chronological reading order on the next page, his website or any of his social media accounts. <u>**Follow him online for all sorts of groovy goodies, giveaways, and new release updates:**</u>

Get Down with Shayne Online
www.shaynesilvers.com
info@shaynesilvers.com

- facebook.com/shaynesilversfanpage
- amazon.com/author/shaynesilvers
- bookbub.com/profile/shayne-silvers
- instagram.com/shaynesilversofficial
- twitter.com/shaynesilvers
- goodreads.com/ShayneSilvers

Printed in Great Britain
by Amazon